D0801433

Michael Allegretto

THE WATCHMEN

SIMON & SCHUSTER
New York   London   Toronto   Sydney   Tokyo   Singapore

SIMON & SCHUSTER
Simon & Schuster Building
Rockefeller Center
1230 Avenue of the Americas
New York, New York 10020

Designed by Deirdre C. Amthor

Manufactured in the United States of America

10 9 8 7 6 5 4 3 2 1

Library of Congress Cataloging in Publication Data

Allegretto, Michael.
The watchmen / Michael Allegretto.
p. cm.
I. Title.
PS3551.L385W37 1991
813'.54—dc20   91-22462
ISBN 0-671-73643-4   CIP

FOR MY GRANDFATHER MIKE

Thanks to Ronda Rolain, landscape architect,
for sharing her expertise.

Special thanks to my editor, Patricia Lande,
who helped shape this book.

The watchmen found me
as they went about in the city;
they beat me, they wounded me . . .
those watchmen of the walls.

—Song of Solomon

THE WATCHMEN

1

LAUREN CAYLOR was not alarmed by the man, but she was intrigued.

She'd stepped out of the air-conditioned, fluorescent-lit confines of the San Miguel municipal building into the warm, hazy California sunshine, glad the workday was over. It had been long and tedious, and most of her time had been spent hunched over a drafting table. She'd entered the parking lot with her fellow workers—planners, civil engineers, technicians, drafters, and secretaries. They'd waved and dispersed to their cars.

As Lauren had made her way across the warm asphalt lot, one car caught her attention. Not the car, actually, but the enormous, white bird dropping that graced its shiny, dark blue hood.

Bombed by a monster sea gull, she'd thought, smiling.

And that's when she'd seen the man.

He was sitting at the wheel, hiding his face behind a paperback book.

Lauren assumed he was waiting to pick up a city employee after work, perhaps his wife. But there were people walking past him and car engines revving up throughout the parking lot, and the man seemed totally unconcerned. He just sat, roasting in the mid-May afternoon sun with his engine off and the windows up, reading a book.

Lauren walked to her car, glancing back once at the man. His face remained buried in his book.

She climbed in her four-year-old Honda Civic and quickly cranked down the windows to let out the sun-baked air. Then she drove slowly from the parking lot, falling in line with the other cars turning into the parkway, which was flanked by majestic palm trees.

13

At the intersection of Santa Rosa Avenue Lauren turned left toward the Pacific Ocean. It was barely discernible a mile away, showing itself as a hazy blue line between treetops and white stucco buildings. The Spanish-style homes that fronted the avenue were set well back from the street and protected by low stone walls covered with lush vines and wild roses. Lauren passed before them, staying in the flow of traffic until she reached Ocean Boulevard.

As she turned left, she glanced in her side-view mirror.

The dark blue car with the bird dropping on the hood was entering the boulevard behind her.

Lauren was surprised that the car had caught up with her so quickly, since when she'd left the lot the driver had seemed engrossed in his book, apparently still waiting for someone. But now he was close by, partially hidden in the traffic behind her.

She continued along Ocean Boulevard, bounded by the sea on the right and by restaurants and condos on the left.

Lauren wondered if she was acquainted with the man's passenger, whoever it was he'd picked up after work. She tried to look, but the car was now totally hidden in traffic. So Lauren shrugged and did what she usually did when she drove along this stretch of roadway—she let her gaze sweep over the ocean and the smooth, soothing sandy beach.

A mile later the nearest car behind her pulled over to turn. The movement in the mirror caught Lauren's eye. And now she saw that the dark blue car was directly behind her.

The driver was alone.

Lauren frowned. She couldn't help feeling mildly annoyed by the continued presence of the car. Forget about it, she told herself, it means nothing. She focused her full attention on the traffic before her, which seemed to grow thicker with each passing block. A few miles later she approached her intersection. She eased into the left-hand lane, waited for a break in the oncoming traffic, and turned.

She looked into her mirror. The dark blue car was turning behind her.

Lauren felt a brief chill. Is this guy *following* me?

Don't be ridiculous, she told herself. Although she knew there were lots of crazies around. And some of them were vicious. She'd seen plenty of news stories about women being raped and sometimes murdered by total strangers.

14

failed in his or her attempt to "protect" the patient from the surgeor
always be stressed to the patient that he or she will have an even gro
for physical therapy after surgery and that the goals of both sur~~,~~ ...u
therapist treating the shoulder are exactly the same.

PREHABILITATION, REHABILITATION, MAINTENANCE, AND TRAINING

These concepts need to be clear to physician and therapist because they involve short- and long-term goals, indications, and expectations.

Prehabilitation

This term usually implies strengthening and stretching in anticipation of an
insult, usually surgery. A prehabilitative function is served by most rotator
cuff and shoulder girdle strengthening for a number of reasons. First, surgery
is often technically superior in the patient who has done long-term shoulder
exercises for these structures. The mechanical strength of the remaining rotator cuff tissues, deltoid muscle, and capsular structures of the glenohumeral
joint does seem to be superior in patients who have worked hard
preoperatively. This means that they are easier to delineate and manipulate,
hold sutures more securely, and probably heal a bit faster. Surgeons worry
less about soft tissue failures, such as the deltoid muscle pulling off the
acromion or the repaired rotator cuff or subscapularis pulling off the humerus,
in an athletic shoulder that has done effective preoperative exercise. Second,
because the tissues are stronger to begin with, it is generally possible to advance strengthening and motion goals more quickly after surgery in the well-
prehabilitated shoulder. Third, because most of the postsurgical exercises are
fairly similar to the presurgical ones, the patient is more adept at them in the
postoperative period, when he or she is dealing with added pain and weakness.

When a new shoulder patient does not seem to be responding to physical
treatment and thus begins the consideration of surgery, it is good practice to
stress the prehabilitative value of the therapy he or she is doing, both as a
motivational device and to have the patient understand the team approach
that is used. The "therapy versus surgery" battle lines will not be drawn if this
team approach is emphasized. The physical treatments will also not be considered wasted if an operative plan is eventually adopted.

Rehabilitation

The term implies recovering from the effects of an insult, which, again, may
be surgery. Practitioners in physical medicine are well aware of their role in

rehabilitative therapy; those in orthopaedics and internal medicine may not be as understanding. In contrast to the prehabilitative situation, it is the physicians who need to be "kept on the team" in the rehabilitative setting. Implicit in the rehabilitation concept is a definite improvement that is expected over the course of treatment. In treating postsurgical shoulder patients, more often than not there is an unwelcome period of functional deterioration that may be accompanied by increased pain. The physical medicine practitioner who conveys a sense of trust in the surgeon and the surgical procedure performed does much to help the patient through these periods. The surgeon needs to play an active role during these periods of temporary dehabilitation, sometimes by changing or decreasing physical therapy, changing medication, or utilizing bracing.

These setback periods are so common as to be the norm for patients in postoperative rehabilitation. They are not to be considered surgical complications. Surgical repairs can and do sometimes fail, and early and late surgical complications may ruin what seemed to be a good result. Although the physical medicine practitioner must be able to recognize these occurrences, it is properly the surgeon's role to diagnose and treat surgical failures and complications. It is by no means appropriate for physical medicine practitioners to trivialize or hide surgical complications, but it is devastating for the patient to be told that a surgical complication has occurred when in fact it has not. Trust in the entire team is lost, and the psychic effect is for the patient to anticipate greater and greater symptoms without hope of cure. It is also unlikely that a physical medicine practitioner will have seen enough surgical complications to be able to diagnose them reliably. There is a good chance that what he or she feels is a retearing of the repaired cuff is early overuse or eccentric stretch or that the wound infection is a sterile inflammatory reaction to absorbable suture material. Regardless of whether there truly has been a complication, the job of announcing it to the patient and then dealing with it belongs to the surgeon. Much anguish may be avoided by observing this rule.

The person with whom concerns about surgical complications and failures should be discussed first is always the surgeon. The surgeon should then evaluate and make treatment recommendations accordingly, explaining the situation to the patient. A therapist who announces that a surgical failure or complication has occurred can seriously compromise the patient's rehabilitation potential, independent of the presumed complication itself.

Maintenance

The idea of maintenance therapy, designed to prevent relapse or deterioration, has greater appeal to many patients who have just successfully completed a course of physical treatment for a painful shoulder problem. It does not appeal to many postsurgical patients, probably because they chose a surgical remedy in hopes of being able to stop physical treatments altogether. One must be specific in defining maintenance therapies. "Get some shoulder exercise every week" is not a maintenance program for prevention of frozen shoulder, just as "eat something every day" is not a maintenance program for the prevention of starvation. The greatest problem with maintenance programs is patient compliance. Cost reasons usually rule out outpatient therapy for the rest of one's life. This leaves home therapies. By being specific with a home maintenance program, there is a greater chance of patient compliance. The usual finding with maintenance programs for common shoulder problems, however, is that either they are not truly maintenance programs because they are not effectively treating the problem or they are not followed because the problem stops producing symptoms.

Given that few patients can or need to stay in a permanent muscle strengthening program, it is generally range of motion exercises that make up the maintenance therapy with which patients are left. The key factor with these range programs is that they be easy to perform. Three range drills performed daily in the shower or by a specific caregiver before bedtime (for institutionalized patients) can be done in less than 1 minute. This type of instruction has a much greater chance of actually being carried out than, for instance, a 10-minute drill done three times a week because it becomes integrated into routine.

The other implicit understanding about maintenance therapies is that they come at the end of a successful therapeutic course. The indications for stopping physical treatments may be difficult to define. Certain criteria are easy: The pain may be completely gone, and range of motion may be normal. Others are vague: When is the subscapularis strong enough to prevent future subluxation of the glenohumeral joint? Leaving a patient in maintenance therapy obviates this question. It means that strengthening never really ends. The experienced practitioner realizes that it does, however. Without monitoring and encouragement, open-ended strengthening programs rarely produce true increases as rehabilitation does. This introduces the other option at the end of rehabilitation: training.

Training

Adaptation to and preparation for a set of specific functional performances constitute training. This process may involve athletic trainers, coaches, family members, or no one other than the patient. Training, by definition, goes beyond rehabilitation in that its goals of improved performance in specific tasks, usually sports, are optional and voluntary. The number of patients who request training at the conclusion of a successful course of physical or surgical treatment seems to be increasing, and with this practitioners in physical medicine have in many instances met the need by declaring themselves to be practitioners of sports medicine. This vaguely defined term seems to be medicine practiced with the goal of maintaining or enhancing performance in sports and games.

Physiatrists, podiatrists, chiropractors, physical therapists, athletic trainers, internists, orthopaedic surgeons, and nurses have all declared themselves to be practitioners of sports medicine. It is no secret that sports medicine is generally profitable and continues to attract new adherents from all areas of the health care field. The practice of sports medicine, without involvement in the training process, seems impossible because some type of training is necessarily involved in all athletics.

Regarding care of the shoulder patient, much input into specific training techniques has come from completely nonmedical sources. These are the specialty coaches and trainers of college and professional throwing athletes, swimmers, and competitors in weightlifting. Yet, high-level throwing athletes have attracted the interest of many of the best-known shoulder surgeons, with the result that sports followers in the general public may have a greater familiarity with arthroscopic shoulder and knee procedures than many medical doctors. Having a famous professional athlete under one's care is certainly apt to be good for one's practice. Because of factors such as these, many practitioners have felt compelled to get in on the sports medicine movement.

The shift in emphasis from rehabilitation to training that goes along with this can be, in the case of established physical medicine and orthopaedic practices, detrimental to some of the patients. The goals of rehabilitation and training are different, despite the fact that the parameters used to describe them may be the same. The psychologic appeal of training and sport is strong. Consciously or not, training methods have been worked into the rehabilitation setting for many shoulder and knee patients. Frustration, prolongation of the clinical course, and suboptimal results have been the product of this practice. The clearly specified practice of athletic training has an important place in today's market, and many patients may benefit from it after they are no longer patients but rather clients. Physical medicine is practiced on those with pathology. When the practitioner trades his or her hat for one labeled *sports medicine trainer*, he or she no longer treats disease. It is important that there be no disease left in the patient when he or she does this.

Part II

Specific Shoulder Disorders

Chapter 7

Frozen Shoulder and Adhesive Capsulitis

DEFINITIONS

Frozen shoulder is a lay term that has been taken into the professional vocabulary to describe the loss of passive range of motion. There are a number of pathophysiologic entities that can produce a loss of passive range, one of which is the distinct phenomenon of adhesive capsulitis. To make things less clear, the term *frozen shoulder* is commonly used in the medical literature to describe a specific, common, and probably temporary inflammatory condition of the glenohumeral, subacromial, and scapulothoracic articulations that results in adhesive capsulitis. This specific frozen shoulder problem is referred to as idiopathic adhesive capsulitis (IAC). It is a subset of adhesive capsulitis, just as tabby is a subset of house cats. Similarly, adhesive capsulitis is properly a subset of frozen shoulder, as house cat is a subset of felines.

It is quite important to understand why passive range of motion has been lost because it makes a big difference in how one goes about restoring it. Three large categories of frozen shoulder may be defined according to underlying pathology. Bony blocks to motion should be considered first. They are usually discernible on X-rays. Bony blocks include fusions, congenital malformations, deformities produced by fracture or arthritis, heterotopic bone formations, and (although not truly bony) surgical hardware that blocks motion (Figures 7–1 and 7–2). Second, consider soft tissue restraints to motion. These are most common. They include contractures of the joint capsule and capsular ligaments, shortening and contractures of the rotator cuff and subscapularis tendons, and the adhesion of these joint structures by scar or abnormal bursal tissues. Although it should not properly be included under the term *capsulitis*, there may be similar adhesions of the scapula to the thorax. Soft tissue blocks to motion can be spontaneous, as in IAC, or caused by infection, trauma, inflammatory disease, surgery, or simply disuse.

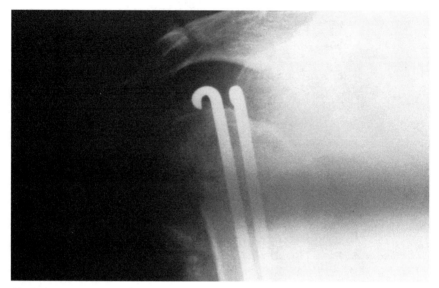

Figure 7–1 Intramedullary fixation hardware blocking motion by acromial interference (hardware impingement).

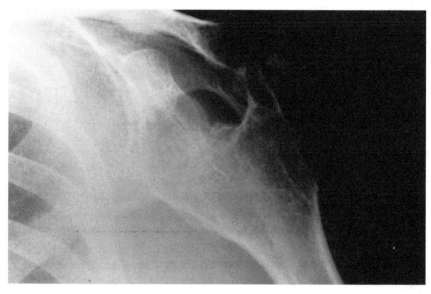

Figure 7–2 Glenohumeral fusion. This was a spontaneous, unnoticed occurrence in a 50-year-old woman with childhood polio.

Third, consider neuromuscular diseases that produce frozen shoulder. Here, motion loss may simply be a result of weakness and disuse, which eventually produce soft tissue contracture. This would be seen after a peripheral nerve injury or with hemiplegia. With many neurologic problems, however, there is initially an active contracture of the joint. This is seen after some cerebrovascular accidents, head injuries, or tumors. It may be the result of many other neurologic diseases such as multiple sclerosis, muscular dystrophy, amyotrophic lateral sclerosis (Charcot's syndrome), Parkinson's disease, and others. The neuromuscular frozen shoulder starts as an active contracture, but eventually soft tissue contractures (the second group) form. These patients still must be kept in the neuromuscular category, despite the soft tissue component that inevitably develops, because their treatment is generally different: The neuromuscular problem remains even after the soft tissue contracture has been addressed.

ADHESIVE CAPSULITIS

Adhesive capsulitis is a final common pathway through which motion loss becomes permanent in many disease states. The image evoked by this title involves the sticking down of the capsule onto the humeral head or other joint structures, preventing motion. Although this is an oversimplification, it does serve as a starting place for understanding the pathology involved in this common shoulder ailment.

Pathoanatomy

The anatomy of the shoulder capsule has been studied extensively in the past 10 years because of increased interest in shoulder instability.[1] The shoulder with adhesive capsulitis unfortunately has exactly the opposite problem, and it is likely that its pathologic capsular anatomy is quite different from the unstable glenohumeral joint's. Surgical descriptions of what is found in and around the shoulder with adhesive capsulitis are generally bland. The shoulder with adhesive capsulitis does not often require open surgery, but with the abundant utilization of the arthroscope in work-up and treatment of shoulder problems sufficient surgical data have been collected regarding the condition of the intraglenohumeral and subacromial structures in adhesive capsulitis to draw reliable conclusions about the pathoanatomy of this disease state.

The inferior pouch of the glenohumeral joint extends downward from the inferior margin of the glenoid labrum for about 2 cm (Figure 7–3). It is this

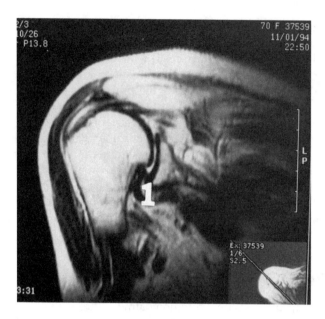

Figure 7–3 Magnetic resonance image of the inferior capsular pouch (1).

capsular redundancy that permits the glenohumeral joint to be abducted without actually stretching the capsular fibers. This pouch can be seen, filled with contrast material, on most arthrographic radiographs of the shoulder (Figure 7–4). It can also be easily visualized arthroscopically in most shoulders that are not involved with adhesive capsulitis. The single most constant patho-anatomic finding in the shoulder with adhesive capsulitis is obliteration of the inferior pouch. It does not fill with contrast on arthrography (Figure 7–5), cannot be visualized on arthroscopy, and does not admit the surgeon's fingertip at open surgery. The underlying idea is that the inner surfaces of the capsular pouch become inflamed and then stick to each other by means of synovial reaction, fibrin deposition, or scar.

Anterior to the glenohumeral joint margin, the superior margin of the subscapularis tendon meets the anterior margin of the supraspinatus tendon (of the rotator cuff). Both these tendons insert on the humerus at the lesser and greater tuberosities, respectively. They blend together laterally near their bony insertions, but medially, directly anterior to the glenohumeral joint line (with the shoulder in anatomic position), they come apart into two distinct tendinous structures. More medially, they are both red, muscular filets and are separated by the coracoid process of the scapula.

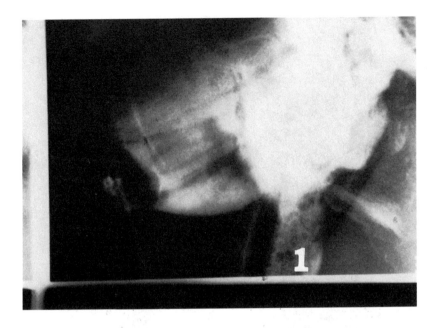

Figure 7–4 Arthrogram showing the inferior capsular pouch (1).

As the subscapularis and supraspinatus tendons separate, a V-shaped opening is left in the continuous sheet of tendon that covers the humeral head. This is referred to as the rotator interval (Figure 7–6). It is a normal structure. The capsule of the shoulder joint closes the rotator interval, but it is normally quite thin, pouching out a bit to join with a fibrous band that runs from the base of the coracoid process to the greater tuberosity. This band, called the coracohumeral ligament (Figure 7–7), strengthens the upper aspect of the anterior shoulder capsule. It is normally rather flimsy and mostly blended in with the rotator cuff. It may be seen as only a thickening of the edges of the rotator interval. During an open surgical procedure it can be appreciated that external rotation of the humerus does tighten the coracohumeral ligament, making it stand out from the cuff tendons. Thickening and contracture of the coracohumeral ligament are other fairly constant surgical findings in adhesive capsulitis. This is readily understood to be a cause of internal rotation contracture. Surgical release, however, usually improves the forward elevation range also. It is thus understood to be a soft tissue restraint to glenohumeral flexion as well.[2]

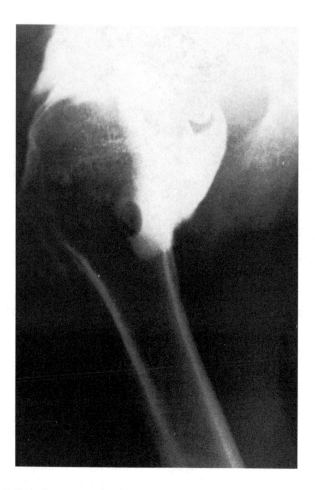

Figure 7–5 Arthrogram of a frozen shoulder showing decreased volume of the capsular pouch.

Other intra- and extracapsular structures are known to be involved in adhesive capsulitis. The capsule itself is divided into a number of thickenings, which are referred to as the glenohumeral ligaments. That these are contracted, preventing motion, is concluded from the observation at surgery that they are often ruptured after forceful, closed manipulation under anesthesia (MUA) of a frozen shoulder. The subdeltoid and subacromial bursae, normally thin and pliant, are often thick, inflamed, and tough. They may contribute to the loss of motion by externally sticking the rotator cuff and subscapularis to the acromion and deltoid.

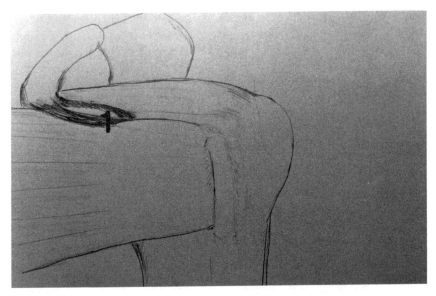

Figure 7–6 Rotator interval (1) and coracohumeral ligament surrounding it (dark shading).

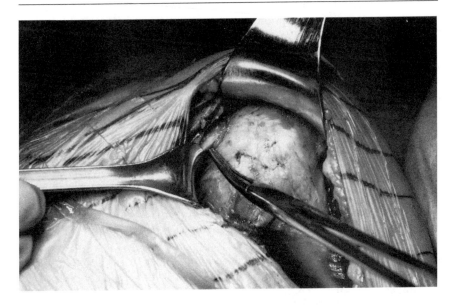

Figure 7–7 Operative photograph showing the coracohumeral ligament under the tip of the clamp. The coracoacromial ligament (a structure that impinges on the anterior rotator cuff, as appreciated here) is seen directly above the clamp.

Surgical dissection of the scapulothoracic articulation is not a procedure done for treatment of adhesive capsulitis. There is some feeling among shoulder practitioners that mechanical sticking down of the scapula to the chest is involved in adhesive capsulitis/frozen shoulder. This has mostly been supported by the fact that scapular mobilization techniques have met with clinical successes in treating some frozen shoulders. The concept that freer scapular motion decreases mechanical stresses at the glenohumeral articulation, permitting a more natural movement pattern, certainly has theoretical appeal. Because of the lack of any pathoanatomic findings supporting this concept, however, and the fact that many frozen shoulders resolve spontaneously, this type of clinical data is at best supportive of the scapulothoracic concept of adhesive capsulitis.

Inflammation of the biceps tendon (long head) has often been implicated as a cause of adhesive capsulitis.[3,4] It is certainly a common clinical observation that the anterior glenohumeral joint area, which is difficult if not impossible to distinguish from the bicipital groove on physical examination, is the most tender part of the shoulder in (some) patients in the early inflammatory phase of IAC. Local anesthesia of the biceps groove area may result in improved motion, and there have been reports suggesting intense bicipital tendinitis as the only underlying pathology in a subset of patients with adhesive capsulitis.[4] More detail than this is not accurately known. Frozen shoulders that are tender anteriorly are not uncommon, and the same inflammatory condition that affects the capsule and cuff may affect the biceps tendon as it pierces and rubs against these structures. One cannot ignore the possibility of misdiagnosing hot bicipital tendinitis (which inhibits shoulder motion through pain) as adhesive capsulitis, which may then be cured by a steroid injection around the biceps tendon.

Subacromial impingement per se seems unlikely to be a true cause of frozen shoulder because the time course and natural history of frozen shoulder are so different from those of rotator cuff impingement. That impingement is somehow related to frozen shoulder has often been suggested. The frequency of impingement, the fact that it is successfully treated by exercises that also treat frozen shoulder, and the concept of impingement's local irritation of cuff and bursal tissues acting as the spark that ignites the fire of adhesive capsulitis all support the relationship. The histopathologic character of IAC is distinct from that of impingement disease, however. Impingement is mechanical, and IAC is more a neurometabolic phenomenon. Not only does frozen shoulder occur in the absence of impingement-increasing activities, it also usually disappears without actual treatment of the impingement. Certainly, surgical correction of impingement in a tight frozen shoulder is likely to prolong, not shorten, the duration of the contracture. That the two problems often exist in the same shoulder is undisputed, but that they are causally related is unproved.

Pathophysiology

What makes the pouch stick closed, the coracohumeral ligament thicken and contract, the capsular ligaments contract, and the subdeltoid and subacromial tissues stick to the cuff tendons? When the answer to this question seems clear, such as in cases of raging infection in the glenohumeral joint, chronic hemorrhage into the joint from hemophilia, or gross inflammation of intra- and extraarticular structures from psoriatic arthritis, the diagnosis of secondary adhesive capsulitis is made, and treatment is begun with the underlying cause of the problem kept in mind. When the answer is not at all clear, the diagnosis of IAC is made by default. Most cases of frozen shoulder treated today are likely to be left with the IAC diagnosis. The actual pathophysiology of IAC is assumed to involve an inflammatory process producing a periarthritis or inflammation around the shoulder joint that occurs and resolves spontaneously, leaving the contractures described above.

The facts that seem best established regarding the pathophysiology of IAC are that insulin-dependent diabetics get it most often and are hardest to treat, that patients are most likely to fall in the 40- to 60-year-old group, and that physical treatments are likely to restore motion in most patients.[5] The diabetic frozen shoulder is also likely to exhibit greater loss of internal than external rotation compared with other frozen shoulders. IAC is a clinical diagnosis of exclusion, and thus the observation of concomitant shoulder pathology is problematic insofar as the causal link between it and IAC cannot be established deductively. The most frequent difficulty with this problem is encountered in the patient who presents with IAC and is successfully treated (with full return of motion) but has a positive impingement sign and some mild impingement symptoms. Did the impingement problem cause the frozen shoulder?

In the orthopaedic world, some eager arthroscopists have made it a practice to perform arthroscopy on large numbers of patients with "resistant" IAC.[6] Peeking into the subacromial bursa and making an impingement diagnosis based on the appearance of the subacromial space, they have performed arthroscopic acromioplasty to prevent the recurrence of impingement and its assumed sequela, the frozen shoulder. Although many orthopaedists (including the author) might question this practice, the facts regarding its logic are simply not known. Impingement is a clinical, not a visual, diagnosis that cannot be made with surety in the absence of a positive impingement sign. It does not seem highly plausible that mild subacromial impingement would cause

IAC because the impingement phenomenon primarily takes place on the high ranges of forward elevation, which are lost early on during the course of IAC.

Adhesive capsulitis secondary to a well-established primary diagnosis is often simply considered a stiff shoulder that arises from inactivity. There are some pathologic findings that can support this view. The tissue changes that accompany trauma, infection, inflammatory arthritis, and even noninflammatory arthritis may be remarkably similar. The most frequently treated secondary adhesive capsulitis is probably that which follows nonoperative treatment of proximal humerus fractures. In this situation, the shoulder has been necessarily immobilized to permit bone healing. Soft tissue trauma and blood in the shoulder joint and subacromial spaces are present at the beginning of the period of immobilization. The surgical findings in this type of shoulder are often more striking than those in IAC. True webs, mats, and clumps of scar and granulation tissue are present around the cuff tendons and inside the capsule. Thickening and contracture of the capsular ligaments may be worsened by the fracture's distortion of their underlying bony anchor points. The tensile strength of the healed fractures is likely to be less than that of the scar–granulation–bursal tissue around it, making forceful MUA a dangerous prospect.

Although the underlying causes of secondary adhesive capsulitis vary widely, and with them the actual pathophysiology of the contracture, the post-traumatic case described here can function as a basic model. It is a situation commonly encountered at surgery because a large number of patients with fractures that are best treated operatively initially refuse surgery, only to change their minds when it is apparent to them that their shoulder is not getting better. This usually occurs between 2 and 4 months after the fracture. The surgical treatment at this point is technically most difficult because of the scaring and distortion mentioned above. Disuse makes the humeral bone so soft that it is often incapable of being fixed securely with surgical hardware.

The surgery does provide a good opportunity to study the pathophysiology of secondary adhesive capsulitis, however. What is seen, beyond the obvious traumatic changes, is not extremely dissimilar to the IAC shoulder, the arthritic shoulder, or the (long-time) postinfectious shoulder. There are only so many reactions that the local tissues can muster to noxious stimuli. It should therefore be appreciated that the same set of stretches and mobilization techniques can be used effectively for a wide variety of shoulder problems that end up causing adhesive capsulitis. It is the final common pathophysiologic pathway for a variety of diseases of the shoulder.

NEUROMUSCULAR DISORDERS

Frozen shoulder is clinically associated with a number of neuromuscular and metabolic disease states, such as diabetes, Parkinson's disease, and hyperparathyroidism.[7] Whether there is an intrinsic neurologic phenomenon that produces a frozen shoulder or merely inactivity that produces a secondary joint contracture is not known. Practitioners with experience in maintaining passive range in stroke patients know that the tendency toward contracture in some of these patients is much stronger than inactivity alone would create. There would logically seem, therefore, to be some neurologic factor increasing joint stiffness. (It is indeed tempting to try to explain IAC as a primarily neurologic phenomenon somewhat akin to a localized reflex sympathetic dystrophy of the shoulder.)[8] Regardless of our poor understanding of the pathophysiology, the clinically relevant point is that it is hard enough to treat the developing passive contractures in patients with neurologic disease without having to fight against muscle spasm and pathologic tone. The difference between success and failure with the neuromuscular frozen shoulder often depends on the use of muscle relaxation techniques and drugs to the same extent as it does on one's solid determination to stretch the joint passively.

The pharmacologic agents in current use as antispasmodics may be quite effective against the spastic tone and rigidity seen with some cases of multiple sclerosis and spinal cord injury. The most commonly used agent is probably baclofen, which is an analog of the inhibitory neurotransmitter γ-aminobutyric acid. Its dosages and side effects vary significantly, and the physiatrist or neurologist prescribing the drug needs to monitor the patient under therapy carefully. The rigidity of parkinsonism can usually be decreased appreciably with proper drug therapy. Pharmacologic treatments for Parkinson's disease have expanded in the past few years. Patients having difficulty on their longstanding drug program should be referred for a fresh neurologic evaluation if the stiffness and rigidity are a problem. This concept applies to all treatments of the neuromuscular frozen shoulder. The physiatrist or neurologist must be involved throughout treatment because the underlying drug therapy can be so important to the success of physical treatments. Direct pharmacologic treatments for the pericapsular fibrosis that ultimately affects the frozen shoulder are limited. Aminobenzoate (Potaba) has been used as an antifibrotic agent with moderate success in patients with systemic sclerosis (scleroderma). Its possible efficacy as a treatment for frozen shoulder has not been established, although a number of well-known practitioners in physical medicine are involved with its use.

BONY BLOCKS TO MOTION AND GLENOHUMERAL FUSION

It is not unusual to find a patient with solid, bony fusion of the glenohumeral joint who has never had shoulder surgery. This phenomenon was probably more common in years past, when long periods of immobilization were routinely prescribed. It can occur after infection, arthritis, or trauma. The shoulder is likely to be comfortable but to have a significantly decreased range of motion. An X-ray makes the diagnosis of spontaneous fusion. Bone trabeculae, the tiny lines on the X-ray that show the fine structure of spongy bone, will be seen crossing from the humerus to the glenoid, and there will obviously be no appreciable joint space (see Figure 7–2).

Surgical fusion of the glenohumeral joint is performed infrequently today. There are still some definite indications for this operation, however. Deep-seated bone infection and total paralysis of the shoulder girdle muscles are among them. The patient who has had a surgical fusion of the glenohumeral joint often has other orthopaedic and neurologic problems with that upper extremity. This is a salvage procedure, and limited goals in rehabilitation will be clear. In treating patients with spontaneous and surgical fusions of the shoulder, it must be kept in mind that the scapula and humerus are one bone. Some patients, especially those with spontaneous fusion of the shoulder, may demonstrate an extraordinary apparent range of motion, achieved through increased scapulothoracic movement and lumbar spine movement. These patients, besides having an interesting physical examination, give practitioners and their other, less fortunate shoulder fusion patients an example of successful functional adaptation to what is generally a rather disabling condition.

Bony blocks to joint motion, especially shoulder motion, tend to be (from an orthopaedist's point of view) overdiagnosed by physiatrists and physical therapists. They do occur, and they do produce a range of motion end point that has a bony, solid, and sudden quality. It is nevertheless not unusual for soft tissue contractures to produce this same feeling. The most common bony block is produced by a fracture of the greater tuberosity that heals in a somewhat displaced position. The tuberosity, being thus elevated, impinges against the acromion as the arm is elevated, producing typical impingement symptoms as well as an impingement sign on physical examination (Figure 7–8). The pain during the impingement test may come at much lower degrees of forward elevation, however. (Note that this is a looser usage of the term *impingement sign*. Properly, an impingement sign, as described by Neer,[9] cannot be recorded unless full forward elevation is achieved.) Without permitting the terminology to dominate understanding, when the protruding tuberosity hits the acromion, pain is felt, and motion stops.

Another fracture that commonly leaves a bony block to motion is the surgical neck (or subtuberous) fracture that heals with the upper fragment abducted. This tends to happen in nonoperatively treated fractures because the rotator cuff, which is still attached to the upper fragment, rotates the fragment, and it heals in this rotated position. As expected, the motions that are usually lost in this situation are abduction or forward elevation and external rotation,

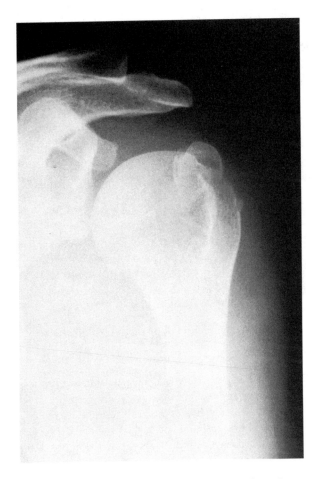

Figure 7–8 Radiograph showing fracture of the greater tuberosity.

the motions produced by the rotator cuff muscles (the subscapularis, which is also attached to the upper fragment, is relatively weak in comparison to the rotator cuff). This rotation of the upper fragment and the greater tuberosity displacement described above are readily seen on standard X-ray views (Figure 7–9).

The common bony blocks to shoulder motion often seem to operate through compression of adjacent soft tissues rather than through actual bone-against-bone abutment. This is felt to be true for two reasons. First, the end points in motion often change (ie, motion improves) with therapy. No doubt exists

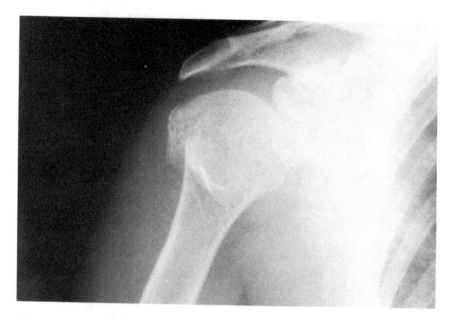

Figure 7–9 Radiograph showing healed, displaced subtuberous fracture.

about the ability of therapy to affect the periarticular soft tissues, but it is unlikely that even the most aggressive progressive range program changes bony configuration. Second, X-ray views taken at the end of the range generally fail to demonstrate actual bone-to-bone contact. These are the basic reasons why the orthopaedist often disagrees with a therapist's diagnosis of insurmountable bony block to motion.

True glenohumeral osteoarthritis is still another cause of a common bony block to motion. Osteophytes typically grow at the inferior and posterior articular margins of the humeral head. The dome of the humeral head also decreases in height, being ground down through frictional wear over the years. This combination of mechanical factors tends to produce a block to external rotation by means of the osteophytes' impingement against the posterior edge of the glenoid. An anterior capsular contracture also forms in most osteoarthritics. It can be quite severe, involving the capsule, coracohumeral ligament, and commonly the tendon of the subscapularis muscle as well. This is probably a secondary contracture, however, because the primary disease process affects the joint. The true osteoarthritic with advanced changes on X-rays does have a significant bony block to external rotation. This patient is unlikely to improve his or her external rotation range significantly with physical therapy.

A problem that is in many respects quite similar to bony impingement is hardware impingement. Many patients are encountered whose shoulder fractures have been treated with surgical open reduction and internal fixation techniques, which leave various rods, screws, and bone plates projecting from the upper humerus. The actual limitation to motion that is created by the hardware depends, of course, on its extraosseous configuration. The two common findings are intramedullary rods or pins (which are placed down the long axis of the humerus) sticking straight up superiorly and protruding screw heads from screw-and-plate constructs (used for proximal humeral fractures) projecting out of the lateral aspect of the upper humerus in the area of the greater tuberosity (see Figure 7–1). These situations block forward elevation and external rotation, respectively. In distinction to the physical examination findings with real bony blocks to motion, hardware blocking motion produces distinct feelings of something hard hitting bone. The patient and therapist are likely to be correct when they think that hardware is blocking shoulder motion.

The intrinsic problem with all bony blocks to motion is that they are unlikely to respond to stretching or mobilization techniques. The hard, sudden, or bony end point to motion is particularly uncomfortable when pushed against. It is, in general, unwise to work aggressively against a bony end point. As mentioned above, however, there are cases in which what seems to be an impassable bony block to motion yields to physical therapy just as a soft tissue contracture would. The important decision to push on despite what seems to be a bony block needs to be made as a team, with good X-rays made in the end point positions. This approach will tend to minimize patient disappointment and maintain realistic goals for nonsurgical therapy.

TREATMENT OPTIONS

Treatment of most frozen shoulders should be nonoperative. Although a precedent has been set in a number of large American shoulder practices for the use of shoulder arthroscopy in the routine treatment of adhesive capsulitis, this must not cloud the fact that, given enough time (up to 1 year), most cases of adhesive capsulitis respond well to physical treatment. Many other treatment techniques with good success rates have been described. These include hydraulic distention of the glenohumeral joint followed by manipulation, steroid injection of the periarticular structures with and without manipulation, scapular manipulation, pure massage techniques, extended use of insonation, pure home therapy exercise techniques, and even nontreatment consisting of mild analgesics and instructions to use the shoulder as well as possible. In modern American practice, it is unlikely that a patient with frozen shoulder will ever be treated without some progressive range of motion therapy. Because this is the mainstay of treatment, it is described in greatest detail.

Progressive Range of Motion Therapy

Patients in progressive range of motion treatment for IAC can generally expect to spend about 2 months in therapy. The aggressiveness of each individual session is determined by the therapist and patient, but it is found repeatedly that, with well-established IAC, vigorous passive end point pressures produce the greatest motion gains in a given session and the quickest returns of motion. The patient who reports the sound of "something breaking in there" almost never has been fractured. This is the sound of the adhesions of adhesive capsulitis breaking. During MUA, these sounds are frighteningly loud, and although an X-ray is always ordered after the manipulation, a fracture is rare.

Two schools of thought exist regarding progressive range therapy. Gentle, frequent stretching that is nearly viscoelastic in nature to produce an elongation of contracted capsular structures is the goal of one school. A version of the orthopaedist's manipulation, with forceful overpowering of the contracted structure's mechanical properties (sometimes termed brisement), is the goal of the other. Although the stretching school is currently more popular than the breaking school, the patients who are considered to have resistant frozen shoulder requiring MUA and arthroscopic debridement are nearly always failures of the gentle treatment.

Because progressive range therapy is the mainstay of treatment for adhesive capsulitis, its technical details are important. Each session with the patient should begin and end with range of motion measurement in forward elevation, external rotation, and internal rotation. Heating modalities are first applied. A moist heating pad is generally sufficient; ultrasonation (pulsed) of the deltoid, capsule, cuff muscles, and trapezius may be of greater value in patients with thick subcutaneous fat. Active scapular protraction and retraction, elevation, depression, and rotation are then done with the arm supported to establish a proprioceptive basis for glenohumeral isolation. This is also effective in increasing scapulothoracic range. The forward elevation range is then worked, advancing from the end of the extension range to the comfortable end of the forward elevation range. Eight to 12 repetitions, with maximal pressure placed on the forward elevation end point at the sixth repetition, are done in active assisted mode. This is followed by 6 to 12 repetitions in passive mode, with the practitioner pushing progressively harder as pain permits with each repetition. Most patients are best kept supine with two folded towels under the scapula for this. The exceptions are those with congestive heart disease, pulmonary disease, and morbid obesity, all of whom may be too uncomfortable when flat. They may be treated in 45° head-up beach chair position, again with the scapula stabilized against the mat.

Direct axial traction on the humerus during all these forward elevations is the key to pain reduction and avoidance of fracture. This is the single most important element of these maneuvers. By keeping the ipsilateral hand high on the humerus and the contralateral hand around the elbow, good tactile feedback and control of rotation and traction can be achieved from the bony contact in the supracondylar area, and moderated force can be applied by the short-lever hand close to the axilla. Pain reduction techniques may be used here. Transcutaneous electrical nerve stimulation and cryotherapy help a bit in some patients. Of more reliable value is an oral narcotic taken 40 minutes earlier, however. It is good to feel or hear the pops and cracks of adhesions breaking as one works against the end point. This is by no means necessary for advancement, though.

The next range to be worked is either adduction or external rotation, whichever is more limited. If there is acromioclavicular joint tenderness, little force should be used in adduction because it is likely that acromioclavicular arthritic pain will be worsened. Modalities to the infraspinatus and teres minor during adduction ranging may help relax these antagonist muscles. Although the actual increase that is desired may be small (10° is often all that is needed for functional adduction to the opposite axilla), adduction range can be quite difficult to improve. This may be due to soft tissue impingement between the humeral neck and the coracoid. Plasic deformation in compression is difficult to achieve, and anterior pain during the adduction stretching maneuvers may be intolerable. If this is the impression gotten during adduction stretching, application of deep cold to the anterior shoulder, in the area of the coracoid, is occasionally helpful in permitting advancement of the adduction range.

The external rotation progressive range maneuvers are performed similarly to the forward elevation maneuvers, with somewhat less axial traction being necessary. Pure passive external rotation tends to be less fruitful than forward elevation because so many strong internal rotators have generally been trained to protect against pain by limiting external rotation. Deep heating techniques on the anterior capsule may be helpful here.

Scapulothoracic immobilization, with a pad of folded towels under the supine patient's scapula or even by direct manual pressure on the spine of the scapula, may improve the efficiency of glenohumeral ranging maneuvers in some patients. In many, especially those with thick subcutaneous tissue and tight shoulders, however, this is impossible. Scapulothoracic mobilization specifically is quite important to improve functional movement of the arm. As mentioned earlier, it may also improve glenohumeral joint mechanics. It is good general practice to work on scapular motion in patients with frozen shoulder. Despite this, many practitioners do treat IAC successfully without ever really concentrating on the scapulothoracic articulation, considering only the positions of the arm relative to the body and allowing the motions to divide as they will between the scapulothoracic and glenohumeral articulations.

A home therapy instruction set should supplement every progressive range program. These are the basic self-elevation, external rotation, and internal rotation exercises. They are generally done daily for about 20 minutes. Pulley exercises may be quite beneficial for some patients. These are really an active assisted exercise. They are most valuable when working on the higher ranges of forward elevation (above 120°). Large pendulum or hanging circle exercises are an excellent warm-up drill for the home program.

All members of the team treating the patient with frozen shoulder should have a good idea of the sequence of alternatives that are planned if progress is not being made in progressive range therapy. Although many orthopaedists recommend MUA, if progress is not visible after 6 weeks in therapy there are other options. A useful one is a variation on MUA: hydraulic distention with local anesthetic. In this technique, one injection is made from a posterior approach into the glenohumeral joint, and one is made into the subacromial space. The frozen shoulder generally admits less than 20 mL of fluid; a large-bore needle is used to permit more pressure transmission into the joint. A long-lasting anesthetic in dilute solution (eg, 0.125% bupivacaine) is used, occasionally with an added steroid, although this has not been shown to have any benefit. The injection of the subacromial space is done in the standard fashion from a lateral or posterolateral approach. After a wait of about 10 minutes for the anesthetic to work, the shoulder is manipulated in much the same manner as it would be for MUA. This procedure may be repeated every other day if necessary. It is effective in patients for whom pain is a big issue.

The concept of hydraulically distending the glenohumeral joint to open up the axillary pouch is quite appealing but probably mostly theoretical. Although there is some arthrographic evidence that the capacity of the capsule can be increased this way,[10] it is countered by the consistent arthroscopic observation that joint volume increases little until MUA has been performed, no matter how much fluid pressure is used to distend it.

MUA is utilized frequently as a way to decrease the inconvenience and expense of prolonged progressive range therapy. Concentrated motion therapy, usually five times per week, is necessary after MUA to preserve the gains achieved. The technique of MUA is quite similar to the progressive range technique described above, but of course rather more aggressive. Patients are quite sore after MUA. There is invariably a large hemarthrosis. Cold applications are quite gratifying, and strong pain medications are often given. Although the risk of fracture is decreased by good technique, it is not eliminated, so that X-rays are always ordered after MUA. The neurocirculatory examination of the upper extremity is also followed after manipulation because arterial, venous, or nerve injuries have been reported. Despite undergoing this procedure to save time, the patient should expect at least 3 weeks of physical therapy after MUA. There is a reliable decrease in the pain and next-day soreness of therapy sessions after MUA.

The reasons for failure of MUA to improve passive range include the occurrence of a fracture necessitating immobilization, the inability to break up the contractures despite anesthesia because of the tissues' extraordinary strength, and an underlying, undiagnosed neurologic problem providing an active element to the frozen shoulder. It is in the first two situations that arthroscopic assist has the most logical place in treating the frozen shoulder.

When the shoulder surgeon finds himself or herself pushing too hard without achieving an increase in range with the patient under anesthesia, arthroscopic distention of the glenohumeral joint followed by capsular releases as necessary (done from inside the joint) is a safer, better tolerated technique than pure brute force. The actual amount of tissue that needs to be divided to achieve motion may be surprisingly little. This may indicate that the hydraulic distention used during arthroscopy is providing some benefit. Arthroscopy of most frozen shoulders is technically rather difficult, however. Visualization is impeded by the presence of much blood, distorted intracapsular anatomy, and the decreased overall volume of the joint. When the surgeon finally can see, he or she is often confronted with massive quantities of scar and synovium, labral and capsular pathology, and frequently a torn rotator cuff. The surgical strategy is generally to debride first, reattempt manipulation, and then start releasing the contracted capsular ligaments one at a time until satisfactory motion is achieved. It is possible to release too much and end up with instability, even true dislocation, when one is surgically treating the frozen shoulder. The common presence of rotator cuff tears in shoulders examined arthroscopically during treatment for adhesive capsulitis may be due to some relationship between rotator cuff tears and the development of adhesive capsulitis. Theories about this have been advanced.[11] It may also be due to tearing of the cuff during manipulation and stretching, or it could be an unrelated phenomenon due only to the frequency of rotator cuff tears.

The physical therapy program used after surgical release of the frozen shoulder is essentially the same as that used after MUA. Information from the arthroscopy, such as the report of a cuff tear, may cause the practitioner to delay the advance to active motion (which should otherwise be done as soon as tolerated) with the idea of protecting the remaining cuff. The practitioner is cautioned not to be overly impressed by the arthroscopic pictures, despite their grim appearance. The clinical evaluation of the shoulder's stability and the strength of its rotator cuff must still come from careful physical examination. Similarly, effective treatment is ultimately physical here. Frozen shoulder must be treated with motion.

OPEN VERSUS CLOSED KINEMATIC CHAIN EXERCISES

A mechanical concept that is useful in treatment of frozen shoulder, as well as in many other phases of shoulder rehabilitation, is the kinetic or kinematic chain. This refers to a system of rigid links, linearly connected by joints, so that motion at one linkage may be affected by motion at the other linkages. Ankle–knee–hip, wrist–elbow–shoulder, and even the vertebral column are examples. If the ends of the chain are fixed or controlled in such a way that the motion of proximal linkages is determined by the motion of distal linkages, the system forms a closed kinetic chain. The classic example is that of the weight-bearing ankle, whose dorsiflexion produces knee flexion and hip flexion. A classic open kinematic chain is seen in the dorsiflexion and volar flexion of the wrist in waving. Elbow and shoulder motion are completely independent of the non–weight-bearing wrist's motion.[12]

The usual, functional motions of the limbs involve simultaneous motion of many joints along the kinetic chain and many muscles around each joint. Proprioceptive, kinesthetic, and joint senses control agonists, antagonists, and stabilizers to produce useful movement in such a way as to avoid overloading muscle and joint structures. Although the true complexity of this rather beautiful process is only appreciated by the unfortunately mute cerebellum, a good bit of research on the lower extremity has shown decreased strains on supporting structures (such as the anterior cruciate ligament) and improved clinical results when weight-bearing, proprioception-enhancing exercises are employed in rehabilitation after knee and ankle injury or surgery.[13]

Because the lower extremities are primarily weight bearing, much of their functional use is in closed chain modes. Although the application of closed chain exercise has been studied extensively in knee rehabilitation, much is still being learned regarding closed chain exercises in shoulder rehabilitation. Presenting one of the most difficult rehabilitation challenges faced by the shoulder practitioner, the frozen shoulder has been a testing ground of sorts for closed chain kinetic shoulder exercises, which have in some cases proved to be helpful when little else has been effective.

Closed chain shoulder exercises include those that are truly fixed-hand weight bearing (eg, quadrupedal walking), various push-ups, push-ups plus, press-ups (from the floor, wall, or incline board), and press-outs leaning on a chair back. For the reasonably athletic patient with a frozen shoulder, especially if there is a significant component of active contracture or splinting against capsular or cuff pain, these may be tried as primary range exercises with or without passive stretching and modalities. The ultimate exercise of this first type is the pull-up or chin-up from a dead hang. Needless to say, this requires excellent strength and is an aggressive motion exercise.

Next in the range of closed chain shoulder exercises are those that involve somewhat less mechanical constraint and partial body weight support. Side-to-side sliding in various single planes with hands leaning on a Fitter, similar motions in three planes while leaning with the hands on a BAPS board, body weight–balancing pull-up machines, and three-joint motions using an isokinetic apparatus are examples of these. Clinical experience with these is still limited in the author's practice because this approach has only been employed for a year at the time of this writing. It has been commonly observed, however, that the bearing of body weight in these complex, physiologic motions often does something immediately to reduce pain and improve range and scapulothoracic–humeral coordination.

The least closed of the closed chain exercises are those that use more advanced proprioceptive feedback tasks with significantly reduced body weight or other (lighter) resistive loads. Variations on ball (Physioball) rolling (up inclines, against a wall, in alphabet patterns) and body weight translation with the arms used to propel the patient while sitting or lying prone on the Physioball are examples. Although useful in cuff and scapular muscle rehabilitation, these are less useful in gaining range.

The closed chain, integrated proprioceptive and functional motion enhancement approach to shoulder rehabilitation is being utilized, with good results, by an increasing number of practitioners. The place for these exercises in rotator cuff–injured, arthritic, and destabilized shoulders is quickly being established. There is a generalized feeling of safety with their use because of the high level of feedback control. In simpler terms, it is hoped that the pain of cuff tearing or glenohumeral subluxation will prevent these problems during this type of exercise. Quite sorely lacking, however, are electromyographic and arthrokinematic data on cuff and capsular stresses during these exercises. As such data are acquired, there will certainly be a greater safety margin associated with the use of these active maneuvers in the injured shoulder. This leaves the frozen shoulder patient as the current, ideal candidate for closed chain rehabilitation techniques.

REFERENCES

1. Turkel SJ, Panio MW, Marshall JL, Girgis FA. Stabilizing mechanism preventing anterior dislocation of glenohumeral joint. *J Bone Joint Surg Am.* 1981;63:1208–1217.
2. Warwick R, Williams P. *Gray's Anatomy.* 35th ed. Philadelphia, Pa: Saunders; 1973.
3. Pasteur F. Shoulder pain and physical therapy. *J Radiol Electrol.* 1932;16:419–426.
4. Lippman RK. Frozen shoulder and bicipital tenosynovitis. *Arch Surg.* 1943;47:283–296.
5. Neer CS. *Shoulder Reconstruction.* Philadelphia, Pa: Saunders; 1990.
6. Bigliani L. Frozen shoulder etiology and treatment. Lecture at American Association of Orthopedic Surgeons' course on the shoulder; March 1994; Marco Island, Fla.
7. Leffert RD. The frozen shoulder. *Instr Course Lect Am Assoc Orthop Surg.* 1985;34:199–203.
8. Steinbrocker O. Frozen shoulder: present perspective. *Arch Phys Med Rehabil.* 1968;49:388–395.
9. Neer CS. Anterior acromioplasty for chronic impingement syndrome in the shoulder. *J Bone Joint Surg Am.* 1972;54:41–50.
10. Helbig B, Wagner P, Dohler R. Mobilization of the frozen shoulder under general anesthesia. *Acta Orthop Belg.* 1983;49:267–274.
11. Murnaghan JP. Frozen shoulder. In: Rockwood CA, Matsen FA, eds. *The Shoulder.* Philadelphia, Pa: Saunders; 1990.
12. Norkin CC, Levangie PK. *Joint Structure and Function.* 2nd ed. Philadelphia, Pa: Davis; 1992:69–70.
13. Yack HJ, Collins CE, Whieldon TJ. Comparison of closed and open chain kinetic chain exercise in the anterior cruciate ligament deficient knee. *Am J Sports Med.* 1993;21:49–54.

Chapter 8

Rotator Cuff Disease and Impingement

SUBACROMIAL IMPINGEMENT

Clinical Presentation

The patient with symptomatic impingement may present with any number of an exceptionally wide range of complaints. That this is by far the most common shoulder problem for which professional help is sought should be borne in mind by every practitioner treating shoulder patients. The classic presentations are discussed in Chapter 1. These are expanded on here to include the less common clues and complaints.

The 40- to 60-year-old patient with night pain, pain with overhead work, and difficulty maintaining the arms at horizontal probably has impingement. He or she is likely to have a positive impingement sign, positive subacromial injection test, and positive magnetic resonance (MR) scan for cuff irritation or tearing. There are some situations, however, in which this classic presentation can accompany nonimpingement rotator cuff disease. Serious overuse of the rotator cuff muscles may produce exactly the same combination of signs and symptoms. There are some unusual, tumorlike conditions of the subacromial bursa that present the same way. These produce masses of heavy, collagenous, but nonmalignant reactive bursal tissue that irritates the cuff. Direct trauma to the cuff or cuff muscles may do this as well. All these less common phenomena still involve rotator cuff damage, however. There is nothing extraordinary about the impingement phenomenon itself; it is simply the frictional abrasion of the flat tendinous tissue of the rotator cuff by harder tissues close by. The reaction of the irritated cuff tendons is also typical: Inflammation, swelling, thinning, and tearing occur in roughly that order, with the reactive bursal tissues around the cuff typically hypertrophying and becoming inflamed.

The unusual thing about rotator cuff disease is the range of symptoms that it produces. It is common in clinical practice to perform a subacromial injection (from a posterior approach, with excellent bony landmarks) and have the patient report pain, paresthesia, or numbness that shoots down the arm into the wrist or hand when the needle is placed into the subacromial space. There is no nerve that runs along this route. The referral of pain from the subacromial space and the rotator cuff may be distal, producing deltoid insertion area, supracondylar, wrist, or medial scapular pain, or proximal, as in the cases of impingement-produced trapezius, neck, or head pain.

The clinical presentations of impingement with which the practitioner ought to be familiar may be divided into the typical and the atypical. No pretense of an anatomic or physiologic explanation for these observations is made. Atypical impingement most often presents with subacromial cervicalgia. This is neck pain and limitation of motion marked by worsening during overhead or prolonged horizontal work, night pain, and the physical examination signs of neck pain increased by the impingement maneuver and decreased significantly by subacromial injection of local anesthetic.

As noted earlier, there is a strange tendency for any irritating phenomenon in the extremity to be intensified by mild proximal compression of the nerves supplying that extremity. The patient with subacromial cervicalgia will therefore often have a concomitant cervical radiculopathy. The nerve compression may be visible on MR imaging of the cervical spine and indeed may have already been treated surgically with a cervical discectomy. If true subacromial cervicalgia is present, however, it is unlikely that the neck surgery was successful in relieving the patient's neck pain. Patients themselves are often unwilling to believe that their neck pain is caused by a shoulder problem; the shoulder itself may be truly pain free. More often, there are mild shoulder symptoms of night pain and pain with overhead work in subacromial cervicalgia patients, although the neck pain predominates their list of complaints.

Supracondylar humerus pain is another presentation of atypical impingement. This pain is similar in character to the aching felt in the fleshy upper part of the arm that characterizes deltoid insertional pain. It is somewhat more distal, however, and is often confused with the pain of lateral epicondylitis (tennis elbow). Unlike lateral epicondylitis, supracondylar atypical impingement pain is not associated with tenderness in the supracondylar area and does not change with resisted motion of the wrist. The impingement maneuver does intensify this pain, and subacromial injection of local anesthetic decreases it. The frequency of biceps tendinitis in patients with distal humerus pain from impingement is high enough to suggest that referral of the pain along the course of the biceps muscle is involved. This distal arm pain usually responds well to exercises that strengthen the humeral head depressors (ie, the rotator cuff and biceps).

Pain felt below the elbow is the least common presentation of atypical impingement. A concomitant paresthesia, felt in the ulnar dorsum of the wrist, often accompanies the forearm pain. Variable numbness, without any reproducible findings on pin prick testing, may be another complaint in these patients. Patients with this presentation of atypical impingement pain are the most likely to report painful sensations that run down the arm during a subacromial injection. The pain relief produced by subacromial anesthetic injection takes somewhat longer to develop in these patients; although the typical impinger notes relief in less than 1 minute after injection, the forearm pain patient may not feel the pain subside until 5 minutes after injection.

Anatomy

The anatomy of subacromial impingement was originally described by Neer in 1972.[1] An enormous body of research done since that time has done little to change our essential understanding of this mechanism. The physical and surgical treatment of impingement must start with an appreciation of the concept of the supraspinatus outlet.

The three muscles of the rotator cuff originate on the scapula and insert on the greater tuberosity of the humerus. The supraspinatus, infraspinatus, and teres minor are, in common surgical terminology, considered the rotator cuff muscles. They have no true agonists. The subscapularis, although listed as a rotator cuff muscle in most anatomy texts, is usually mentioned separately and not included under the term *rotator cuff*. The subscapularis is an internal rotator, inserting on the lesser tuberosity. Its many agonists and entirely different biomechanical milieu have led to its glossologic separation from the other three muscles by those who treat problems of the rotator cuff.

The supraspinatus muscle, taking its origin in the upper, or supraspinatus, fossa of the scapula, travels laterally and becomes flat and tendinous, forming the anterior margin of the rotator cuff. It blends in at its posterior margin with the infraspinatus tendon. The infraspinatus muscle originates in the inferior, or infraspinatus, fossa of the scapula. The third and most posterior tendon of the rotator cuff is the teres minor muscle. The teres minor originates from the lateral scapular border and then, traveling laterally, becomes flat and tendinous, blending in with the infraspinatus.

From front to back, the rotator cuff itself comprises the confluent tendons of the supraspinatus, infraspinatus, and teres minor, which insert on three rather indistinct facets of the greater tuberosity of the humerus. If one could sit on the insertion of the supraspinatus tendon and look back along the direction of its fibers, one would see an arch of bone and ligament passing obliquely over the supraspinatus. Laterally, this arch is composed of the acromion and the inserting fibers of the coracoacromial (CA) ligament. More medially, the acromio-clavicular (AC) joint usually bulges downward a bit (more in cases of AC arthritis), lowering the arch. Although there is no true foramen, tunnel, or retinaculum that surrounds it, the supraspinatus tendon is bounded above by this arch and below by the superior aspect of the glenoid with its labrum and, of course, the humeral head. The supraspinatus outlet is therefore a confluence of structures, all of which are relatively immobile, that form the passageway for the anterior rotator cuff.

Looking at the supraspinatus outlet from the side, the shape of the acromion can be appreciated. Acromia vary enormously in their relative size and shape.[2] The anterior beak of this bone may slope upward or downward or stay flat, continuing the direction of the flat midsection. The flat midsection itself may be nearly vertical in some people and nearly horizontal in others. The relative length of the acromion varies as well. The acromion may project out 2 cm past the anterior border of the lateral clavicle, or it may stop at the clavicle. Classic impingement occurs when the acromion, the CA ligament, or the undersurface of the AC joint rub against the rotator cuff, specifically the anterior cuff (Figure 8–1), producing abrasion of the cuff tissue, inflammation, and

A

Figure 8–1 Mechanism of subacromial impingement on the rotator cuff. **(A)** Diagram of impingement of the inferior acromion on the underlying rotator cuff tendon. Arrow shows motion of the humerus during forward elevation.

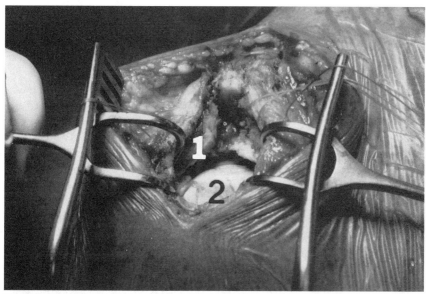

B

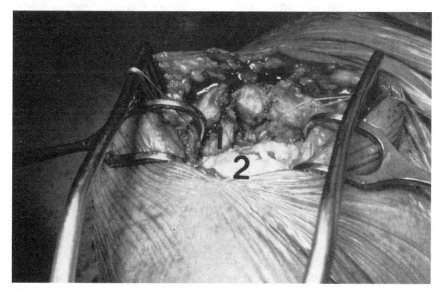

C

Figure 8–1 (B) Surgical exposure showing the space between the acromion and the humeral head with downward traction on the arm. 1, acromion; 2, humeral head. **(C)** Elevation of the humerus causes the acromion (1) to hit the humeral head (2). The rotator cuff is torn and retracted, leaving a bare humeral head.

pain. The relationship between the anatomic factors above and the impingement phenomenon should be clear. The greater the inferior projection of the acromion, the greater the mechanical interference with the supraspinatus tendon. Similarly, a downward-sloping acromial body and anteriorly projecting acromial tip produce more impingement.

An AC joint that is enlarged and irregular will also impinge on the cuff tendons, although at a somewhat more medial and posterior location. The damage done to the rotator cuff by the inferior aspect of the AC joint is usually seen at the musculotendinous junction of the supraspinatus (Figure 8–2). The involved cuff tissue here has a beefy, macerated appearance. This type of cuff tear, which is seen in younger, muscular patients, is qualitatively different from the typical acromial impingement tear. Subacromial impingement produces an atrophic, "worn away" appearance of the cuff tendons, which are frequently retracted (Figure 8–3). AC impingement tears usually do not retract. Regaining range of motion during postoperative rehabilitation of this type of tear is easier because there is no tension in the repaired cuff. Nonsurgical treatment should not stress anterior cuff strengthening because muscular hypertrophy increases the mechanical impingement against the AC joint (Figure 8–4).

There are other mechanical causes of impingement in the subacromial space. A poorly healed fracture of the greater tuberosity leaves bone projecting upward from the humerus. The projecting bone tends to impinge against the acromion, producing similar symptoms. This is not classic outlet impingement, though, because as described earlier, this involves bony impingement against bone, not the cuff tendon. In actual fact, there is often seen to be classic acromial bone-on-cuff impingement occurring in those people who, after tuberosity fracture, have continued symptoms.

Wheelchair users may develop subacromial impingement because of the constant upward pressure on their arms. The action of raising one's weight with the arms at the side is certainly not considered an impingement-producing maneuver, as overhead activities are, yet if there is upward translation of the humerus relative to the glenoid acromion-on-cuff impingement may occur.

The most subtle variation on the mechanical impingement phenomenon is termed complex impingement. This is best understood as a dynamic phenomenon involving some degree of anterior and possibly superior instability of the glenohumeral joint. It is seen primarily in throwing athletes who develop rotator cuff pain but have negative classic impingement signs. In complex impingement, the rotator cuff is irritated either by the superior aspect of the glenoid (from inside the joint)[3] or by a more posterior part of the acromion making contact with the cuff (from the outside). Although complex impingement is included under the anatomy section, there is little evidence of any anatomic peculiarity or abnormality that causes it, beyond the mild instability

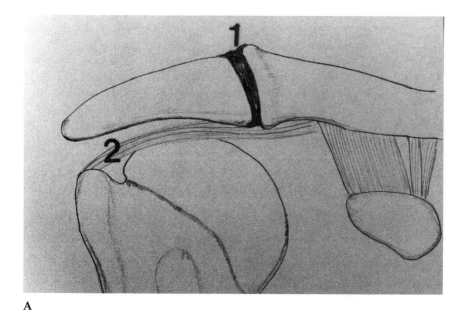

A

B

Figure 8–2 AC joint impingement. **(A)** Diagram showing an enlarged AC articulation impinging on the rotator cuff. 1, AC joint; 2, cuff tendons. This usually takes place at the musculotendinous junction of the supraspinatus. **(B)** MR image of same. 1, inferior, impinging aspect of the AC joint.

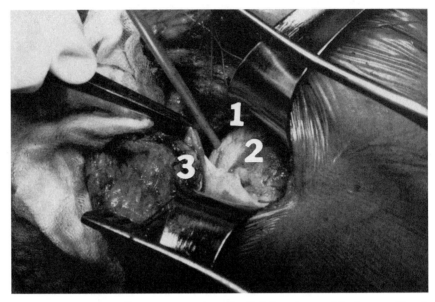

Figure 8–3 Rotator cuff tear. 1, torn edge of cuff; 2, bare bone of the humeral head; 3, anterior acromion.

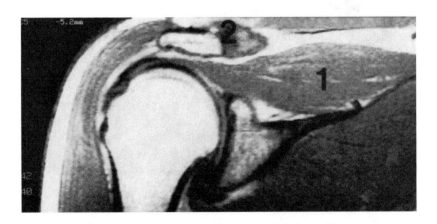

Figure 8–4 MR image showing hypertrophy of the supraspinatus muscle (1) and AC joint impingement (2).

mentioned above. The surgical findings in patients with complex impingement are most often changes of the glenoid labrum posterosuperiorly. Some degree of rotator cuff abrasion is often present, however. Complex impingement has been termed glenoid impingement, instability-associated impingement, and pitcher's shoulder. It is discussed in greater detail in Chapter 12.

Pathophysiology

The exact pathologic process involved in the creation of rotator cuff disease has been the topic of rather vigorous debate in the surgical community. Impingement, as described, is believed by most authorities to be the underlying cause of most rotator cuff tears. This is difficult to argue against because the surgical findings of rotator cuff abrasion or tearing at the exact area of acromial contact is so common. Two other mechanisms have been advanced, though, and they are likely to account for some (small) fraction of the cases of rotator cuff tear.[4,5,6]

Pure mechanical failure of the otherwise normal rotator cuff is believed by some to account for the occurrence of sudden, traumatic rupture of the rotator cuff in patients with no history of shoulder pain. This must be the simple material failure of the cuff tendons when overloaded in tension. Eccentric contraction of the cuff muscles, as would be observed in a patient putting an arm out to break a fall, is far more likely to produce a pure tensile failure than concentric contraction. Greater forces can be generated this way than by concentric contraction because the energy of the fall is added to the system. The cuff muscles pulling one way and the humeral insertion point moving the other leave the cuff in the middle; it is then simply pulled apart. The most convincing evidence for this happening is, again, the appearance of some (few) completely avulsed cuffs at surgery. After a true traumatic episode, usually a fall that is broken by the affected upper extremity, a cleanly and entirely ripped off cuff is found that bears absolutely no signs of impingement abrasion. Tissue analysis of the edges of the cuff tear is in agreement in these cases; no chronic inflammatory changes or other signs of wear are seen. These patients generally advance rapidly after a secure repair. Because they are not recovering from the slow, primarily degenerative process whereby impingement produces cuff tears, they are not slowed down by the need to restrengthen the cuff muscles and reverse the changes caused by chronic irritation and inflammation in the subacromial space. The other clinical corollary of this is that, once identified, the pure tensile failure cuff tear should be fixed soon. It is unusual to achieve a good result in this situation with nonoperative treatment.

The other pathophysiologic mechanism that has been advanced to explain the high prevalence of rotator cuff disease involves poor blood circulation to the rotator cuff.[5] The cuff is thus believed to fail because of an intrinsic hypoperfusion state, which renders the cuff weak and unable to remodel and strengthen in response to normally applied stress. Supporters of this theory maintain that the mechanical impingement phenomenon is basically a normal occurrence; it is the cuff tissue's inability to heal and strengthen normally that makes it unable to tolerate the normal mechanical challenges of impingement and moving of the humerus. The scientific evidence cited for this is found in microscopic studies of the blood supply to the cuff tissues. Indeed, the circulation to the cuff tendons, in comparison with that of most other structures around the shoulder, is quite poor. The rotator cuff is made of white, dense, collagenous tendon tissue. It is chronically under tension, making blood flow through it more difficult. Most supportive of this theory, the circulation is poorest in the part of the cuff that usually tears first. It seems likely that poor circulation plays a role, at least in some cases. The problem with drawing this conclusion from these microcirculation studies is causation; it is not clear whether the observed decrease in local microcirculation in the area of cuff damage is the cause of the damage or the result of the damage produced by chronic impingement.

The microcirculatory failure theory of rotator cuff disease does not directly explain the success of surgical measures that reduce impingement in reversing the disease. It is probably a more important factor than most American surgeons recognize it to be, however. The effect of stretching and strengthening on the cuff and cuff muscles is difficult to isolate from the effect of impingement reduction done through either increasing the tone of the humeral head depressors or surgery. There are, nonetheless, many reasons to believe that the physical treatments used on the cuff muscles produce greater microcirculation in the tendons. Tendinous tissues do respond to the application of controlled stress with increased circulation and, eventually, hypertrophy. The debate is somewhat academic because the same physical maneuvers can be expected to produce both impingement reduction and increased microcirculation. Appreciation of this pathophysiologic principle is nevertheless important to the underlying goals of physical treatments of the cuff.

ROTATOR CUFF TEARS

The pathophysiologic mechanisms described above create a few classic pathoanatomic patterns of cuff tearing. Somewhat different nonoperative, operative, and postoperative management of the different tear patterns should be employed. Management should also be tailored to the estimated age of the tear. Consideration of tear patterns begins with the fracture of the greater tuberosity, or the cuff tear through bone (Exhibit 8–1).

Exhibit 8–1 Rotator Cuff Tear Classification

Greater tuberosity fracture
- Nondisplaced
- Displaced
- With glenohumeral dislocation

Impingement tears
- Partial thickness
- Full thickness
  1. Small
  2. Large
  3. Massive
  4. Ancient
  5. Recurrent

Pure traumatic tears
- Avulsion
- Laceration

Pathologic tears

For what is usually a small, nondisplaced apophyseal fracture, the nondisplaced greater tuberosity fracture is often rather difficult to treat. Apophyses are terminal protrusions from bone into which tendons insert. They are subject to tension and generally have the ability to heal under conditions of tension. This is mentioned because tension at a fracture site generally produces distraction and failure to heal. Greater tuberosity fractures usually exhibit a linear fracture pattern, indicative of failure of the bone under tension. Because the greater tuberosity is the insertion site of the rotator cuff, the tension to produce this fracture is generally thought to be produced by the cuff muscles. (The major exception to this is in cases of greater tuberosity fracture with anterior dislocation of the glenohumeral joint. In the case of anterior dislocation, the greater tuberosity may be sheared off by the anterior edge of the glenoid as the shoulder dislocates.) The tendinous tissue of a normal rotator cuff is extremely strong. In producing a greater tuberosity fracture, the cuff is failing through bone. If nondisplaced (ie, properly localized in its original, anatomic position), the fracture may be accompanied by a rotator cuff tear, which becomes quite symptomatic after healing. This is because impingement often becomes severe after the fracture heals.

The tuberosity fracture generally heals with a few millimeters of increased height of the tuberosity, representing fracture displacement and soft tissue reaction. This seems to be enough to create impingement pain and to render symptomatic any rotator cuff tearing already present (or produced by the trauma that caused the fracture).

A displaced greater tuberosity fracture must be accompanied by some degree of tearing of the cuff,[5] at least a dissociation from the anterior tendon of the subscapularis. The majority of these fractures are avulsions of part of the tuberosity. These leave a tear between the cuff elements attached to the avulsed fragment and those still attached to the undisturbed part of the tuberosity. These tears are quite different in character from impingement tears, however (Figure 8–5). They are linear, along the lines of force normally present in the cuff. They are often repaired surgically at the time of the tuberosity fracture repair. Tears of this type do not need the degree of protection during postoperative rehabilitation that transverse impingement tears require. It is the strength of the fracture repair that governs the amount of stress to which this type of surgical reconstruction can be subjected. Because the fixation used in the surgical repair of a tuberosity fracture is secured in bone (heavy suture or wire is often used), early use of the cuff muscles and a relatively accelerated rehabilitation course may be chosen. As with the nondisplaced fractures, impingement may complicate the rehabilitation

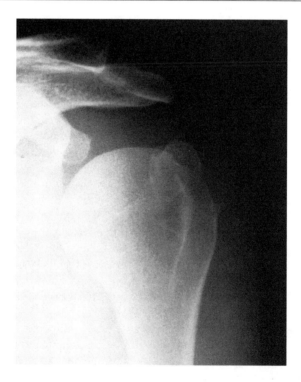

Figure 8–5 Tuberosity fracture associated with a longitudinal cuff tear.

course after repair of a displaced tuberosity fracture unless steps were taken to prevent this during the surgical procedure (eg, acromioplasty and lowering of the tuberosity fragment).

The greater tuberosity fracture that is seen in association with anterior glenohumeral joint dislocation (a fracture-dislocation) is a slightly different clinical entity. It is often possible to reduce the dislocation nonsurgically, after which the tuberosity may reduce as well. After it heals, this fracture usually does not leave residual impingement, and there is only rarely a problem with residual anterior instability. Although high-energy injuries, irreducible fracture-dislocations, and dislocations with concomitant fractures of other parts of the upper humerus and scapula are not as straightforward in their pathophysiology, the greater tuberosity fracture-dislocation can be viewed as a complete cuff avulsion through bone. When anatomically reduced, good function can be expected because the cuff, in its entirety, is intact. The balance of forces among the three cuff tendons is maintained because they all insert onto the tuberosity fragment. The major rehabilitation concerns are thus avoidance of active use of the cuff muscles until bone healing is secure and avoidance of abduction–external rotation to prevent recurrent dislocation. Motion can be started earlier if there has been a secure surgical repair of the tuberosity.

Classic impingement tears are the most commonly encountered. These all start out as partial-thickness tears. A more appropriate term for this might be *rotator cuff abrasion.* If impingement continues, the local abrasion of the cuff deepens and becomes a full-thickness tear. The full-thickness tear then might be a stable one that remains for years without growing much, or it may progress, getting larger and producing greater pain and weakness until the entire function of the cuff is lost. A shoulder that has had no rotator cuff function for years may be painless. Often it is still the source of some pain, which is increased by attempted use. People with a large or massive and ancient tear generally are unable to elevate actively or even to maintain a passive elevation of the shoulder.

Residual function of the remaining, untorn bits of the cuff varies considerably among patients. It probably depends most on the patient's ability to recruit other muscles (deltoid, trapezius, pectorals, latissimus dorsi, and scapular rotators) as well as the glenohumeral joint's intrinsic (or passive) ability to resist axial elevation of the humeral head. These are both important concepts involved in both nonoperative and postoperative rehabilitation. It is the rotator cuff muscles that turn the glenohumeral articulation into a fulcrum around which the deltoid produces torque and thus active elevation of the arm. If one looks at a radiograph or skeleton and knows the origin and insertion of the deltoid, it is obvious that its contraction alone should mostly produce shear, generating upward slipping of the humeral head on the glenoid. The cuff prevents this by initiating some rotation and by keeping the humeral head centered in the glenoid.

One of the goals of rehabilitation of patients with cuff tears is to enhance the humeral head's depressive function of the remaining cuff and the biceps (whose long head tendon crosses the humeral head, exerting a downward force on it during contraction). Doing this not only strengthens the remaining cuff but also enhances the ability of the deltoid to function as an elevator of the humerus. The actual kinematics involved in elevation of the arm in the presence of a cuff tear is not well established but seems to involve use of the scapular rotators. Subtle motions of rotation and protraction are used by some people with no cuff function to position the glenoid in such a way as to provide more of a fulcrum using bone and other passive soft tissue joint elements (labrum and capsule). This can be observed by watching the scapulae during active elevation in these (few) patients without a cuff who are still capable of elevating actively.

Surgeons have classified cuff tears according to size.[7] The difficulty encountered in repairing (and rehabilitating) most cuff tears is directly proportional to the size of the hole. Size is related to the age of impingement tears as well. Because of the tendency of the cuff to retract after it tears and for the cuff muscles themselves to shorten and develop fibrofatty degeneration from disuse, a poor functional outcome is also associated with large, old tears. Tears are considered small if they are less than about 2 cm in maximal diameter. Small tears are roughly oval in shape, and because a good amount of untorn tendon remains on both sides of the tear (ie, anteriorly and posteriorly) they can be repaired simply by bringing the edges together with sutures. Many shoulder surgeons will still place a suture through the bone of the greater tuberosity for security when repairing a small tear. Either way, the speed of rehabilitation is limited mostly by the surgical repair of the deltoid (which has to be detached from the acromion to some degree during the procedure). A small cuff tear takes 6 to 12 weeks to heal. Active use of the cuff should therefore not be started until at least this long postoperatively. A partial-thickness tear, which is not actually repaired, may sometimes take longer to rehabilitate than a small, full-thickness tear. This is because thinned, damaged tissue still transmits the force of the cuff muscles. It is expected that, as long as it is protected from overuse, the abraded cuff tendon will thicken and strengthen once the impingement process is stopped. This may take many months, however. In cases of extensive partial-thickness tearing, a carefully graduated, light resistance program should be used to encourage strengthening of the cuff tendon itself. Muscular strengthening of the spinati and teres minor is considered secondarily.

A large tear is 2 to approximately 5 cm in maximal diameter. Most surgically treated tears are in this range. The nonoperative treatment of large tears is a subject of some controversy. Nonoperative measurement of tear size is, in the first place, quite inaccurate. Arthrograms are useful in determining the presence of a tear but help little with size estimates. The experienced radiologist reading a shoulder MR image may be capable of estimating tear size, but this is simply not a dependable estimate. The MR image can give a reliable indication of whether a tear is small, large, or massive, however. Little valuable information is to be had in the comparison of the size of large tears. The secondary changes produced by rotator cuff tears begin to play a significant role when tears are large. Elevation of the humeral head may be apparent on plain radiographs (Figures 8–6 and 8–7). This is believed to produce bony impingement (there is no cuff tissue interposed because of the tear) of the humeral head and greater tuberosity on the acromion.

Advanced retraction of the rotator cuff tendons often imbalances the forces on the greater tuberosity. The supraspinatus tendon nearly always tears first, followed by the infraspinatus. The posterior cuff (teres minor) plays a different role physiologically, and its direction of pull makes it more of an external rotator when the arm is at the side. This can make coordination of the deltoid and the remaining cuff difficult, resulting in poor residual ability to elevate the arm. The long-term presence of reactive bursal tissue in the glenohumeral joint, unresisted shear forces from the deltoid, and the constant loss of joint fluid contribute to the development of cuff tear arthropathy, a type of glenohumeral arthritis that may be a serious problem with old, massive tears.

Tears that recur after surgical repair pose a difficult clinical challenge. A symptomatic, complete, recurrent cuff tear is a clinical entity that must be distinguished from a somewhat painful postcuff repair shoulder that has a positive arthrogram or MR scan. It must be understood that the MR scan of a shoulder after completely successful cuff repair surgery is likely to be interpreted as demonstrating a rotator cuff tear. Scar, healing cuff, and reactive tissues from surgery are likely to give an abnormal signal that is interpreted as a tear. Similarly, although a watertight repair is sought at open surgery, pumping in contrast with a syringe and needle may show a leak in an otherwise well-repaired cuff. Arthrograms therefore have little use after cuff repairs because they have a high rate of positivity. Shoulders are also commonly painful with rotator cuff weakness for long periods after rotator cuff repair. The criteria for diagnosing recurrent cuff tear requiring rerepair are therefore clinical, and the practitioner must be aware of this specific clinical entity. The recurrent cuff tear is usually traumatic. It most often is caused by a sudden eccentric load, such as catching oneself while falling. A pop may be heard, and there is sudden, complete loss of cuff function. Pain with this is variable but is not often severe. Little improvement in cuff function occurs with time after this injury. The treatment is surgical and the rehabilitation long and difficult, especially because the specter of still another rupture of the repaired cuff haunts every member of the team.

Traumatic cuff tears are those produced by direct trauma to the cuff. Most often knives and bullets produce these. Although no particular pattern is rec-

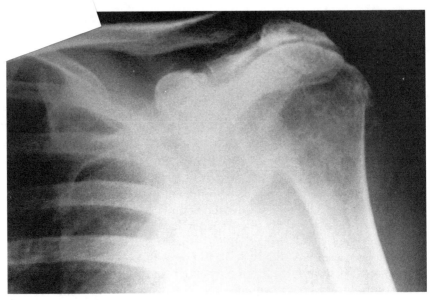

A

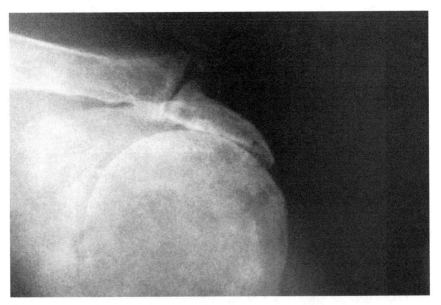

B

Figure 8–6 **(A)** Humeral head elevation with cuff dysfunction. **(B)** Detail of bony impingement of the humeral head on the acromion.

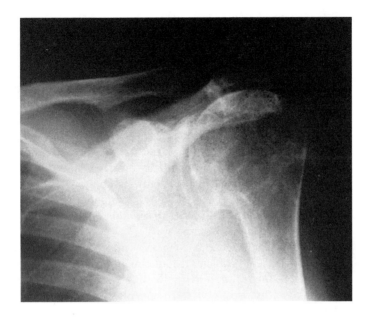

Figure 8–7 Same case as in Figure 8–6 after acromioplasty, AC arthroplasty, and debridement.

ognizable in these injuries, they are mentioned to note the fact that, with no underlying impingement disease, cuff tears heal quicker and stronger. Of course, great damage can be done with shrapnel or an axe, but the most common traumatic cuff injuries are rather neat knife and bullet holes. Those injuries whose acute surgical exploration or debridement permits easy closure of the cuff generally do well in rehabilitation, but those knife- and gunshot-induced cuff tears that are not repaired surgically do well also. Simply maintaining passive range of motion until healing has taken place is the most important element of rehabilitation in these (hopefully rare) cases.

Pathologic cuff tears are caused by infection, inflammatory disease, metabolic disease, or tumor that damages the cuff tissues or muscles. They are nearly impossible to repair surgically. Maximal medical treatment of the causative disease is desirable. Physical treatments must be, above all, gentle. Whatever bits of the cuff are still functional must be preserved. The pathologic milieu around the cuff favors the extension of tears. Until the underlying disease process is controlled, maintaining function and achieving comfort might be the most appropriate goals of physical treatment. Resting the joint and the occasional use of a shoulder sling to decrease pain are two old-fashioned treatments that may still be useful in the treatment of pathologic tears.

The rheumatoid patient with cuff disease is sometimes considered under the pathologic cuff tear category. The destructive enzymes and cellular processes of rheumatoid arthritis may destroy any structure around a joint; bone and cuff tendon are not immune to this process. It is not universal, however, that the rotator cuff is destroyed in shoulders affected by rheumatoid disease. The articular surface cartilage generally is attacked first, and the patient may have tremendous pain from arthritis per se, but the cuff is intact and functional. Cuff rehabilitation and strengthening may certainly be hampered by the presence of the underlying articular surface destruction. The decision to treat the rheumatoid shoulder as pathologic cuff disease is aided by MR evaluation of the shoulder. If the cuff signal is entirely abnormal, only minimal strengthening is employed. If there is a significant amount of intact cuff, however, the shoulder is treated for arthritis. Cuff function can then be expected to respond to properly graduated exercise.

The pathologic cuff tears seen after long-term infection and gouty arthropathy are difficult treatment problems. Motion maintenance is a primary concern here because meaningful cuff strengthening is difficult to achieve and surgical cuff repair nearly impossible. This type of end-stage rotator cuff disease is similar to advanced cuff tear arthropathy in its treatment and outlook. Surgery is hampered by the intrinsic weakness of the cuff tissues; they are more likely to tear than stretch when pulled together, and the sutures used to hold them in place are likely to cut through the issue. Physical treatments can make an important difference by controlling pain and maximizing function. This is done by reducing stiffness and strengthening the noncuff shoulder girdle muscles. Improving the strength of the cuff itself is attempted, but in the case of true pathologic cuff deficiency it is unlikely to be effective.

Cuff tear arthropathy, seen primarily in the older population, is the long-term result of an untreated rotator cuff tear.[8] It is not common enough to be a clear danger to every patient with a torn rotator cuff, but its distinct pathophysiology makes it a possibility. The chronic presence of a hole in the rotator cuff and joint capsule of the glenohumeral joint is believed to be responsible for loss of joint fluid and, with it, joint nourishment and lubrication. As mentioned above, increased shear at the articular surfaces and the action of reactive bursal tissues on the articular surfaces may also play a role in the development of this arthritis. In later stages, the friction of the humeral head moving against the undersurface of the acromion undoubtedly plays a role in creating pain and humeral surface destruction.

Cuff tear arthropathy takes years to develop. It is not known whether early physical treatment to decrease impingement can slow or prevent its occurrence. From a surgical point of view, by the time significant cuff tear arthropathy has developed it is too late to improve things simply by stopping impingement and repairing the cuff. Joint surface irregularity now dictates joint replacement, and chronic retraction and fibrosis of the cuff muscles greatly diminish the chances of good cuff function after any possible repair. Cuff tear arthropathy patients can become chronically dependent on physical therapy. A significant percentage of them can be kept nearly pain free, with shoulder function adequate for their activities of daily living, by aggressive use of modalities, ranging, and strengthening. Because of the age, weakness, and arthropathy of these patients, home programs have been much less successful than outpatient therapy. When physical therapy is stopped, symptoms often recur. During therapy, however, relief is sufficient to obviate the need for surgery. This situation creates a semipermanent therapy requirement that can become quite taxing to all involved with the patient's care.

The surgical treatment of cuff tear arthropathy is another controversial area. With articular surface disease and rotator cuff tearing as the essential mechanical problems, the obvious solution is to replace the joint surfaces and repair the cuff. Patient satisfaction with this treatment is about 50%. Recurrent cuff tear, failure of the repaired cuff to function, and failure actually to repair the cuff at the time of surgery are problems that result from the long-term presence of the tear. Relief of the pain produced by joint surface irregularity is reliable after joint replacement; if physical examination reveals pain generated primarily by the glenohumeral articulation, much benefit can be expected from the surgery. The outlook concerning return of cuff function is not as bright. Two major rehabilitation issues attend the patient after cuff repair and joint replacement: permissible motion range and muscle use.

Technically, repair of an old cuff tear involves making a number of compromises. The subscapularis tendon is often transposed superiorly and posteriorly into the cuff (supraspinatus) deficit. The reattachment of the subscapularis tendon weakens and effectively shortens it somewhat. This makes external rotation more difficult and painful. To avoid stress on this part of the repair, the early external rotation range is limited. The posterior cuff tendons are also stretched anteriorly, and the anterior cuff is stretched in a lateral direction. Getting the retracted cuff to its bony anchor point is facilitated by abduction. This brings the bone of the greater tuberosity to the cuff tendon. Postoperatively, the patient may therefore require a brace that maintains an abducted position of the arm. This is used to keep tension off the repair while the cuff tissues stretch and heal. The greatest degree of abduction is attained with braces called airplane splints (because the arm is held out like an airplane wing). There are others, known as abduction pillow braces. Much less elevation of the arm is achievable with the pillow type braces, but they are usually better tolerated by patients. Especially if the cuff repair was tight, dropping the arm down below the brace may be dangerous. Elevation of the arm above the brace is permissible, however, and is safe for the repair as long as pure passive motion is utilized. Full elevation may not be attainable because of the tendon transpositions used to close the cuff. Both the subscapularis transfer posteriorly and the often used trick of attaching the supraspinatus a bit medial to the greater tuberosity (so that it does not have to be stretched quite as far) prevent full forward elevation. Although this does permanently limit the ultimate elevation range, it is usually not a functional problem for this group of patients.

The other early rehabilitation issue to be considered after surgical repair for cuff tear arthropathy is muscle use. A taut, degenerative tendon stretched out over a metal ball does not heal, remodel, or strengthen quickly. One of the most difficult concepts of which one must convince patients (and some therapists) is that the feeling of strength and shoulder well-being 4 months or so after this type of reconstruction does not at all indicate good strength of the repaired rotator cuff. A large cuff tear repaired over a replaced humeral head can be expected to be weak for at least 1 year. Strict discipline in avoidance of active, and especially eccentric, cuff use must be observed if retear is to be minimized.

DIAGNOSIS OF ROTATOR CUFF DISEASE

Physical Examination of the Rotator Cuff

Examination of the rotator cuff is absolutely essential to shoulder diagnosis. It is specifically this group of tendons and their unique function that make the shoulder biomechanically distinct among the body's bony articulations. The basics of the cuff examination are described in Chapter 2. Some further specifics are important, however, to differential diagnosis and decision making regarding proper advancement in rehabilitation.

The supraspinatus isolation (SSI) maneuver (forward elevation of the maximally internally rotated arm) is the most reliable indicator of supraspinatus strength (Figure 8–8). Pain felt during this maneuver or with resisted, internally rotated forward elevation is not a specific sign but is notable because it is a sensitive indicator of cuff disease. The best way (short of subacromial injection testing) to distinguish true cuff pain from other glenohumeral pains during SSI is to note how the pain changes as the internally rotated, forward elevated arm is slowly rotated to neutral and then externally rotated, all while active forward elevation is maintained.

Estimates of the strength of the anterior cuff are done with resistive feedback testing in SSI position. After repair of even a small cuff tear, SSI may be quite weak and painful for 4 to 6 months despite complete symptomatic relief and functional return, including return to sports. This is probably due to the training effect of postoperative therapy on the other shoulder girdle muscles, which take over much of the torn supraspinatus' load. The patient exhibiting

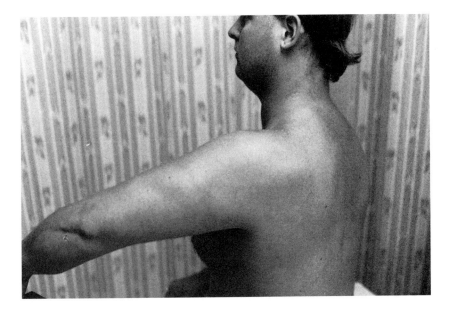

Figure 8–8 SSI maneuver with a full supraspinatus fossa.

this phenomenon should be studied carefully because he or she is showing the examiner an example of pure cuff tendon pain. Nonoperated patients generally have ongoing impingement and subdeltoid bursitis. Impingement produces cuff pain, but there is also pain from the acromion and even the bursal tissues (which have significant innervation), all of which are participating in the pathomechanics of impingement.[9] The operated patient presumably has had an acromioplasty, subdeltoid bursectomy, and resection of the CA ligament; therefore, mechanical impingement is no longer occurring. The cuff is still healing, stretching, and strengthening for many months, however. It is what still hurts. The nature of this patient's pain on SSI (after wound and deltoid healing) is therefore pure rotator cuff pain. It is most similar to the pain of pure cuff overuse, seen typically in the weekly tennis player who plays 4 hours of singles in a 1-day tournament. Appreciating this can make sorting out the various elements of the next sore shoulder under treatment much easier.

The classic impingement test is another absolute basic in the physical evaluation of rotator cuff disease. As explained earlier, it is performed with the patient seated by holding down the acromion and raising the humerus in forward elevation (Figure 8–9). This causes the anterior cuff to jam into the anterior acromion, and it will produce the patient's typical pain if the pain is due to impingement. The most common false positive on impingement testing

Figure 8–9 Impingement maneuver, detail of inferior pressure on the acromion.

is produced by a mild degree of adhesive capsulitis. The frozen shoulder designation is difficult to apply when there is only a 10° to 20° motion loss in the arc of forward elevation. A mild, passive contracture of the glenohumeral joint may, nevertheless, produce what appears to be a positive impingement sign. In the presence of overhead work pain and night pain, this may lead to an incorrect diagnosis of rotator cuff disease. The best way to get the sense of whether glenohumeral joint contracture or subacromial impingement is producing pain with the impingement maneuver is to vary the downward pressure applied with the contralateral hand on the acromion while passively elevating the humerus a number of times. In the presence of true impingement, taking downward pressure off the acromion will decrease the pain felt at the terminal elevation of the humerus. With a mildly frozen shoulder there will be little difference in pain with or without the acromion forced downward.

Can both entities, a mild joint contracture and subacromial impingement, exist in the same joint? Certainly they do. Although the classic teaching is that impingement cannot be diagnosed in the presence of a joint contracture that prevents full forward elevation, it is often not possible to achieve full forward elevation during therapy because of impingement pain. The same technique may be used to clarify the situation. Varying pressure on the acromion will mostly affect the impingement component of pain during elevation. Firmly lowering the acromion (actually rotating the scapula a bit into the sagittal plane) can produce impingement pain at lower levels of humeral elevation, one hopes within the joint's passive range. This impingement pain then can be blocked with a subacromial anesthetic injection, establishing the impingement diagnosis.

Some practitioners in both orthopaedics and physical medicine believe that the subacromial impingement phenomenon can be demonstrated in a variation on the impingement test, in which the fully abducted arm is rotated from internal to external rotation. If this is done on a skeleton, the greater tuberosity will be seen to rotate up against the acromion, ostensibly producing impingement. This maneuver is indeed painful in many shoulders that exhibit classic impingement. It is also painful in shoulders with instability, glenohumeral arthritis, superior labrum anterior posterior (SLAP) lesions of the biceps tendon, bicipital tendinitis, and labral tearing. This maneuver does not produce rotator cuff impingement. The cuff tendons in this position are less elevated than the greater tuberosity. It is the greater tuberosity that most closely approaches the acromion during this maneuver. Reactive bursal tissue may be present in the subacromial space (because of chronic true impingement), and this may be pinched between the tuberosity and the acromion, but the relationship between this (possible) mechanical phenomenon and the patient's symptoms is not causal. The humeral head skids down inferiorly during the abduction–external rotation maneuver, permitting subacromial clearance of the tuberosity. This can be readily observed at open surgery. Impingement in abduction is not a clinical source of symptoms, and testing for it on physical examination is unlikely to aid diagnosis.

Posterior capsular contracture is believed by some practitioners to produce subacromial impingement by preventing posterior and inferior translation of the humeral head during elevation.[10] Although some mild cases of impingement do respond to posterior capsular stretching exercises, it has most often been seen that impingement symptoms continue unless humeral head depressors are toned and strengthened. Most shoulders in the author's practice that come to surgery for impingement do not have passive horizontal adduction unless AC arthritis is present. AC joint pain is more likely to limit adduction than posterior capsular contracture in the impingement population.

The other false positive to be aware of on impingement testing is that produced by a recently injured shoulder. Mild tearing of the capsule or cuff, fresh intraarticular blood, a tiny fracture of the greater tuberosity, or even damage done to the anterior deltoid may (temporarily) produce a positive impingement sign. The only reliable way to avoid misdiagnosis in this situation is to reexamine the shoulder after a suitable interval of rest. The historical detail of recent trauma is obviously important in this instance.

Despite the preponderance of impingement disease underlying most rotator cuff dysfunction, the examination of the cuff should be done with other possible causes of cuff pain and weakness in mind. Suprascapular nerve entrapment is rare but recognizable because of two signs. Tenderness at the scapular notch, where the suprascapular nerve gains access to the supraspinatus fossa, is not at all subtle. Palpation with a fingertip posterior to the midbody of the clavicle will discover an extremely tender spot. Resisted external rotation is weak because the infraspinatus is affected; SSI is also weak, but the impingement sign is negative or at least unimpressively positive (there may be a bit of pain with the impingement maneuver, but much less than one would expect with this degree of cuff weakness; this is the tip-off). Reports of suprascapular nerve palsy being more frequent in competitive volleyball players have been made in the sports medicine literature[11] (neither of the two patients with this condition treated by the author was an athlete).

Pure traumatic tearing of the cuff usually involves avulsion of the entire structure, resulting in a weak shoulder that exhibits the drop sign: The arm cannot even be maintained in neutral external rotation but drops back to the seated patient's lap when released by the examiner. The fullness of the supraspinatus fossa eventually decreases after a complete cuff avulsion, but early after the trauma the fossa may be even more full than it is normally because of the bulk of the retracted muscle.

Tenderness of the rotator cuff tendons is nearly impossible to be sure about on physical examination. The adjacent joint structures are just as likely to produce pain when pressed, and the ability of any examiner to apply pressure to cuff tendons without pressing on the underlying joint is suspect. Tenderness of the anterior subacromial space, which is the primary impingement zone in most patients, is sometimes pronounced. This tenderness is generally unchanged by rotation, elevation, or extension of the shoulder. It is therefore unlikely that the cuff itself is the source of this tenderness. The change in anterior subacromial tenderness with subacromial anesthetic injection is confirmatory of (although not necessary for) an impingement diagnosis. Tenderness and small muscular nodes in the supraspinatus and infraspinatus fossae are commonly seen in the presence of cuff disease, but because they are such nonspecific signs they need only be noted for a clinical record of how they are affected by treatment. The cuff muscles can become sore with overuse. Soreness of the cuff muscle bellies may be distinguished from that of the trapezius by moving the scapula around; especially when the scapula is depressed inferiorly, the spinatus fossae are some distance away from the proximal trapezius, where soreness and spasm are most likely to be a problem.

Shoulder crepitance is a sign and symptom commonly reported by patients. The examiner should be familiar with two types. The common type of crepitance is that associated with subdeltoid and subacromial hypertrophic bursitis. It may be quite loud but is not often painful and is of a low-frequency quality. Patients are often convinced this is due to loose bits in their shoulder joints, but this is rarely the case. The other type of crepitance is that associated with the glenohumeral joint per se. It is a high-frequency sensation felt when the humeral head is moved about on the glenoid, especially in rotation. The feeling is of the head skidding or grinding across the glenoid; squeaking may even be noticed. This glenohumeral crepitance is observed nearly exclusively with glenohumeral arthritis.

Radiography

The clinical diagnosis of most rotator cuff disease is straightforward enough that radiographic confirmation of impingement or rotator cuff tear is not always immediately necessary. For patients who achieve symptomatic relief with initial conservative treatment, especially in physical medicine practice, radiographic examinations may never be necessary. Few patients, however, are treated for shoulder problems by orthopaedists without radiographs, consisting of plain films, at least; there are areas of the country and surgical practices in which nearly every patient gets an MR examination of the shoulder. Why is this the case, given that impingement and rotator cuff disease are clinical diagnoses?

Medical, legal, and financial reasons exist for radiographic work-up of cuff disease. In a purely medical sense (ignoring cost), it is ultimately difficult for an orthopaedic surgeon to justify not getting a full radiographic work-up on most patients because there is simply more information available if a work-up is done. All biologic systems are extremely complex, and although a purely clinical diagnosis may be statistically supported, there can always be an unexpected radiographic finding that changes one's diagnosis. A small tumor, a congenital anomaly, or an unexpected fracture are examples of rare occurrences that may be completely undetectable on history and physical and yet produce rotator cuff symptoms. The medical cost (ie, the risk of producing physical harm) of most radiographic tests is essentially zero, but there is a definite statistical medical benefit: the possibility of the radiographs correctly changing an initially incorrect clinical diagnosis. One might be able to argue that another medical cost must be weighed against the medical benefit of the tests; this is the statistical possibility of the tests incorrectly changing an initially correct clinical diagnosis. Part of the practitioner's responsibility when a test has been ordered, however, is to interpret its results in light of all other information available. Thus, positive MR findings that have nothing to do with a patient's clinical presentation require medical interpretation as to their significance. This last factor notwithstanding, the medical reasons for doing expensive radiographic work-ups of cuff disease (in modern practice this means the shoulder MR scan) may be simply understood.

The legal reasons for doing MR imaging on patients with cuff disease revolve around two issues: delay of diagnosis and failure to diagnose. A small tumor that is missed on physical examination and plain films might have been diagnosed on MR imaging. A patient with a poor result after attempted repair of a massive, ancient tear may sue, claiming that he or she had no tear at all before surgery because his or her shoulder felt better then than it does now. There is no preoperative study showing the tear. Although negligence is purported to be necessary for there to be a successful malpractice suit, every successful personal injury lawyer and most physicians know that the only truly necessary ingredient is a negative outcome. With or without negligence, these will occur, and every possible issue can and will be raised by a plaintiff's lawyers making arguments against professionals before a jury of laypeople. One cannot be held at fault for ordering a test, but one can be held at fault (and can lose one's house and car) for not ordering it. This is not a theoretical concern but a reality with which surgeons work every day. It often explains the policy of getting MR scans on all surgical patients.

The financial reasons for MR imaging being done on patients with cuff disease can be obvious if the ordering physician profits from the test itself, but this is not commonly the case with orthopaedists. A common reason is that many insurance carriers insist on a confirmatory test before elective surgery can be authorized. Arthrograms are uncomfortable and, in the case of a partial-thickness tear, may come back as negative, in which case authorization may be denied (many insurance companies understand cuff tearing but deny the existence of impingement). The orthopaedist is essentially told by this that an MR scan must be done if any surgery is to be paid for.

The impact on physical medicine of such a large percentage of shoulder patients having "MR-proved" diagnoses of, for example, impingement is to detract from the importance of the physical examination in the mind of both the patient and the practitioner. This must be avoided. Although the financial and legal issues surrounding imaging studies for cuff patients have much less significance for most physical medicine practices, the medical issues are still quite salient. The level of confidence to be placed in radiographic shoulder diagnosis should be clear to the practitioner in physical medicine. It is with this in mind that the specific imaging modalities are described in reference to rotator cuff disease.

Plain Film Radiographs

The most reliable signs of cuff disease on plain film radiographs develop, unfortunately, only when the disease is severe and has been present for a long time. The humeral head is kept down in the glenoid by the normally functioning cuff. A large tear or neurologic dysfunction of the cuff results in this humeral head depressing effect being lost. The high-riding humeral head is thus a fairly reliable sign of rotator cuff insufficiency or dysfunction. If this high riding of the head continues for years, the undersurface of the acromion may become eroded by the motion of the humeral head. This, too, can be seen on plain films. It is a specific sign of long-term cuff disease, but it also suggests that it is too late to begin treatment expecting a perfect result.

Early signs of rotator cuff disease on plain films are much less reliable diagnostically. These signs are consistent with, but not diagnostic of, cuff disease. The thick acromion with anterior bony spurring is actually the structure most often responsible for rotator cuff impingement. It is readily visible on plain films and is comforting to see when the diagnosis of impingement is suspected. The major caveat about using it in the diagnosis is that an enormous number of people have it and have no problem with impingement whatsoever. Osteophytes and spurs of the AC joint also produce impingement. These can be clearly seen on plain films, with the same caveat. Other signs are even less reliable. Increased radiolucency (darkening on the film due to a decrease in the local bone density) of the tuberosities is one of these. Calcifications within the cuff tendons themselves are another. Because plain films are relatively cheap and practically harmless, they are obtained regularly and do function to rule out many possible problems with the shoulder's bony architecture. They do not give specific information about the cuff, however, and except for cases of advanced arthritis or fracture they can only support, not make, a definitive diagnosis.

Arthrograms

As described earlier, the arthrogram is simply a series of plain film radiographs performed after an intraarticular injection of contrast solution that is opaque to X-rays is given. A practically definitive test for rotator cuff tear, the arthrogram of the shoulder is being supplanted by the MR image. There are, as a result, fewer radiologists performing them and fewer physicians, in general, with great expertise in interpreting them. Experienced arthrographers can give fairly reliable information about intraarticular pathology (eg, loose bodies or articular surface irregularity), the biceps tendon, and even the glenoid labrum. These radiologists are uncommon today, though. The basic question that the arthrogram answers is therefore still whether there is a full-thickness cuff tear.

Ultrasonography

Ultrasonography of the rotator cuff may be capable of answering the same questions as the arthrogram without the need for an injection or X-rays. Radiologists skilled in performing and interpreting these studies are even harder to find than good arthrographers. Few treatment decisions are made today on the basis of ultrasound findings.

Computed Tomography

Although it provides excellent detail of bony structures about the shoulder, computed tomography uses X-rays to image the shoulder in a single geometric plane. It therefore does not image the cuff well at all and is not a typically performed test in the diagnosis of rotator cuff disease.

MR Imaging

Costing nearly as much as some shoulder surgical procedures, the MR image has taken a dominant role in shoulder diagnostics in the eyes of many health care providers. The major difficulty with MR diagnosis is image interpretation. The same image showing the rotator cuff, AC joint, and acromion may often be interpreted as showing a complete tear, partial tear, and no tear by three different board-certified radiologists. This problem arises not only because of differences in the radiologists' training but also because of the intrinsic nature of MR imaging. Radio wave signals produced by the tissues themselves under the influence of extremely intense magnetic and electrical fields are the basis on which MR images are produced. These signals correspond not only to the physical shape of the object being studied but also to its chemical composition. Bruising, swelling, or inflammation of tendon material may be interpreted as tearing. Similarly, an actual tear may be interpreted as inflammation. Although it is certainly true that, as a whole, the field of radiology is becoming technically better at interpreting shoulder MR images, there is still quite a bit of variability in individual radiologists' accuracy when one compares actual surgical findings with preoperative MR reports. The ability to diagnose cuff disease is also affected strongly by the generation of the scanner used to create the images. The most modern machines do produce much more useful images than earlier models, many of which are still in heavy service (these machines cost millions of dollars and so are kept in use as long as possible).

Although the ultimate responsibility for interpretation of MR images traditionally belongs to the radiologist, it is good for all members of the shoulder treatment team to be familiar with the basics of the shoulder MR image. Many patients keep copies of their scans. Reference to these pictures for purposes of mental imagery during therapy is often quite useful. The major obstacle to be overcome in understanding the MR image is orientation. A knowledge of the basic musculoskeletal anatomy is all that is necessary to begin piecing together the information present on the scan. The planes in which the images are made are now standard, but it is unlikely that one is familiar with thinking about the anatomy in these planes unless one has experience with MR images.

Starting with the frontal plane images (the nearest equivalent to the anteroposterior projection on the standard shoulder X-ray), the bony anatomy is fairly easily to make out (Figure 8–10). Humerus, glenoid, acromion, and clavicle are sought first when one is looking at a shoulder scan. There are usually two or three images in which a clear outline of all these can be found. The deltoid muscle is seen surrounding the humeral neck, and the subacromial space is (obviously) under the acromion and above the humeral head. Looking at the subacromial space, one is seeing the signal from the rotator cuff, the subacromial bursa, and any fluid that may be here. In the scan of a young person without rotator cuff disease, a reasonably distinct dark horizontal line is seen in the subacromial space. This is learned as a normal rotator cuff signal. Other cuff images are then mentally compared to this, the first question being asked about the cuff on scan always being, Is it normal? A clear-cut interruption in the cuff signal may then be interpreted as a tear.

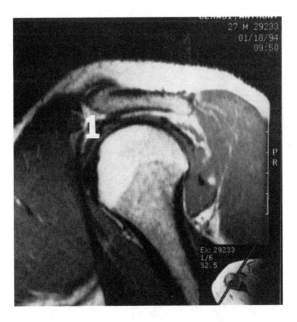

Figure 8–10 Parasagittal MR projection showing anatomic detail of an intact rotator cuff (1). Impingement of the anterior acromion against the anterior rotator cuff (supraspinatus tendon) as shoulder is elevated.

Most of the time, however, the cuff signal changes are not a clear-cut break in the dark tendon signal but rather some degree of inhomogeneity, an admixture of lighter signals within the dark tendon signal. The subtleties of interpreting these are quite complex, but there are some useful aids. A number of different MR techniques can be used in making the same projection images in most shoulder studies. These produce various signal intensities (brightness on the images) in different tissues, enhancing the contrast among tissues and changing their relative brightnesses. Without going into greater specifics on these, it will suffice to appreciate the fact that cuff tendon, when normal, appears dark with all the commonly used techniques. An interruption, inhomogeneity, or other alteration of this dark line is usually interpreted as rotator cuff disease. Three examples are provided as illustrations in Figures 8–11 through 8–13.

Images in other planes are useful for examining the cuff as well as intraarticular structures, specifically the labrum. Reference to these is probably beyond the ability of most patients. The oblique, sagittal plane views are helpful for estimating the size of tears and their location with respect to the AC joint. Horizontal plane views are most useful for glenohumeral joint imaging, offering little useful information about the cuff.

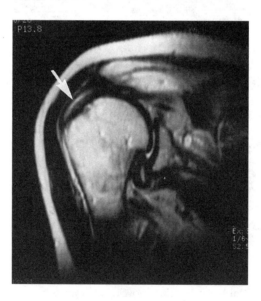

Figure 8–11 MR scan showing a definite cuff tear.

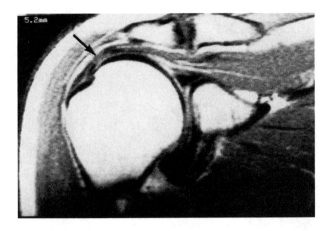

Figure 8–12 MR scan showing what appears to be rotator cuff tendinitis or a partial-thickness tear (abrasion), denoted by the inhomogeneity (see arrow) in the cuff signal. This turned out to be a partial-thickness tear at surgical exploration. Enlargement of the AC joint and impingement on the medial aspect of the cuff are also demonstrated in this projection.

Although it may now seem to be outside the scope of practitioners in physical medicine, MR imaging is so quickly becoming a mainstay of shoulder diagnostics that a basic familiarity may soon become as necessary as a knowledge of shoulder pathoanatomy. It is with this in mind that practitioners should take every opportunity to examine a shoulder while seeing its MR image. The proper function of this imaging technique is to add to the information gained from physical examination. By taking a minute of his or her time, on a regular basis, to try to correlate the patient's physical findings with the MR images, the practitioner can painlessly begin to integrate this rich source of information into his or her assessment. Just as the surgeon who regularly correlates his or her surgical findings with MR images is able to relate to the images in terms of the physical reality they represent, the practitioner in physical medicine has a similar opportunity.

TREATMENT OF ROTATOR CUFF DISEASE

Treatment Options

Once a diagnosis of impingement with or without cuff tear has been made, the question of treatment hinges on the actual morbidity of the particular cuff

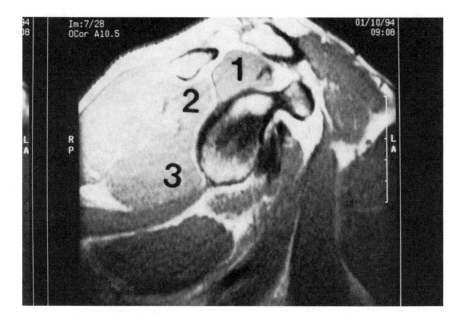

Figure 8–13 Parasagittal MR image showing the three cuff muscles: supraspinatus (1), infraspinatus (2), and teres minor (3).

disease for the particular patient. The overwhelming majority of human beings with rotator cuff disease require absolutely no treatment, nor do they seek any. Autopsy studies have shown a high rate of cuff tears in older people with no history of shoulder problems. One may see many patients with a rotator cuff tear whose shoulder pain is generated by muscular overuse or cervical radiculopathy. These patients do not require treatment of the rotator cuff disease that might be discovered by MR imaging. The clinical diagnosis, therefore, must reflect the patient's symptoms; these are the major determinant of whether rotator cuff disease is to be treated.

Assuming that symptomatic cuff disease is present, pain and dysfunction must be discussed with the patient before embarking on treatment. These are separate issues in many people. Older patients with lighter functional demands on the shoulder may be concerned only with pain relief. It is often surprising how little shoulder function is necessary for some people to live what they consider normal lives. If pain is truly the only issue, activity modification to prevent any cuff use or impingement-producing activities, liberal use of an arm sling, and medications (both nonsteroidal agents and possibly subacromial injectable steroids) may be the only treatment required to satisfy the patient. This shoulder will probably become stiff (if it is not already stiff at presentation). Basic, functional range exercises are appropriate for this type of patient. Typically this is an institutionalized or caregiver-assisted senior whose attendants can be taught internal rotation, external rotation, and forward elevation drills to maintain approximately low lumbar internal rotation, 40° of external rotation, and 90° of forward elevation. This type of maintenance therapy is better if monitored by someone from the shoulder team at long but regular intervals (2 to 6 months) for 1 year after presentation. Besides keeping the attendants vigilant, this monitoring serves to alert the team if this most basic treatment plan does not work.

The average patient with rotator cuff disease, and even the low-demand senior above who fails to be relieved with the rest-and-range routine, should be treated with shoulder education, physical therapy, and occasional antiinflammatory pills and injections. The specific shoulder education here concerns the concept of impingement, the functions of the cuff, the long-term consequences of cuff disease, and the functions of the therapy being undertaken. The mainstay of physical therapy is strengthening and toning of the rotator cuff and biceps. These are the humeral head depressors, the muscles that can best decrease the impingement phenomenon. The cuff tendons may also respond to exercise by getting stronger and tougher, one hopes reversing the changes produced by impingement that is making them thinner and weaker.

Exercises to change the scapular carriage have been employed by some practitioners in the treatment of subacromial impingement.[12] The idea behind these is somewhat akin to a reverse impingement test. Just as depressing the anterior edge of the acromion increases impingement, elevating it is believed to decrease impingement. Exercises are therefore given to maintain scapular retraction and acromial elevation. Some therapists advocate the use of skin tapes to achieve these same goals. The acromion is a rigid, bony process of the scapula, so that scapular retraction and any possible sagittal plane rotation (rotation of the acromion and upper scapula posteriorly) may tend to decrease the impingement forces on the cuff in a given angle of forward elevation. It must be acknowledged that clinical improvement in pain does sometimes attend treatments that include strengthening of the muscles of scapular movement, improvement of posture (ie, increasing retraction in scapular carriage and cervical and lumbar lordosis), and increasing scapulothoracic motion. This is largely because elevation of the acromion permits a higher degree of forward elevation of the humerus to be achieved before impingement occurs. This is exactly the same reason for which an impinger can bring the arm to a vertical position without pain while supine but not while standing. Anatomic considerations make it highly unlikely, however, that this mechanism of decreasing impingement actually operates during functional activities. With the exception of the pectorals and the latissimus dorsi, all the important mechanical connections of the humerus to the chest are through the scapula. The deltoids, subscapularis, rotator cuff, teres major, and all the capsular ligaments arise on the scapula and insert on the humerus. The relationship of the cuff to the acromion may thus be changed in a given degree of forward elevation by having a greater percentage of the motion take place at the scapulothoracic articulation, but for a given degree of glenohumeral elevation the relationship of the acromion and humeral head (and thus the cuff) remains fixed by the bony architecture and the stability of the glenohumeral joint.

The other anatomic reality that makes impingement treatments focused on scapular alignment less useful is the limited rotation of the scapula in the sagittal plane. This flat bone is normally applied quite closely to the thorax. An examiner's fingers or a skin tape might pull the acromion up a bit for a short time, but this is achieved by compressing the muscles under the scapular body. This cannot be maintained for long. In clinical terms, if the impinger is taught to elevate the arm by using increased scapular motion, he or she may experience less impingement pain. Scapular motion exercises may also improve cuff and shoulder girdle tone, reducing impingement pain. The place for scapular rotation in the treatment of impingement is secondary, however. Cuff, biceps, deltoid, and trapezius strengthening are far more likely to improve impingement symptoms in most patients.

Exercises for cuff strengthening in those with cuff disease must always be performed well within the comfort range for a given patient on a given day. As with any other musculotendinous unit, overuse produces tissue damage that can slow the strengthening process considerably. In considering the rotator cuff in particular, there is the added worry about subacromial impingement. The ongoing impingement makes natural remodeling and repair of the cuff tendons much less likely to occur after any insult. Put more directly, the cuff has enough problems already; it should not be damaged further by over-aggressive exercise.

The patient, and certainly the shoulder practitioner, should clearly understand the concepts of eccentric and concentric muscle contraction during rehabilitation of the rotator cuff. Concentric contraction occurs when a given muscle shortens as it actively contracts. Eccentric contraction occurs when the muscle lengthens as it actively generates tensile force. The term *eccentric contraction*, although commonly used, is a bit misleading because it does not actually involve physical contraction, or shortening, of the muscle. There is, nonetheless, active work using metabolic energy done by the muscle during an eccentric contraction.

Damage to a musculotendinous unit is more likely to occur during eccentric than concentric contraction. This may be appreciated in a number of ways. Tearing of muscle or tendon is most likely to occur as the ends of the muscle move apart while the central, contractile portion of the unit tries to pull them together. The energy going into tearing of the musculotendinous unit during concentric contraction must come from the muscle itself. During eccentric contraction, the energy of whatever is causing elongation is added to the equation. This can be greater than the muscle's active and passive elements are capable of absorbing without permanent deformation, thus producing musculotendinous damage. The typical example of this is seen in acute rotator cuff tears or avulsions and greater tuberosity avulsion fractures. These usually occur during a fall as the patient puts out a hand to break the fall. The kinetic energy of the patient's falling body is absorbed by the rapidly contracting cuff muscles, which, having no true agonists, must in some positions of the arm act nearly alone in this function. Rehabilitative exercise of the cuff, weakened by the abrasion (impingement) or disuse or having been recently repaired, must start in the active mode only. It is only after cuff strength and tone have been restored and the protective proprioceptive functions of both the shoulder girdle and the scapular mobilizers have returned that significant eccentric work should be used on the cuff.

The concentric mode of contraction should be emphasized in resistive cuff isolation exercises until anterior and posterior cuff strengths are normal and the patient is asymptomatic. So many difficulties in cuff patients can be avoided by observing this that it may be a safer policy to avoid primarily eccentric mode isolation exercises altogether. The patient should be taught the concepts of eccentric, isometric, and concentric contraction. Placing a small weight in the patient's hand and having him or her concentrate on the biceps muscle, which is easy to visualize, makes this easier. Lifting the weight, the biceps does work; it shortens, and the elbow bends. This is the concentric contraction. Holding the weight elevated, the biceps continues to work; it still bulges, but the elbow does not move. This is isometric work. Letting the weight down, the biceps is still working, but it is lengthening, and the elbow is straightening. This type of eccentric work is the most dangerous for the cuff. This explanation is also especially important for patients after cuff repair. Now, because nearly every repetitive resistive exercise includes a recovery that involves eccentric contraction of the muscles being strengthened, it is necessary to do some eccentric work if any practical exercises are to be done. When possible, however, the eccentric backstroke of resistive exercises with weights or elastics is done quickly and smoothly using maximal, coordinated contraction of an entire muscle group. This is the opposite of the concentric work contraction, which is done slowly with attention to isolation of the specific part of the cuff being trained.

The basic plan that is followed with nonsurgical cuff patients is first to eliminate joint contracture with passive and active assisted range exercises, avoiding impingement at the top of forward elevation range as much as possible. After range has been maximally improved, it is safest then to begin cuff strengthening with coordinated contractions of the cuff, specifically upper cut, shoulder extension, and scapular elevation exercises. The most efficient impingement-reduction exercises are then begun; these are the SSI exercises (raising the internally rotated arm in the scapular plane to about 70° against increasing resistance) and the posterior cuff isolations (external rotation against resistance of the arm held at the side of the body). The biceps is strengthened with coordinated contraction of the cuff. Reverse curls (curling a straight bar with palms down [ie, hands pronated]) are useful in addition to standard curls because they emphasize anterior cuff setting. True biceps isolation, as on a machine, is not used with impingers until the posttherapy training phase.

Exercises are started as active assisted motions and then are advanced to gravity only, elastic resistance, and finally isotonic exercises with weights. A typical session comprises 30 minutes of exercise with 15 minutes of warm-up, cool-down, instruction, and modality use (as necessary). Home sessions of half this length may be started once the patient is working smoothly through each segment. There is a distinct advantage of using the supervised, outpatient setting for most cuff patients in the early phases of treatment, however. Most people have no idea what their rotator cuff is or does. The number of ways the exercises can be modified to do the motion without using any cuff muscles is also remarkable. Cuff patients often have been unconsciously training themselves for years to perform daily functions without using the cuff, and they become used to adapting activities to their painful shoulder. Handed a sheet of exercises and given a 10-minute demonstration, they have much smaller likelihood of successfully strengthening the rotator cuff than if they regularly attend supervised sessions.

The patient who does not achieve satisfactory symptomatic relief with 2 months of serious shoulder exercise is unlikely to be improved by further exercise. This rather hard fact is based on the experience of many patients who continue on with therapy past the 2-month mark, trying to avoid surgery. A small percentage do get better later, but by 2 months it is generally clear whether the therapy is helping. This does not necessarily mean that surgery is therefore the only option. For many patients surgery is seen as an absolutely last resort, and the option of living with the pain is viable.

Two particularly difficult issues are commonly raised after physical treatment for cuff disease. The first is the option of trying large doses of injectable steroids. This is safest if accompanied by cessation of work on cuff strengthening because the risk of cuff rupture is probably increased after a steroid injection. Patients who have worked hard to eliminate their pain are sometimes happy to try the rest-and-steroids routine. Of course, there will be no healing of a cuff tear, but pain relief, at least temporarily, is achieved by some. The important consideration that the steroid injection raises is surgical timing. Rotator cuff repair surgery should not be undertaken for at least 1 month after subacromial steroid administration, and a 2-month wait is safer still. The prehabilitative value of a well-done course of exercise is considerable. This is lost if steroids and rest are used at the end of an unsuccessful course of physical treatment. Trying steroids before a course of therapy with a 2-week wait after injection is likely to be a safer course.

The other issue is that of the patient losing confidence in physical therapy because of its perceived failure to eliminate symptoms. This is particularly problematic with shoulder patients because their reliance on therapy postoperatively will be even greater than before surgery. This is primarily a communication issue among the members of the treatment team. The patient who understands the rather difficult task of therapy in decreasing impingement force ought to understand readily the possibility of it not working. If a positive but still expectant attitude is maintained throughout the course of nonoperative treatment by both the surgeon and the therapist, the idea of something more being necessary to correct the problem will not be as difficult for the patient to accept.

Surgical Treatment

Decompression of the rotator cuff is the term frequently given to the surgical procedures used to eliminate subacromial impingement. Most surgery done for rotator cuff disease includes some type of decompressive procedure followed by closure of the defect in the cuff, if there is one. Decompression includes the bony acromioplasty, or removal of the subacromial and subdeltoid bursal tissues (which usually become quite thick and hypertrophic in impingers), removal of some or all of the CA ligament, and removal of some or all of the AC joint. These are explained individually.

Removal of the anterior aspect of the acromion, especially the undersurface, is the most effective part of the subacromial decompression because it is this part of the acromion that is responsible for most of the impingement force on the cuff. Various parts of the acromion have been removed by surgeons over the years, but the operation designed by Neer[1] has been clearly the most successful in relieving pain and avoiding surgical complications. Neer's anterior acromioplasty is done by removing bone from the anterior third of the acromion's undersurface. Most patients with impingement have visible, obvious cuff damage that is maximal in the area of the cuff that touches this part of the acromion (Figure 8–14). Neer used a chisellike osteotome to remove this piece of bone in one or two chunks. Many surgeons now use a high-speed bone-cutting bur for this purpose. The piece of bone removed is quite small, about the size of a cashew in most patients.

This anterior aspect of the acromion is the origin of part of the anterior deltoid. Many techniques are used to reattach the deltoid to the anterior acromion after this is done through open surgery. Sutures placed through the bone of the acromion are generally secure, but the deltoid muscle itself is soft and does not hold the suture material reliably. Sutures pulling out of the muscle is what the surgeon hopes to avoid by the various repair techniques. By using the somewhat tougher trapezius and deltoid insertional tissues (through which these muscles insert onto the acromial bone), a reasonably secure repair can

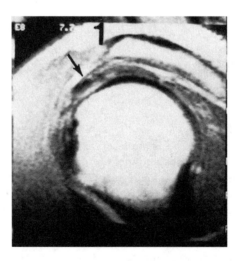

Figure 8–14 MR image showing the anterior acromion (1) with the projecting CA ligament (arrow). Both are producers of cuff impingement.

generally be achieved. A danger that must nevertheless always be considered in postoperative rehabilitation is pulling the deltoid off the anterior acromion.

Avoidance of anterior deltoid stresses during postoperative therapy is a key concept for all cuff patients. This is true after arthroscopic acromioplasty (in which no repair of the deltoid is made) as well as open surgery. This is achieved is early postoperative therapy through passive forward elevation, avoidance of extension beyond neutral, and active assisted extension of the forward elevated position back down to neutral. The patient is also carefully instructed in avoidance of anterior deltoid use postoperatively. Pulling off of the deltoid is a rather difficult complication to treat. It is often detectable by the presence of a depression inferior to the anterior acromion, although loss of the subcutaneous fat in the surgical site can produce the same appearance and is harmless. The best way to check for deltoid pull-off is to palpate the muscle carefully while having the patient actively set the anterior deltoid. The depression can be clearly appreciated as being muscular with this approach. It is also important to do this gently to avoid pulling the muscle off with this examination. A large pull-off of the deltoid requires rapid surgical repair to avoid permanent weakness. A small pull-off may be asymptomatic. They are all best avoided.

The acromioplasty is quite frequently performed arthroscopically. In this approach, the undersurface of the bone is visualized via the arthroscope placed in the subacromial space (the interval between the rotator cuff and the acromion; Figure 8–15). Motorized shavers are used to remove the bursal tissues, which obscure visualization as well as contribute to the impingement process. Pressurized solutions are necessary to keep down bleeding and carry away debris during this procedure. The motorized bur is then used to remove acromial bone, roughly producing the same acromioplasty as described above. Because work is done exclusively from the undersurface of the acromion, the deltoid origin is believed to be disturbed less, and therefore the fact that no repair of the deltoid is done is believed to be tolerable. There have been few reports of anterior deltoid complications after arthroscopic acromioplasty. There have been quite a few reports of continued impingement, pain, and weakness after this procedure, however. The reason for this probably relates to the actual shaping of the acromion that is possible in the arthroscopic procedure. Anatomically, there are acromia whose shape is such that some of the anterior deltoid origin is involved in producing impingement. The anterior projecting length of the acromion is also related to its tendency to impinge on the cuff. One can appreciate that a trade-off can exist between removal of sufficient acromion to guarantee elimination of impingement and maintaining enough acromion to make open repair of the deltoid to it unnecessary.

Figure 8–15 Arthroscopic views during acromioplasty.

Two other structures in the area immediately above the rotator cuff are recognized to cause impingement similar to that caused by the anterior acromion: the CA ligament and the AC joint. The CA ligament is a firm band of ligamentous tissue that runs from the anterior aspect of the acromion to the coracoid process, a distance of about 2.5 cm. It is actually continuous with the clavipectoral fascia, a thin layer of dense connective tissue that separates the more superficial deltoid from the deeper cuff, subscapularis, and strap muscles (biceps short head and coracobrachialis). The CA ligament certainly is closely applied to the anterior cuff and seems to be capable of causing some degree of impingement pain itself. European shoulder surgeons have reported successfully treating impingement simply by transecting the CA ligament and doing nothing else. Although this experience has not been duplicated in the United States, most surgeons here do resect the CA ligament when doing a subacromial decompression operation. It is possible to do a conservative acromioplasty and leave some of the CA ligament intact, but it also quite straightforward technically to take the whole thing out during the acromioplasty. The CA ligament is believed by some surgeons to play a role in increasing anterior stability, especially after joint replacement. To the end of preventing anterior subluxation of the glenohumeral joint, it is left in place by those who believe that it has a physiologic function. Because this ligament is between two processes of the same bone (the scapula), its structural role is not obvious; some believe that it is vestigial. The CA ligament does become thickened, cartilaginous, and even bony in some patients with chronic impingement. These are changes that would be expected from chronic abrasion by the cuff.

Although performed less frequently today, CA ligament resection is a procedure occasionally done on younger patients with signs and symptoms of subacromial impingement. They are advanced in exactly the same pattern as bony acromioplasty patients. Because there is actually much less deltoid detachment done in this procedure, however, the rapidity of deltoid return is greater. Because no acromioplasty has been done on this type of patient, it is well to avoid the upper ranges of forward elevation, especially with the scapula depressed, to avoid bringing on symptoms of bony impingement. The CA ligament can be sectioned arthroscopically as well as with an open procedure. CA ligament resection is nearly always done at the time of arthroscopic acromioplasty (Figure 8–16). It is indeed often difficult to perform a proper acromioplasty without detaching the CA ligament.

The rehabilitation issue arising from the open versus arthroscopic acromioplasty debate is most closely related to deltoid protection. An awareness of anterior deltoid function, stresses in the muscle, and the possibility of loss of strength due to pull-off must be maintained in the patient after arthroscopic decompression. This is often an issue to which surgeons are not particularly sensitive because they have not actually taken down the deltoid in the surgical approach. Highly accelerated postoperative rehabilitation is one of the chief advantages of the arthroscopic procedure touted to patients considering this rather than traditional surgery. Although this may be the case with some, the individual patient and deltoid must be followed carefully in the postoperative period. Slower advancement to active deltoid use is warranted by signs of weakness and muscular pain. Anterior deltoid pain and supraspinatus pain may be quite difficult to tell apart. Both structures are irritated after the arthroscopic procedure. The safest course to take is to keep motion passive until pain is significantly decreased. It is sometimes helpful to use abduction pillow splints in postoperative patients who seem to have anterior deltoid pain and tenderness. If the deltoid origin in the area of the

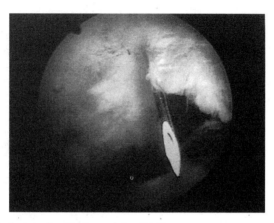

Figure 8–16 Arthroscopic view of the CA ligament.

acromioplasty is distinctly tender and painful with any extension, the slight degree of flexion maintained by the splint can be comforting and may prevent deltoid pull-off.

The other impingement-producing structure in the shoulder is the undersurface of the AC joint. As is explained in Chapter 12, the AC joint enlarges considerably in some patients with degenerative joint disease. The inferior aspect of the AC joint is less than 2 cm away from the offending anterior aspect of the acromion, directly over the anterior cuff (supraspinatus) and near the myotendinous junction. It may produce impingement symptoms quite distinct from the pains of AC arthritis by rubbing against the cuff directly below. Some (the undersurface) or all of the AC joint is commonly resected during subacromial decompression surgery. Resection of the AC joint actually entails removal of the distal 2 to 3 cm of the clavicle. Because the medial aspect of the anterior deltoid arises from this part of the clavicle, more deltoid origin is detached if the entire joint is resected. Decreased postoperative deltoid stress is therefore indicated if the entire joint is removed. Removal of the entire distal clavicle is termed a formal AC arthroplasty (Figure 8–17). Using a bur or bone-nibbling tool to take away a bit of bone from the AC joint's undersurface (which is the primary area producing impingement on the cuff) is called a modified AC arthroplasty. This is nearly always done as an addition to a bony acromioplasty. The modified AC arthroplasty does not require postoperative rehabilitation materially different from that used after acromioplasty because no additional deltoid origin is violated.

Although deltoid issues frequently may be ignored in cuff patients during their postoperative rehabilitation, the advancement of stress on the cuff

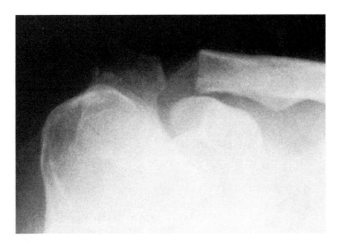

Figure 8–17 Radiograph after AC arthroplasty. Note the resected distal clavicle.

muscles is usually considered quite carefully because of the present danger of rerupture of the cuff. The actual mechanical quality of the cuff tendons and their repair is only appreciable during surgery. It is the surgeon who therefore must direct the specific advancement of cuff stresses. Explanation of the actual methods of repair illustrates this.

After resection of the impingement-producing parts of the acromion, AC joint, and CA ligament, the repair of the rotator cuff is begun. The surgeon must first identify and tag the margins of the torn tendons with multiple heavy sutures that allow traction to be placed on the cuff's edge without tearing it (Figure 8–18). The retracted cuff is then mobilized by freeing it as much as possible from surrounding bone and soft tissues to which it may be adherent. The cuff is finally closed or reattached, usually to bone, immediately adjacent to the cartilaginous articular surface. In some cases of small tears the cuff can be closed to itself, the hole being closed simply with tendon-to-tendon sutures.

The two most important factors in cuff repair are tissue quality and tension. Good-quality cuff tendon is strong and tough. It can be pulled hard without tearing, and a suture placed through it will not be able to slice through the tissue and cut out. A tendon is made of living fibrous tissue that responds to gradually applied stresses by getting stronger. In the case of longstanding cuff tears, the tendon has not felt stress for a long period and thus tends to lose mechanical strength. A person's genetic make-up also influences the quality of the cuff tendons, as does the presence of many systemic diseases. The cuff

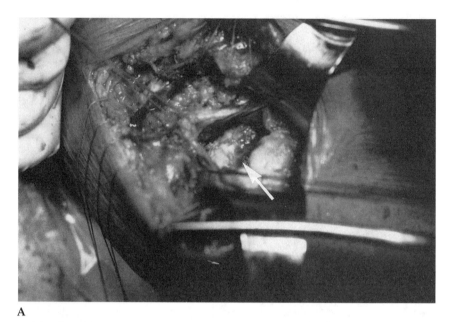

A

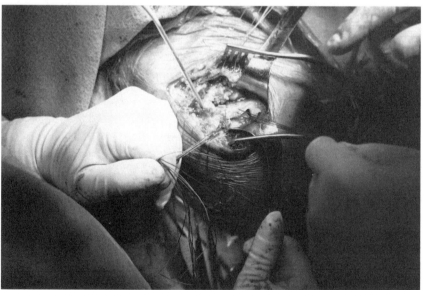

B

Figure 8–18 Rotator cuff repair. **(A)** Sutures are placed into the torn edge of the cuff. A trough (see arrow) is made in the bone to receive the cuff. **(B)** The retracted cuff tissue is released and stretched to reach the trough.

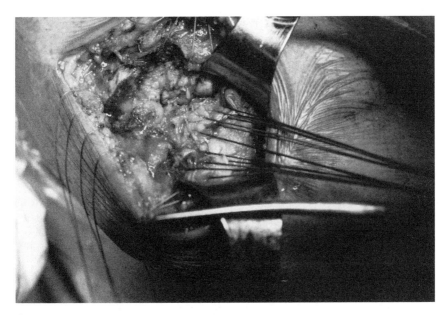

C

Figure 8–18 (C) Restored to length, the cuff is ready to suture to holes in the bone of the tuberosity.

becomes weaker after infections and inflammatory conditions such as rheumatoid arthritis. Also important in rheumatoids, the long-term use of steroidal drugs is associated with global loss of tissue quality, affecting bone, muscle, tendon, and skin. Although an appreciation of cuff tendon quality is immediately gained at surgery, one can anticipate poor-quality tendon material with a greater tendency to rerupture in many patients based on their clinical presentations. A slower and gentler postoperative cuff strengthening course would therefore be appropriate for a slightly built, prednisone-dependent rheumatoid after repair of a tear that became symptomatic 5 years earlier.

Cuff tension is another important factor influencing surgical repair and postoperative rehabilitation. The surgeon tries to mobilize, or free up, the cuff from surrounding tissues so that there is as little tension as possible in the repaired tendons when the arm is in sling position. Large, longstanding tears can be difficult to mobilize with the cuff muscle and tendons having become shortened, more fibrotic, and stiffer. There are numerous surgical techniques used to close the cuff in cases of large tears that simply cannot be closed by the method described above. Partial transfer of the subscapularis tendon into the anterior aspect of the cuff defect is one commonly employed strategy. Little trouble is caused by this if the transfer is small (1 to 2 cm). A large transfer may be accompanied by difficulty in rehabilitation, however. The balance of forces about the humeral head after this is done may be quite different than in the normal shoulder, resulting in difficulty with external rotation and forward elevation. As with any cuff repair, healing of the tendons must take place before they are stressed. Passive motion is begun soon after surgery, though, and with a subscapularis transfer forward elevation is easier and safer with the humerus internally rotated.

The surgeon should give external rotation limits based on the tension of the transferred tendon at surgery. The initial limit, which is generally the passive external rotation range achieved without undue stress on the repair (with the patient anesthetized), may be difficult to regain postoperatively in neutral elevation; working on the passive external rotation range in slight flexion is usually better tolerated after a subscapularis transfer. Increases in the external rotation limit are then made gradually (usually by the surgeon) after the initial operative limit is gained.

The cuff tendons are completely adherent to the underlying shoulder joint capsule. In attempts to mobilize the tendons, it is often necessary to release (ie, cut) the capsular fibers from inside the joint. The surgical terms used for this may vary but usually include the words *capsular* or *intracapsular release, cuff mobilization,* or *slide.* Capsular releases do not clinically destabilize the glenohumeral joint in most patients (suggesting alternative mechanisms to those commonly held regarding glenohumeral instability). It is nonetheless a safe policy to avoid abduction and external rotation in these patients' postoperative rehabilitation. The safety of abduction movements for the shoulder patient in general is the topic of some controversy.

The use of shoulder abduction, either active or passive, is attended by risks that many shoulder surgeons (including the author) feel outweigh the potential benefits of the exercises in most patients. The arguments against abduction are easily summarized. Few functional activities are done in abduction, and the overhead position can be achieved safely through forward elevation. Abduction increases glenohumeral joint reaction forces, places unshared stress on the anterior cuff and capsule, and, of course, is the position of anterior dislocation. The classic painful arc sign felt in the intermediate segment of the active abduction arc is well appreciated to be nonspecific for rotator cuff disease, active abduction being able to elicit capsular, glenohumeral, and labral pain quite easily. Although abduction maneuvers are regularly used by many practitioners, they are avoided by many as well. It is certainly possible to treat shoulders successfully without ever using abduction.

The occasional patient has had the rotator cuff repaired with a salvage or desperation strategy, such as a free tissue graft or latissimus dorsi transfer, or has had the repair done with the cuff tendons so tight as to require the use of an abduction cast or brace (because the tendons would rip away if the arm were brought to the side). The most important, controllable element of rehabilitation in these cases is time. Retear of the cuff is common after such extraordinary measures have been taken and may occur no matter what rehabilitation course is used. A tenuous closure of the cuff is less likely to fail, however, after a good, long period of healing has taken place. This means that motion must remain passive for longer than most patients and therapists find acceptable. After the surgical pain has subsided and the passive range is comfortable, it sometimes feels a bit silly not to advance to active muscle use. It must nevertheless be the surgeon who orders this advance when his or her judgment indicates that sufficient healing has taken place. Significant liability is associated with this decision, and it is the specific surgical technique employed, not the patient's clinical course, that is the major factor in deciding when to permit range increases and active muscle use.

A number of prominent shoulder surgeons have advocated cuff debridement and decompression without actual repair of the tear.[13] Good clinical results have been reported with this strategy, and it certainly simplifies postoperative rehabilitation. The decompress-and-debride strategy is used by a number of other surgeons in cases where closure is technically difficult or impossible without resorting to extraordinary means. Although it is not possible to say that clinical results with this strategy are the same as when a functional cuff is completely repaired, relief of much pain is reliably achieved. During rehabilitation, the same sequence of passive and then active motion is employed, and to the greatest extent possible the cuff tear is ignored. As soon as deltoid healing is secure, active assisted cuff strengthening is begun. Cuff functions are never isolated, though; deltoid rehabilitation is concomitant with all the cuff strengthening maneuvers, and it is likely to be extraordinary training of the deltoid that permits good functional recovery in the absence of the intact rotator cuff.

POSTOPERATIVE REHABILITATION

Immediate Goals after Rotator Cuff Surgery

A dry, healed wound and a healthy patient are the first goals that are sought after all surgery. Although the rotator cuff procedures described above frequently take a long time to perform (up to 6 hours in some cases), they generally involve little blood loss and much less overall trauma to the patient than open hip or knee surgery. These patients have nevertheless had a long period under anesthesia, which is usually general, and are likely to be somewhat weak, confused, irritable, and in pain when first confronted for postoperative rehabilitation.

Despite this, most patients should begin postoperative therapy on the first postoperative day. This consists of passive forward elevation; internal and external rotation; elbow, hand, and wrist motion (active); pendulum exercises; and ambulation. Pendulum exercises may be done actively from the outset; truly passive pendulum exercises (Codman's exercises) are quite difficult to achieve with a postoperative patient because of the strong tendency to splint a painful joint. No problems seem to have been caused by this small bit of active work. Forward elevation is generally the most difficult, and most important, of the postoperative maneuvers. It may be done seated or supine, according to patient comfort. Many patients having trouble with forward elevation in one position will find it easier in the other. The utilization of active assisted extension from the forward elevated position back to the sling position does greatly help reduce the pain of motion in the early postoperative phase. The newly postoperative patient nearly always has a sling. It is another great relief for most patients to remove the sling and place the elbow and forearm on a big pillow kept at the side and on the abdomen. Nearly all patients may safely use the hand on the operated side for limited self-help in eating and grooming.

The patient seen postoperatively after arthroscopic subacromial decompression is usually an outpatient. Exactly the same early passive motion techniques are used. Pulley elevation exercises may be started earlier if there has not been a cuff repair. Pulleys may be used by the third week after an arthroscopic subacromial decompression. The practitioner must know clearly what procedure the patient has undergone. It is the policy of some surgeons to perform arthroscopy on the shoulder before doing any open surgical procedure or to perform open cuff repairs after an arthroscopic subacromial decompression through an incision referred to as a miniarthrotomy. These patients may report that they have had arthroscopic surgery, and they have, but the rehabilitation is dictated by the open surgery, which they have had as well. There are some few surgeons performing truly arthroscopic rotator cuff repairs. This is technically quite difficult and not likely to be done with longstanding or large tears. Although the patient appeal of these apparently less invasive techniques is great, the presumed medical advantage of arthroscopic or mini cuff repairs lies in decreased trauma to the deltoid. The principle of early passive motion with protection of the deltoid followed by gradually increased active stress on the cuff should still be applied to any of these combination open and arthroscopic procedures. It is again emphasized that deltoid protection after arthroscopic procedures is a key to smooth rehabilitation, the deltoid's pain and strength always dictating the advancement of its rehabilitation.

Protection of the Repair

Protecting the deltoid in the early postoperative period is generally not difficult because of the pain associated with its use. The deltoid is red muscle that is highly vascularized, and it heals well. The rotator cuff, on the other hand, heals much more slowly and must be protected through all the phases of postoperative rehabilitation. The repair of cuff tendon to bone probably does not reach its full, ultimate strength for at least 1 year after the surgery, and the cuff muscles themselves are likely to gain strength for 18 months or longer. Of course, all these times are estimates because the duration and size of the tear, as well as the individual patient's medical status and the particular technique used to perform the repair, all affect the healing period. Advancement of motion from passive to active assisted is the first major step in the patient's postoperative rehabilitation course. The next step, to active forward elevation, is achieved almost automatically as the active assistance is decreased. When to permit this advancement is obviously an important clinical decision that depends on input from all members of the shoulder treatment team. The responsibility for this decision should ultimately rest with the surgeon, however, because he or she has handled the cuff itself and will bear the blame if the repair fails.

Activity and Life Style Modifications after Cuff Repair

Practitioners in physical medicine are often looked to for advice on many activities not directly involving the shoulder during both postoperative and nonoperative rehabilitation. For nonoperative patients with impingement-related rotator cuff disease, the most important element of any activity to be evaluated is whether it produces impingement or rotator cuff strain. Certain sports activities, such as swimming, throwing, tennis, squash, and racquetball, are cuff intensive and are largely performed in the impingement position. These should obviously be discouraged until impingement pain has been controlled. Any prolonged use of the unsupported arms at chin level or higher is likely to exacerbate cuff symptoms. Impingers in pain should be encouraged to sleep semiupright, in any easy chair if necessary, with the arm supported by a pillow. They should be taught what the cuff does and what positions are likely to stress it so that they are able to judge for themselves whether a given activity is to be avoided. A classic story is the patient with mild shoulder symptoms developing acute pain after reaching into the back seat of the car from the driver's seat. A well-instructed impingement patient should know not to do this. Falls and other accidents are associated with the appearance of cuff symptoms in some patients (many of whom have legal representation).

Although it is silly to recommend that a patient avoid accidents, both nonoperative and, more important, postoperative cuff patients are encouraged to maintain shoulder awareness in their daily lives. The use of the arm to break a fall is a rather common mechanism of cuff tear and retear; it is good policy to let patients know this.

The postoperative patient generally has life style questions centered on the issue of when he or she can safely return to the activities that the cuff disease made impossible. After a large cuff repair, any sporting activity, even running, must be evaluated carefully before it is permitted. Although an arthroscopically performed decompression can permit some running within the first week, an open repair should be followed by at least 3 weeks of no running, and in many cases surgeons ban sports entirely for 6 weeks after an open repair. There is little science underlying this decision, but the shoulder girdles are active during running and jogging; the jarring caused merely by walking is painful to many patients in the first postoperative week. The use of a sling makes walking more comfortable, but there is no equivalent that can be used during running.

The resumption of other activities after surgery should be based on the level of shoulder involvement, the extent of the surgery, and the individual patient's rehabilitation course. If there has been no cuff repair, 6 weeks is generally a sufficient time period for deltoid reattachment to be secure. Sporting activities below the horizontal are generally permitted at this time, with advancement to activities above the horizontal occurring at 10 to 12 weeks. If there has been a major cuff repair, cuff-intensive sports should be out of the question until the cuff strength is normal both posteriorly and anteriorly and cuff stress is completely painless. It is common to wait 1 year after repair of a full-thickness tear to permit return to tennis in a 60-year-old. Many patients will, of course, not comply with this advice, and they may not experience setbacks as a result. The number of these noncompliant patients who do reinjure their cuff is high enough, however, to justify the conservative approach to sports resumption, which is based on a nearly perfect physical examination.

PITFALLS IN REHABILITATION OF THE ROTATOR CUFF PATIENT

Sympathetically Mediated Cuff Pain

A phenomenon of persistent rotator cuff soreness and pain, often associated with decreased range of motion, is observed in a number of patients after both open and arthroscopic cuff decompression or repair. A nonoperative cuff patient may develop this same type of stiffness, hypersensitivity, and pain, although it is usually less dramatic. A typical patient experiencing this syndrome has had subacromial cervicalgia or a shoulder fracture in the past. Concomitant cervical radiculopathy is also common in the history. The first 2 to 3 weeks of the postoperative course is usually smooth, with little pain and good motion advancement. A rather sudden recurrence of cuff symptoms with active contracture of the shoulder girdle musculature then occurs, generally without a clear precipitating cause. These patients can be trying for all members of the shoulder care team. If there has been a cuff repair, it is probably thought to have failed, producing anxiety about the prospect of revision surgery. If there has not been a cuff repair, the impingement diagnosis, on the basis of which treatment has been performed, comes under question, producing yet greater anxiety.

The surgeon's usual response to this occurrence is to push even harder with physical therapy for motion, and the therapist's reaction to decreasing range and increasing complaints of pain is to push less aggressively. The actual pathophysiology of this phenomenon is not understood, but because the use of sympatholytic drugs tends to improve these patients it is considered a sympathetically mediated pain syndrome, somewhat similar to reflex sympathetic dystrophy. Cutaneous hypersensitivity is often present in these patients, as are other vague signs of local nerve involvement, such as feelings of hot or cold around the shoulder and that common tip-off to sympathetic pain, the complaint of a burning feeling around the surgical site. Sheer persistence is important to the successful treatment of this problem. With the underlying problem of impingement and cuff tear removed, the pain and stiffness will eventually resolve with continued, gentle motion therapy. If there is yet a problem with true impingement, it is unlikely that symptoms will resolve without surgery, but surgery should be delayed until signs of sympathetic dystrophy (hypersensitivity, active contracture, burning, and disproportionate levels of pain) have resolved. These patients are often treated with a steroid pulse. This is occasionally helpful, but sympatholytic agents are more likely to be beneficial. The steroid pulse is more useful in the early postoperative phase if signs of dystrophy are returning.

Of course, not every sore rotator cuff, especially after surgical repair, is due to sympathetic mediated pain. The rate of recovery after the same surgical repair varies tremendously among patients; some appear ready to return to throwing sports by the second week, whereas others may be highly symptomatic at 3 months yet experience total symptomatic relief by 6 months. Active cuff strengthening nearly always is permitted by 2 months, despite poor motion. The switch to active cuff use helps with motion in some patients. Physiatrist evaluation for sympatholytic treatments, such as parenteral medications and local sympathetic blocks, is extremely useful when sympathetic mediated pain is suspected. The encouragement of resumption of functional activities is also helpful. Sports are, of course, impossible, but shoulder-intensive activities of daily living are not forbidden after cuff healing has taken place. Gentle desensitization of the surgical wound and entire shoulder area has been used successfully with some patients, although the distinction between desensitization and irritation may be difficult to judge; when in doubt, desensitization of such proximal joints is probably best abandoned. An extremely unwelcome complication, sympathetically mediated shoulder pain may persist for 18 months before resolving.

Therapeutic Noncompliance

Some cuff patients refuse postoperative therapy or advance their activities despite warnings against this. Although this small subgroup of surgical cuff patients has done surprisingly well in the author's practice, the potential exists for persistent loss of motion and cuff retear. These patients present a real problem when they come back for treatment after a lapse of a few months. The shoulder with postsurgical stiffness may be quite resistant to stretching maneuvers. If it is determined that the patient will become compliant if given a second chance, a manipulation under anesthesia followed by intensive therapy (minimum three times weekly for 1 month) is usually successful in restoring motion. The pitfall to be avoided is performing the manipulation if the patient again will not follow through with therapy. It must ultimately be recognized that successful shoulder treatment, whether surgical or nonsurgical, cannot be performed against a patient's will.

Cuff Tear Arthropathy

A longstanding cuff tear can produce degenerative changes of the glenohumeral joint that themselves produce pain with motion. This type of glenohumeral arthritis, termed cuff tear arthropathy, may necessitate joint replacement and quite altered rehabilitation. The disease and its treatment are considered in Chapter 11.

REFERENCES

1. Neer CS. Anterior acromioplasty for chronic impingement syndrome in the shoulder. *J Bone Joint Surg Am.* 1972; 54:41–50.
2. Morrison D, Bigliani L, April E. The clinical significance of variation in acromial morphology. *Orthop Trans.* 1987;11:234.
3. Walch G, Liotard JP, Boileau P, Noel E. Posterosuperior glenoid impingement: another shoulder impingement. *J Radiol.* 1993;74:47–50.

4. Codman EA. Rupture of the supraspinatus: 1834–1934. *J Bone Joint Surg Am.* 1937;19:643–652.

5. Rathbun JB, Macnab I. The microvascular pattern of the rotator cuff. *J Bone Joint Surg Br.* 1970;52:540–553.

6. Neer CS. Impingement lesions. *Clin Orthop.* 1983;173:70–77.

7. McLaughlin HL. Rupture of the rotator cuff. *J Bone Joint Surg Am.* 1962;44:979–983.

8. Neer CS, Craig EU, Fukuda H. Cuff tear arthropathy. *J Bone Joint Surg Am.* 1983;65:1232–1244.

9. Rowinski M. Afferent neurobiology of the joint. In: Gould JA, ed. *Orthopedic and Sports Physical Therapy.* St Louis, Mo: Mosby; 1985:50–64.

10. Matsen FA, Arntz CT. Subacromial impingement. In: Rockwood CA, Matsen FA, eds. *The Shoulder.* Philadelphia, Pa: Saunders; 1990:637.

11. Collins K, Peterson K. Diagnosing suprascapular neuropathy. *Physician Sportsmed.* 1994;22:59–66.

12. Brewster CE. Rehabilitation of the shoulder. *Phys Ther.* 1994;74:130–133.

13. Rockwood CA, Burkhead WZ. Management of patients with massive rotator cuff defects by acromioplasty and rotator cuff debridement. *Orthop Trans.* 1988;12:190–191.

Chapter 9

Instability of the Glenohumeral Joint

CLINICAL SPECTRUM OF INSTABILITY DISORDERS

Shoulder instability is a blanket term that describes the underlying pathomechanics of a broad range of clinical problems. Instability of the sternoclavicular and acromioclavicular joints is responsible for a number of clinical problems as well, but in common usage the term *shoulder instability* refers only to instability of the glenohumeral joint. Exhibit 9–1 provides a framework within which the various clinical problems that stem from glenohumeral joint instability may be considered. New patients whose history and physical examination seem to be pointing toward an instability-related diagnosis may be classified as specifically as possible based on this framework. Although *instability* is a broad term covering a range of disorders, the disorders themselves are quite distinct. Focusing therapy on the specific type and direction of instability that is producing a specific symptom is a key to successful treatment.

Instability: Definitions

The presence of glenohumeral joint laxity on physical examination is not, of itself, indicative of symptomatic instability. There are many people with remarkable instability on physical examination who have never had a shoulder complaint. One basic rule of the examination is therefore always to examine the other side. It may certainly be true that both shoulders exhibit instability while only one is symptomatic. Normal stability on the asymptomatic side, however, does suggest that the observed instability of the symptomatic shoulder is an actual cause of the patient's symptoms. Symptomatic instability is a clinical diagnosis that depends on history (symptoms) and examination

162

Exhibit 9–1 Diagnoses Produced by Shoulder Instability

Labral tears
Complex or glenoid impingement
Symptomatic subluxation
    Anterior
    Posterior
    Multidirectional
Dislocation
    First-time dislocation
        Without cuff tear
        With cuff tear
    Unusual dislocations
        Posterior dislocation
        Luxatio erecta
    Recurrent dislocation
    Chronic dislocation
    Arthritis of dislocation

(signs). Although it can be an incidental finding in patients with other shoulder diagnoses, instability is nevertheless a rather common cause of shoulder symptoms and should be considered in every patient evaluation.

Labral Lesions

The range of instability disorders begins with lesions of the glenoid labrum. Labral pathology has come to be accepted as a legitimate cause of shoulder pain by most shoulder specialists, especially those who perform arthroscopy.[1] There are still some, however, who do not believe that labral tears produce pain. These practitioners maintain that surgical resection of a torn labral flap is unnecessary. Their belief is based on the fact that labral resection itself has not been proved to produce the symptomatic relief that is known to be achieved by arthroscopic procedures, which include labral resection. Because a blinded trial would involve sham surgery, it is difficult to argue against this point of view; all must admit, however, that intermittent, catching pains associated with the presence of labral tears are effectively relieved by arthroscopic procedures, which include resection of the tears. Labral pathology (which is described in greater detail later) is believed to arise from both overuse and instability, the labrum being torn by the humeral head riding over it on its way out of the glenoid fossa.

Complex or Glenoid Impingement

Complex or glenoid impingement is the next related problem in the range of instability disorders. Occurring primarily in throwing athletes, this is a rotator cuff tendinitis that is caused by impingement of the posterosuperior glenoid and glenoid labrum on the rotator cuff.[2,3] The patient with complex impingement exhibits both impingement and rotator cuff signs as well as signs of symptomatic instability. The currently held theory about the causation of complex impingement regards instability as the initiating factor. The cuff is somehow overused during throwing to compensate for the lack of normal passive stabilization. This has been shown on dynamic electromyography (EMG); the rotator cuff is surprisingly inactive during throwing in shoulders with normal stability. The activated cuff then impinges inferiorly against the upper posterior glenoid during throwing. Anteroinferior translation of the humeral head is responsible both for the increased activation of the cuff muscles (which are doing extra work to keep the humeral head properly located in the glenoid) and for the cuff's increased proximity to (and thus impingement against) the superior glenoid.

Symptomatic Subluxation

Symptomatic shoulder subluxation is more obviously related to chronic instability. Although anterior subluxation is by far the most common problem, a significant proportion of these patients have multidirectional instability, and some few have symptoms from primary posterior subluxation. A history of shoulder dislocation is common but by no means universal in patients with chronic subluxation symptoms. This group presents a clinical range of complaints from minor, function-specific discomfort to chronic and continuous pain, dysfunction, and even neurologic compromise related to traction on the brachial plexus. Painful subluxation commonly is a primary residuum of shoulder dislocation. Proper initial management and rehabilitation of the first-time dislocation is believed by many (including the author) to decrease the probability of a dislocation resulting in chronic subluxation.

OVERVIEW

The most obvious presentation of shoulder instability is true dislocation. A first-time shoulder dislocation is an extremely painful and traumatic event. Subsequent dislocations are also painful, but in general, as the total number of dislocations of a given shoulder increases, the pain and dysfunction produced by a given dislocation decrease. The first time a shoulder "goes out," a visit to an emergency department is necessary for X-rays, pain medications, and reduction of the joint by a physician. By the 10th time, most patients are able to reduce the joint themselves and have little pain afterward. Nearly all recurrent dislocators exhibit a degree of symptomatic subluxation. The frequency with which first-time dislocators become recurrent dislocators or symptomatic subluxators is a topic of considerable current debate. There is here a marked difference of opinion between those in sports medicine and practitioners of traditional physical medicine or orthopaedics.

Sports medicine and arthroscopy enthusiasts point to research showing that well over half the patients who return to active lives after an initial dislocation go on to dislocate again and develop symptoms of subluxation.[4,5] In the opinion of these practitioners, this justifies arthroscopic (but, curiously, not open surgical) evaluation and repair after a first-time dislocation. The rest of the orthopaedic and physical medicine community bases its understanding on other, equally valid research showing a much lower rate of symptomatic instability after proper rehabilitation of the initial dislocation.[6,7] These practitioners only rarely recommend arthroscopic surgery for active patients who have had one dislocation. This issue becomes a clinical concern quite frequently in modern shoulder practice because so many patients, especially the athletically inclined, have come to feel that "I've had a dislocation and therefore need an operation to prevent it from happening again." This obviously affects the enthusiasm with which nonoperative rehabilitation will be undertaken. The evidence and pathophysiology on both sides of this issue are addressed later. The treatment of first-time dislocators is significantly different (and much more commonly performed) than treatment of multiple dislocators. Separate discussions are devoted to these topics as well.

Anterior Dislocation

Anterior dislocation is so much more common than inferior and posterior dislocations that, unless these latter two are specified, the term *dislocated shoulder* is taken to imply the anterior direction. The humeral head may exit the glenoid through the inferior capsule and produce what is referred to as luxatio erecta. The patient with this dislocation presents to the emergency department with the arm over the head and is unable to bring it down. This inferior dislocation of the humeral head is not rare. It is an injury produced by severe trauma and has a high rate of associated injuries to nerves around the shoulder and the rotator cuff. Most anterior dislocations result in the humeral head being somewhat more inferior than normal; the usual X-ray view does show the humeral head to be lower than, or inferior to, the glenoid. These are not true inferior dislocations, however; the humeral head exits through the anterior capsule. The luxatio erecta dislocation leaves the humeral head caught under the inferior rim of the glenoid; although there is some component of anterior capsular damage in this case as well, it is reasonable to think of it as a primarily inferior dislocation.

Posterior Dislocation

The other type of dislocation, posterior, is unusual. Posterior dislocation is a commonly missed diagnosis because of its rarity and the fact that the standard shoulder X-ray views taken in most emergency facilities may fail to demonstrate the dislocation. The patient also may not present for treatment for quite some time after a posterior dislocation because the shoulder may not be painful. The shoulder also may retain a fairly functional range of motion despite being posteriorly dislocated. The essential finding with posterior dislocation is inability to rotate the shoulder externally actively or passively. An axillary X-ray view, which shows the glenohumeral joint from a top-down "bird's-eye view," demonstrates posterior dislocation clearly. Missed posterior dislocations may go unrecognized for years; this should always be suspected in a new patient who lacks external rotation.

Posterior Subluxation

Posterior subluxation is not rare; it can be discovered in many shoulders by careful shear stress examination. Symptomatic posterior subluxation can therefore be a difficult diagnosis to make. It is suggested by a history of pain with activities that drive the humeral head posteriorly. Bench press, push-ups, breast stroke, and kayaking are among the activities that have been seen to produce symptoms in patients with posterior instability. The actual subluxation takes place with the arm forward elevated to about 80°; reduction takes place as the arm is externally rotated and abducted. This is, as might be expected, exactly the opposite situation of anterior subluxation.

Elongation of the posterior capsular ligaments and posterior labral injuries can be observed on magnetic resonance (MR) imaging of the shoulder, but this is a clinical diagnosis. Patients are usually quite specific about the position of the arm that elicits the feeling of "being about to go out." They may also demonstrate the reductive "thunk" that occurs as the arm is abducted. Symptomatic posterior subluxation is much less common than anterior or inferior symptomatic subluxation.

Anterior and Posterior Mechanisms of Anterior Dislocation

Anterior dislocation of the shoulder in the elderly age group (older than 60 years) is often (but not always) associated with tearing of the rotator cuff. In younger patients, the cuff is usually intact after a dislocation. There is quite a difference in optimal postdislocation care with and without a cuff tear. The terms *anterior mechanism* and *posterior mechanism* have been applied by Neer[8] to dislocations occurring without and with disruption of the cuff. These terms refer to a theory of how the dislocation occurs, but they have created a philosophy of treatment of the two types of dislocations as well.

The anterior mechanism of dislocation involves disruption or detachment of the anterior capsule and/or labrum, permitting the humeral head's egress through the weakened anterior tissues. This is the typical younger patient's shoulder dislocation. The posterior mechanism assumes the presence of some degree of laxity of the anterior tissues (capsule and labrum), but this does not produce a problem until the cuff tears traumatically (or the greater tuberosity fractures off the upper humerus). When the cuff is disrupted, the humeral head is no longer restrained by this more posterior tissue (the cuff) and thus dislocates. This is a rather theoretical distinction for at least two reasons. First, surgical observation has shown that cuff tears of a particular geometry (longitudinal, linear tears along the interval between the subscapularis and supraspinatus) are clearly caused by the dislocation itself. These linear rotator interval tears are fresh, sometimes still bleeding, when acute dislocations are surgically explored. This type of cuff tear clearly cannot be a cause of dislocation. Second, autopsy studies have shown that rotator cuff tears are common in the older population. The reported incidence of full-thickness rotator cuff tears in cadavers older than 70 years ranges from 15% to 50%.[9] It is therefore possible that posterior mechanism dislocations are simply dislocations in patients with preexisting tears. Although the anterior/posterior mechanism theory may not be completely accurate, it is nevertheless important to monitor the cuff during rehabilitation of older patients after a dislocation. Exceptions exist, but a safe rule with dislocators is to work primarily on the subscapularis and cuff, emphasis being put on the subscapularis with younger patients and on the cuff with older patients.

Recurrent Dislocation

Recurrent dislocation of the shoulder is most often a problem in younger and more active patients. As noted earlier, the pain and dysfunction produced by successive episodes of dislocation tend to decrease, so that a significant proportion of recurrent dislocators learn to live with their "trick" shoulder, avoiding maneuvers that produce dislocation and reducing the joint by themselves when it does come out. Quite a few recurrent dislocators develop joints so loose that the shoulder dislocates during sleep or can be dislocated voluntarily.

Categories of Anterior Dislocation

Distinguishing volitional from nonvolitional dislocation is necessary when one is evaluating the patient with recurrent and voluntary dislocation. Within the category of volitional dislocators, it is also important to distinguish two types of patients. There are those who can dislocate their shoulder on command but do not have psychologic reasons for doing so (ie, they do not like to dislocate). These patients are truly bothered by their shoulder's instability and would gladly lose their special ability to dislocate a major joint. The other group of voluntary dislocators derive some sort of satisfaction from being able to dislocate the shoulder. They may complain of some symptoms, but they will give the sensitive examiner the definite impression that they like being able to dislocate their shoulder. The classic example is the teenage patient, smiling with the shoulder out of joint, with onlooking parents squirming in horror. Distinguishing these groups of recurrent dislocators is especially important for practitioners in physical medicine because most voluntary dislocators are ultimately referred for therapy. Serious physical treatment is only appropriate for the unhappy dislocators, however.

Chronic Dislocation and Arthritis of Dislocation

At the far end of the spectrum of instability-related disorders is chronic dislocation (permanent dislocation of the glenohumeral joint) and arthritis of dislocation. These are both relatively rare conditions. A chronic dislocation may be the result of a dislocation that was never diagnosed, a mental problem, or a great number of recurrent dislocations. Older patients and those with mental problems are the most frequently seen with chronic dislocations. Clinically, one is often surprised at how well these patients function with their shoulder out of joint. For those who actually seek treatment, management of a chronic dislocation can be extremely difficult. The arthritis of dislocation is a posttraumatic arthritis (similar to osteoarthritis) that is usually seen in the presence of a cuff tear. It also tends to be a management problem because of its chronicity.

SHOULDER INSTABILITY: DIAGNOSIS

Subluxation of the Glenohumeral Joint: Symptoms

Subluxation is a rather common shoulder problem that is increasingly being recognized and treated aggressively in sports-oriented practices. This is a diagnosis that is easy to over-call because so many shoulders display a degree of glenohumeral joint laxity on physical examination. Consistent agreement, on two or three examinations, of historical details and physical examination signs is sought when one is trying to make a reliable diagnosis of symptomatic subluxation. Reviewing the historical criteria, the practitioner should look for the presence of specific details. These include documented dislocation, pain with carrying loads such as a suitcase, pain with combined abduction and external rotation, a feeling that the shoulder is about to "go out of joint" (many patients do sense this even though they have never had a true dislocation), throwing pain that is not associated with much discomfort later on, pain with certain weightlifting exercises (specifically flies, reverse flies, and bench press), pain with swimming freestyle and butterfly, and pain with putting on a heavy coat. There is no consistent location of anterior or inferior subluxation pain. The pain is not typically described as being in front, in back, in the trapezius area, or in the deltoid insertion area. The pain is most certainly in the shoulder, however. Radiation of subluxation pain is uncommon.

Posterior Instability

Posterior instability in the absence of anterior instability is most reliably indicated by the patient giving a history of documented posterior dislocation, and this is rare. In athletes, a history of strangely severe, sharp posterior shoulder pain with bench press or push-ups or in the follow-through of a golf swing can be a sign of posterior subluxation. Surgeons tend to classify instability problems as traumatic or atraumatic in origin. Because this distinction becomes blurred by many patients who, knowingly or not, are compelled to assign fault for their symptoms, it is often impossible to know with certainty whether there actually has been an episode of significant trauma. The difficulty with the posterior subluxation diagnosis is similar to that with isolated inferior instability: One will examine many patients whose humeral heads can be posteriorly subluxated with ease yet who have no complaints referable to this instability. The symptoms of posterior subluxation per se do not always include the feeling that "my shoulder is coming out the back." The recognition of posterior subluxation produced during the physical examination as "the thing that bothers my shoulder" is an important sign, however. Posterior instability is even less likely than anterior instability to be diagnosed from the history alone.

Physical Examination in Subluxation

The physical examination of patients suspected to have symptomatic subluxation should start with the postural description. Although it seems that there should be, there is no true tendency for droopy shoulders to exhibit symptomatic subluxation. There is, however, quite an overlap between the symptoms produced by chronic poor posture (and poor shoulder girdle tone) and mild symptomatic subluxation. Chronic protraction and depression of the scapulae are associated with various muscular aches felt in the trapezius, rhomboids, base of the neck, and posterior glenohumeral joint area. The major distinction between these and subluxation pain is found in the provocative testing for instability during the rest of the examination.

The range of motion of an unstable shoulder is generally full. A common finding in subluxators is an increased external rotation range accompanied by relative tightness (decreased passive range) in internal rotation. Some practitioners believe this to be evidence of a pathophysiologic mechanism, whereby anterior instability is slowly created by posterior capsular tightness. Little else supports this theory, and other mechanisms can be postulated whereby anterior instability, or maneuvers that tend to create anterior instability, also create posterior capsular contracture. Some benefit does result from posterior capsular stretching in these patients, however. The ranges of internal and external rotation (with the arm at the side) and forward elevation should therefore be checked at every examination. Checking external rotation range in abduction is not recommended in general and specifically is not recommended in subluxators. The creation of an anterior capsular contracture is one goal of treatment when one is dealing with anterior instability. The abduction–external rotation range check always shows a soft end point; it is the anterior contracture that one is feeling, and probably undoing, when pushing against this end point.

Muscle Testing

Muscle strength testing of shoulders with symptomatic instability is done as part of the general shoulder evaluation. Because there are large numbers of competitive weightlifters with symptomatic instability and even recurrent dislocation, it should come as no surprise that weakness of the shoulder girdle musculature is neither a sign nor a true cause of glenohumeral instability. Despite every muscle of the shoulder girdle, including the subscapularis and the cuff, being strong, the shoulder can still have symptomatic instability. Weakness of the posterior cuff, seen as below-normal strength in external rotation with the arm at the side, is believed by some to be characteristic of anterior instability. This probably has more to do with the pain that external rotation produces in subluxators than with any anatomic lesion of the posterior cuff. Weakness in external rotation with the arm at the side is nonetheless common in subluxators and should be noted, if present, on physical examination.

Tests of Glenohumeral Stability

The application of shear stress across the glenohumeral joint underlies most instability tests. Direct tests of stability involve judging the actual translation of the humeral head with respect to the glenoid or scapula by palpation of these bones during application of subluxation-producing stress (Figure 9–1). Provocative instability tests involve either pushing the humeral head out of the glenoid and producing (provoking) pain or pushing the head back into the glenoid and stopping pain. The humeral head can be pushed out of the glenoid through the front (anteriorly), the bottom (inferiorly), or the back (posteriorly). Shoulder instability is therefore described as existing in one, two, or three directions. The term *multidirectional instability* has been given to the pathologic phenomenon of symptomatic subluxation in more than one direction. Like the subluxation diagnosis itself, multidirectional instability may be over-called by the examiner who notes a degree of inferior joint laxity in many patients whose only symptomatic subluxation is anterior.

Many asymptomatic shoulders exhibit a sulcus sign (Figure 9–2). It is a painful sulcus sign that is diagnostic of symptomatic inferior instability. A difficult and rather inexact judgment must be made in the gray area between the incidental (ie, completely asymptomatic) inferior instability finding and the diagnostic painful sulcus finding. Many patients fall into this category; they have pain with anterior subluxation maneuvers and some discomfort with inferior stress, although the amount of inferior translation is about equal in the

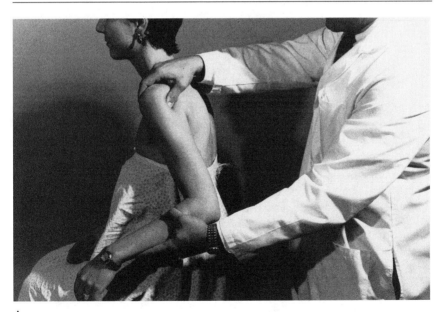

A

Figure 9–1 (A) Shear stress testing in anterior direction.

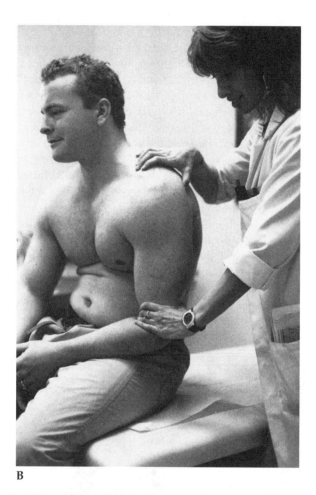

B

Figure 9–1 (B) Shear stress testing in inferior direction.

contralateral shoulder. When in doubt, it is safer to label this situation multidirectional instability, although treatment is harder and restrictions are greater.

Shear Stress Tests

The physical examination for instability is reviewed with specific attention to the shear stress tests because there are a number of similar tests in use that go by different names. The classic test for anterior instability and subluxation is the anterior apprehension test. To perform this, the examiner, standing behind the seated patient, puts the patient's shoulder into 90° of abduction and

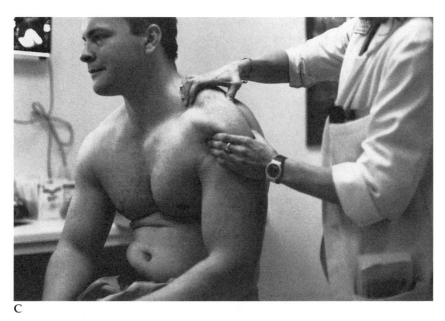

C

Figure 9–1 (C) Shear stress testing in posterior direction.

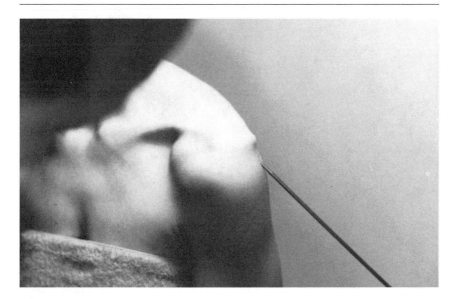

Figure 9–2 Sulcus sign. It is pathologic only if painful or if it produces apprehension.

maximal comfortable external rotation and then asks the patient to relax. The patient's arm is supported by the examiner's ipsilateral hand. The contralateral hand then pushes the proximal humerus straight forward, a bit suddenly. This pushes the humeral head forward against the anterior capsule. In a shoulder with normal anterior restraints, there will be no tightening of muscles in response to this maneuver (Figure 9–3). In a shoulder with anterior instability and symptomatic subluxation, there will be an immediate, involuntary tightening of the entire shoulder girdle to prevent the subluxation. There may also be some pain and a grimace, the so-called apprehension sign. In a shoulder with many recurrent dislocations there may be a frank (and frankly embarrassing) dislocation if this maneuver is done too briskly.

It is partly for this reason, and also because some patients will not relax the shoulder girdle musculature sufficiently to permit the apprehension test to be performed accurately, that the more experienced examiner tends to rely on the subtler shucking test (see Figure 9–1A). This is done with the patient seated and the examiner's ipsilateral hand supporting the arm in the same way. The arm is kept in slight abduction (about 20°) and in neutral to 20° of external rotation, with firm support being provided to promote relaxation of the shoulder girdle. The examiner's contralateral thumb is kept on the posterior hu-

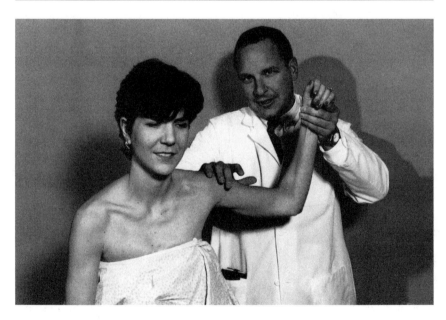

Figure 9–3 Anterior apprehension test with the patient seated.

meral head with the fingers wrapped over the acromion. The humeral head can then be slowly and gently pushed forward with much better feedback for the examiner about how much subluxation has actually taken place, minimizing the possibility of dislocating the joint. Anterior subluxation may not be recognizable in some tense patients until they are placed supine with the shoulder projecting off the side of the mat, the abducted and externally rotated arm hanging from the examiner's supporting hand on the wrist. The humeral head may then be lifted up out of the anterior glenoid in the so-called lift test (Figure 9–4). The relocation test (Figure 9–5) is done by externally rotating the abducted arm of the supine patient until pain is felt and then applying a straight posterior (downward in this case) force to the upper humerus. The test is positive if the pain is eliminated by the applied posterior force.

The push-pull test, the jerk test, the shift test, the drawer test, and the fulcrum test are variations of shear force application that may be useful in individual patients. The anteroposterior shift maneuver, in which alternating anterior and posterior shear force is applied to the humeral head, is sometimes the only way to judge stability in patients who are apprehensive or unable to relax the shoulder girdle. By suddenly changing the rhythm of anterior and posterior pressure applications, the examiner can catch the respective guard-

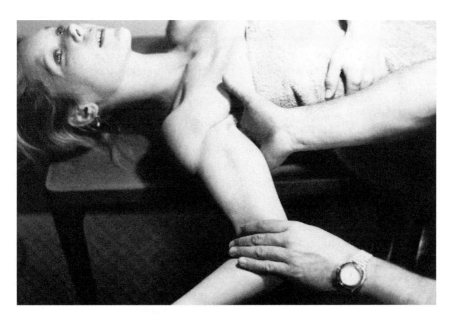

Figure 9–4 Supine anterior apprehension test (lift test).

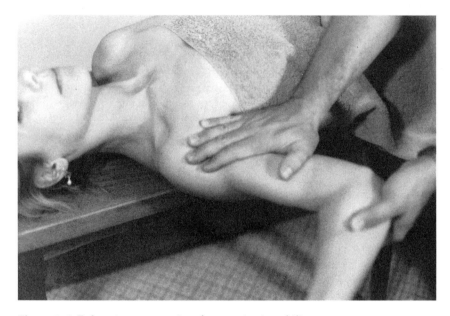

Figure 9–5 Relocation test, supine, for anterior instability.

ing muscles "off guard" for a moment, permitting some palpable subluxation. Posterior instability may only be noticeable in a specific range of forward elevation, and therefore shear tests for posterior subluxation should be done in multiple degrees of elevation.

The push-pull test (Figure 9–6) is done with the patient supine. The slightly abducted arm with the elbow at a right angle is suspended from the wrist by the examiner's upward, pulling hand while the other hand is pushing down on the proximal humerus, creating posterior shear forces that will palpably posteriorly subluxate a posteriorly unstable glenohumeral joint.

The anterior version of the push-pull test has been called the fulcrum test. The fulcrum test is done on the supine patient with the shoulder abducted and externally rotated, the examiner's ipsilateral hand pushing up on the proximal humerus while the other hand forces the arm into still more abduction, extension, and external rotation (Figure 9–7).

The jerk test is a relocation test that is mostly used for posterior instability, the jerk happening as the internally rotated shoulder is elevated above or extended below the range in which subluxation occurs. A sudden, noticeable shift during subluxation or reduction of the joint is a sign of posterior subluxation (Figure 9–8). Some posterior axial loading makes the jerk more noticeable as the arm is swept through the horizontal plane in abduction/ad-

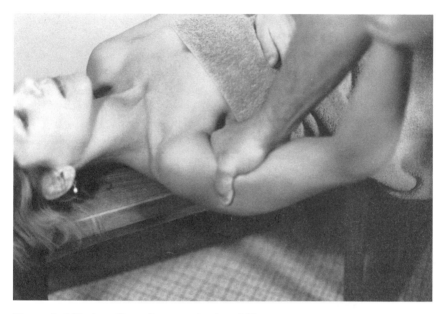

Figure 9–6 Push-pull test for posterior instability.

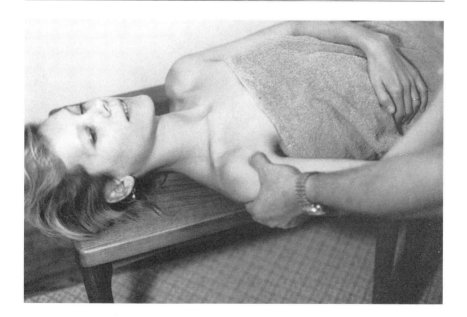

Figure 9–7 Fulcrum test for anterior instability.

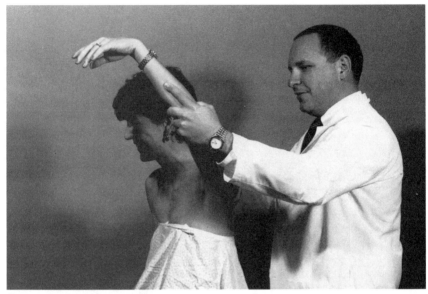

A

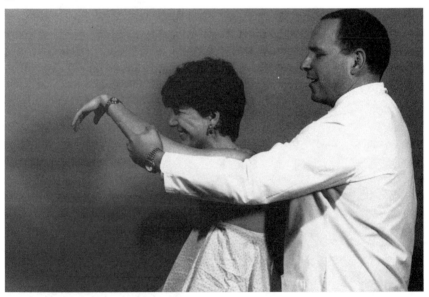

B

Figure 9–8 Jerk test for posterior instability: Sudden reduction or subluxation as the arm (with a posteriorly directed load) is swept through the horizontal or vertical plane. The sudden shift is felt as the arm is moved from the position in **A** to the position in **B** and back.

duction and the vertical plane in elevation/extension. The posterior subluxation takes place in adduction or elevation; the reductive jerk then occurs during abduction or extension.

Other Instability Tests

Many patients with shoulder instability will be seen to have a degree of scapular winging on inspection; this is especially noticeable during forward elevation of the shoulder. This has been termed pseudowinging by some practitioners because there is no true dysfunction of the serratus anterior. The theoretical explanation of this phenomenon generally involves the involuntary attempt to keep the glenoid face more orthogonal to the force being applied to the humeral head, decreasing shear across the joint. Although little empiric evidence for this explanation exists, it is plausible because the winging often does stop after successful treatment of the underlying instability.

Pain with gently forced external rotation of the arm while held at the side is another sign of anterior instability (Figure 9–9). This is a rather nonspecific test, being positive in cases of glenohumeral arthritis and acute rotator cuff tear as well. It is nevertheless easy to perform and, in a younger patient, is quite suggestive of an anterior instability diagnosis because of the decreased

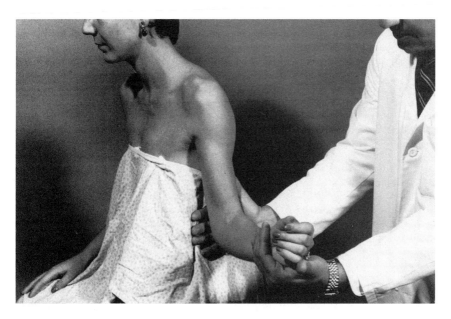

Figure 9–9 Forced external rotation test for anterior instability. This is often painful in the presence of symptomatic anterior instability.

likelihood of these other two problems. Considered anatomically, the forced external rotation test is a variation on the anterior apprehension test. The humeral head, which normally points backward (posteriorly) about $35°$ when the arm is in neutral rotation, is rotated anteriorly when the external rotation of the arm is greater than $35°$. This drives the humeral head against the anterior capsule and glenoid labrum, reproducing the patient's anterior subluxation pain.

Inferior Instability: Considerations in Testing

Inferior instability is nearly always described in conjunction with anterior or posterior instability. The classic physical examination sign of inferior instability is the sulcus or inferior drawer sign (see Figure 9–2). Visible on patients who are neither too fat nor too muscular, this is a depression, or sulcus, that forms just inferior to the lateral aspect of the acromion when the shoulder girdle is relaxed and the humerus is pulled down with straight axial traction. The reason why inferior instability is rarely diagnosed as an isolated entity becomes apparent as many patients are examined for the presence of a sulcus sign; it is a common finding in shoulders with and without symptomatic instability. All shoulders have an inferior capsular pouch; this is the capsular redundancy or looseness that permits abduction and forward elevation of the humerus. Inferior translation of the humeral head into this pouch is resisted by passive elements of many musculotendinous groups (the cuff, subscapularis, and deltoid), but the active function of the deltoid clearly has an enormous mechanical advantage in elevating the humeral head. This dynamic inferior stabilization of the humeral head by the deltoid is likely to play a significant role in preventing symptomatic inferior instability. Physical examination tests of inferior stability judge only passive restraints. This may partly explain the great prevalence of the positive sulcus sign. The existence of symptomatic, pure inferior instability is uncertain. If it does exist, it is certainly rare because nearly every patient with a painful sulcus sign has either anterior or posterior signs as well.

Patients who experience pain with downward axial humeral traction are likely to have symptomatic inferior subluxation. This is not necessarily true, however, and other causes of pain with inferior humeral traction do exist. Any acute shoulder injury may produce glenohumeral capsular or synovial irritation, which can be painful during axial traction. The deltoid muscle can be stretched a bit by this maneuver and may produce traction pain if it is sore from overuse or tear. A large rotator cuff tear may produce pain with downward traction as well. In this case, the humeral head may be starting out abnormally high on the glenoid (herniating up through the cuff defect) and then produces pain either by stretching the remaining cuff and capsule or via pressure on the inferior capsular structures, which tighten because of the chronic abnormally high position of the humeral head. Other signs and symptoms will be present if a cuff or deltoid diagnosis is responsible for a patient's inferior traction pain. Similarly, if an instability diagnosis is responsible, there are nearly always other signs and symptoms to suggest this.

Posterior Instability: Physical Examination

Posterior instability producing symptomatic posterior subluxation is being recognized with increasing frequency as more examiners become sensitive to it. It is nevertheless rather uncommon and needs to be confirmed by multiple examinations before it can be trusted as a primary diagnosis. The classic test for posterior instability is performed by elevating the arm in neutral rotation to horizontal and applying straight posterior, axial pressure from the patient's elbow while palpating the posterior joint line with the other, contralateral, hand, feeling for increased prominence of the humeral head (Figure 9–10). Varying degrees of rotation, elevation, and abduction are necessary to make this test sensitive. It is also possible for the patient to protract the scapula, bringing the glenoid face forward, and foil the examiner's efforts to apply a

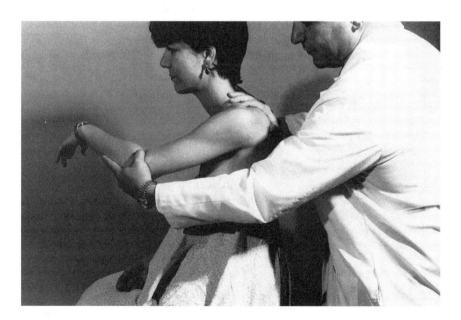

Figure 9–10 Posterior translation (instability) test, the classic test for posterior instability.

shear force across the glenoid's face. Greater sensitivity to posterior subluxation is probably achievable through the use of a direct posterior shear test, similar to that used during examination under anesthesia before surgery.

The shucking test that is done for anterior instability is easily adapted to test the humeral head's posterior capsular restraints. The examiner is again standing behind the seated patient. The thumb rests on the posterior joint line, and the middle and index fingers of the examiner's contralateral hand can apply increasingly firm posterior pressure and feel for the humeral head's travel across the face of the glenoid and up onto its posterior rim. Many patients will not mind this happening even though the humeral head moves posteriorly more than half its diameter. If this posterior subluxation is uncomfortable, it is suggestive of symptomatic posterior subluxation; if it produces the patient's pain, it may be diagnostic. Arthroscopic examination of patients with this presentation has led to some understanding of an important issue in the physical diagnosis of posterior subluxation: the relationship between the symptoms of subluxation and those of glenoid labral tears.

Labral Signs

It is entirely possible that the pain reported by a patient on anterior or posterior shear stress testing for instability is produced entirely by forces placed on a torn anterior or posterior glenoid labrum. Labral pathology is a frequent sequela of instability, and the two are likely to be present together. Distinguishing labral signs from those of instability requires some subtlety and depends largely on the tactile feedback received from the hand on the humeral head. A mild clunk or low-frequency click is often produced by the humeral head moving over an unstable labrum. Large labral tears can be detected on MR imaging. Repeated examination of patients with a known large labral tear can help one develop sensitivity to the labral click. The other distinction between labral and instability signs is less reliable but should be inquired about nonetheless. This is the time course of the patient's pain as the humeral head is subluxated and reduced. Capsular pain of subluxation is maximal when the humeral head is in the position of maximal displacement from the glenoid. It decreases when the humeral head is reduced. Labral pain is greatest when the forces on the torn labrum's attachment points are greatest; it hurts on the humeral head's way out and again on its way in.

Recurrent Dislocation

The physical examination of symptomatic subluxation is essentially similar to that of recurrent dislocation. This diagnosis is not difficult to make; the patient complains that the shoulder keeps dislocating. Care to avoid dislocating the shoulder during the physical examination is necessary, and dislocation may be avoided by use of direct palpation instead of provocative tests of stability. Although few cases of recurrent posterior dislocation exist, there are quite a few patients who experience painful posterior subluxation, and the degree of subluxation can be large enough that at least the patient feels as if the shoulder is actually dislocated. These patients know how to reduce the subluxation themselves. Many posterior subluxators can produce and reduce the subluxation voluntarily by using the posterior cuff and deltoid. It is helpful to ask patients whether they can put the shoulder "out of joint" by themselves and then to have them perform the maneuver if they can while palpating the glenohumeral interval to judge the direction of subluxation.

Recurrent dislocation is almost exclusively anterior. The posterior subluxation described above is reducible and not a true dislocation (posterior dislocation is not generally self-reducible). Inferior subluxation is an element of either anterior or posterior symptomatic instability. The inferior dislocation that has been described (luxatio erecta) is a high-energy, severe, acute injury; there is not an entity of chronically recurrent inferior true dislocation. The primary exception to these rules is patients after total shoulder reconstruction in whom components have been placed in unusual positions of height or rotation. Dislocating total shoulders may come out inferiorly or posteriorly as well as anteriorly (which is still most common). The problems of the artificial shoulder joint are considered in a separate discussion.

A final consideration on the topic of instability is frequency. Although a comparatively large amount is written here and elsewhere about posterior instability, it is much less common than anterior instability. The overwhelming majority of patients under treatment for instability-related pathology have simple anterior glenohumeral subluxation, labral pain, or recurrent dislocation. The medical adage "the more written, the less known" is convincingly illustrated in the current literature on posterior shoulder instability.

Subluxation Radiographic Signs: Hill-Sachs and Bankart Lesions

As mentioned above, the diagnosis of symptomatic instability is clinical. Plain films are routinely made on most shoulder patients. These quickly and simply rule out many diagnoses, such as fractures, dislocations, tumors, congenital defects, and arthritis. Other tests (MR imaging, computed tomography [CT], and arthrography) are also available, but when one is dealing with an instability-related problem the history and physical examination generally provide sufficient information to make most diagnoses. Tests beyond plain films are appropriately obtained when some diagnostic confusion exists, response to treatment is poor, or a surgical decision must be made. The small number of common radiographic signs of instability-related pathology with which the shoulder practitioner needs to be familiar are described. There are many more that are less common or less specific and therefore clinically less important.

Hill-Sachs and Bankart lesions are the primary radiographic stigmata of shoulder instability. Most important clinically is the Bankart lesion because repairing it is the goal of much instability surgery.

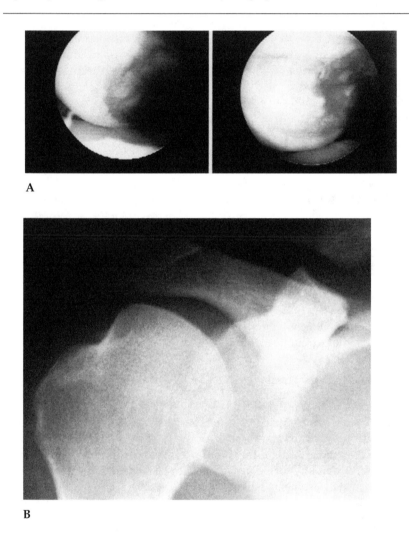

A

B

Figure 9–11 Hill-Sachs lesion. **(A)** Arthroscopic views. **(B)** Radiographic view.

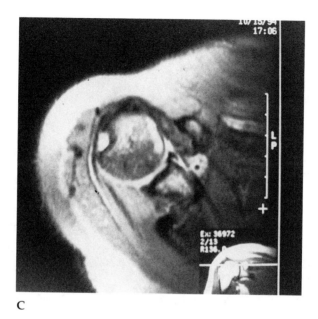

C

Figure 9–11 (C) Hill-Sachs lesion MR appearance.

The Hill-Sachs lesion is a posterior humeral head indentation fracture produced during anterior dislocation by the anterior edge of the glenoid, which is jammed with great force against the posterosuperior aspect of the humeral head (Figure 9–11). It is a classic radiographic sign of anterior shoulder dislocation. It is, of course, not absolutely specific, but if a patient presents with a large Hill-Sachs lesion on the plain film and the shoulder is bothersome, there is a good chance that the pain is related to anterior instability.

The Bankart lesion is the other classic finding in anterior instability. It consists of detachment of the anterior capsule and labrum from their normal insertion on the anterior glenoid (Figure 9–12). This was originally a surgical finding that was noticed repeatedly during operations for recurrent dislocation. Modern radiographic techniques can demonstrate the Bankart lesion noninvasively with MR imaging or CT arthroscopy. A subgroup of the Bankart lesion can be demonstrated on plain films. The axillary or "bird's-eye" view of the shoulder may show a fractured piece off of, or a flattening down of, the anterior lip of the glenoid. This is referred to as a Bankart fracture or bony Bankart lesion. The Hill-Sachs lesion is bony damage done to the humeral head by the glenoid; the bony Bankart lesion is bony damage done to the glenoid by the humeral head. The standard (not bony) Bankart lesion itself is a

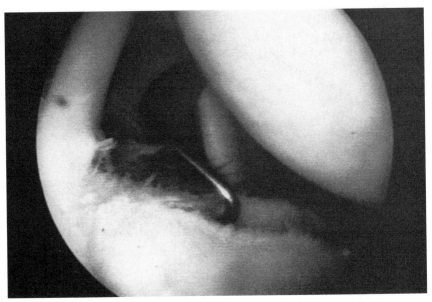

A

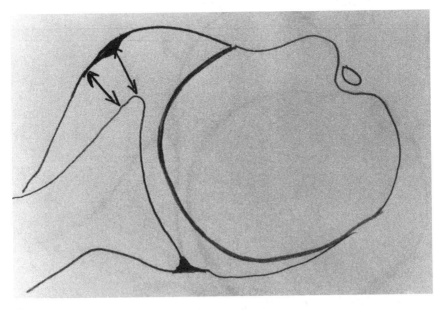

B

Figure 9–12 Bankart lesion. **(A)** Arthroscopic view and **(B)** diagram.

common, although not universal, finding after anterior dislocation. It may be present in subluxators who have never had a dislocation. The classic Bankart lesion involves tearing away of the anterior capsule and labrum from the neck of the glenoid. An anterior labral tear, with mostly intact glenocapsular attachments medially, is believed by some to be a variation of the Bankart lesion.

Some Bankart lesions are visible on MR scans and some on arthrograms. CT arthrograms are most sensitive but are not performed frequently. Many Bankart lesions are discovered during arthroscopy or surgery, having been missed on preoperative imaging studies.

TREATMENT OF SHOULDER INSTABILITY AND RELATED DISORDERS

The Treatment Decision

Not every patient with glenohumeral instability ought to undergo treatment; this is true even for conservative treatments such as exercise. As mentioned earlier, the relationship between the patient's symptoms and the instability of the shoulder must be reasonably well established before one embarks on a course of treatment. Voluntary, "happy" dislocators, who derive some psychologic benefit from being able to dislocate their shoulder, will continue to dislocate regardless of treatment; their dislocations are not painful and therefore do not require physical therapy or surgery. Similarly, ancient (older than 1 year), chronic dislocations in older, demented patients are likely not to be the cause of significant functional loss. Treatment is difficult and may produce bone or nerve damage. These, too, may be better off untreated if they are not painful. The decision to treat an instability-related problem hinges on physiologic factors as well; a denervated shoulder girdle with dislocation of the glenohumeral joint offers little with which to work on strengthening, and neither surgery nor physical therapy would be expected to produce significant functional return. Although functional help with activities of daily living might be achieved by working around the shoulder problem, little benefit would be expected from treatment of the shoulder itself in this case (Exhibit 9–2).

Practical Goals of Treatment

Although the practical advice "try therapy first, then surgery if it fails" is well taken with instability-related problems, the practitioner in physical medicine needs to be realistic about the achievable goals of nonoperative treatment in some cases. A patient with chronic dislocation will not achieve relocation

Exhibit 9–2 Treatment of Shoulder Instability and Related Disorders

The treatment decision
Clinical role of instability
Goals
Acute treatment
• The acute examination
  –Labral tears
  –Acute subluxation
  –Acute dislocation
• Immobilization
  –Functions of immobilization
  –Positions and devices
  –Isometrics
• Concomitant injuries of the destabilized shoulder
  –Nerve injuries
  –Cuff injuries
  –Fractures
• Mobilization

Treatment of chronic instability-related problems
• Labral tears
• Subluxation
  –Motion
  –Strengthening
  –Proprioception and neuromuscular performance
• Dislocation
  –Initial
  –Recurrent
  –Chronic
• Surgical repairs for instability
  –Open
  –Arthroscopic
  –Surgical indications
• Postsurgical rehabilitation

and a full range of motion with physical treatment alone. He or she can be helped with pain and function through increasing scapulothoracic motion and strength, but this patient should understand from the outset of treatment that the shoulder will still be dislocated. Similarly, the patient who has had 50 or more dislocations may improve with physical treatments and have less pain or less frequent dislocations. Both patient and practitioner, however, should expect that the shoulder will continue to dislocate despite tremendous muscle strengthening and that, if stopping dislocations is the primary goal of treatment, the initial treatment should be surgical.

Life style modification is a treatment option that may be often overlooked. It can be successful and well tolerated in many cases of symptomatic instability. Despite having a sports medicine practice, it is quite often reasonable for practitioners to recommend cessation or change of sport to some patients whose only symptoms are produced by a particular game. Although all throwing and racquet sports make heavy use of the shoulder, the most commonly seen "optional" sport that is a patient's sole source of instability symptoms is usually tennis. "Stop playing tennis" is another, often forgotten, treatment option. Not every patient bases his or her entire quality of life on sports participation. In more than a few instances, patients have given this author the distinct impression of relief that they can (must) stop playing, on a physician's orders.

Sports Modifications

Tennis, baseball, racquetball, and swimming are particularly apt to bring out symptoms in unstable shoulders. For those who are uninterested in stopping, there are some sports modifications that occasionally reduce pain. These are not suited to high-level athletes but can be helpful to recreational players. Athletic modifications may be worked out on an individual basis once the underlying pathophysiology of the particular symptoms is understood.

There are a few typical changes to try. In tennis, the two-handed backhand and even forehand keep the arms closer to the body and stable, reducing instability symptoms (Figure 9–13). Trading a fast or twist serve for a slower slice serve accomplishes the same thing. An occasional swimmer with anterior instability can be freed of shoulder pain by changing strokes. Butterfly and freestyle seem to be the worst for anterior instability patients; changing to the breast stroke may permit a comfortable workout. Those with primary posterior instability, on the other hand, may benefit from switching away from the breast stroke to freestyle. Weightlifters are routinely counseled to avoid flies and reverse flies. This is a semipermanent restriction; these two exercises place the glenohumeral joint in a position of tremendous compressive and simultaneous shear load. They are commonly the cause of labral tears and capsular injuries. There are many other ways to work the deltoids, cuff, and trapezius; flies are best avoided.

Workplace Modifications

Outside of athletics, many patients with symptomatic instability find that job-related tasks produce or increase their shoulder pain. Workplace maneuvers that produce subluxation symptoms may occasionally be modified to be less painful. Although each application obviously must be considered separately, useful modifications for anterior subluxators generally involve keeping the arms closer to the body and minimizing abduction and external rotation positioning in each task. Multidirectional subluxators should also avoid prolonged vertical loads, both overhead and with the arm at the side. Disability and compensation issues often so cloud the picture in these situations, however, that honest efforts by well-meaning practitioners can be a waste of time.

Nontreatment, partial treatment, and life style modification will by no means become mainstays of practice. They are to be kept in mind as possibilities, however. Although most patients with instability-related problems are fairly straightforward in their diagnosis and treatment, a few are not. These few do have a greater likelihood of ending up as "terminal referrals" to physi-

A

B

Figure 9–13 (A) One-handed and (B) two-handed backhand strokes. Although it decreases reach, the two-handed backhand provides increased control in follow-through with decreased abduction and external rotation of the dominant shoulder.

cal medicine departments unless these issues and options are well understood.

Treatment Considerations

Two factors that must be kept in mind throughout evaluation and treatment of instability-related shoulder problems are the severity and the time course of the instability. As mentioned earlier, many shoulders have a bit of instability on physical examination. This instability may permit an episode of subluxation in which a capsular or labral tear is sustained. The patient's presenting complaint would then be capsular or labral pain and weakness with recent trauma. Although the patient clearly has an instability-related problem, it is not appropriate to treat this patient's instability at this point. Early on, tears of the capsule and labrum have good healing potential. They are best treated with a period of immobilization, during which sufficient healing, scarring, and contracture of the capsular structures might take place to produce an asymptomatic shoulder. Treating the actual subluxation at this early period in the time course of the underlying instability problems would be unwise. Done early in the course, muscle strengthening exercises involving motion would probably interfere with contracture of the anterior capsular structures, making permanence of the symptoms more likely. The other side of this argument is illustrated by the patient with a multiyear history of instability-related symptoms, labral catching, and a few frank dislocations. Immobilization for 6 weeks after further episodes of subluxation or dislocation would be unnecessary because little scarring or contraction is to be expected; as mentioned earlier, the later dislocations are far less traumatic and produce less tissue reaction. This period of immobilization would be likely to increase instability symptoms through weakening of the cuff and subscapularis.

Severity of symptoms is an obvious guide to the appropriate aggressiveness of treatment. The factor that may complicate this relationship in treating shoulder instability is the severity of instability. It must be kept in mind that instability is generally a sign and, except in cases of recurrent dislocation, not a symptom. An illustration is the case of a patient with an extraordinarily unstable shoulder who presents with mild pain and discomfort after pitching an entire baseball game. The actual diagnosis turns out to be complex impingement of the cuff on the superior glenoid, an instability-related diagnosis but one that usually responds to mild treatments, in this case 1 week of rest, antiinflammatories, and some gentle posterior capsular stretching. The immediate reaction of the practitioner on examining such an unstable shoulder might be to diagnose severe symptomatic subluxation, immobilize for 1 month, and follow with aggressive strengthening and no sports for 3 months. The clue to this diagnosis and proper treatment is (as usual) in the history. The symptoms were new and rather mild; the instability, in contrast, was pronounced and most likely of long standing. The pathomechanical role played by the patient's observed glenohumeral instability in the production of actual symptoms should thus be considered in every treatment decision.

A final point regarding the age and severity of instability problems is that older, established patterns of instability-related pain are more likely to require surgical correction. This is true for the multiply recurrent dislocator, the subluxator who has been symptomatic for many years, and even the labral tear patient who has had catching symptoms for years. A course of physical treatment should be started with a somewhat more expectant attitude in this type of patient. Unless special circumstances exist, thought should be given to surgical treatment after 1 to 2 months of unsuccessful treatment rather than 6 or 8 months. These special circumstances would include extraordinary weakness of the cuff and subscapularis and the (unusual) patient who, despite an instability-related problem, lacks full range of motion.

Treatments in Chronic Instability

The long-term patient with pronounced weakness may be helped by a long course of physical treatment that breaks the cycle of instability, pain, disuse, weakness, and increased instability. Goals in this type of situation should be based on strength parameters until the stabilizing muscles are maximally improved. Working through pain (as long as exercises are not actively subluxating the joint) is necessary for this treatment to be effective. The stiff, yet unstable shoulder most often has an external rotation or abduction contracture. Tightness of the posterior capsule can be resistant to stretching maneuvers; a strong posterior cuff may also be difficult to relax during these sessions. Although this type of physical treatment can take more than a few months, the relief of actual instability symptoms that it brings is variable and sometimes minimal.

The less common unstable shoulder with decreased elevation range is more likely to respond well to long-term physical therapy. This situation usually results from acute trauma, such as a traumatic subluxation, leaving the anterior capsule and/or labrum torn and then secondarily contracted. The contracture prevents external rotation and forward elevation, but instability is still noted on shear testing. A prolonged course of physical treatment for this patient, first regaining a normal range of forward elevation, then achieving a limited (30°) external rotation range, then working on strengthening of the stabilizers, may effectively relieve instability-related symptoms.

Instability Treatment: Goals

Working with one's patients toward specific short- and long-term goals is an intelligent way to structure one's practice. As mentioned earlier, short-term goals in instability patients may be based on strength parameters. A variety of force- and energy-measuring machines may be used for this; none is as portable or adaptable as the examiner's own hands used in isometric resistive feedback testing. For those patients (or practitioners) who are interested in knowing maximum measurements, a specific number can be generated equally reliably with an expensive machine or a dumbbell. It is wise to avoid specific numbers whenever possible, however. There is a real danger of straining the muscles and tendons of the shoulder girdle in the course of this type of goal-driven strengthening exercise. The symptoms of overwork are also easily confused with those of instability-related pathology. To avoid these problems, therapeutic exercise should be closely supervised, and single-repetition maximums should be absolutely avoided. Staying away from numeric output machines is a safe policy with shoulder patients.

One's choice of actual strength goals is somewhat arbitrary. It involves the estimated deficit and the patient's general habitus, compliance, and enthusiasm. Goals should be achieved on a regular basis to maintain patient confidence. The biggest danger with strength goal emphasis is the occasionally tenuous relationship between strengthening and reduction of instability symptoms (the implicit, overall goal). Many patients with unstable glenohumeral joints remain quite symptomatic despite having developed strong, toned, and supple shoulder girdle musculature.

It is especially important when one is treating instability-related problems that the course of physical treatment begin with establishment of a long-term goal of treatment. This may simply be pain relief, but often there is a desire for some type of functional enhancement, which may involve pain relief as a perceived incidental (eg, "I don't care about the pain, I just want to be able to play in the finals"). The range of long-term goals of treatment within the instability population is wide. Some patients' goals seem entirely functional: to get back a fastball or twist serve or to resume windsurfing, kayaking, or rock climbing, all with no mention of shoulder pain. Others are more mundane: carry a briefcase comfortably, sail a boat, put on a heavy coat, or sleep through the night without dislocating the shoulder. It is good practice to stay in touch with the patient's pain symptoms despite his or her aggressive insistence that athletic performance is the only goal. As one's relationship with the patient grows, it may become clear that relief of pain is quite an important goal to him or her, just somewhat difficult to admit.

Performance Issues in Athletics

High-level athletic function is perhaps the most difficult goal to achieve with shoulders that require surgery. Performance athletes may be overcompliant with exercise treatment plans; they are naturally goal oriented and more often require holding back than urging on. Goal emphasis need not be strong with this group, especially in the postoperative period. More than strengthening, the shoulder after open instability repair needs protection while the capsular tissues heal and mature. The first goal here is healing of the surgical repair; only after this is accomplished can stretching, strengthening, and sports-specific training become goals.

Termination of Therapy

A final consideration regarding treatment goals in instability is termination of therapy. In the absence of normal passive stabilizing structures about the glenohumeral joint, effective therapies may work through maintenance of what may be regarded as a supraphysiologic level of strength and tone in the rotators and subscapularis as well as enhanced joint position sense reflexes. The long-term goal of preventing instability symptoms may only be attainable through constant exercise. It should be an understood goal of one's treatment program eventually to stop therapy. A home exercise plan may be permanent, but visits with a practitioner should eventually stop. Without surgical stabilization, a good number of instability patients may seek permanent physical treatment, which can be quite effective in reducing subluxation symptoms.

Shoulder Instability: Acute Treatments

The Acute Examination

Examining a shoulder within minutes or hours of injury may be necessary in sports situations, outside of practice, or in the emergency setting. Although the complete emergency medical management of upper extremity trauma is beyond the scope of this book, the shoulder practitioner should be able to recognize a dislocated shoulder, perform the basic neurologic and vascular evaluations of the upper extremity, and understand the acute treatment. Similarly, the shoulder that has recently undergone a traumatic subluxation or has a fresh capsular or labral tear can be recognized and treated. Specifics on the early examination of the acutely dislocated or subluxated shoulder are thus included here rather than with the general physical examination material presented in Chapter 2.

Neurologic checks. Although shoulder dislocation is not always obvious, patients with a fresh dislocation often do know that their shoulder is out of joint, especially if they are younger. This can make the diagnosis of shoulder dislocation trivial. Older patients, who may stay home for a few days after dislocating the shoulder "to see if it gets better," are not rare, however. When a dislocation is suspected, check the extremity's neurovascular status first. Ask the patient to move the fingers on the affected side. Fanning them tests the ulnar nerve, curling them into a fist tests the median, and dorsiflexing the wrist tests the radial. These are the three nerves that run into the hand. The other two nerves commonly injured after dislocation of the shoulder are the axillary and musculocutaneous. These can be grossly tested by evaluating light touch sensation over the lateral head of the deltoid (this area is provided with sensation by the axillary nerve) and the lateral or radial aspect of the forearm (supplied by the lateral antebrachial cutaneous nerve, a terminal branch of the musculocutaneous).

Strength testing to screen for nerve injury can be done in the acute setting but can be difficult and deceiving in the presence of an acutely dislocated shoulder because the great pain of the dislocation can make any motor activity difficult. Although the acute management will not be changed in most cases, it is important to document carefully the acute neurologic examination. Neurologic injuries are quite common after shoulder dislocation. Most are neuropraxias (the equivalent of a nerve bruise) and reverse themselves with time. The possibility of nerves being damaged by the maneuvers used to reduce the dislocation is small but present. A dislocation with acute injury to the axillary nerve, brachial plexus (the confluence, found at the base of the neck, of all nerves to the extremity), or one of the peripheral nerves is a somewhat more urgent problem than the dislocation alone. The (theoretical) reason for this is that the nerves involved may be under severe compression or stretch while the shoulder is dislocated and may only be able to tolerate the mechanical load for a short time before permanent damage, and a permanent neurologic deficit, result. This same increase in urgency to reduce the dislocation exists when there is a loss of circulation (diminished pulses) to the hand below the dislocated shoulder.

The skin over the lateral head of the deltoid (the "epaulet region"), with its sensation supplied by the axillary nerve, is especially important to check for light touch when there is a dislocation. Any pattern of nerve injury can occur with a dislocation, but most common is axillary nerve injury. Axillary nerve function is important to shoulder rehabilitation because this is the nerve to the deltoid muscle. As noted above, one should always check for the radial pulse and compare it with that of the other side if it is weak. Reduction of the glenohumeral joint usually improves the weak pulse. Peripheral vascular disease is probably more likely to be the cause of a weak radial pulse than acute injury to the axillary artery; nevertheless, these injuries do occur and must be kept in mind.

Musculoskeletal examination. While standing behind the patient, if possible, palpate the top, front, and sides of both shoulder girdles simultaneously. Feel first for soft tissue contour, turgidity, and tenderness and then deeper for fractures of the clavicle, acromion, upper humerus, and shaft. Even slight crepitus on palpation indicates a high likelihood of clavicular or acromial fracture. While feeling for bony detail from behind, there will be some increased fullness anteriorly if the shoulder is dislocated. This is not a particularly reliable physical examination sign of dislocation. Simultaneously if possible, or sequentially if need be, palpate the posterior angle of the acromion and feel for the fullness of the humeral head 2 cm below. This area feels empty when the shoulder is dislocated anteriorly and too full when dislocated posteriorly. This sign (emptiness of the posterior joint line) is a much more reliable indicator of anterior dislocation than increased anterior fullness. The entire examination can be done with the arm in a sling, so leave the sling on if it has already been applied. If the results of a cursory examination suggest acute dislocation, the shoulder is best put gently into a sling and X-rays obtained as soon as possible.

After an episode of acute subluxation, the same examination is performed and followed by immobilization and plain films. The finding of anterior glenohumeral joint line tenderness is rather nonspecific. The usefulness of shear stress tests in the acute period is questionable because muscle spasm and guarding are likely to be intense. As with dislocators, many acute subluxators will know that their shoulder "started to come out," which will suggest the diagnosis. A safe and reliable test for subluxation in this situation is gently forced external rotation with the arm at the side. This is quite painful if there has been a recent subluxation with capsular or labral damage.

Acute treatment and immobilization. Little thought needs to go into acute treatment of most instability injuries: Immobilization should be applied immediately to prevent further injury; rapid assessment should be performed to check for neurologic, vascular, or bone injuries; appropriate radiographs should be obtained, and reduction should be performed if there is a dislocation. Immobilization is easiest with an arm sling. The type with a second strap that goes around the patient's waist is most secure. Many other devices are satisfactory, however; a muslin triangular bandage or even a large bandanna worn as an arm sling is adequate.

The immobilizer should take the weight of the upper extremity. The type of immobilizer that straps around the waist with two small cuffs attached to prevent motion of the arm and forearm does not do this and should not be used. An immobilizer can be ineffective if it is too small; there is usually no problem if it is too big, so that one should use a larger size if there is any question. All necessary acute radiographic studies can be performed with the arm in the sling. A dislocated shoulder must be reduced as soon as possible, but X-rays must be obtained and evaluated before any reduction is ever attempted.

Reduction of dislocated shoulder. The reduction procedure is most commonly performed in a hospital emergency department. Many practitioners routinely give narcotics and muscle relaxants before reducing the dislocation. Some (including the author) almost never do. A variety of methods for reducing anterior shoulder dislocations are popular. Each has its potential drawbacks and advantages. All methods work better if the patient is calm and obeying instructions; getting the patient's attention and cooperation is the first part of every reduction. It must also be realized that modern anesthesia is quite safe, and if attempts at reduction with the patient awake are repeatedly unsuccessful there is little harm in closed reduction under a brief general anesthetic.

The commonly utilized reductive techniques for anterior dislocation are illustrated in Figure 9–14. The most commonly used method is traction-

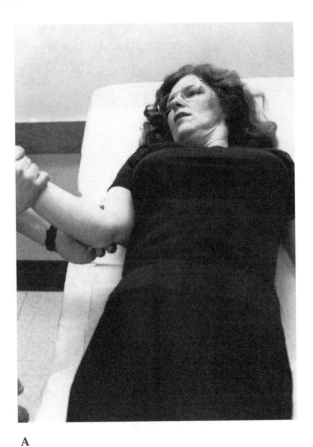

A

Figure 9–14 Anterior dislocation reduction maneuvers. **(A–C)** The Milch maneuver: Assisted external rotation followed by elevation with traction and then internal rotation.

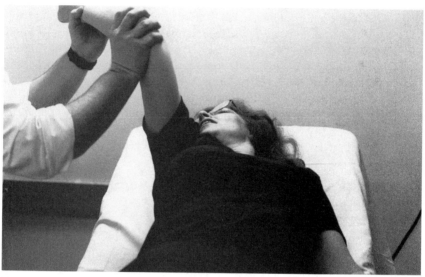

B

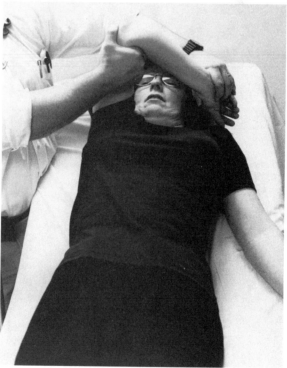

C

D

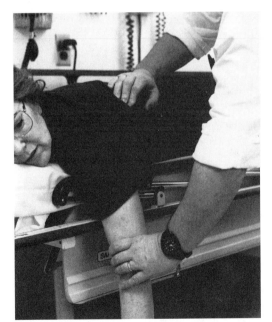

E

Figure 9-14 (D) Traction-countertraction method. **(E)** Stimson method: Prone traction with elevation of the medial scapula.

countertraction. To do this, the patient is kept supine with some elevation of the back (chaise lounge position). A bedsheet under the axilla of the affected side provides superior countertraction (an assistant pulls on the ends of the sheet) while inferior axial traction is applied to the arm with the elbow kept at 90° of flexion. This is continued until the girdle muscles relax sufficiently to unlock the humeral head from the front of the coracoid. Reduction of the glenohumeral joint is usually not subtle; the clunk is palpable and even audible in many cases. Although the reduction itself is painful, the patient will generally know immediately that the shoulder is "back in place," and the pain he or she was having with the dislocation soon begins to disappear.

The traction-countertraction method, and other axial traction methods of reducing anterior dislocations, are likely to require narcotics or muscle relaxants to be effective. They are, nonetheless, among the safer reduction methods because little twisting or bending force is used. There is little danger of fracturing the humerus with axial traction. The author's preferred technique was originally described by Milch.[10] This involves external rotation of the arm while held at the side to unlock the humeral head's posterior aspect from the anterior glenoid. The arm is then elevated as high as possible and then internally rotated, reducing the joint. The danger of fracturing the humerus with this technique is lessened considerably by making all these movements active assisted. The patient must be cooperative for this technique to be used safely.

Difficulty with reduction is likely to be encountered only with shoulders that have been dislocated a small number of times. As the capsule of the glenohumeral joint becomes looser and looser, the anterior glenoid more worn down and stripped of its capsular attachments, and the labrum more attenuated, the humeral head can slip out and back into the glenoid more easily. Some patients who have dislocated many times are able to reduce the joint by themselves.

Immobilization

Functions of immobilization. After an acute injury, the shoulder is immobilized to prevent further damage to the joint and to help control pain. After reduction, immobility still helps control pain but is also important to permit healing and contraction of the injured capsular tissues. As people who spend a great deal of time working against contractures of capsular tissues, many practitioners in physical medicine question the benefit of prolonged (up to 6 weeks) immobilization after shoulder dislocation or even the 2 weeks of immobilization that is often prescribed after an early episode of traumatic subluxation. There is no doubt that stiffness, weakness, and proprioceptive loss are to be expected, for a time, after immobilization of an injured, blood-filled joint with such an enormous physiologic range of motion. A number of research papers have been presented claiming no improvement in long-term stability with early immobilization of dislocations.[11,12] Because immobilization is a basic physical treatment, its efficacy must be understood as accurately as possible. This understanding can then form the basis for a treatment plan for the acutely dislocated shoulder.

Immobilization background literature. The classic studies of recurrence rates after initial anterior shoulder dislocation are those of McLaughlin and Cavallero[4] and Rowe and Sakellarides.[12] The recurrence rate for anterior dislocation in the teenage group was nearly 90% in these early studies. These, and more recent studies done by Hovelius et al,[11] indicated that little benefit results from 3 to 4 weeks of immobilization. The rate of recurrence of anterior dislocation in two groups of more than 100 patients was equal; one group received 3 to 4 weeks of immobilization, and the other was allowed to use the shoulder ad lib as soon as pain permitted. This recurrence rate was also quite high, more than 50% in the youngest age group (<22 years). The incidence of redislocation in nearly all published studies is always highest in the youngest age group (teenagers and those in their early 20s), higher in more athletic subgroups, and higher in men. These are the highest-demand shoulders, subject to the highest uncontrolled stresses.

The 90% rate for recurrence of anterior dislocation in the young, athletic, male population became a medically accepted figure that not only justified surgical repair after initial anterior dislocation in this population but also made immobilization and rehabilitation seem useless to many practitioners. This trend started to change, however, when studies began to be published in the early 1980s showing significantly lower recurrence rates after more carefully supervised and enthusiastically monitored immobilization and rehabilitation protocols. Yoneda et al[6] in 1982 reported on 124 men with an average age of 21 years who were treated with 5 weeks of immobilization and 6 weeks of exercise, avoiding external rotation; the recurrence rate was 17%. Aronen and Regan[7] in 1984 reported a 0 rate of recurrence in a 3-year follow-up study of 20 naval recruits averaging 19 years old at the time of dislocation. Their study involved the most vigorous and specific rehabilitation protocol of any nonoperative study up to that time as well as 3 weeks of initial immobilization. A clear difference between these results and those obtained in the 1950s and 1960s suggests that the physical treatments being used in the earlier period were not truly the same as those used in the 1980s. This may be seen in the early studies of Row and Sakellarides[12] in as far as they were conducted by orthopaedic surgeons interested in surgical repairs for dislocation; consciously or not, nonsurgical treatment was not likely to be monitored as closely as surgical treatment. The protocol of Aronen and Regan,[7] on the other hand, was quite specific, with specific strength parameters that had to be met before activities were advanced as well as a strict regimen of strengthening exercises, starting with isometrics and then going to isotonic and finally isokinetic strengthening, all well supervised in the military setting.

Further light can be shed on the question of immobilization and rehabilitation after dislocation by the history of surgical procedures used to treat recurrent dislocation. These are explained in detail below, but it is notable here that more than 20 procedures have been used to prevent recurrent dislocation, with great variation among them as to what is actually done to the structures around the joint. Despite this wide variation, quite satisfactory results, with respect to stopping further dislocation, have been achieved with nearly all of them (strength, motion, and pain results have differed quite significantly). Hippocrates, in the millennium before the birth of Christ, reported satisfactory results with his surgical procedure for recurrent dislocation, which consisted of placing a white-hot poker into the anteroinferior glenohumeral joint followed by a long period of immobilization in sling position. It becomes apparent that anterior injury to the unstable glenohumeral joint, inflicted by almost any type of surgery, followed by immobilization for an extended period of time is effective in stopping recurrent anterior shoulder dislocation.

The response to injury includes scarring and local contraction of tissues. This contraction and scarring is an important element in preventing recurrent dislocation, and, as might be guessed at this point, it can be initiated by the dislocating injury itself. Early immobilization takes advantage of the natural reaction to injury by allowing it to contract the anterior capsular tissues, laxity of which is a major cause of recurrent dislocation. This is a major theoretical justification for early, prolonged immobilization after an initial anterior dislocation. The early scarring and contracture in response to the dislocation may be as effective as a surgical procedure in preventing further dislocation.

Treatment decisions. Immobilization in the sling position is therefore recommended after initial anterior dislocation. Younger, more flexible, more athletic, and male patients should be immobilized for a longer time. Older, less athletic, and less flexible patients need less time. Although clinical judgment must be individualized, 6 weeks is the longest period used; this is how long to hold a 17-year-old throwing athlete (dominant side) with marked ligamentous laxity. A 60-year-old with otherwise tight joints is held for 1 week, and a 30-year-old recreational athlete with normal joints is held for 4 to 5 weeks. Isometric drills can be safely started in the second week. At first, these consists of isometric adduction, internal rotation, and flexion. By the fourth week, isometric external rotation and extension may be safely added. Isometrics are well tolerated at 60% of maximal effort held for 20 seconds and repeated three to five times per set. Careful, daily elbow motion and hand and wrist motion ad lib may be started the day after reduction.

Immobilization is quite satisfactorily maintained in a standard shoulder sling. This keeps the anterior tissues loose and shortened. It is not necessary for patients to maintain 90° of elbow flexion while in the sling; many patients find the sling more tolerable with the elbow kept at around 110°. There has been some use made of casts and orthoses that can maintain a degree of flexion during immobilization. The most convincing rationale for their use has been based on the concept of the zero position[13] for the joint, in which the anterior and posterior capsular tissues are equally stress free and the humeral head's central axis is aligned with the central axis of the glenoid. The theoretical problem with this is that anterior dislocation does not symmetrically involve the shoulder capsule but rather preferentially involves the anterior structures. The practical problem with immobilization in anything other than a sling is that flexion or abduction orthoses are ungainly and awkward. There has not been any clinical evidence that their use is advantageous.

Immobilization for posterior dislocation. After a posterior dislocation, it is best to use a cast to immobilize the shoulder in neutral or slight external rotation. A pillow type abduction orthosis may more comfortably maintain the same position in those people for whom a shoulder spica cast is not practical. It must be appreciated, however, that for the posterior capsular tissues to be kept loose, so that they can contract in response to the injury of posterior dislocation, the internally rotated position maintained by an arm sling is unsatisfactory.

CONCOMITANT INJURIES OF THE DESTABILIZED SHOULDER

Nerve Injuries

As mentioned earlier, neurologic injuries accompanying shoulder dislocations are usually neuropraxias that resolve completely after prompt relocation. The axillary nerve, which innervates the deltoid muscle, is the most frequently involved. The radial nerve has been next most commonly affected in the author's practice. Any of the other nerves to the upper extremity may be involved, however. The greatest clinical value of knowing this is being able to give a reason for poor or slow rehabilitation progress after dislocation and being able to assure patients that nerve function usually returns with time. Rarely is there anything specific that can be done to correct these nerve injuries; an expectant attitude and patience in rehabilitation are the most helpful elements of successful treatment. Axillary nerve injuries are more common in older patients and may involve the deltoid innervation without significant loss of skin sensation. The patient's ability to set the deltoid should be followed after anterior dislocation, and axillary nerve injury should be suspected if it is decreased or absent despite intact light touch over the deltoid's lateral head. Beyond making this diagnosis (which requires an EMG), there is little else to do about the neuropractic nerve injuries that accompany anterior dislocation. Because return of nerve function is eventually expected, continued attempts at strengthening are justified.

Permanent weakness of the deltoid may have to be accepted if nerve function does not return before denervation changes (fibrosis and fatty infiltration) occur in the deltoid. These are generally considered irreversible. There has been no convincing clinical evidence that galvanic stimulation of the deltoid can prevent these changes. Consultation with a neurologist is often sought in this setting. Although this is often for medicolegal purposes, there is real value in definitive establishment of the injury as a neuropraxia. In the (extremely rare) instance of true nerve disruption or avulsion (called neurotmesis), there is evidence that reparative surgery on the affected nerves can improve ultimate function.

Rotator Cuff Injuries Accompanying Dislocation

Older patients also experience a higher incidence of rotator cuff injury after anterior dislocation. These tears are usually large and are more likely to explain poor return of shoulder function after dislocation in an elderly person than nerve injury. Both can happen, however. It is also quite possible for the cuff tear that is noted after dislocation to have been present before the dislocation. Recurrence of dislocation is less common if there has been a cuff tear (see Chapter 8). An anterior dislocation with a large cuff tear is generally a disabling injury. Early surgical repair of the rotator cuff should be considered if the patient cannot maintain the arm in neutral rotation and slight abduction by 6 weeks after the dislocation. MR scans after the shoulder has been dislocated are more likely to be falsely positive for cuff tears because of traumatic changes in the cuff tendons and blood in the joint. An arthrogram is always reliable for the diagnosis of cuff tear and may have a greater advantage in this setting. The postdislocation patient with marked weakness of the anterior or posterior cuff (they tend to come off together after dislocation) should be worked up both neurologically and radiographically for denervation and cuff tear.

Fractures

The common fractures that accompany shoulder dislocation are generally noted at the time of relocation on plain film radiographs. Tuberosity fractures (the greater tuberosity for anterior dislocations, the lesser tuberosity for posterior dislocations) usually reduce themselves when the humeral head is reduced because the fragment of tuberosity is held in place by the rotator cuff and/or subscapularis. Tuberosity fractures that remain displaced after reduction of the joint generally require surgical replacement and internal fixation both to restore rotator cuff power and to prevent impingement and motion loss. The Hill-Sachs impression fracture of the posterior humeral head is associated with chronic instability. There is little to be done about it besides limiting the external rotation and abduction range that is permitted during rehabilitation. Fractures of the glenoid rim, both anterior and posterior may be difficult to appreciate on some plain film radiographs. The axillary view visualizes the anterior and posterior rims well, as does CT. Glenoid fractures are well tolerated in older patients unless they are large and displaced, in which case surgical fixation is necessary to restore painless motion. Rehabilitation is often unaffected by the presence of a small, minimally displaced glenoid rim fracture in the elderly patient. In the younger, more active patient, the rim fracture, often referred to as a bony Bankart lesion, is associated with a greater likelihood of recurrence of dislocation and continued subluxation symptoms. It is one of the more legitimate reasons for surgical repair of first-time dislocators.

The other fractures that can accompany shoulder dislocation can be considered somewhat independently. Humeral shaft and neck fractures, acromial fractures, coracoid fractures, and clavicular fractures may all occur in the setting of a dislocated shoulder. The most important rehabilitation concept involved with these is that fracture healing takes precedence over motion and strength. The great majority of these fractures will be treated nonoperatively with an additional period of immobilization. Even isometric exercise is contraindicated in the presence of most of these fractures. Weakness and stiffness must be accepted and worked on after bone healing is secure. Nonunion of humeral neck and clavicular fractures can be the result of inadequate immobilization.

MOBILIZATION AFTER DESTABILIZING INJURY

After the initial period of immobilization and isometrics, the first-time dislocated shoulder will be fairly stiff. Mobilization of both the glenohumeral and the scapulothoracic articulations is begun with the goal of completely restoring forward elevation and internal rotation before starting on external rotation beyond neutral. Abduction, and especially abduction with external rotation, are best avoided in rehabilitation of anterior dislocators; patients are shown that this position (abduction with external rotation) is most likely to make the shoulder chronically unstable and possibly dislocate again. They usually recall the arm being in that position at the time of dislocation and have little trouble understanding that the position is a dangerous one. If questioned carefully, many first-time dislocators admit to having tested the waters with a little anterior apprehension test on their own. This generally convinces them of the legitimacy of our warnings.

Motion Loss

Concerns about permanent loss of motion after dislocation are not unfounded; there are many patients with measurable loss of elevation and rotation after dislocation. These patients tend not to be high-demand athletes, however. It is the older patient who most commonly has a permanent motion deficit after dislocation. Only occasionally is this loss of motion in the dislocated shoulder a patient complaint. In view of this, a bit too much emphasis is often placed on regaining full range of motion after immobilization for dislocation. Many moderate- to high-demand patients regain their motion in the course of resistive strengthening exercise, without spending any rehabilitation time solely on progressive motion therapy. The value of regular isometrics while in the sling is apparent when mobilization is begun. Patients whose compliance with the isometric program was poor advance slower with motion and strengthening when the sling comes off.

Strengthening after Immobilization

Contrary to the usual routine of "motion first, then strength," muscle strengthening of the rotator cuff and subscapularis is best worked on early, during mobilization. This is done because of the nature of the injury under treatment. The cuff and subscapularis are stabilizing muscles; they tend to keep the humeral head centered on the glenoid. The residual instability that is present after dislocation impedes range of motion therapy because the weak, stiff, and uncoordinated cuff and subscapularis tend to resist passive range maneuvers; they first obey the most primitive reflex, which is to resist subluxation, and thus they resist motion. By simultaneous enhancement of voluntary control and tone in these muscles, glenohumeral range is restored more rapidly and comfortably. It is therefore an order for active assisted cuff and subscapularis strengthening with progressive forward elevation, internal rotation, and external rotation to approximately 15° that is given after sling immobilization is discontinued.

The Shoulder Leash

Avoidance of abduction and external rotation is a significant element of the mobilization period program. Most patients can do this on their own during waking hours. Control of the arm during sleep can be maintained by use of the sling, by pinning the sleeve of the patient's nightclothes to the body, or, most easily, by use of a shoulder leash. This is a length of cord or string tied from the wrist of the affected side to the waist with about 50 cm of slack in between (Figure 9–15). It permits the patient to touch the face and rest the arm at the side while preventing the abduction–external rotation position in which so many people sleep. The shoulder leash is also helpful for chronically unstable shoulders that dislocate during sleep. It does not seem to help impingement-related night pain as much. The leash does not prevent the inferior subluxation that tends to occur when there is an inferior component of instability, and it does permit quite a bit of motion. It is thus not appropriate for the initial immobilization period if true immobilization is the objective.

Pain during Mobilization

There is pain to be expected during the mobilization period. Some help with this is afforded by the modalities, especially ultrasonation. Pain often prevents advancement of motion and functional goals; medication, including some narcotics, may be necessary during this phase of rehabilitation for some patients.

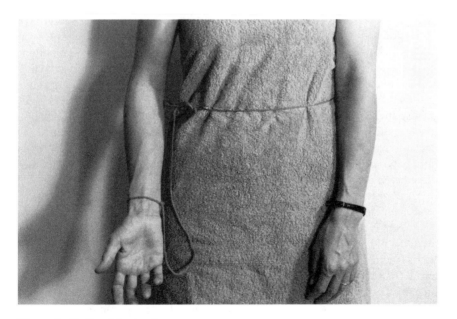

Figure 9–15 Shoulder leash.

Diagnostically, it is important for the practitioners to be sensitive to the presence of excessive pain during mobilization. There is, of course, no objective measurement of this, but even within the shifting boundaries of individuals' differences in communication and display of pain-associated behaviors, clinical experience soon teaches one to realize when a given patient is having more than average pain.

A number of possibilities beyond random variation must be considered in the dislocator who has excessive pain during the mobilization period. For one, instability may be severe if there has been loss of the stabilizing muscles, with pain being produced by subluxation when motion is attempted. This can be determined by looking for similar pain on shear stress testing and active versus passive motion pain. Rupture of the subscapularis accompanying anterior dislocation can present this way. The subscapularis isolation maneuver (lifting the dorsum of the hand off the back) helps diagnose this. A large cuff tear may be similarly painful and will produce cuff weakness on examination, less pain being noted with the same motion performed passively than actively.

Stiffness after Immobilization

An element of idiopathic adhesive capsulitis may be present after dislocation or subluxation and immobilization. This is more likely to be the case if the patient is a diabetic, even if blood glucose levels are well controlled. Poorly understood, this is believed to be a capsulitis or pericapsulitis that leaves the tissues around the glenohumeral joint highly sensitive to stretch. The patient splints (resists motion actively to prevent pain) and has pain with both active and passive motion. This situation is often accompanied by signs that are suggestive of a reflex sympathetic dystrophy. These include cutaneous hypersensitivity and skin temperature changes around the shoulder. This is also the one case in which instability is likely to be associated with radiating pain into the neck or arm. The pathophysiology of this easily recognized pain syndrome is not known but certainly seems to involve a neuropathic or autonomically mediated element.

Another common cause of excessive pain during mobilization is an intraarticular fracture or cartilaginous loose body that may or may not have been recognized earlier. A particularly large labral tear, a bony Bankart fragment from the anterior glenoid rim, or a cartilaginous fragment from the Hill-Sachs fracture can each produce severe pain with attempted motion. A minimally displaced fracture of the greater tuberosity is often associated with increased pain and stiffness during mobilization of the dislocated shoulder, although this is likely to involve subacromial impingement rather than intraarticular pain.

Treatment Modifications during Mobilization

The modifications of treatment during mobilization because of excessive pain depend, of course, on the underlying cause. A loose body in the joint may need to be removed surgically (arthroscopically). This is not always the case for loose bodies in general because with time they often become trapped by the joint's synovial lining and fixed in place, thereby being rendered asymptomatic. Loose bodies that are symptomatic after a long period of sling immobilization, however, seem to have a decreased likelihood of becoming safely trapped. The idiopathic capsulitis mentioned above is a good reason for consultation with physiatry or a pain service. It may respond to neuropathic pain medications such as carbamazepine, prazosin, or steroids (see Chapter 5). Intermittent nerve blockade administered by injection around the brachial plexus of long-acting local anesthetics or adrenergic blocking agents such as guanethidine (which temporarily cut off sympathetic innervation to the entire upper extremity) are quite useful with cases of postimmobilization idiopathic adhesive capsulitis. These injections not only permit manipulation under anesthesia, which can painlessly remove any passive elements of contracture in the hours after administration, but also may have a lasting effect on the hypersensitivity, somehow tending to rebalance the sympathetic tone around the joint.

Regardless of the use of nerve blocks or medications, careful, extremely persistent physical therapy is the absolute mainstay of treatment in these and all cases of idiopathic adhesive capsulitis. Active and passive motion, thermal modalities, and transcutaneous electrical nerve stimulation must be continued until symptomatic relief and functional goals are achieved. This may take a year in difficult cases. True desensitization therapy may not be applicable to these shoulders because hypersensitivity is not usually a major element of the presentation. Progressive ranging that is ultimately successful does, however, take on an aspect of cuff desensitization. Of note is the observation that only rarely is residual instability of significant clinical importance when there is a postdislocation capsulitis. The high degree of rotator cuff and subscapularis stiffness does seem successful in eliminating instability.

Rehabilitation with Tendon Disruptions

Shoulders in which there is a large tendinous disruption after anterior dislocation are unlikely to regain normal function without surgical repair. Rehabilitation modifications that have been attempted include prolonged cuff and subscapularis strengthening; concentration on strength and flexibility of the scapulothoracic musculature, latissimus dorsi, and pectorals; and highly prolonged immobilization in an effort to create glenohumeral ankylosis. Functional improvement with these efforts is expected to be moderate at best. The large cuff or subscapularis tears that accompany dislocation remove extremely important stabilizing forces from the glenohumeral joint. Nonsurgical rehabilitation of these injuries is essentially teaching patients how to get along without a functioning shoulder. Even after surgical repair of the tendons, rehabilitation is slow. Improvement is seen for more than a year in many cases.

Distinction must be made between these cases and greater or lesser tuberosity fracture-dislocations. Although it is true that these are, in a certain mechanical sense, identical injuries because the tuberosity fractures are cuff (or subscapularis) tears through bone, their prognosis, once the shoulder has been reduced and the tuberosity has healed back in place, is much better. The tuberosity fracture-dislocations usually regain full function and stability much more rapidly and reliably than the tendon avulsion-dislocations.

Maintenance after Destabilizing Injury

Prevention of recurrent dislocation is the primary purpose of the maintenance therapy with which patients are treated after range and strength goals have been achieved in the mobilization phase. A set of shoulder girdle exercises with the major emphasis on the cuff and subscapularis is helpful. Perhaps as important as keeping the muscles strong, toned, and coordinated is avoidance of activities and positions that produce subluxation. This can be thought of as a mental shoulder leash. It is useful for all patients except those whose livelihood depends on activities performed in abduction and external rotation. Outpatient physical therapy is generally stopped at the end of the mobilization phase. The last few sessions should anticipate this and include teaching on the activities and positions that produce subluxation and how to avoid them.

Activity Modifications

Some degree of activity modification, which is more or less permanent, should be recommended for all recurrent dislocators, even those who have undergone surgical reconstruction. Although most patients will eventually go on to resume unmodified activities after they have been symptom free for a few years, recurrences are less frequent in patients who are careful with their shoulders. This degree of modification is actually rather slight. It consists of avoiding high-level abduction–external rotation stress and overhead abduction positions whenever possible. Some people will be unwilling or unable to do this on a permanent basis, and they will certainly test repairs and treatments. Accidents, such as falls, can always result in recurrence of dislocation (or severe subluxation) after successful treatment is concluded. Proper rehabilitation after an initial destabilizing injury or a secure surgical repair after multiple dislocations does greatly reduce the likelihood of this occurring. This fact notwithstanding, there should never be an understanding that any treatment, whether surgical or nonsurgical, can absolutely eliminate the possibility of dislocation. Maintenance exercises should be continued for at least 1 year, longer in high-demand shoulders that are treated nonoperatively.

Athletic Issues

The high-demand athlete who intends to return to throwing sports, tennis, or football must be advanced from mobilization to training phase exercise. These include the same cuff and subscapularis strengthening exercises as well as sports-specific exercises, such as graduated throwing drills, serving practice at increasing speeds with increasingly less side spin, and resistive work with free weights. Although these patients are more likely to have undergone a surgical repair, they, too, are best protected by maintenance of a supranormal level of strength in the stabilizing muscles, pectorals, and deltoid.

SPECIFIC TREATMENTS FOR CHRONIC INSTABILITY-RELATED PROBLEMS

Labral Tears

The torn glenoid labrum (Figure 9–16) may produce symptoms of instability as part of the Bankart lesion, direct labral pain when it is pulled by the humeral head, or loose body symptoms (catching, clicking, and locking) as a partly attached or completely detached free intraarticular object. Most of the glenoid labrum is mechanically tough enough to be an obvious source of pain when loose pieces of it become intermittently jammed between the humeral head and glenoid articular surfaces. The actual anatomy of the labrum is quite different from that of other, analogous structures in other joints, such as the meniscus of the knee or the acromioclavicular joint.[14] Little fibrocartilage (the material of which the knee meniscus is composed) is found in the labrum. It is mostly made of the same tissue as the capsule and may be considered a thickened, wedge-shaped fold of the capsule that runs around its perimeter, functionally deepening the glenoid fossa and improving the stability of the glenohumeral joint.

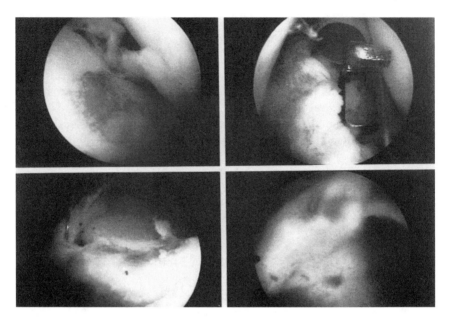

Figure 9–16 Arthroscopic views of the torn glenoid labrum. A surgical instrument resecting torn tissue is seen at the upper right.

The Superior Labrum Anterior Posterior Lesion

The superior labrum is the attachment site for the tendon of the long head of the biceps. The fraying and detachment of this superior aspect of the labrum is popularly termed the superior labrum anterior posterior (SLAP) lesion (Figure 9–17). The name was coined by Snyder et al[15] and describes how the damage to the labrum begins posterior to the biceps tendon's insertion and ends anterior to it. It is a common finding in throwing athletes. Throwers, swimmers, and tennis players are the patients who are most likely to present with labral tear problems of any sort. It does take quite a lot of shoulder use to make labral tearing a significantly painful problem. Nonetheless, because of the large sports medicine population, much attention is currently paid to labral tear pain and especially to the SLAP lesion.

It is not currently clear whether the SLAP lesion is caused by over-pull of the long head biceps tendon or by the action of the humeral head and rotator cuff on this confluence of tendon and labrum. It is also unclear whether the SLAP lesion is the product of shoulder instability or simply overuse. The diagnosis may be suggested by the simultaneous presence of signs and symptoms of labral tear and anterior biceps tendon–related pain. Some radiologists be-

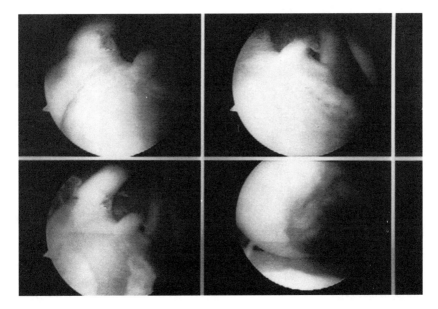

Figure 9–17 Arthroscopic views of the SLAP lesion: tearing at the confluence of the tendon of the biceps and the superior glenoid labrum.

lieve that they can visualize the lesion on MR arthrography by injecting a gadolinium-containing contrast medium (which produces a characteristic MR signal in a manner similar to the radiopaque contrast media used in standard arthrography). These studies have not been widely employed; neither have they been extremely accurate in this author's limited experience (consisting of two MR arthrograms, one false negative and one false positive).

SLAP Lesion Treatment

The SLAP lesion is most often discovered during shoulder arthroscopy. It is then ignored, debrided (with every effort made to preserve the attachment of the biceps tendon to the glenoid), or repaired. The debridement procedure consists of trimming back the torn and hypermobile edges of the labrum-tendon confluence, possibly making it less likely to be caught and pulled by the moving humeral head (Figure 9–18). The repair procedure is fairly easy to do arthroscopically. It consists of anchoring the labrum and biceps back to the bone of the superior glenoid with sutures placed directly into bone. As with other lesions of the glenoid labrum that are treated arthroscopically, good clinical results have been achieved with various treatments, suggesting a high

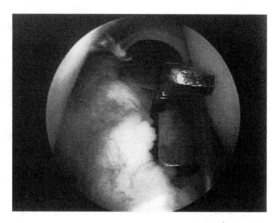

Figure 9–18 Arthroscopic view showing trimming of a SLAP lesion.

mechanical threshold level at which instability of the torn labrum produces symptoms. There is no currently accepted conservative treatment of the SLAP lesion because it is only (reliably) discovered at surgery.

Other Labral Lesions

The treatment of other labral lesions should be tailored to the clinical situation in which they are discovered. It is certainly true that labral symptoms in high-performance throwing athletes have been treated successfully with surgical arthroscopy to debride torn labrum, loose bodies, and hyperplastic synovium. Removal of unstable, interposing tissues may also prevent or slow the wearing of articular surface cartilage. This does not mean that all patients with labral symptoms should be treated arthroscopically, however. The bulk of shoulder practice does not consist of caring for high-performance athletes. Low-performance golfers, bowlers, swimmers, car polishers, and hedge trimmers may also present with signs and symptoms of labral pathology.

Immediate shoulder arthroscopy is not the first treatment recommendation in the moderate-demand population; a rational plan of physical treatment is. This includes early rest followed by a graduated range and strengthening program. The ends of the forward elevation/external rotation/internal rotation (FE/ER/IR) ranges as well as abduction and extension are avoided until there are no symptoms in the FE/ER/IR range representing about 80% of the normal range. This means, for example, that if there is a 180°/80°/T-8 range on the other side work should stay within 145°/60°/T-12 until labral signs have been absent for 2 to 3 weeks. The rationale for these motion restrictions is that the forces that tend to displace the labrum tend to occur at the ends of range and in anterior/inferior translocation of the humeral head. There is no nonsurgical therapy that directly trims or mends the labrum, but by letting whatever healing (and stabilizing) potential there is occur in a milieu that still includes significant motion, clinical improvement is usually achieved. Rehabilitative treatment for 1 to 2 months is standard for this. Arthroscopic surgery of the glenohumeral joint may then be elected with these patients if the physical treatments are not being tolerated or have been ineffective.

Specific Treatment

The first treatment for suspected labral pathology in the moderate-demand shoulder is rest. If there is distinct anterior or anteroinferior glenohumeral instability on examination, a sling may be used for up to 10 days. This is not the continuous, 24-hour-per-day immobilization that is used after a severe subluxation or dislocation but a somewhat more casual use of the sling in bed and during waking hours as a place to rest the arm instead of on the back of a sofa or behind the head. The arm can be removed from the sling for meals, desk work, washing, and the like. It is hoped that this period of sling rest will permit the initial healing potential that is present in the damaged labrum to be realized, preventing further separation of the torn surfaces by the continued intrusive action of the moving humeral head.

After 2 weeks of rest, careful glenohumeral motion in elevation and internal and external rotation with the arm at the side is begun. The 80% limits described above are used. This motion is ideally passive or with strong active assist and is started with gravity traction across the glenohumeral joint. Prone elevation with the arm hanging off the side of the table is excellent here (Figure 9–19). Conceptually the opposite of the glenohumeral grinding maneuver used to detect labral tears, this passive motion with gravity traction attempts to avoid forces that would tend to catch the torn labral edge while establishing gliding surfaces that, it is hoped, will smooth with time and repetition. After 3 weeks of this, it will be apparent if the tear or loose body is still unstable. Significant catching pain, locking, or painful clunking at this point should be evaluated with MR scan, CT arthrography, and/or arthroscopy. If symptoms have diminished by week 5, gradual return to activity may be permitted. At least half these patients return happily to their prior activities without surgical intervention. Most of these eventually will have some recurrence of their symptoms. The same program may be started again if symptoms and signs are of sufficient magnitude. It is most often the case, however, that labral symptoms in moderate-demand patients are fairly mild and can be managed quite successfully with physical methods.

Arthroscopic Treatment of Labral Tears

Despite the implicit warning that surgical arthroscopy is often not necessary, it is an extremely effective treatment for symptomatic labral pathology.

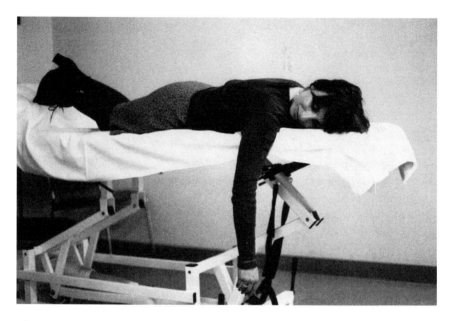

Figure 9–19 Prone (hanging) elevation.

The arthroscope is an optical lens system contained in a tube about the diameter of a drinking straw. In years past, the surgeon's eye was placed up against the instrument as if looking through a telescope; today a small video camera at the outside end of the tube puts the images seen through the scope on a television screen. The inside end of the arthroscope is positioned within the glenohumeral joint, through a small (less than 2 cm) surgical incision on the posterior shoulder. This entry site, called a portal, is about 2 cm inferior and medial to the posterior corner of the acromion. Its location is on the posterior joint line, well away from the axillary nerve. The portal pierces the posterior rotator cuff (at the border of infraspinatus and teres minor) near its musculotendinous junction. Although technically the procedures creates a rotator cuff tear, there is no retraction when the puncture is in this location; it heals well and has not been a source of significant symptoms through many thousands of cases. Other portals are created on the anterior and lateral aspects of the shoulder to permit use of a variety of small surgical instruments within the joint or to permit replacement of the arthroscope to visualize other areas within the joint. Portal scars are generally small and do not often create painful skin adhesions.

Arthroscopy if performed under general anesthesia or regional block (a technique in which local anesthetic is injected around the brachial plexus, creating temporary anesthesia and muscle relaxation of the entire shoulder girdle). Strict surgical sterile technique must be observed; septic arthritis can easily be a complication if the joint is contaminated during the procedure. The glenohumeral joint is most easily visualized when traction is maintained on the arm to open up the space between the humeral head and the glenoid. Occasional transient neurologic problems, presumably due to traction on the brachial plexus, have been seen after arthroscopic procedures. The joint is also distended with saline or a similar solution to increase the space within and to decrease bleeding from cut or abraded surfaces. Bleeding, which obscures visualization, can be quite a problem during shoulder arthroscopy. Pharmacologic agents (such as epinephrine) are sometimes added to the distending solutions to decrease this local bleeding.

The glenoid labrum is one of the most easily seen structures within the shoulder joint. It is also easily resected with small hand instruments or motorized suction shavers, whose rotating blades cut off tiny bits with each revolution and then vacuum them out of the joint in a stream of irrigating fluid. Free or loose bodies within the joint are also easily removed with small grasping instruments. Free bodies may be quite difficult to find during arthroscopy, however. It is not unusual for there to be no trace of a bony free body on careful arthroscopic examination of the joint, even though it is plainly visible on X-rays. This is usually due to the tendency of the joint's lining tissue, the synovium, to cover over and incorporate loose intraarticular objects. It can be impossible for the synovium to do this with semiloose objects, such as torn labral tags, because of their location at the actual joint interface. These semiloose bodies are unable to float off to a remote recess of the joint and become incorporated into the synovial lining. They are more likely to remain symptomatic as a result.

Rehabilitation after shoulder arthroscopy for labral lesions. After shoulder arthroscopy, it is common for the shoulder to be enlarged by large amounts of the irrigating fluid, which leaks out of the joint into the subcutaneous tissues. This fluid is harmlessly reabsorbed, and the shoulder returns to normal size in 1 to 2 days. The arthroscopic portals are normally closed with sutures, which are removed in 3 to 10 days. Most surgeons send patients home on the day of surgery with the arm in a sling. The sling may be discontinued by the evening of the first postoperative day or sooner if desired. Motion exercises, which are passive at first and advanced to active as tolerated, are begun on the first postoperative day as well. Large dressings may be changed to adhesive bandage strips on the second day; this helps with motion. The shoulder is quite sore after arthroscopy, and this soreness may persist for up to 1 week or longer if more work, such as extensive removal of synovium, has been done. Rehabilitation after glenoid labral tear resection does not have to wait for any massive muscle or tendon healing to be complete before advancing, however. Active motion is advanced in most patients, as tolerated, from the second day. Labral tear symptoms of catching and sudden positional pain are usually gone by the time full motion has been regained.

If resection of labral tear was the primary surgical procedure performed during the shoulder arthroscopy, it should be anticipated that rehabilitation will be rather quick and that a high functional level (usually sports participation) is being sought by the patient. Postoperative physical therapy in this group can be advanced as patient comfort permits. Because there has not been an acromioplasty, the deltoid origin should not have been damaged at all. There need not be significant protection of the anterior musculature. Active assisted FE/ER/IR is therefore advanced as tolerated to pure active. When the active range (FE/ER/IR) is full, resistive strengthening of the entire shoulder girdle is used until sports-specific functional and coordinating maneuvers are begun. A typical physical therapy prescription after arthroscopic labral resection lasts for 1 month or less in the outpatient setting with 1 to 2 months of supervision of home therapy or training.

Understanding the primary arthroscopic procedure. An issue that is often faced in the postarthroscopic outpatient therapy course is which of the many procedures listed on the patient's operative note was primary. This affects both the anticipated postsurgical course and the recommendations for therapy. It is unfortunately true that a good bit of arthroscopy has been done with less than scrupulous indications, and "We did a little bit of everything" can be the reported surgical procedure when in fact "We had a hard time seeing anything and didn't do much" was the case.

The first person to consult regarding this is the surgeon. Asking directly what the primary procedure was or, more specifically in this case, whether the labral resection was the primary procedure might steer rehabilitation effectively. There are some surgeons who perform an arthroscopic subacromial decompression every time they do an arthroscopy. This ought to raise the caveats (see Chapter 8 regarding rehabilitation of arthroscopic subacromial decompression) about the anterior musculature and should significantly slow the rehabilitation course from the otherwise brisk pace that is possible after labral resection. Given the large number of patients who have undergone such treatment with no radiographic evidence of having had a bony acromioplasty, a retroactive history may need be taken to decide whether the patient was an impinger (most likely) or was operated on for labral symptoms. Postoperative physical examination is always more difficult to draw conclusions from because of diffuse soreness, but if subacromial and cuff tenderness and pain predominate, it is likely that the subacromial surgery was the more significant of the two procedures.

It is certainly possible for a patient to have symptomatic problems both above and below the rotator cuff, but the primary reason for the arthroscopic procedure is usually one or the other. Most surgeons have this primary diagnosis in mind when performing the procedure, and it is quite helpful to know this during subsequent rehabilitation. Labral tearing is held to be primarily related to glenohumeral instability. This is true of anterior tears and Bankart lesions, the posterosuperior tears seen in complex or glenoid impingement, and even the SLAP lesion. Subacromial impingement has a different pathogenesis. The desire not to miss anything that might cause pain later and possibly the insurance company's reimbursement structure might underlie the practice of performing subacromial decompression when surgeons treat symptomatic labral tear. Impingement, however, remains a clinical entity that cannot be diagnosed arthroscopically (although rotator cuff tear, which is most commonly the result of impingement, certainly can).

The other side of this issue is seen when the primary diagnosis is actually impingement, and an arthroscopic look into the glenohumeral joint makes the (necessarily) pathologic diagnosis of labral tear. Because resecting this tear is technically easy and carries with it little additional postoperative pain, it is done routinely. This is the so-called incidental labral tear resection. There cannot be such a thing as a beneficial labral tear, and any unstable fragment within the joint does carry the possibility of producing symptoms at some time. This argument does seem to justify this type of secondary labral tear resection. Little if any change in postsurgical rehabilitation is warranted after such a resection. The course can be dictated entirely by the subacromial decompression.

Arthroscopic Treatment of Subluxation and Dislocation

The arthroscopic treatment of patients with truly symptomatic instability is still evolving at the time of this writing. This topic relates to the actual restoration of stability to the glenohumeral joint. Resection of labral tears and free bodies may be considered arthroscopic treatment for secondary problems produced by shoulder instability, but these procedures are not actually treatments for the underlying problem of instability, which, to the best of current understanding, causes the labral damage. Much has been written in both the sports medicine and the orthopaedic literatures about the proper role of arthroscopic procedures in the treatment of symptomatic instability[16]; conclusions are few but include the following generalities:

- Patients with lesser degrees of instability have better clinical results than those with recurrent frank dislocation when treated with arthroscopic stabilization procedures.
- The postsurgical rehabilitation course is quicker after arthroscopic stabilization procedures than after open surgical stabilization procedures.

- Open surgical stabilization is significantly more likely permanently to prevent dislocation and symptomatic subluxation than arthroscopic stabilization. Arthroscopic repairs have a higher failure rate.

Arthroscopic Stabilization Techniques

The arthroscopic procedures in use today for stabilization of the anteriorly unstable glenohumeral joint most often address the Bankart lesion. This ripping away of the capsule from the anterior glenoid neck accompanies most cases of truly traumatic dislocation. Its repair, via an open surgical procedure, is a reliable method of stopping recurrent anterior dislocation. The shoulder that has had multiple episodes of highly traumatic anterior dislocation is unlikely to exhibit significant inferior or posterior instability. A distinction, somewhat artificial, has been adopted in a large segment of the orthopaedic community between unidirectional (anterior) and multidirectional instability syndromes. The former is seen as being purely due to trauma, pathophysiologically related primarily to the Bankart lesion, and less likely to be treated successfully without surgery (ie, traumatic, unidirectional, Bankart, surgery necessary: TUBS). The latter is pathophysiologically related to underlying joint laxity, usually produces symptoms of multidirectional instability in both shoulders, has a better chance of being successfully treated with exercise alone, and requires a capsular shift procedure if surgery is necessary (ie, atraumatic, multidirectional, bilateral, rehabilitate, inferior capsular shift: AMBRI)[17] (Figure 9–20). In clinical practice, many patients are seen not to obey these rules (eg, with pure anterior instability, without a Bankart lesion, and multidirectional instability with a Bankart lesion). Careful nonsurgical treatment of pure traumatic anterior instability (most first-time dislocators) is successful more often than not. The TUBS/AMBRI distinction does therefore seem to be a bit of an oversimplification of the pathophysiology. Nevertheless, it is useful to consider pure anterior instability more closely related to pathologic change of the anterior capsule. In as far as the Bankart lesion is the primary pathologic problem and not the bagginess of a stretched capsule, a simple procedure whose only goal is to reattach the anterior capsule to the glenoid would appear to be effective in eliminating this type of instability.

The arthroscopic Bankart repair consists of abrading the bone of the anterior glenoid and then cauterizing or mechanically irritating the detached capsule. The capsule and labrum are then kept together with sutures, screws, metallic tacks, or absorbable polymeric tacks or with simple immobilization until the tissues have healed together with sufficient strength to prevent further subluxation or dislocation. Technically, this is not difficult to do arthroscopically. The traditional open surgical Bankart repair accomplishes a similar reattachment of the anterior capsule and labrum, albeit in a somewhat more controlled

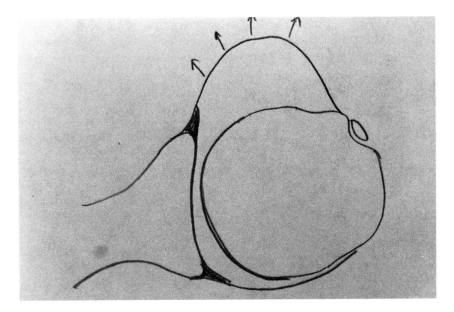

Figure 9–20 Diagram showing anterior capsular laxity. In the absence of a Bankart lesion, increased anterior capsular volume may produce symptomatic anterior instability.

and mechanically stronger manner. The open surgical repair also creates significantly more capsular scar and soft tissue reaction. The success rates that have been reported for the various arthroscopic repair techniques range from 70% to 100% when recurrence of dislocation is the only measured parameter of success.[18] Data regarding the success of arthroscopic stabilization techniques in eliminating symptomatic subluxation are less conclusive because postoperative rehabilitation can have such a significant effect on control of instability symptoms and because the symptoms themselves are rather subjective. The technical and theoretical advantages and disadvantages of the arthroscopic repairs commonly used can be readily understood in light of comparison with the highly reliable open techniques.

Arthroscopic Stabilization: Physiologic Considerations

There is no doubt that the long-term effectiveness of arthroscopic stabilization relies on the body's reaction to the selective tissue damage created by the surgical procedure. This is true of successful open surgical stabilization and even successful nonsurgical rehabilitation. The most basic arthroscopic repair technique, glenoid abrasion and capsular escharification, may be thought of as a subtler version of Hippocrates' white-hot poker. Contraction of the local capsular tissues and their adherence, through scarring, to the anterior glenoid neck represent the only mechanism whereby this technique can be effective in reducing glenohumeral instability. The various tacks, screws, staples, and sutures that can be used to hold the capsule fast to the glenoid while healing takes place can only be thought of as providing temporary fixation; none of them can provide sufficient mechanical holding power to resist the subluxating forces present in an athletic shoulder. Little use is currently made of tacks or staples that are visible on X-rays. This is because they were frequently seen to come out of the bone of the glenoid and migrate into the joint, where they could cause significant damage. The absorbable tacks in use today have holding power in bone that lasts for 2 to 3 weeks. They break down, fall out, and are absorbed, one hopes after some solid scarring down of the Bankart lesion has taken place. Sutures used to hold the capsule to the anterior glenoid are usually nonabsorbable but can be expected to break or cut through the tissues they are holding if healing and scarring do not create a strong mechanical bond of the capsular tissues to the glenoid bone.

Activity after Arthroscopic Stabilization

The clinical significance of these technical details of arthroscopic anterior stabilization surgery is summarized in a strong warning against subjecting any shoulder to anterior subluxating forces in the 2 months after anterior stabilization surgery. This holds true for open surgical repairs as well. As a result of the extensive surgery associated with open repairs, pain and soreness may prevent premature stressing of the repair. This is not the case after an arthroscopic stabilization. Strict, repeated teaching on avoidance of subluxatory force is therefore an essential part of postoperative therapy. Preoperative teaching is beneficial with these patients; everyone should well understand the "forbidden positions" of the arm before the surgery is undertaken.

Arthroscopic stabilization procedures are well tolerated by most patients; there is a short period (less than 1 week) of postoperative pain. Rehabilitation after this type of repair is rarely pain limited. Some surgeons who perform these procedures regularly permit patients relatively unrestricted activity within 2 weeks of surgery. These features can make the arthroscopic procedure quite attractive to sports-oriented patients. Other surgeons (including the author) use a longer period of postoperative sling immobilization (up to 6 weeks in young patients). This is done for all the same reasons that sling immobilization is used after initial dislocations; scarring and capsular contraction are essential to the success of the procedure. The sling is left on long enough to ensure maximum tissue response. Although patients are more comfortable after the arthroscopic procedure than the open procedure, the long immobilization period makes this comparative advantage smaller.

Comparison of Arthroscopic and Open Stabilization

The primary technical disadvantage of the closed (arthroscopic) Bankart repair is that it does little to improve the anteroinferior capsular laxity that is nearly always found to be present (to some extent) when open surgical repairs are performed. This laxity can be related to continued subluxation or dislocation despite the Bankart lesion having been addressed. Techniques that currently are being tried to address this problem include large-scale use of laser cautery on the anterior capsule to scar and shrink it and closed capsular plication techniques that attempt to fix anteroinferior capsular tissue medially and superiorly, up to the glenoid neck.[19] Insufficient surgical experience throughout the country has been gained with these techniques thus far to judge their relative benefit. Excellent results have been reported by a small number of surgeons. They may ultimately prove to be quite effective. From a simplified technical point of view, however, some insecurity about the glenohumeral stability achieved by arthroscopic repairs is understandable. In clinical shoulder practice, it is the shear stress examination that measures instability. After a secure open repair, the shear stress test done on the operating table palpably demonstrates the improvement in glenohumeral stability. It would be a great improvement if an arthroscopic repair could create this immediate, palpable resistance to subluxatory force.

Although there have been a number of series reported with high percentages of successful outcomes,[19,20] few surgeons would recommend an arthroscopic stabilization for a high-demand shoulder that has undergone multiple true dislocations. The arthroscopic repairs now in use do enjoy their best outcomes in patients with marginal surgical indications; the general thinking about their usefulness is that they are reliable if all one needs to do is tighten up the capsule a little. Prolonged activity restriction and much toning and strengthening of the stabilizing muscles are essential after arthroscopic anterior stabilization. The benefits of arthroscopic repair over open surgery are real, but most of them are realized in the first 2 postoperative weeks. The distinction between the true medical advantages and the selling points of arthroscopic stabilization should thus be understood.

Rehabilitation after Arthroscopic Stabilization

Rehabilitation after arthroscopic anterior stabilization is similar to that used after an open anterior surgical repair. It is accelerated by the decreased surgical pain associated with the arthroscopic technique but relies on tissue healing and scar maturation to a similar, if not greater, degree. Abduction and external rotation, which stress any anterior repair, should therefore be avoided for as long as the patient can tolerate this. Initial sling immobilization should be for at least 4 weeks, the sling being removed for bathing, elbow exercise, and quiet meals. Isometrics in all six degrees of freedom (internal and external rotation, abduction/adduction, flexion, and extension) can be started immediately postoperatively. After sling discontinuation, motion in forward elevation and internal rotation is advanced as tolerated, starting as active assisted and advancing to active within 1 week. Scapulothoracic stretching, strengthening, and coordination exercises are especially important in the athletic population. A mobile scapula with well-toned supporting musculature is itself a partial safeguard against shear stress on the glenohumeral joint; increasing the motion of the entire shoulder girdle can decrease motion at the glenohumeral joint.

Surgical Complications

The complications that attend all orthopaedic surgery, such as infection and anesthetic reactions, can certainly happen after shoulder arthroscopy, but these occurrences are quite rare. Neurologic damage and recurrence of instability are the most common complications related to the surgical procedure itself. The nerve problems associated with the arthroscopic techniques are also relatively rare but should be considered if there is cuff weakness and a transglenoid suture has been used to correct a Bankart lesion. The suprascapular nerve, which supplies motor power to the supraspinatus and infraspinatus muscles, can be encircled and damaged by this suture, which is inserted from behind the scapula and through the glenoid to hold the capsule to its anterior surface. Severe cuff weakness in this case needs to be evaluated with EMG and the nerve conduction velocity test (see Chapter 2). External rotation, although active, must be limited to approximately 30° for as long as the patient will tolerate this. Without the stabilizing influence of rotator cuff tone, full external rotation is more likely to produce recurrent anterior instability. An internal rotation contracture is a reasonable method for avoiding recurrent anterior instability in this case.

Returning to Sports

Abduction is not actively pursued during physical therapy unless there is a functional necessity for this in the patient's life, such as the need to throw. In this case it is permitted only after full forward elevation has been achieved, and external rotation in the abducted position is only progressed actively. A true throwing athlete who has had an anterior repair must be advanced slowly and carefully. Tossing and low-speed throwing may be well tolerated, but the final test of this type of repair is high-speed throwing. This places great stresses on the repair and must only be attempted after all other stabilizing influences and reflexes have been absolutely optimized. A 6- to 12-month time frame for this is not unrealistic.

Open Surgical Repairs for Anterior and Inferior Instability

The Bankart Repair

Much has been written about the long and complex history of surgery for instability. Numerous procedures have enjoyed popularity at various times and are incorporated, in some part, by many surgeons today. Two procedures are in common use today, and there are two others that are done frequently enough to be of interest to all shoulder practitioners. As mentioned above, the Bankart repair is probably the most frequently performed and statistically reliable operation for recurrent dislocation of the shoulder. A formal Bankart repair[21,22] is done by passing one to six sutures from the anterior edge of the glenoid's articular surface to the anterior glenoid neck (the area of stripping away of the capsule–labrum complex). These sutures are then passed on needles through the detached capsule and tied outside the capsule to fix this securely to the abraded glenoid neck, creating a soft tissue block to subluxation/dislocation and obliterating the space into which the humeral head goes while dislocated.

The Capsular Shift

The capsular shift operation is the other commonly performed procedure.[23] It is often performed with a simultaneous Bankart repair (which indeed should be done whenever there is a significant Bankart lesion). The capsular shift decreases the volume of the capsule, taking out the bagginess that is associated with anterior and inferior instability. It also reinforces the anterior capsule by doubling its thickness. The shift procedure can be extended to eliminate posterior capsular bagginess as well. The standard anterior/inferior capsular shift involves isolating the capsule (which itself is reinforced with a partial thickness of the subscapularis tendon) and then cutting and plicating it to decrease its bagginess. This involves shifting the anteroinferior capsular pouch upward (hence the name of the procedure). The inferior flap of capsule is thus brought up over the superior flap, giving the anterior tissue reinforcement. The capsule is then reattached to the humerus, from which it had been detached at the beginning of the procedure. The capsule is sutured back to the humerus and held fixed against the bone at the margin of the articular cartilaginous surface of the humeral head. This bone is abraded beforehand to encourage healing to the capsular tissue. Full maturation and healing of the capsular tissues to themselves and the bone of the humeral head takes a long time, probably 1 year or more.

Other Capsular Reduction Procedures

Some surgeons accomplish the same goal of reduction of the capsule's volume by detaching the capsule not from the humerus but from the glenoid.[24]

Because the humeral attachment of the capsule is much larger than the glenoid attachment, significantly less capsular volume reduction is achieved with this method of shifting on the glenoid. It can be accomplished without detaching the subscapularis from its humeral insertion, however, which is an important, although theoretical, advantage because any muscle is weakened by being removed from its insertion, and the subscapularis is an important stabilizer of the glenohumeral joint. A Bankart repair is also an integral part of this approach; securing the capsule to bone accomplishes both the shift and the reattachment.

The Putti-Platt Procedure

The Putti-Platt procedure was quite popular in the past.[25] It is less commonly performed today because there is evidence that it may produce glenohumeral arthritis, and it does limit external rotation permanently. It is a fairly easy repair technically, however, with shorter surgical times and somewhat less dissection around the glenohumeral joint. The Putti-Platt is still used in some patients with low-demand shoulders. Many surgeons add a modified Putti-Platt to other procedures done for instability. This generally means that something was done to shorten the subscapularis tendon (usually overlapping of the repair) after it was cut to give access to the glenohumeral joint. The subscapularis tendon lies on the anterior capsule of the glenohumeral joint and must be cut in some way to gain surgical access to the anterior shoulder. If it is put back in such a way as to tighten it, the term *Putti-Platt procedure* is commonly used.

The formal Putti-Platt procedure involves a simple shortening of the subscapularis tendon, which tightens the anterior capsular structures and limits external rotation by creating an instant subscapularis contracture. Of rehabilitation significance is the need to recognize and not work against the internal rotation contracture that is caused by the Putti-Platt. The surgeon must be asked for the external rotation limit that was set on the operating table. This will be an approximate guide during the first 6 months of rehabilitation. A bit more external rotation is usually achieved as the repair stretches out, but this is not actively sought during therapy. The contracture is a primary mechanism whereby this repair is successful in decreasing anterior dislocation.

A simple Putti-Platt is not usually the procedure of choice for patients with an inferior component of instability. Inferior instability noted in postoperative rehabilitation should be treated with prolonged sling use and cuff strengthening. Internal rotation, being accomplished by many other muscle groups besides the subscapularis (eg, the pectorals and latissimus dorsi), can be safely begun at the active level by 3 weeks after a Putti-Platt. Subscapularis isolation (hand off back) is not permitted for 2 months, however.

The Helfet-Bristow Procedure

Finally, the Helfet-Bristow procedure[26] is a transfer of the coracoid process, which is the origin of the short head of the biceps and coracobrachialis, to the anterior glenoid neck. The mechanism by which this stops further dislocation is the subject of some debate, but the bony block of coracoid probably does not simply block the egress of the humeral head from the glenoid. The dynamic sling of the biceps and coracobrachialis muscles, which are yet attached to the transferred tip of the coracoid, may exert some posterior force on the humeral head. There is also a Bankart repair effect caused by local scarring of the capsule to the glenoid around the base of the coracoid block as well as a considerable "hot poker" effect from this procedure. It is done when significant damage to the bone of the anterior glenoid is present. A bony Bankart lesion may leave a large anterior bony defect in the glenoid. The Helfet-Bristow fills this in nicely and seems to have a bone block effect in this case. Clinical results with the Helfet-Bristow have often been disappointing, with shoulder pain and weakness as well as recurrent instability occurring in up to 10% of patients.[27] The primary use of this procedure is in cases of glenoid bone loss.

Surgical Repairs for Posterior Instability

Recurrent posterior dislocation is an uncommon diagnosis and its milder form, recurrent posterior subluxation, is not likely to remain symptomatic after a proper course of physical therapy. There are, nonetheless, patients who, despite long and careful rehabilitation, continue to have symptomatic posterior instability and require surgical stabilization. The pathomechanics of posterior instability are in many ways similar to those of anterior instability. There is an equivalent of the Bankart lesion, a tearing away of the normal posterior capsular attachments of the glenoid. This posterior Bankart lesion must be quite extensive to produce instability symptoms. Normal shoulders can exhibit quite a bit of capsular redundancy in the area of the posterior glenoid. There is, however, a distinct stretching of the posterior capsule in most cases of posterior glenohumeral instability. This is visible on MR scan.

Arthroscopic repair of the posterior Bankart lesion can be accomplished in much the same way as is done anteriorly. It has been quite successful in eliminating symptoms in both of two such repairs the author has had the opportunity to perform (this is not a common problem). Posterior shear stress testing was not done immediately after the surgery in both cases for fear of ruining the repair. Three months later, neither shoulder was posteriorly subluxatable. Although anecdotal, these results after simple arthroscopic abrasion of the posterior glenoid followed by 6 weeks of immobilization in slight flexion and external rotation were especially encouraging in light of the open procedures that would have been done had they failed.

Fairly extensive operations have been performed for open repair of posterior instability.[28] These have included capsular shifting from a posterior approach, addition of bone block grafts to the posterior glenoid, and cutting off and anteriorly angulating the entire glenoid process of the scapula. The standard inferior capsular shift used for anterior and inferior instability can be extended to decrease the posterior capsular volume as well. This is probably the most commonly utilized surgical approach to posterior instability.[29] It involves the same creation of capsular flaps, but the inferior flap is followed all the way around, being detached from the anterior, inferior, and posterior humeral attachments. After abrasion of the bone at the articular margins all the way around, the flap is pulled up in the front, thereby decreasing posterior, inferior, and anterior capsular volume. This procedure is fraught with hazards both during surgery (the axillary nerve is pushed out of the way to get to the inferior and posterior capsule and can be damaged in the process) and afterward (anterior instability and excessive capsular tightness can be caused by the procedure).

Rehabilitation after Posterior Stabilization

Rehabilitation after posterior stabilization should be cautious and slow. The posterior cuff and posterior deltoid are the elements of the shoulder girdle musculature to be strengthened in particular. Posterior subluxatory force is, as described earlier, greatest in internal rotation, flexion, and mild adduction. This position is to be avoided, as is any posteriorly directed force along the humerus. When passive ranging is begun, care is taken to keep the anterior deltoid (which exerts a posterior force) quiet. More than the usual axial traction is used, and the elevation is done with the patient sitting or prone, not supine, to avoid the weight of the arm producing a posterior force. A cast or orthosis is usually on for at least 1 month after surgery, and these shoulders will be quite stiff when they come out. Horizontal adduction is, of course, the last range to be restored, and because this is not usually difficult to achieve it can wait until posterior cuff strength has come back. External rotation strengthening with the arm at the side can therefore begin in the range above neutral in the fifth week. Full motion, without working purposefully on horizontal adduction, should be achieved at about 3 months, and resistive strengthening should continue for at least 6 months. Exercises that produce posterior force (eg, push-ups) are forbidden for at least 1 year.

Surgical Approaches and Complications in Instability

Surgical Approaches for Anterior Instability

With the exception of the posterior approaches mentioned above, all the commonly used stabilization procedures are done through the same surgical approach. This is termed the limited deltopectoral approach. It utilizes a skin incision that starts in the fold that rises out of the axilla when the arm is held relaxed at the side. Immediately beneath this is the interval between the deltoid and the pectoralis major (a large vein, the cephalic, usually marks the interval). These two muscles are gently massaged apart and retracted to expose the strap muscles that originate on the coracoid (the short head of the biceps and the coracobrachialis). These are retracted medially to expose the subscapularis and anterior glenohumeral joint. No muscles are transected to get to the shoulder in this way, but a number of nerves may be stretched or even transected in these approaches. Both the deltoid and pectoralis are sore and weak after this surgical approach. Shoulder stabilization procedures can be long and tedious, commonly taking 4 hours and sometimes longer. The deltoid and pectoralis must be pulled vigorously for the entire duration of the procedure; the interval between them snaps closed as soon as the retractors are removed. Those who have been in the operating room for these procedures are never surprised at the generalized muscular soreness that patients feel for the first few postoperative days.

Anatomic Considerations of Surgery

The musculocutaneous nerve leaves the brachial plexus and joins the strap muscles within 2.5 cm or so of the coracoid. It can be damaged by the retraction of strap muscles if retraction is overly vigorous. Numbness of the lateral forearm and weakness of the biceps can be caused by injury to the nerve. These symptoms are usually due to a traction neuropraxia and resolve on their own. They should be noted and reported to the operating surgeon if encountered. Similar risks exist with this approach for the axillary nerve. The axillary nerve, as mentioned earlier, runs on the anterior subscapularis and then wraps around the humeral neck, just under the inferior insertion of the capsule. It must be pushed out of the way when the inferior capsule is isolated and cut. Axillary nerve function in patients who have had multiple dislocations is often somewhat diminished. Traction neuropraxias usually resolve spontaneously, but nerves that have already been damaged by recurrent dislocations do tend to recover less reliably and more slowly. Checking for deltoid setting and sensation in the area of skin over the insertion of the lateral head of the deltoid is therefore an important part of postoperative therapy sessions.

REFERENCES

1. McMasters WC. Anterior glenoid labrum damage: A painful lesion in swimmers. *Am J Sports Med.* 1986;14:383–387.
2. Rossi F, Ternamian PJ, Cerciello G, Walch G. Posterosuperior glenoid rim impingement in athletes. *Radiol Med.* 1994;87:22–27.
3. Jobe FW, Pink M. The athlete's shoulder. *J Hand Ther.* 1994;7:107–110.
4. McLaughlin HL, Cavallero WU. Primary anterior dislocation of the shoulder. *Am J Surg.* 1950;80:615–621.
5. Rowe CR. Prognosis in dislocation of the shoulder. *J Bone Joint Surg Am.* 1956;38:957–977.
6. Yoneda B, Wesh RP, Macintosh DL. Conservative treatment of shoulder dislocation in young males. *J Bone Joint Surg Br.* 1982;64:254–255.
7. Aronen JG, Regan K. Decreasing the incidence of recurrence of first time anterior shoulder dislocation with rehabilitation. *Am J Sports Med.* 1984;12:283–291.
8. Neer CS. *Shoulder Reconstruction.* Philadelphia, Pa: Saunders; 1990.
9. Matsen FA, Arntz CT. Rotator cuff tendon failure. In: Rockwood CA, Matsen FA, eds. *The Shoulder.* Philadelphia, Pa: Saunders; 1990:650.
10. Milch H. Treatment of dislocation of the shoulder. *Surgery.* 1938;3:732–740.
11. Hovelius L, Eriksson K, Fredin H. Recurrences after initial dislocation of the shoulder: Results of a prospective study of treatment. *J Bone Joint Surg Am.* 1983;65:343–391.
12. Rowe CR, Sakellarides HT. Factors related to recurrences of anterior dislocation of the shoulder. *Clin Orthop.* 1961;20:40–47.
13. Saha AK. Mechanism of shoulder movements and a plea for the recognition of the "zero position" of the glenohumeral joint. *Indian J Surg.* 1950;12:153–165.
14. Moseley HF, Overgaard B. The anterior capsular mechanism in recurrent anterior dislocation of the shoulder. *J Bone Joint Surg Br.* 1962;44:913–927.
15. Snyder SJ, Karzel RP, Del Pizzo W, et al. SLAP lesions of the shoulder. *Arthroscopy.* 1990;6:274–279.
16. Tibone JE. The facts about arthroscopic stabilization. Presented at the American Association of Orthopedic Surgeons course on the shoulder; March 1994; Marco Island, Fla.
17. Matsen FA. Anterior glenohumeral instability. In: Rockwood CA, Matsen FA, eds. *The Shoulder.* Philadelphia, Pa: Saunders; 1990:535–536.
18. Ellman H, Gartsman GM. Arthroscopic treatment of glenohumeral instability. In: Ellman H, Gartsman GM, eds. *Arthroscopic Shoulder Surgery and Related Procedures.* Baltimore, Md: Williams and Wilkins; 1993:273–298.
19. Wolf EM. Arthroscopic anterior shoulder capsulorraphy. In: Paulos L, Tibone JE, eds. *Operative Techniques in Shoulder Surgery.* Gaithersburg, Md: Aspen; 1991:65–70.
20. Morgan C. Arthroscopic transglenoid Bankart suture repair. In: Paulos L, Tibone JE, eds. *Operative Techniques in Shoulder Surgery.* Gaithersburg, Md: Aspen; 1991;71–77.
21. Bankart ASB. Recurrence of habitual dislocation of the shoulder joint. *Br Med J.* 1923;2:1132–1133.
22. Bankart ASB. The pathology and treatment of recurrent dislocation of the shoulder joint. *Br J Surg.* 1939;26:23–29.

23. Neer CS, Foster CR. Inferior capsular shift for involuntary inferior and multidirectional instability of the shoulder: A preliminary report. *J Bone Joint Surg Am.* 1980;62:897–907.

24. Jobe FW, Flousman RE. Anterior capsulolabral reconstruction. In: Paulos L, Tibone JE, eds. *Operative Techniques in Shoulder Surgery.* Gaithersburg, Md: Aspen; 1991:127–134.

25. Osmond-Clarke H. Habitual dislocation of the shoulder: The Putti-Platt operation. *J Bone Joint Surg Br.* 1948;30:19–25.

26. Helfet AJ. Coracoid transplantation for recurring dislocation of the shoulder. *J Bone Joint Surg Br.* 1958;40:198–202.

27. Torg JS, Balduini FC, Bonci C, et al. A modified Bristow-Helfet-May procedure for recurrent dislocation and subluxation of the shoulder. *J Bone Joint Surg Am.* 1987;69:904–913.

28. Hawkins RJ, Koppert G, Johnston G. Recurrent posterior instability (subluxation) of the shoulder. *J Bone Joint Surg Am.* 1984;66:109–174.

29. Tibone JE. Posterior capsulorraphy for posterior shoulder subluxation. In: Paulos L, Tibone JE, eds. *Operative Techniques in Shoulder Surgery.* Gaithersburg, Md: Aspen; 1991:143–147.

Chapter 10

Disorders of the Acromioclavicular Joint

Shoulder separation is the lay term for any disruption of the acromio-clavicular (AC) articulation. AC joint injuries are common and often create permanent instability of this simple diarthrodial joint. Painful AC arthritis can be a late complication of AC instability. Mild but chronic nonarthritic shoulder pain is also a common problem in patients with longstanding AC instability. Not only does abnormal motion of the joint produce pain, but the increased functional activity of the muscles that stabilize the scapula to the axial skeleton (especially the trapezius and levator scapulae) can produce aching and a sense of weakness in overhead work.

The causal relationship between AC instability and AC arthritis is by no means universal. Most cases of symptomatic AC arthritis occur without gross instability. There often is a questionably related history of trauma in AC arthritis patients; it might be argued that a low level of instability, created by this trauma, is responsible for the existing AC arthritis becoming symptomatic. This is difficult to establish with surety.

Arthritic enlargement of the AC joint is a common cause of impingement pain and rotator cuff disease. Good familiarity with AC instability and arthritis is essential for the shoulder practitioner not only because these problems are common but also because they present concomitantly with so many other shoulder ailments.

It is easy to overlook the AC joint when one is pursuing other, more complex shoulder pathology; in the face of a large rotator cuff tear, a shoulder dislocation, or a grossly arthritic glenohumeral joint, the simple, subcutaneous articulation of the clavicle and medial acromion may fail to attract much of the patient's or the examiner's diagnostic attention. The AC joint must be considered in every shoulder patient, however. The symptoms produced here may be severe, and, as with other shoulder pathology, they can be so poorly localized as to be mistaken for symptoms from other nearby structures.

The classic example of this often occurs with the seemingly ubiquitous finding of mild subacromial impingement. An impingement sign and some rotator cuff soreness are often noted on physical examination, although the patient's primary pain is that of AC arthritis. Cuff strengthening and humeral head depression techniques fail to relieve symptoms, so that (usually arthroscopic) subacromial decompression is undertaken, which is similarly unsuccessful. The difficulty here arises because a hot and tender AC joint can produce a (temporarily) positive impingement sign. This joint does abut the rotator cuff, irritating it and producing cuff pain. Rotator cuff impingement also does commonly produce some pain on forced horizontal adduction, further obscuring the correct diagnosis of AC arthritis, the cardinal features of which are AC tenderness and painful horizontal adduction.

Some mild subacromial signs and symptoms may also be present independently in patients whose primary pain generator is the AC joint. Differential injection testing is an absolutely necessary part of the physical examination when this situation is expected. Repeating the physical examination twice, first after a subacromial anesthetic injection from a posterior site and then after an anterosuperior injection directly into the AC joint, can tell the examiner exactly which signs and symptoms are due to subacromial impingement and which are due to AC joint pain. A simple injection of corticosteroid into the AC joint usually treats the latter problem quite effectively.

Continued shoulder pain after otherwise successful treatment of any other shoulder problem is quite often due to the untreated element of AC pain. The term *AC joint pain* is often more accurate than *AC arthritis* or even *symptomatic AC instability* when the instability is low grade. Arthritis, implying inflammation of the joint, is certainly present in a number of cases, but the AC joint can be a source of typical arthritis symptoms without any sign of inflammation being present on radiographs or even microscopic analysis of the tissue. Although they are confirmatory of an AC arthritis diagnosis in many cases, radiographic signs of arthritis of the AC joint (joint enlargement, joint space narrowing, osteophytes, or destructive bony changes adjacent to the joint) do not correlate well with the presence of symptoms or positive physical signs of AC arthritis[1,2] such as joint tenderness or horizontal adduction pain.

AC INSTABILITY

Clinical Presentations

Patients with primary complaints stemming from AC instability may present early (after an injury) with acute pain and deformity of the shoulder or later on with chronic complaints of pain with load carrying and overhead work or inability to sleep on the affected side. A late presentation might be AC arthritis or even rotator cuff disease caused by AC joint impingement on the cuff.

The acute, high-grade AC injury is usually not difficult to diagnose because the patient is aware of the joint's disruption and is usually able to put a finger on the joint and say "it hurts most right here." The nearly universal history is a fall onto the point of the shoulder (the acromion) with the arm kept by the side. A rare patient will sustain an AC separation when a heavy object falls onto the acromion. Some patients recall a pop, which may have been the sound of the coracoclavicular ligaments of the AC joint capsule tearing. A crack or crunch tends to indicate a clavicular fracture. These are often produced by the same type of trauma and may be present concomitantly. Certain clavicle fractures, as will be seen, are the functional equivalents of AC separation.

The most important element of an AC separation pathomechanically is disruption of the tissues connecting the scapula and the clavicle. This includes, to a lesser extent, the AC joint capsular tissues, which connect the clavicle with the acromial process of the scapula, and, to a greater extent, the coracoclavicular ligaments. Certain clavicle fractures must also be considered under the heading of AC separation (although the AC joint itself may be unaffected) because they share a similar mechanism and produce a similar clinical problem. These clavicle fractures, just medial to the insertion of the heavy coracoclavicular ligaments (called type II clavicle fractures) produce a functional AC separation or an AC separation through bone.

The coracoclavicular ligaments (Figure 10–1) connect the coracoid process of the scapula to the clavicle, providing the major passive suspensory element to the entire scapula and shoulder girdle. There are two distinct ligaments here: the conoid and trapezoid. They are quite stout and strong and obviously subject to heavy loading in the physiologic state. (They do not, however, look anything like cones or trapezoids, to this author's eyes.) It is the lack of this passive suspension that is probably the cause of the tiredness of the shoulder of which patients with chronic AC instability complain. They must use active elevators (the trapezius, levator scapulae, and rhomboids) to a greater extent when the coracoclavicular ligaments are no longer there to hang the scapula from the clavicle. Similarly, when there has been a type II clavicle fracture, the distal clavicle can fall forward and down with the shoulder girdle, to which it is still well connected, while the proximal clavicle rides upward under the influence of the trapezius. The resultant clinical deformity looks much like an AC separation but presents with the bony crepitus (the well-defined sensation of broken bone ends rubbing against each other) that is associated with clavicular fracture.

Chronic, symptomatic AC instability is most often seen in patients with a clear history of injury to the shoulder. Many patients are seen with some de-

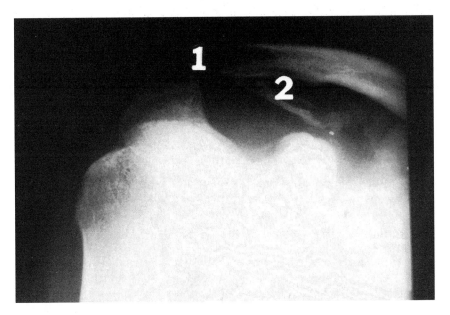

Figure 10–1 AC joint (1) after repair of separation with the coracoclavicular ligaments (2) calcified.

gree of AC instability on physical examination; this may increase somewhat during life as a result of ligamentous stretching or destruction of the AC joint capsule by inflammatory arthritis. This type of slowly progressive AC instability is only rarely the cause of true instability symptoms. Symptoms from this type of AC joint are more likely to be those of arthritis.

The actual symptoms produced by chronic instability of the AC joint are quite variable. It is the patient with a high-grade AC separation, left unrepaired, who is most likely to complain of actual instability symptoms. These are often rather vague, consisting of aching in the posterior deltoid and trapezius area that is intensified with overhead work or carrying of loads at the side. The sensation of the AC joint subluxating and reducing as the shoulder girdle is raised and lowered (the symptom—instability—as opposed to the sign) is also uncomfortable. An occasional patient with chronic AC instability has neurologic symptoms of tingling and numbness in the arm when downward force is placed on the arm. This is possibly due to the inferior slumping of the shoulder girdle causing traction on the brachial plexus. This symptom can be caused by a number of other, more common neurologic problems, however. The possibilities of the initial causative injury having produced an acute traction injury of the brachial plexus or of an underlying cervical nerve root compressive problem therefore must be explored. This entails a careful neurologic examination and examination of the neck. Consultation with a neurologist is appropriate if tingling, numbness, or weakness are the predominant symptoms.

It is absolutely necessary to obtain plain films of the shoulders and clavicle whenever AC injury is suspected. Not only are fractures common, but the droopier appearance of the shoulder girdle may be caused by glenohumeral dislocation. Special stress films with the arm weighted with 10 to 20 lbs are sometimes obtained to demonstrate the maximal downward displacement of the acromion with respect to the clavicle (Figure 10–2). These are useful in low-grade injuries if the AC joint is tender and seems a bit unstable on physical examination but regular films fail to reveal a distinct depression of the acromion. Weighted films exaggerate the deformity of AC separation by pulling the shoulder girdle down. They should be made of both shoulders whenever they are used because native ligamentous laxity in some patients can produce significant downward displacement of the acromion when a weight is hung from the relaxed arm. This weight is hung with a cloth or leather loop, not held in the hands, to relax the muscles completely. The trapezius and the

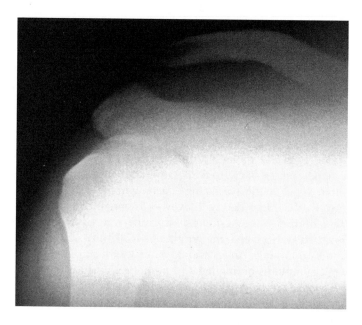

Figure 10–2 AC separation: weighted view.

other elevators can raise the shoulder girdle sufficiently to hide the AC separation, even with the arm weighted, if the patient is not specifically instructed to relax the shoulder and arm completely.

Having just sustained an AC separation, the patient characteristically cradles the injured side to support its weight. The profile of the shoulder is abnormal; in fact, the acromion and entire shoulder girdle become displaced inferiorly, causing the shoulder to droop somewhat. Early after injury, however, trapezius spasm and splinting often produce the appearance of the distal clavicle being displaced upward. On comparison of the shoulder with the opposite side, it usually becomes apparent that the shoulder girdle is downwardly displaced, the clavicle having been "left behind" as the ligaments that have held it fast to the coracoid and acromial processes of the scapula have been torn. There are situations in which the distal clavicle actually is left superiorly displaced despite good muscular relaxation; this may occur when it penetrates the trapezius superiorly and becomes held up in the soft tissues that it has impaled.

Physical examination of the shoulder with AC instability is fairly straightforward. As mentioned above, the contour and overall appearance of the shoulder girdle are often diagnostic in more severe AC separation injuries. The seated patient is best examined from behind and above, posterior displacement of the clavicle is best appreciated from above, and inferior displacement of the shoulder girdle is best seen from the front with the examiner's eyes at the level of the shoulders, both of which should be observed simultaneously so that side-to-side differences can be noted. The sternoclavicular joint is palpated, and the examiner's fingers are walked out along both clavicles until the AC joints are encountered. These are checked for tenderness, and then both distal clavicles are checked for stability. The clavicles are pushed down in a vertical plane and then moved forward and backward in a nearly horizontal plane. Motion in excess of that present on the normal side is recorded as mild, moderate, or severe instability of the clavicle to stress in the particular direction. It is convenient for the examiner to keep the heels of the hands (the hypothenar eminences) on the patient's acromia while moving the clavicles to judge better the relative motion of the clavicle with respect to the acromion.

The horizontal adduction test is always done when one is evaluating the AC joint. Shear stress testing of the AC joint is then performed, again from behind the seated patient. With the contralateral hand palpating the lateral shaft of the clavicle, the index and thumb carefully straddle the AC joint while the ipsilateral hand cradles the elbow, which is flexed to about 90°. The patient is asked to relax the entire shoulder girdle, and the examiner applies firm upward axial pressure to the humerus while feeling for reduction in the prominence of the distal clavicle. This is held for a few seconds, and then firm downward pressure is applied while feeling for any increase in the vertical separation of the clavicle and acromion. The specific examination of the AC joint thus tests for tenderness, pain with compression of the joint, and instability in the horizontal and vertical planes (Figures 10–3 through 10–5).

Little need for magnetic resonance (MR) evaluation of the shoulder exists when AC separation is strongly suggested by clinical evaluation and plain film radiographs. A reflexive response to obtain MR scans on every shoulder patient contemplating surgery is apt to generate unnecessary worry about the rotator cuff in patients with acute AC injuries. The presence of blood in the subacromial space is readily detected on MR imaging, as is some bruising of the cuff tendons, which may occur during the AC injury. These are apt to be interpreted as indicating a degree of cuff tear. Cuff pathology may in fact be present, but if there has been an acute injury and the AC joint is tender and unstable, the AC injury is much more likely to be the source of the patient's symptoms. Concomitant AC separation and rotator cuff tear is more often due to a preexisting cuff tear at the time of AC separation. The mechanisms by which cuff tears occur generally involve the application of force to the hand or arm, whereas AC separations are produced by forces applied to the shoulder

Figure 10–3 Horizontal adduction test.

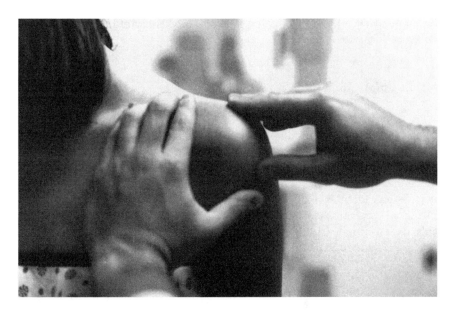

Figure 10–4 Testing for vertical stability of the AC joint.

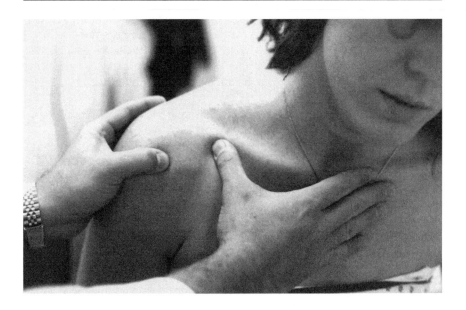

Figure 10–5 Testing for anteroposterior stability of the AC joint.

or, more specifically, the acromion. The specific history of injury is therefore well worth careful elucidation.

Grading of AC Joint Injuries

AC joint injuries are commonly given a clinical grade to communicate severity and direction of displacement. A great deal of attention in the orthopaedic community has been given to the grading of all sorts of injuries in the past 15 years. Some grading systems seem natural, are easy to remember, and enhance communication and decision making among involved practitioners. The grading system used for more than 20 years[3] classified minimally displaced separations of the clavicle and acromion as type I. These mild injuries are essentially sprains of the AC joint capsule without injury to the coracoclavicular ligaments. Tenderness of the AC joint is the dominant physical finding with type I injuries. Type II injuries produce noticeable but slight separation of the AC interval on X-rays; complete disruption of the weaker AC joint capsule and some stretching of the coracoclavicular ligaments are seen. With type II injuries one can just begin to feel the bump of the distal clavicle and notice abnormal motion (compared with the other side) at the joint when upward and downward force is applied to the humerus. Type III injuries involve complete disruption of the coracoclavicular ligaments and complete dislocation (as opposed to subluxation) of the AC joint. There is obvious slumping down of the shoulder girdle, and the AC joint can be felt to reduce when the clavicle is held down and the humerus is pushed upward. The end of the clavicle is generally detached from the trapezius and deltoid muscles by a type III injury.

In recent years, three additional categories[4] have been adopted for more severe and somewhat less common injuries: type IV for complete AC dislocation with posterior displacement of the end of the clavicle through the trapezius, type V for gross upward displacement of the clavicle, and type VI for inferior displacement of the distal clavicle. Although the last of these, type VI, is rather rare and does demand quite different treatments, the type IV and V AC separations may be considered, for surgical purposes, as more severe type III injuries. These injuries were, in the past, lumped together in the type III category.

Although memorizing this grading system can be useful, it is not absolutely necessary. A practical way to consider the case and communicate effectively with most shoulder practitioners (who may or may not remember the entire system) regarding AC separations is to consider the AC or coracoclavicular distance on stress films. The injuries may then be described as nondisplaced, mildly displaced, or severely displaced.

Treatment of AC Joint Injuries

Any treatment system based on the above grading system for AC separations will be controversial because there is no universal agreement among orthopaedists about the best treatment for complete dislocations of this joint. There is fairly good agreement about nondisplaced and mildly displaced AC separations. These are rarely, if ever, treated surgically. Type I and II injuries may be treated according to a standard joint sprain paradigm of (sling) immobilization until initial healing has taken place (indicated by decreased or absent tenderness at the joint) with subsequent exercise of the protecting musculature (the scapular elevators particularly) and gradual reexposure of the injured ligaments to stress until they have matured and strengthened.

Trapezius exercises, in particular, are useful for nondisplaced or mildly displaced AC separations because good tone and strength of the trapezius do seem to guard against the development of the aching symptoms of AC instability. A strong trapezius may also decrease the likelihood of a further injury to the already weakened scapuloclavicular connections. Reinjury of low-grade AC separations is fairly common, perhaps because these injuries tend to occur most often in young, athletic men. Hand weights, lifted with shrugs in internal rotation, horizontal abduction, and slight extension, can be started as soon as the shoulder is comfortable against gravity in this position. The protraction and elevation of the scapula in this position seem to be well tolerated by the unstable AC joint; in this position, the amount of separation of the AC interval is also somewhat decreased. Latissimus pull-downs (and, later on with strong patients, pull-ups) may be used effectively for shoulder girdle strengthening without subjecting the scapuloclavicular suspension to increased inferior stress. Overhead weights, military press, and bench press are obviously not to be used in this strengthening program.

The controversy regarding the best treatment for completely displaced AC separations has developed because excellent functional results have been reported with large series of patients treated both operatively and nonoperatively.[5] Considering type III separations only, the most simple nonoperative treatment (termed minimal, symptomatic, benign neglect, or, most interestingly, skilled neglect) consists of sling immobilization for comfort only (3 to 10 days) followed by gradually increasing use of the shoulder for normal daily activities without any specific strengthening or activity restrictions. This usually results in a functionally adequate and mostly pain-free shoulder. The problems of a permanent bump on the top of the shoulder, the typical dull aching pain of AC instability under moderate to heavy loads, and an increased likelihood of painful AC arthritis in years to come are the only usual drawbacks associated with this type of conservative treatment. There is even some feeling among orthopaedists that the type III injuries are less apt to cause chronic AC pain than type II injuries because the clavicle and acromion are more widely separated and therefore less likely to produce AC arthritic symptoms.

A number of studies have been published in which orthopaedic authorities have been polled about how they would manage a type III separation in a young, athletic patient.[6] Surgical management was chosen by the majority in 1974, whereas minimal treatment was the majority's choice in 1984. Polling of colleagues in attendance at a large shoulder conference by this author in 1994 seemed to indicate that surgical repair was becoming more popular again. These vacillations have occurred during a period in which there have been no major changes in the actual surgical options available (ie, no new operations have been invented) for treatment of displaced AC separations. Surgical correction of the anatomic deformity of type III and higher AC separations is chosen by many patients today purely for cosmetic appearance; the surgical scar is usually less objectionable than the bump of the clavicle, and the depressed shoulder girdle can give the head and shoulders an asymmetric appearance. To many practitioners, it makes basic sense simply to correct the dislocation of such an important joint of the upper extremity; that satisfactory results can be achieved with the dislocation unreduced is surprising to many. It should be clearly understood, however, that nonsurgical management of type III AC separations is an acceptable form of treatment for all, including athletic, shoulders. Surgical treatment of this problem is therefore an elective decision based on the anticipated impact of this permanent and rather gross distortion of normal shoulder anatomy on a particular patient. This may be illustrated by the finding that few surgeons, even the most conservative, would recommend nonoperative treatment of a widely displaced AC separation in a career baseball pitcher's or tennis player's dominant arm.

The next step up in aggressiveness in the treatment of type III AC separations, beyond the minimal treatment described above, is the use of some sort of reductive device to maintain reduction of the AC joint while healing and scarring take place. An enormous number of these have been tried. The most widely used today is the Kenny-Howard splint (Figure 10–6). This is a slinglike device that uses a tight strap over the distal clavicle to hold the AC joint more or less reduced. It works by pushing down on the clavicle and up on the arm.

The problem that is often encountered with the Kenny-Howard brace is that the clavicle strap must be quite tight to reduce the separation, so tight that it causes skin damage. Skin maceration and even necrosis can result from wearing this strap too tightly for too long; when first applied, this strap must be removed and the skin checked every 4 hours. If redness or blistering is begin-

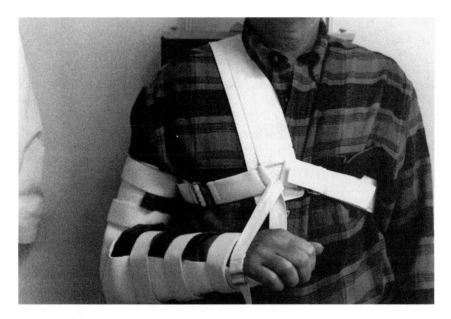

Figure 10–6 AC joint reductive brace (Kenny-Howard).

ning, the strap must be loosened. The interposition of soft tissues between the clavicle and acromion, as occurs with type IV and V AC separations, makes reduction of the joint much more difficult and skin damage more likely. Skin damage on top of the clavicle is not merely a cosmetic problem; it precludes both surgical repair and the continued use of a reductive harness. Despite this obvious problem, careful management of the Kenny-Howard brace, with frequent checks for tightness and skin condition as well as good padding of the clavicle strap (a standard dishwashing sponge works well under the strap), can result in a healed, reduced AC joint after type III AC separations.

The effectiveness of the AC reductive brace treatment depends on the healing and scarring reaction that takes place while the joint is held reduced. It is not always sufficient to stabilize the joint. Great disappointment has followed 6 weeks of careful, and quite uncomfortable, brace use, when the shoulder girdle falls right back down upon removal of the brace. It is in regard to the likelihood of reductive brace treatment being ineffective that the expansion of the classification system by Rockwood[4] has important value. A type IV or V AC separation is much less likely to be reduced or to stay reduced when treated with reductive bracing. The interposed muscular tissues of the trapezius, through which the end of the clavicle has pierced in these injuries, will invariably prevent proper reduction and strong healing. The Kenny-Howard or other reductive braces are therefore much less appropriate treatments for type IV and V injuries.

Patient compliance is another significant issue with the use of reductive braces. Many simply will not wear the brace properly or full time. Others opt away from it when told that after 6 weeks of bracing there may well be no improvement in the deformity. It is certainly possible to do isometric exercises, but significant weakness and stiffening of the entire shoulder girdle is the rule after 6 weeks in a tightly fitting reductive brace.

In summary, the reductive braces are most useful in milder type III AC separations in which there is believed to be some residual stability (ie, the shoulder does not fall away quite so rapidly when reductive pressure is relieved). They are not used without risk of complication, however, and often fail to achieve a lasting AC reduction.

The surgical treatment of displaced AC separations is based on maintaining reduction of the joint by using hardware, suture, or tapes to hold the clavicle fast to some part of the scapula (the acromion or the coracoid) while healing and scarring take place. Repair of the injured deltoid origin and trapezius insertion is another surgical goal. The element of injury to these muscles sometimes can be the most important aspect of the injury; in type IV (posterior displacement of the clavicle) and type V (wide superior displacement) injuries, the deltoid and trapezius are necessarily avulsed from the clavicle. Significant weakness of the anterior deltoid after high-grade AC separation may be a serious problem in the athletic population.

Surgical timing is another important issue faced in repair of AC separations. AC separations repaired within approximately 1 month of injury may be restored quasi-anatomically because the coracoclavicular ligaments can still be distinguished and actually repaired. The AC joint itself, although damaged, will not have had that long a period of dislocation to cause arthritis-producing changes in the joint surfaces, capsule, and articular meniscus (this interposing ring or disc of fibrocartilage is similar to the meniscus of the knee but more variable in size and shape). The intense scarring and healing reaction present in the early postinjury period may also help achieve a stronger reduction and surgical repair than that obtained years afterward.

Early AC joint surgery is primarily a repair of torn tissues; the joint capsule and coracoclavicular ligaments are still distinct structures that can be sutured back together. Late AC joint surgery is reconstructive; the coracoclavicular ligaments and AC joint capsule are lost in a mass of scar tissue, necessitating transfer of another coracoid-based ligament (usually the AC ligament, rarely a strip of the tendon of the short head of the biceps) to the clavicle to restore the scapuloclavicular suspension. The AC joint is also apt to be arthritic when reconstruction is done late. This necessitates resection of the distal clavicle to prevent AC arthritic pain.

Surgical repair of AC separation is appropriate for selected type III injuries and most type IV and V injuries. With the exception of more extensive suture repairs of the damaged trapezius and deltoid with types IV and V, the repairs used for all three types are the same. Three surgical options are in popular use: direct screw fixation of the clavicle to the coracoid; heavy tape or suture fixation that wraps around the coracoid and over the clavicle; and pin, wire, or screw fixation that goes horizontally across the AC joint. All three options work well to provide fixation of the scapula to the clavicle while healing of the AC capsule and coracoclavicular ligaments (which are generally repaired during the procedures) takes place. The procedures are done through a linear skin incision directly over the AC joint (usually termed a saber incision). Little blood loss and an acceptably low rate of infection and nerve injuries accompany these procedures (Figures 10–7 and 10–8).

Repairs involving metallic screws, pins, or wires generally necessitate a secondary minor surgical procedure to remove these implants. The coracoid suture repairs are technically a bit more difficult and may not achieve the rigidity of reduction that screw techniques do. This is especially true of motion

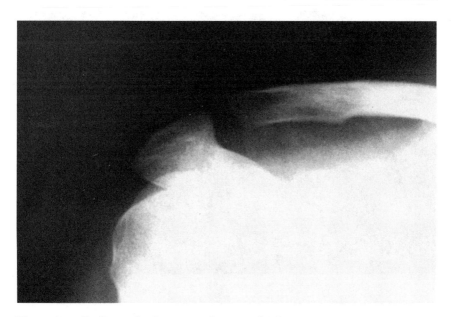

Figure 10–7 Radiograph after surgical repair of AC separation.

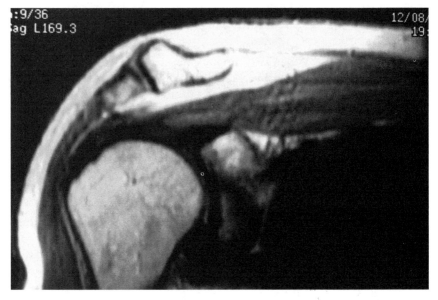

A

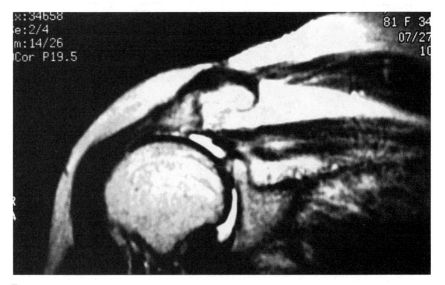

B

Figure 10–8 MR scans comparing **(A)** normal and **(B)** arthritic AC joints.

of the distal clavicle in the horizontal plane. Although this is not clearly a clinical problem, the immediate reason for performing this procedure is to reduce and stabilize the AC joint; anteroposterior instability of the clavicle after the surgery is therefore not a welcome finding. Drawbacks to the screw or pin techniques include the possibility of screw or bone breakage if there is excessive early use of the shoulder, dangerous migration (pins have been removed from the heart, lungs, and even brain) of broken metal parts around the shoulder and elsewhere should breakage occur, and articular surface damage to the AC joint caused by the crossing pins. Such damage may increase the likelihood of late AC arthritis, although this has never been established scientifically.

Late reconstruction for established, high-grade AC instability utilizes similar internal fixation methods as those described above. One of the most popular procedures, called the Weaver-Dunn,[7] involves transfer of the AC ligament to the cut end of the clavicle and a subcoracoid tape or suture to keep the scapula suspended while this transferred ligament heals and strengthens. Resection of the distal 2 to 4 cm of the clavicle is the surgical treatment for AC arthritis. It simply and effectively (and surprisingly safely) prevents painful abutment of the acromion on the clavicle. As mentioned above, a distal clavicular resection is included in most late AC reconstructive procedures to guard against later development of AC pain.

The rehabilitation issue of greatest importance after early or late surgical repair for AC instability is protection of the reconstruction. Orthopaedic complications arising from AC reconstruction are often due to inadequate immobilization. These are not operations on the glenohumeral joint, capsule, or rotator cuff; the stiffness experienced after 6 weeks of sling wear in the AC joint patient is milder and vastly easier to reverse. The surgical pain after AC reconstruction dissipates dangerously quickly. Patients who surmise that, because it does not hurt anymore, it is safe to go back to usual activities may ruin their repair. For most patients, 6 weeks in a sling immobilization with daily elbow stretching and limited use of the hand is an adequate healing period. After this, protected motion in forward elevation, external rotation, and internal rotation is begun at the active assisted level and advances as tolerated to active. Gentle resistive work on the entire girdle may be started when the entire active range is painless, but care must be taken to avoid an exercise that produces shear or separation force at the AC joint. Horizontal adduction, which produces compressive forces at the AC joint, is also generally avoided, although not as strictly.

The long-term protection of these repairs involves avoidance of lifting, both at the side and overhead, and of abduction. These activity modifications should be enforced for at least 3 months after acute repairs and for 4 months after late reconstructions. Patients with pins projecting through the skin should be kept in a motion range that does not produce significant pulling of the skin against the exiting pins. This is both for patient comfort and to avoid loosening of the pins. AC reconstruction is one of the few situations in shoulder rehabilitation in which pendulum exercises are not recommended. This is because of the downward traction and AC joint shear that can be created by a heavy relaxed arm.

Certain caveats may be appropriate from the surgeon in cases of high-grade AC separations. If there has been a large deltoid or trapezius injury, these muscles should be excluded from isometrics while the patient is in the sling and then protected from eccentric work for approximately another month after the sling is discontinued. Some unusual transfers that are done for late reconstructions, such as using a part of the tendon of the short head of the biceps to reconstruct the coracoclavicular ligaments, may demand a longer period of healing and maturation before they are allowed to be stressed.

Final return to unlimited sports activities is permitted when muscle strength has returned to normal and AC vertical shear testing shows good stability without pain. This is usually achieved by the fourth postoperative month. Patients treated with temporary metallic internal fixation devices generally must have had their hardware removed for at least 1 month before returning to unrestricted activity. This is particularly true for those with horizontal pins or screws across the AC joint. These implants are subject to high levels of shear and are quite likely to break if stressed. The broken inner fragments can then migrate internally, causing tremendous damage to nerves and blood vessels. Coracoclavicular screws present a bit less danger. There are still some orthopaedists who do not routinely remove coraclavicular screws, permitting patients to return to full activity with the screw still in place. The originator of this operation did not, in fact, remove the screw unless it was the source of symptoms.[8] Although not a major clinical problem, loss of this screw's fixation in the coracoid is the primary danger of return to full activity with the screw in place. Waiting for strong ligamentous healing before subjecting the screw to high levels of stress is the obvious way to avoid this type of problem. Patients who have had late reconstructive procedures for chronic AC dislocations require a longer period of protected activity; 6 months is recommended.

The AC separation population, as noted earlier, is athletic and notoriously difficult to control. One of the arguments in behalf of a reasonably aggressive strengthening program is that half of one's AC joint reconstruction patients will start to return to sports by 2 months, regardless of instructions. They should therefore be given as much muscular strength as possible in the early postoperative period, it being safer to exercise under control than to return to sports while the repair is still weak. The applicability of this concept must be determined on an individual basis; resigning oneself to a patient's noncompliance may be practical in some cases. The late clinical problem that is most likely to affect patients with AC instability treated operatively or nonoperatively is painful AC arthritis. This is discussed below.

AC ARTHRITIS

Clinical Presentation

Pain generated by the AC joint is somewhat more easily localized than that of the rotator cuff origin, although it is still vague enough to be the cause of many a diagnostic wild goose chase. AC arthritis patients are numerous in shoulder practice; many present for second and third opinions, with $3000 worth of MR images under their arms, to be entirely relieved of their symptoms with a single steroid injection into the AC joint. As mentioned earlier, the AC joint must be considered in every patient whose complaint is shoulder pain. Although often mild, it is quite common.

Pain when sleeping on the affected side and pain when washing the contralateral axilla are probably most typical of the complaints of patients with serious AC arthritic pain. AC joint patients have presented with chief complaints of pain with throwing and tennis serves, overhead work pain, night pain, pain when carrying loads with a shoulder strap, pain while driving, and pain with bench and military press weightlifting. The AC joint is compressed when the arm is brought across the body; this is the basis of the horizontal adduction test that is used to diagnose AC joint pain. It is less well appreciated that, in some patients, the AC joint is also compressed in abduction. The external rotation of the scapula that normally occurs during abduction involves lateralization of the scapula's inferior angle and reciprocal medialization of the acromion (the scapula's lateral angle). Patients with painful AC arthritis often exhibit this sign, although it is a less specific finding than horizontal adduction pain because so many other things can make abduction painful. Painful horizontal adduction is not specific for AC arthritis either. As described in Chapter 8, subacromial irritation of the rotator cuff can produce horizontal adduction pain that is quite severe.

It is useful to ask whether the pain produced by abduction is of the same character as that produced by horizontal adduction. This can help determine the cause of a patient's horizontal abduction pain. Throwing athletes and tennis players are sometimes seen with primary AC joint pain; they have pain at the beginning of the acceleration phase of the throwing motion, when the abduction-induced stress on the joint is high. External rotation of the humerus is necessary for most people to achieve full abduction. This is probably because the greater tuberosity is taken out of the way of the acromion, avoiding impingement thereon. The tender AC joint can also be compressed by the tuberosities and cuff pressing upward and medially on the acromion; the same pain is generally reported with gently forced abduction in internal rotation as with horizontal adduction in AC joint patients.

It is certainly true that patients with generalized arthritis (osteoarthritis, rheumatoid arthritis, and others) have a greater than average tendency to develop AC arthritis. The processes that lead to joint surface destruction go on in the AC joint just as they do in the others. The average patient with AC arthritis, however, does not have multiple joint replacements and a favorite chair in his or her rheumatologist's waiting room. Inactive or infirm patients tend not to move the shoulder enough to make AC arthritis symptoms become severe. Although a particular bout of AC inflammation may continue to be painful despite rest and even immobilization, a sedentary life style tends to make AC arthritis (more properly termed AC arthrosis here; arthritis implies joint inflammation) easier to live with. A large, knobby AC joint that is tender and appears arthritic on X-rays (the AC joint is usually quite well seen on standard chest X-rays) is most often an incidental finding. Few of the millions of older people with these arthritic AC joints have sufficient pain to mention it to their physician. Those patients who do seek help for AC arthritic pain therefore must be carefully evaluated diagnostically. The AC joint's enlargement with arthritis can produce impingement on the rotator cuff. This rotator cuff pain and weakness are often the actual problem for which the patient seeks help. It may also be the intensification of AC joint pain that finally sends the patient with longstanding glenohumeral arthritis to the shoulder practitioner. In both these cases, attention to diagnoses other than the AC joint arthritis is necessary to treat the presenting symptoms successfully.

The specific physical signs of AC arthritis are AC joint tenderness and horizontal adduction pain, both of which are relieved by an injection of local anesthetic into the AC joint. Other positive signs are often present on the AC arthritis patient's examination; frozen shoulder frequently accompanies AC arthritis, as does impingement and rotator cuff tear. Chronic (mild) AC instability is probably the most frequent underlying cause of AC joint pain in the younger population. The degree of instability may be quite low, however, and it is not until the joint is exposed at surgery that its abnormal motion can be appreciated. The pathophysiologic theory for this is based on the idea that with a low degree of instability, due to stretching of the joint capsule and coracoclavicular ligaments (type I and II separations), the joint surfaces and the intraarticular meniscus are still close enough together to grind on each other, producing degenerative changes, tears of the meniscus, and pain. High-grade separations take the surfaces away from each other.

Examination for AC instability in patients with AC joint pain should be performed regularly, especially with an eye toward determining whether the abnormal vertical motion of the joint on shear stress examination causes the patient's characteristic pain. It usually does not, but if it does there is a greater than usual chance that therapy aimed at strength and tone of the scapular elevators will be effective.

Pathophysiology and Radiographic Work-Up

The radiographic appearance of AC arthrosis is typical of any affected diarthrodial joint. Most cases involve a bone-forming (productive or hypertrophic) type of arthritic process. Osteoarthritis is the most common of these; posttraumatic arthritis and the arthritis produced by chronic joint instability are other examples. These may all be variations on the same pathophysiologic process. The joint space becomes narrowed, and the facing ends of the acromion and clavicle widen and produce spurs and lumps of bone called osteophytes. As noted earlier, these radiographic changes are common incidental findings on the chest X-rays of older people.

Inflammatory, destructive, or lytic arthritic diseases, typified by rheumatoid arthritis, also present with their characteristic radiographic changes when they involve the AC joint. Here, the ends of the bone become darker, destroyed, or moth-eaten in appearance on plain film radiographs. On physical examination, the patient's AC joints may be enlarged and tender; this is usually not bony enlargement but synovial hypertrophy. Bone is actually destroyed (osteolysis) by the intense inflammatory reaction occurring at the joint. The term *mixed arthritis* is used when elements of both types, productive and destructive, are present. This should not be as confusing as it sounds; the process of inflammatory arthritis, with the immune system reacting against joint cartilage and ligamentous structures, may go on in the presence of the bone-producing reaction to joint stress and irritation.

An entirely different pathophysiologic mechanism underlies the AC joint destructive process termed weightlifter's clavicle. Properly considered a destructive arthritis due to repetitive trauma, weightlifter's clavicle is more a disease of bone than joint. Also termed distal clavicular osteolysis, it is a rather uncommon problem primarily affecting young male weightlifters who do bench and military press, although case reports have been made involving other sports activities. This patient presents with a tender AC joint and horizontal adduction and often abduction pain. The radiographic appearance of lysis or destruction of the distal clavicle is diagnostic; the outer 1 cm or so seems to be melting away. The (assumed) pathophysiologic mechanism involves repetitive, high-level compressive loading of the AC joint, which somehow produces bone changes leading to increased vascularity and ultimately resorption. Microscopically, the process most closely resembles fracture healing, but healing occurring in different stages simultaneously. The term *microfracture* is used for this process.[9] Unlike other clavicle fractures, which heal reliably, healing and resolution do not always occur when the offending activity is stopped and the shoulder is immobilized. The destructive process of the distal clavicle produces obvious changes at the AC joint, and the AC arthritic character of the disease then dominates the treatment plan.

A few other, less common causes of AC arthritis should be kept in mind when one is evaluating older or debilitated patients with painful AC joints. Septic or bacterial arthritis can affect this joint, especially after an injection with steroid or in a patient with an ongoing infection, such as bacterial endocarditis. Intravenous drug users have been seen with this problem. The local signs of infection—*rubor, dolor, tumor,* and *calor* (redness, pain, swelling, and heat)—will be exaggerated in this case; the patient will usually have a fever, and AC joint tenderness will be severe. A reliable sign of infection is peeling of the skin over the joint. A true septic arthritis is a medical emergency. Drainage of pus must be accomplished as soon as possible. As a subcutaneous joint, the AC articulation may be subject to much local trauma.

Institutionalized patients who are incapable of giving an accurate history may develop a type of direct trauma related AC arthritis after repetitive trauma to the shoulder area. A similar condition is seen in patients who carry loads on the shoulder, resting them on the AC joint. Relief from the offending trauma is curative in most of these cases.

AC joint ganglion is the term given to a large cystic mass that emanates upward from and communicates directly with the AC joint. Although ganglia, or outpouching synovial tissue-lined cysts, of other joints occur commonly as a result of arthritis, those occurring at the AC joint are just as often a sign of chronic rotator cuff tear. The glenohumeral joint fluid that regularly escapes through rotator cuff tears gets up into the inferior AC joint, which is generally eroded by the high-riding humeral head in late-stage rotator cuff disease. This fluid then produces the ganglionic outpouching at the superior surface of the joint. Arthrograms of the shoulder usually are made when AC joint ganglia are encountered. They show communication of the dye from the glenohumeral joint to the subacromial space and up through the AC joint into the cyst. The important treatment principle in these cases is that the cuff must be repaired in addition to the cyst being removed. If the cuff is not repaired, there is a good chance of the cyst recurring. This type of AC cuff tear–ganglion is the most common cause of AC joint cyst. There are AC cysts caused solely by AC arthritis, but they are uncommon.[10]

Other than X-rays and the all-important AC joint injection test, little else is needed to diagnose AC arthritis accurately. MR scans are regularly obtained in AC patients, however, because they often come to require surgery and because the nearby rotator cuff can be torn by the hypertrophic bone of the AC joint. The MR scan does evaluate for rotator cuff tear, and a slightly different surgical approach can be used if no cuff surgery is to be performed. MR imaging does little more than plain films in diagnosing the radiographic changes of AC arthritis, however. As is true of plain film evidence of AC arthritis, there is no correlation between MR evidence of AC arthritis and AC arthritis symptoms. The MR scan does show more of the soft tissue detail of the AC joint; some radiologists believe that they can visualize the articular meniscus or disc that sits between the acromion and the clavicle (see Figure 10–8). The clinical value of this has not been established. The surgical practice of debriding the AC joint by removing its articular meniscus, without resecting the distal clavicle, was used occasionally in the past. Because of the good chance of true painful AC arthritis developing after this procedure, which would necessitate another surgery to resect the distal clavicle, this is not generally done any longer.

Treatments for AC Arthritis

Successful physical treatments for AC arthritis are mostly passive. Simple avoidance of compressive joint stress is probably the most effective activity modification. Muscle strengthening does not play an important role in treatment here; therapies that address joint stiffness and range of motion are similarly ineffective. The reason for this lies with the physiologic behavior of the joint. Twenty degrees to 30° of rotation and a few degrees of abduction/adduction represent the entire normal range of this joint.[11] There are no muscle groups whose primary function is to produce motion here. The AC articulation is a rather unusual joint in as far as it may cause severe, disabling pain when only mildly arthritic, yet it can be either fused solid or completely removed with almost no morbidity. Physical therapy for AC arthritis can be reasonably successful in some cases, however, with the use of little else but modalities.

Direct pain reduction techniques such as transcutaneous electrical nerve stimulation, cryotherapy, trapezius massage, acupressure, heat, and ultrasonation should be utilized expectantly. Little consistent superiority has been demonstrated among these; none has been found to work extremely well in severe cases. A reasonable approach is to try them all and then continue with those that work best. A rather recent addition to the selection of topical agents available in the United States for local pain reduction is a patented eutectic mixture of local anesthetics called eutectic mixture of local anesthetics (EMLA). This drug is basically a combination of two local anesthetic agents that are dissolved in each other, giving local concentrations high enough to create dense cutaneous anesthesia when applied for a sufficiently long time (2 hours or more). The author has had some drastic short-term improvements in AC arthritic pain using phonopheresis with hydrocortisone and EMLA. More is being learned about this technique. It attempts to achieve the benefits of the steroid and anesthetic without injection. Although delivery of these agents to the subcutaneous AC joint by pheresis is an interesting development, the non-surgical treatment that is most effective for AC arthritis is still intraarticular steroid injection.

Injection of long-acting steroid preparations into the arthritis AC joint is an extremely effective treatment. At least three fourths of patients with significant AC arthritic pain respond at least partially to intraarticular steroids.[12] Steroid injections are given with local anesthetic to be sure of needle placement. There are some technical details to the injection process that can often affect the effectiveness of the injection treatment, however.

Some AC joints with productive arthritis are difficult to enter with a needle because of bony overgrowth. It is often helpful to have a plain anteroposterior film in view when one is performing the injection. The slant of the medial acromion and distal clavicle varies quite a bit among patients, and getting the needle between these bones is easier when their radiographic morphology is visible. The normal AC joint will take about 3 mL of injected fluid; some take more, but if much more fluid flows in freely it is likely that a communication exists between the joint and another space (generally the subacromial space) or that needle placement is not within the AC joint. Nearly immediate relief of the patient's typical pain, horizontal adduction and abduction pain, and most of the AC joint tenderness can be expected when local anesthetic is used with the steroid. Increased pain the next day (injection soreness) is a common occurrence when insoluble, long-acting steroid preparations are used. Somewhat less injection soreness has been seen after use of a soluble injectable steroid (dexamethasone), although the actual antiinflammatory effect may not last as long with this drug.

A needle of 22 gauge is used; the heavier needle is somewhat less likely to be deflected by tough capsular tissues and small osteophytes. The direction of needle placement varies with the actual pathoanatomy of the joint (Figure 10–9). In general, the sterile gloved fingers of the examiner's nondominant hand palpate the front and back of the distal clavicle, pushing downward and releasing to give an impression of the actual AC interval (the springing down and up of the clavicle is quite helpful if the subcutaneous fat is not too thick). The needle is directed inferiorly from a point on the top of the front half of the AC interval. Needle direction should reproduce the slant of the AC interval (seen on the anteroposterior radiograph) in the coronal plane and should be

Figure 10–9 AC joint injection.

slightly posterior in the sagittal plane. Resistance to fluid flow will be too high to inject if the needle is placed in the periarticular capsular tissues but will still be higher in the AC joint space than at most other injection sites.

Patients in whom good needle placement is achieved but who fail to be relieved of their typical pain and horizontal adduction pain within 15 minutes or so of injection with local anesthetic and steroid are usually given a subacromial injection of pure local anesthetic next. Subacromial impingement is the process that is most likely to mimic AC arthritic pain, with horizontal adduction pain being caused by stretching a sore rotator cuff and anterior subacromial tenderness passing for AC joint tenderness. Relief of symptoms and negation of these signs with the subacromial injection are diagnostic of a subacromial process (see Chapter 8).

The mechanism whereby intraarticular steroid produces pain relief in the AC joint patient cannot involve correction of the (assumed) underlying mechanical problem: irregularity of the articulating joint surfaces. The steroid decreases local inflammation; in the joint this means decreasing synovial hyperemia, swelling, and production of pain-producing chemical mediators of the inflammatory process. The degeneration of the AC joint's articular meniscus may well be the most painful process that goes on at the AC joint. Debris from this can produce the acute inflammatory response that causes the AC joint to become painful. That the irregularity of the joint is not the ultimate source of pain in many patients is suggested by three observations: Most irregular joints are not, or are minimally, symptomatic; no radiographically apparent change closely accompanies the development of symptoms (ie, the painful, irregular joint generally was just as irregular last year, as seen on old chest films); and steroidal modulation of the local inflammation, with a single injection, often produces long-lasting, sometimes permanent, relief of symptoms.

Oral nonsteroidal antiinflammatory agents are tried in nearly every patient, without medical contraindications, who complains of musculoskeletal pain. These are mentioned in the context of AC arthritis in the same regard as the application of physical modalities. Some cases, generally not severe ones, respond well to them, although generally they are of small benefit. Oral steroidal therapy has not been used for AC joint disease per se by the author because of the large number of systemic side effects that are possible. Anecdotally, quite a few rheumatoid patients already on systemic steroid therapy have developed AC arthritis, which responded quite well to intraarticular injection. The local concentration of injected steroid is enormous compared with the concentrations at the joint achieved with even high-dose systemic therapy.

Surgical treatment of AC arthritis is generally reserved for patients in whom steroid injection fails to achieve lasting relief of AC arthritis symptoms and in whom the physical examination and local anesthetic injection testing continue to indicate AC arthritis as the source of pain. Injections, to be considered effective, must give at least 1 month of symptomatic relief when long-acting steroids are used. Relief that lasts for only a few days is likely to be from the injection volume and local anesthetic effect only; the steroid's antiinflammatory effect can be assumed to be present for at last 2 weeks. This type of patient is referred for surgery early on; further injections are similarly unlikely to help.

The maximum number of injections that should be used in a given time period is not well established. Atrophic changes of the skin and supporting tissues around the joint can accompany excessive use of local steroid, with concerns being raised about the patient's ability to heal and scar after surgery, if it is ultimately required. Three intraarticular injections of 40 mg of methylprednisolone within a 12-month period is the arbitrary maximum used in the author's practice. Injections are effective for most patients with AC arthritis, however. Less than a third of AC arthritis patients ultimately require surgery.

The surgical treatment of AC arthritis is simple. Excision of the distal 2 cm of the clavicle produces excellent results in nearly all patients who have been correctly diagnosed. Distal clavicular excision is termed AC arthroplasty. It is often performed concomitantly with other shoulder surgical procedures if AC arthritic symptoms are present. A good argument can be made for excising the distal clavicle at the time of other shoulder surgery if any signs of AC arthritis are present. The procedure adds little morbidity to most surgeries and does have a reasonably good chance of sparing the patient another surgery and postsurgical rehabilitation course.

There has been some recent enthusiasm for arthroscopic excision of the distal clavicle. This procedure accomplishes most of the same goals as the open AC arthroplasty. Its advantages include a slightly smaller scar and, for some patients, a faster postoperative course, by about 1 week. The disadvantages include a significantly longer operative time (the arthroscopic procedure takes at least twice as long) and the inability securely to repair the deltoid origin from the resected part of the clavicle. This latter factor has a significant impact on postoperative rehabilitation and should be well appreciated.

Open AC arthroplasty, done as a primary procedure, is performed through an incision about 5 cm long over the AC joint. At this location, the trapezius and deltoid origin blend into the periosteum of the superior aspect of the clavicle and the superior capsule of the AC joint. By preserving the tissue at this location, the surgeon is able to suture the trapezius insertion to the deltoid origin, re-creating a mechanical structure that holds the end of the inserting part of the trapezius down and the originating part of the deltoid up. Although it is true that the 2 cm of clavicle that is removed is only a small part of the deltoid origin and trapezius insertion, it is a nonnegligible amount of muscle that is anchored here. Protection of the anterior deltoid and the entire trapezius is therefore a major concern in the first 3 postoperative weeks. Like patients who have had AC joint stabilization procedures, those who have had AC arthroplasty, open or arthroscopic, may have little pain; they must be carefully instructed to maintain only passive motion in elevation and to avoid extension altogether for the first 3 weeks. AC arthroplasty itself does not tend to produce much shoulder stiffness. Early motion in therapy can be much less aggressively pursued than after rotator cuff or glenohumeral arthroplastic surgery. Sling usage for the first 2 weeks is encouraged, although many patients remove the sling on their own before this time.

An anatomic concern that is often raised with excision of the distal clavicle is what happens to the scapuloclavicular suspension after the capsule of the AC joint and the insertion of the lateral coracoclavicular ligament are lost. If there has not been a prior AC separation injury, there is no clinical problem with instability; the medial coracoclavicular ligament seems to be strong enough to take on the entire role of scapuloclavicular suspension without problems. If there has been an AC separation (and there commonly has, especially in younger patients, whose AC arthritis is often due to chronic instability), there will be a problem with scapuloclavicular suspension because the medial coracoclavicular ligament is stretched or torn. Merely excising the distal clavicle in these cases may result in symptomatic AC instability with a badly slumping shoulder girdle and a superiorly protruding bump of distal clavicle. In this case, it is therefore necessary to transplant the coracoacromial ligament to the cut end of the clavicle at the time of surgery and to provide some fort of fixation (a heavy suture, wire, tape, or screw) between the clavicle and the coracoid to keep the stress off the transferred ligament until it has healed and become strong in its new location. This is usually termed a Weaver-Dunn procedure,[7] although it was described by a surgeon named Cadenat.[13] If there has been an AC ligament transfer, this AC arthroplasty should be rehabilitated exactly as an AC stabilization procedure.

REFERENCES

1. Petersson CJ, Redlund-Johnell I. Radiographic joint space in normal acromioclavicular joints. *Acta Orthop Scand.* 1983;54:431–433.
2. DePalma AF. Surgical anatomy of the acromioclavicular and sternoclavicular joints. *Surg Clin North Am.* 1963;43:1540–1550.
3. Tossy JD, Mead NC, Sigmand HM. Acromioclavicular sepsis: Useful and practical classification for treatment. *Clin Orthop.* 1963;28:111–119.
4. Rockwood CA. Acromioclavicular dislocations. In: Rockwood CA, Green DP, eds. *Fractures.* Philadelphia, Pa: Lippincott; 1975:721–756.
5. Harries TJ, Cox JS. Acromioclavicular injuries and surgical treatment. In: Jackson DW, ed. *Shoulder Surgery in the Athlete.* Gaithersburg, Md: Aspen; 1985:121.
6. Powers JA, Bach PJ. Acromioclavicular separation closed or open treatment. *Clin Orthop.* 1974;104:213–223.
7. Weaver JK. Dunn HK. Treatment of acromioclavicular injuries, especially complete AC separation. *J Bone Joint Surg Am.* 1972;54:1187–1197.
8. Bosworth BM. Acromioclavicular separation: New method of repair. *Surg Gynecol Obstet.* 1941;73:866–871.
9. Neer CS. *Shoulder Reconstruction.* Philadelphia, Pa: Saunders; 1990.
10. Burns SJ, Zvibulis RA. A ganglion arising over the acromioclavicular joint: A case report. *Orthopedics.* 1984;7:1004–1007.
11. Inman VT, Saunders J, Abbot LC. Observations on the function of the shoulder joint. *J Bone Joint Surg Am.* 1994;26:1–30.
12. Waxman J. Acromioclavicular disease in rheumatoid practice: The forgotten joint. *J La State Med Soc.* 1977;129:1–3.
13. Cadenat FM. The treatment of dislocations and fractures of the outer end of the clavicle. *Int Clin.* 1917;1:145–169.

Chapter 11

Arthritis and Related Conditions of the Glenohumeral Joint

Glenohumeral arthritis, avascular necrosis (AVN) of the humeral head, and diseases producing mechanical destruction of the glenohumeral joint are considered together in this chapter. The clinical symptoms and signs of glenohumeral joint surface erosion are fairly consistent, although underlying causes may differ. These signs must be clearly recognized by every shoulder practitioner. Just as acromioclavicular (AC) joint arthritis may contribute an element, large or small, of a patient's shoulder pain, glenohumeral arthritic pain may be responsible for all, or only a small part of, a given patient's symptoms. Recognition of the glenohumeral component of pain helps direct treatment effectively.

Physical treatments are useful at every stage of glenohumeral degeneration; early disease may be rendered asymptomatic by this alone. Medical treatment may occasionally play a much more significant role in glenohumeral joint disease than with other common shoulder problems. This is especially true of inflammatory arthritis (eg, rheumatoid disease) of the glenohumeral joint. There is, on the other hand, no stronger indication for joint replacement than high-grade osteoarthritis of the shoulder. Osteoarthritis of the glenohumeral joint, in the presence of an intact rotator cuff, is the purest form of glenohumeral degenerative disease. This is what is properly described by the term *arthritis of the shoulder*. Other disease processes that lead to glenohumeral joint destruction will often be considered in reference to this.

GLENOHUMERAL OSTEOARTHRITIS: CLINICAL PRESENTATION

Pure osteoarthritis of the shoulder is not common. The number of cases of secondary arthritis is much higher. These include cuff tear arthropathy, arthritis of dislocation, postseptic arthritis, posttraumatic arthritis, and the mixed arthritis that may be seen in some rheumatoid patients. With certain exceptions, however, the osteoarthritic pattern of disease does eventually tend to dominate the clinical features of these secondary arthritides. It is a nonspecific reaction of moving joint surfaces to increased local stresses experienced as the normal, marvelously smooth contact surfaces of the humeral head and glenoid become rough. Arthritis is a progressive, degenerative disease. Although patients do present for treatment at all stages of its development, there is a distinct threshold for symptom production in this disease process in each shoulder.

Considering cuff-intact osteoarthritis, the most important pathomechanical element is that the humeral head is tightly held up against the glenoid. A consistently remarkable feature of these shoulders at surgery is how thick and well-developed their rotator cuffs are. With a thick, strong cuff and a capsule that is contracted from decreasing motion, the glenohumeral joint is chronically compressed. The disease therefore progresses as the humeral head grinds away its joint surface, thinning the articular cartilage surfaces and increasing the friction produced by subsequent motion. This wearing process might continue until frictional forces become so high as to generate intolerable pain and severely limit motion.

It is not always this later threshold, though, that brings the shoulder arthritis patient to the practitioner's attention. If an unusually large amount of joint debris is produced, the joint is traumatized in some way, or some balance in the immune system's tolerance of the products of the ongoing joint destruction is upset, an inflammatory reaction may arise within the joint, causing local synovial hypertrophy and capsular pain. An early threshold, inflammatory pain, is crossed in this situation. This would then be a shoulder that presents relatively early in the disease course. Symptoms here might be adequately controlled with antiinflammatory measures, maintenance of motion, and medication. Standard radiographs may be interpreted as normal at this point in the disease (although an axillary view is more sensitive to this early loss of joint surface cartilage; (Figure 11–1). It is even possible that the diagnosis of early osteoarthritis would be rejected because of the normal (standard) radiographs and the good response of the patient's symptoms to modalities and antiinflammatories. The usual threshold for osteoarthritis presentation might not be reached for many years in such a shoulder.

Advanced glenohumeral osteoarthritis tends to be seen in a fairly hearty patient population. These people necessarily have tolerated the entire course of disease development leading up to the late stage of the disease. It is perhaps due to this fact that, on the whole, they do well as shoulder patients. Although their presenting complaints are often related to loss of motion or functional capacity, these patients do have quite a bit of pain. On questioning, it is often described as being in the posterior aspect of the shoulder or upper arm.

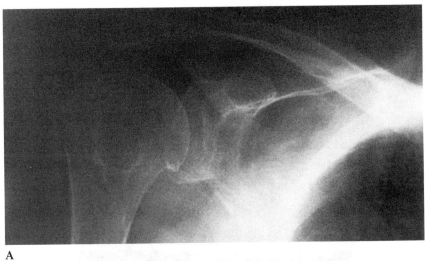

A

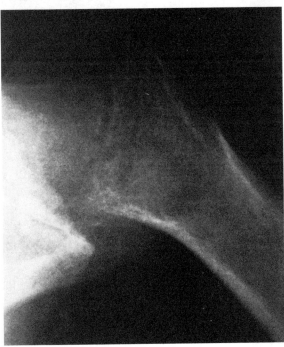

B

Figure 11–1 Rheumatoid arthritis of the shoulder. **(A)** Anteroposterior radiographic projection. The joint space appears to be preserved. **(B)** Axillary projection shows loss of joint space.

C

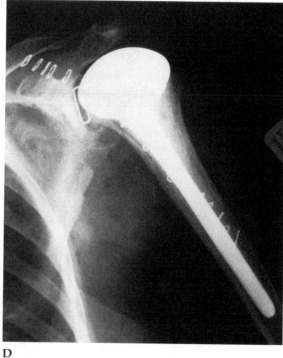

D

Figure 11-1 (C) Clinical photograph of a humeral head specimen from same case, showing erosive, inflammatory destruction of the joint surface. **(D)** Radiograph after joint replacement.

Osteoarthritic glenohumeral pain is not often felt in the trapezius area or neck. The typical osteoarthritic pattern dominates; the pain is greatest when the arm is first moved after a period of immobility, such as sleep. It decreases somewhat as the shoulder warms up with the day's activities. Night pain may be a prominent feature, however, with "I can't find a comfortable position for my arm" being a common complaint. Functional pain is also common; pain when trying to wash the contralateral axilla, perform perineal hygiene, or put on clothing is typical in advanced arthritis of the glenohumeral joint.

Despite all these pain descriptions, many patients with advanced shoulder arthritis present without specific complaints of pain. As mentioned, this is a hearty group. It is often the loss of range of motion that finally forces them to seek help. Thus the presenting complaints are more often of functional disabilities, such as an inability to comb the hair, close the car door, put on a coat, or the like. Some cases produce grinding, popping, or squeaking noises as the humeral head moves against the glenoid. These can be quite loud. "I'm here because the wife can't stand the noise my shoulder is making" was a recent presenting complaint of an arthritis patient in the author's practice.

Physical examination of the osteoarthritic shoulder is most remarkable for loss of motion, particularly external rotation, and tenderness of the posterior glenohumeral joint line and humeral head. External rotation is the one motion of the arm for which scapulothoracic movement is unable to compensate. The scapula cannot externally rotate on the chest. In productive glenohumeral osteoarthritis, osteophytes form at the articular margin of the humeral head. These may become prominent as the humeral head's articular area is lowered by being ground away. This results in actual bony blocks to motion, which become tighter as the osteophytes, under the stimulation of impingement against the margins of the glenoid, become larger and larger (Figure 11–2). Although the shoulder invariably loses elevation as well, rotation is more severely affected by this process. Some elevation can still be performed by the humeral head with this collar of osteophytes because the collar can rotate around an axis through the center of the glenoid without actually having to cross the glenoid articular surface. Significant forward elevation can also be accomplished with scapulothoracic motion.

Internal rotation is also lost in advancing osteoarthritis; it is common to find that the passive range is six to eight segments less than that of the unaffected side. This is not a usual presenting complaint, however, because the sling position, in which most of the osteophytes form, is already internally rotated. Rotation to the hip pocket is usually maintained until late in the disease course. (Complaints about the inability to rotate internally are more likely to be caused by rotator cuff disease or anterior instability. Chronic posterior dislocation should also be kept in mind.) The element of internal rotation that is necessary for horizontal adduction is likely to become painful and eventually

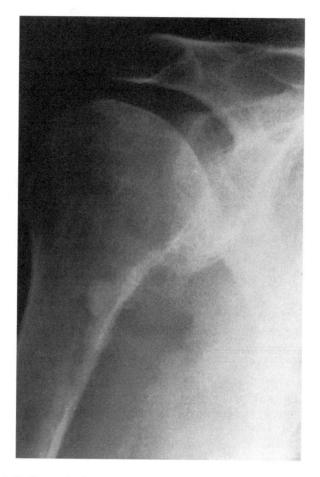

Figure 11–2 Radiograph showing glenohumeral osteoarthritis. Note the free bodies in the inferior pouch.

lost as the disease progresses. This is due to impingement of the anterior marginal osteophytes as well as true contracture of the posterior capsular tissues and posterior rotator cuff tendons. The symptom of inability to wash the contralateral axilla results from this.

Posterior glenohumeral tenderness is the other classic finding in osteoarthritis of the shoulder. This is not a completely specific finding. It occurs with any glenohumeral synovitis or injury of the posterior capsule or cuff tendons. The quality of posterior glenohumeral joint tenderness in osteoarthritis is somewhat different, however. It is as if the humeral head itself is painful when touched. The tenderness is bright, reproducible, and distinctly greater than that of the anterior or superior aspects of the humeral head. This is an area at which the examiner is able to bring finger pressure directly against an osteoarthritic articular surface. The two other places in the body where this can be achieved are the medial condyle of the knee and the medial surface of a large bunion. The quality of tenderness due to rubbing directly on an arthritic surface is similar in these situations.

To the examiner who has developed the subtlety needed to detect signs of glenoid labral tears, the crepitance, skidding, and squeaking of the arthritic humeral head as it is rotated across the glenoid may be overwhelming. Examining, as usual, from behind the seated patient, the clinician's ipsilateral hand rotates the arm as the contralateral hand palpates the joint lines. Whereas a labral click, catch, or grind is usually a low-amplitude, low-frequency sensation that may be eliminated by changing the pressure placed across the joint, the feeling in advanced osteoarthritis is much more pronounced and reproducible with each rotation of the humerus. This is a distinct bony crepitance, not the bursal grinding, labral catching, or synovial crackling produced by the soft tissue structures around the joint.

It is usually not possible to get the arthritic shoulder into the positions necessary to test the strength of all the shoulder girdle muscles in isolation. The supraspinatus isolation maneuver, for example, involves abduction and internal rotation beyond the range of many patients with advanced osteoarthritis of the shoulder. The primary function of muscle testing in these patients is to establish clinical evidence of the integrity of the cuff and deltoid and normal motor function of the cervical nerve roots. Osteoarthritis of the cervical spine is a concomitant disease in many patients with shoulder arthritis (motion of the cervical spine should be recorded in each patient with shoulder arthritis). Fairly good information about the strength of the cuff may be obtained by testing external rotation from sling position to maximal external rotation. The examiner should palpate the supraspinatus fossa while doing this. The deltoid is similarly tested in flexion, abduction, and extension from anatomic neutral. A good idea about subscapularis function can be obtained by forced internal rotation from a position a few degrees short of maximal internal rotation to the maximal position. The trapezius and the scapular positioners are tested in the standard manner.

Injection testing of the glenohumeral joint is of some value when doubts about the relationship of glenohumeral arthritis to the patient's signs and symptoms are present. Intraarticular injection of local anesthetic is easily accomplished here but the potential risks are significantly higher than in cases of AC or subacromial injection. The arthritic joint is a site that is particularly prone to bacterial infection. Absolutely sterile injection technique must be observed to avoid seeding the nutrient-rich, immunologically compromised culture medium afforded by joint fluid laden with bone and joint debris. Septic arthritis that has been clearly caused by joint injection is extremely rare but has been observed. Repetition of the physical examination after the injection is performed, with attention to motion ranges, pain with rotational grind, posterior joint line tenderness, and muscle strength, is useful. It may help establish an extraarticular (ie, subacromial) problem as the source of signs and symptoms or, by diminishing pain and tenderness, may further implicate the degeneration of the glenohumeral joint surfaces. There is usually significant relief of pain and joint tenderness after anesthetic injection into an arthritic glenohumeral joint. Range of motion may change little when disease is advanced because capsular contraction and bony blocks to motion are unaffected.

Although it is occasionally a valuable diagnostic test, injection testing of the glenohumeral joint is not a standard part of the physical work-up of all patients with suspected glenohumeral arthritis. The diagnosis may be established in most patients without injection test, and the threat of septic arthritis can make the test ill advised with this type of shoulder, whose ultimate relief via total shoulder replacement can be rendered impossible by any joint infection. Intraarticular steroid injection, which may be performed concomitantly with injection testing of the joint, is considered separately below.

GLENOHUMERAL ARTHRITIS: RADIOGRAPHIC FEATURES

Like arthritis of the AC joint, glenohumeral osteoarthritis produces characteristic, and even diagnostic, radiographic changes that may or may not correlate with symptoms. As mentioned above, the disease process produces osteophytes at the periphery of the articular surface of the humeral head while simultaneously grinding down the dome of the articular surface. Narrowing and eventually complete loss of joint space (leaving no intervening radiolucent, or dark, interval between the humeral head and glenoid) may only be appreciable on axillary films in some patients because of the tendency of the humeral head to fall away from the glenoid when the shoulder is relaxed in the upright position (Figure 11–3). This is not usually a cause of much confusion in late cases because the build-up of osteophytes is diagnostic of osteoarthritis. In early cases, however, there may be a real need for radiographic diagnostic information because clinical signs of arthritis are still subtle or conflicting. It is primarily in this situation that special studies, such as magnetic resonance (MR) or arthrography, are useful.

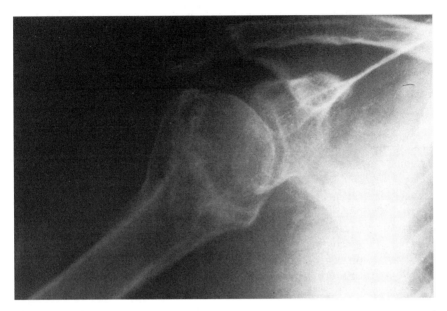

Figure 11–3 Radiograph showing glenohumeral osteoarthritis. Note the ring of osteophytes at the articular margin of the humeral head. These contribute to limitation of motion.

Coating the articular surfaces of the humeral head and glenoid with radiopaque dye, the arthrogram can give somewhat more information about the actual contact surfaces of the glenohumeral joint than plain film radiographs. Arthrography has traditionally been performed for patients with suspected glenohumeral osteoarthritis, both to visualize the articular surface better and to rule out rotator cuff tear. This is still a useful test if early osteoarthritis is suspected and plain films are equivocal. Computed tomographic arthrography is still better at evaluating the joint surfaces and, of course, the presence of labral tears and cuff tears. Both these tests are unnecessary if the classic plain film signs of arthritis are present along with stiffness and posterior joint line tenderness. MR imaging is similarly unnecessary in this case, but because it is so regularly obtained in patients contemplating surgery it has been shown to provide reliable information about the cartilaginous articular surfaces. In cases of nonproductive arthritis, or when a cuff tear or cuff laxity creates a falsely normal impression of the joint space on plain film, the MR scan is valuable in the work-up of patients suspected of having glenohumeral arthritis. By giving an impression of the articular surface as normal, thinned, or absent, the MR image may be an important confirmatory test.

SECONDARY ARTHRITIS OF THE GLENOHUMERAL JOINT

Traumatic Arthritis and Arthritis of Dislocation

Osteoarthritis is the model for both these disorders. They both involve articular surface damage causing chronically increased joint surface forces. The reaction of otherwise normal joint structures to this results in the typical osteoarthritic pattern of disease. In the case of traumatic arthritis, the humeral head or the glenoid (or both) may be initially deformed or merely worn by trauma, which may be acute, as in the case of a fracture of the humeral head or glenoid, or chronic, as in the case of repetitive use injury to the articular cartilage (eg, arthritis in a jackhammer operator). A clinically important element of posttraumatic arthritis is often the concomitant soft tissue injury and resulting scar and contracture. An attempt should be made to distinguish symptoms and signs related to the damaged periarticular tissues from those related to the damaged joint surfaces and their subsequent arthritic degeneration. The amenability of posttraumatic arthritis to physical treatments is highly variable. It depends on the type and extent of injury, the time since injury, associated nerve and soft tissue injuries, and patient age. A complete radiographic work-up is valuable in these cases to help define the exact bony pathoanatomy, the arthritic reactive changes, and the condition of the rotator cuff. The vascularity of the humeral head, which can be appreciated on MR scan, is also an important issue after certain upper humeral fractures.

AVN may affect the humeral head after a fracture of the proximal humerus that separates the articular dome as a free fragment. This may be apparent on plain film radiographs (Figure 11–4). When there is a free avascular segment of humeral head in the joint, it is unlikely that any amount of stretching or strengthening will relieve pain and improve motion. Displacement of the greater and lesser tuberosities, another concomitant finding with many cases of posttraumatic arthritis, may similarly cause pain, weakness, and limitation of motion. The tuberosities may be badly malunited yet permit acceptable clinical results in older patients given slow, persistent motion therapy. A surprisingly large amount of radiographic arthritic change is well tolerated after complex upper humeral fractures as long as a small area of congruent and stable joint surface remains. This is also true of glenoid fractures. Although there are surgical indications for performing open reduction and internal fixation, patients with large displaced fractures have been seen late with radiographic changes of arthritis and truly minor symptoms.

The presumed reason for many deforming fractures of the humeral head and glenoid being well tolerated is that the glenohumeral joint is non–weight bearing. It is primarily when a compressive load is maintained for long peri-

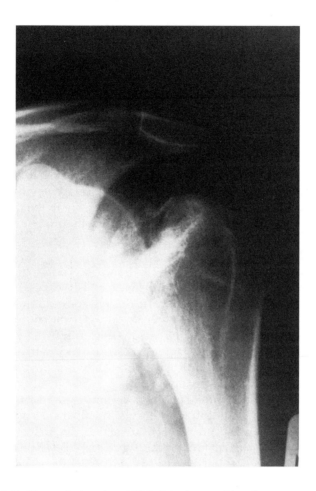

Figure 11-4 Radiograph showing AVN of the humeral head.

ods, as in the case of osteoarthritis with an intact rotator cuff, that the symptoms of glenohumeral osteoarthritis become significant. Shoulder fractures that deform the articular surface also generally weaken the rotator cuff by detaching the tuberosities. These cuff tears through bone then weaken the compressive force across the joint. A rehabilitation principle is demonstrated by this concept: Distraction of the glenohumeral joint, either by gravity (as in the pendulum exercises) or by direct axial traction along the humerus during passive and assisted motion, is quite helpful in decreasing the pain generated by the irregular articular surfaces of arthritic shoulders.

slocations or a chronic dislocation can produce a similar destruc-
rticular cartilaginous surface with repetitive trauma. Again in
these cases, the soft tissue factors (excessive laxity of the glenohumeral capsule, the Bankart lesion, and possibly a rotator cuff tear) may dominate the
clinical presentation and thus control treatment. Arthritis of dislocation is one
of the most difficult and complex problems of the shoulder. Reconstructive
surgery is necessary to provide both congruent joint surfaces and stability.
Rare in the younger population, surgical rehabilitation is done with modified
goals in most patients. It is the stabilizing element of the surgical procedure
that must be considered the limiting factor in mobilization and strengthening.
The surgical approach in these cases is difficult and dangerous; the neurologic
structures are involved in scarring and are quite close to the displaced humeral head. They are thus at significant risk during the procedure.

Rotator Cuff Tear Arthritis and Arthropathy

Cuff tear arthropathy, a term coined by Neer and colleagues,[1] refers to the
semispecific changes in the joint surfaces of the humeral head and glenoid that
occur in the presence of long-term unrepaired tears of the cuff. Much debate
has ensued in the surgical community as to the specificity of these changes and
their pathogenesis.[2] In simple terms, the joint fluid, which normally is responsible for nourishing the living articular cartilage of the glenohumeral joint, is
not contained within the joint because of the perforation in the rotator cuff and
the underlying capsule. This fluid produces the fluid sign of flabby swelling in
the upper arm of long-term cuff tear patients. The fluid's relative absence or
abnormal circulation causes premature death of the living cells of the articular
cartilage and then degeneration of the cartilage surface. Few believe the pathophysiology to be this simple, however. Many other factors may contribute to
the typical pattern of destruction of the joint surfaces. It is necessary to consider the etiology of the cuff tear itself.

Most tears of the rotator cuff are caused by subacromial impingement. The
process of impingement, which produced the cuff tear, continues despite the
tear, now producing wear of the humeral head. The absence of an intact cuff
also creates increased shear forces at the glenohumeral articulation when elevation is attempted. The upward skidding of the humeral head on the
glenoid may thus contribute to increased cartilage wear. The humeral head
cartilage may also be adversely affected by extraarticular structures, namely
bursal tissues, which are able to invade the intraarticular milieu. All these factors may contribute to the degeneration of the glenohumeral articular surfaces. The patient with cuff tear arthropathy is typically older, often in his or
her 80s, and generally unable to perform strengthening exercises because of

the pain produced by movement of the shoulder. This patient has had "a bad shoulder" for many years, however, and presents for treatment at this late date because of increased pain, decreased function, or both. Satisfactory treatment at this point depends in large part on correctly diagnosing that aspect of the disease process that is most responsible for symptoms. In many cases, this is the secondary glenohumeral arthritis.

The arthritis produced by the phenomena mentioned above is not typically as productive as osteoarthritis. Whereas osteoarthritis produces hardening, or sclerosis, of the proximal humeral bone, cuff tear arthropathy is often associated with softening, or porosis. Actual loss of the softened bone stock from the humeral head can be severe. This may be due to a different pathophysiology[3] or to the fact that decreased forces operate across the joint when there is a major cuff disruption, and this leads to disuse osteopenia or bone loss. The glenoid is relatively less affected by cuff tear arthropathy than by osteoarthritis. Loss of the shoulder's passive range of motion is usually less severe than in osteoarthritis. Cuff tear arthropathy takes a long time, at least 10 years, to develop. It also does not seem to develop in every patient with a longstanding cuff tear. (It is for this reason that it is not quite fair to inform patients with cuff tears that they must have them surgically repaired or else suffer the consequences of cuff tear arthritis.) This is a common problem, however, whose best treatment depends on the type and level of symptoms it creates.

The articular incongruity created by cuff tear arthropathy may not be a major source of symptoms. The pain of impingement, in this case impingement of the humeral head on the acromion, may be the primary complaint. Treatment is then directed at strengthening the remaining cuff and biceps (depressors of the humeral head; see Chapter 8) and at relieving inflammation and pressure in the subacromial space. Few patients with cuff tear arthropathy have adequate active elevation of the shoulder; rotator cuff function is generally quite diminished by the time arthritis develops. It is usually a large or massive cuff tear that is seen in patients with cuff tear arthropathy. As mentioned, loss of active elevation may be a presenting complaint. It is the cuff tear, not the secondary glenohumeral arthritis, that is probably responsible for this. By the time arthritic changes of the glenohumeral joint develop, the cuff muscles may have undergone irreversible change, becoming fibrous, inelastic, fatty, and incapable of strong contraction. Even with surgical repair of the cuff, active range may be impossible to restore. Surgical indications in cuff tear arthritis should therefore include shoulder pain because functional return, after the rotator cuff has been disconnected for years, is often small. Better results, with both operative and nonoperative treatment, are obtained for pain relief than for return of cuff functions.

A small but well-respected group of shoulder surgeons has practiced surgical debridement of the remaining rotator cuff along with acromioplasty without any repair of the torn cuff along with acromioplasty without any repair of the torn cuff tendons.[4] This tactic becomes especially attractive when cuff repair is difficult and time consuming, as it often is in cuff tear arthropathy cases (see Chapter 8). The cuff debridement, which consists of trimming the frayed edges of the tear, has reportedly produced good results, but primarily in the hands of one well-known surgeon.[4] It is still an accepted surgical principle, however, that water-tight repair of the cuff to bone, despite the cuff's having been torn for many years, provides the best possibility of resuming nearly normal function. The actual arthritis must be addressed as well when surgery is contemplated.

The decision must be made as to whether it is necessary to replace the humeral and glenoid joint surfaces at the time of reconstruction for cuff tear arthropathy. This is a clinical decision that should be based on the presence of glenohumeral signs on multiple examinations. Differential injections of the glenohumeral joint and subacromial space cannot be done here because the two spaces communicate so freely through the cuff tear. It is only the impression as to whether pain is being generated at the glenohumeral articulation or the subacromial space that can help in making this decision preoperatively. During surgery the articular surfaces can be closely inspected, and this may help somewhat, but the correlation between joint surface condition and pain generation is quite variable.

Significant risk also attends joint replacement in cases of cuff tear arthropathy. The humeral head must be dislocated anteriorly and the subscapularis tendon and anterior capsule divided to perform the procedure. Lasting anterior instability may thus be created, which further diminishes active elevation and compromises function. Nonoperative treatment of cuff tear arthropathy is similarly challenging because both glenohumeral arthritis and cuff insufficiency are present. Nonoperative treatment is described later.

Postsepsis Arthritis

The arthritis produced by bacterial infection of the glenohumeral joint is mentioned in reference to cuff tear arthropathy because it, too, is initially caused by intraarticular conditions that are hostile to the living cartilaginous surfaces of the joint. In this case, it is the toxic products of bacterial growth that produce the articular surface damage. Acute septic arthritis is a surgical emergency, demanding immediate drainage and irrigation of the joint to remove the toxic bacterial products and to prevent the development of deep-seated bone infection or systemic illness. When septic arthritis has occurred in the distant past (ancient sepsis) and there is no sign of continued infection, an arthritic presentation that is quite similar to osteoarthritis may be seen.

It is for this reason that all patients who present with glenohumeral osteoarthritis are asked whether there has ever been an infection in the shoulder. This problem, often seen in a younger population, can be addressed surgically with total shoulder replacement. This is not often done, however, for fear of reactivation of the septic process after implantation of the prosthetic components. This reactivation of an old infection has been seen 30 years after clinical signs of infection have disappeared. It is a disastrous problem if there has been a joint replacement because the prosthesis must be removed, antibiotics must be used for months, and multiple surgical debridements of the joint may be necessary. The patient with postseptic arthritis therefore is often consigned to nonoperative treatments in physical therapy. The treatment is essentially similar to that of the osteoarthritis patient (also described later).

Rheumatoid Arthritis

Rheumatoid arthritis of the glenohumeral joint presents a rather different disease process than that of osteoarthritis. Articular surface degeneration (along with a lytic synovitis that destroys adjacent bone, tendon, and ligament), muscular weakness, and constitutional frailty characterize this disease. The side effects of the drugs used to control the disease process (systemic steroids and antimetabolites, which slow healing and make tissues weak) often pose additional treatment problems.

The rheumatoid shoulder presents with one or both of two separate pain-producing results of the rheumatoid process: inflammatory synovitis and/or articular destruction. *Rheumatoid flare* is the term often used for the intense autoimmune reaction that produces joint pain, swelling, and stiffness. In glenohumeral disease this appears as a puffy and unusually tender frozen shoulder. Prednisone or methotrexate, given systemically, may produce a dramatic reduction in these symptoms. Intraarticular steroids, with the usual caveats regarding infection, are also effective in some instances. This shoulder often displays only minor changes on plain film radiographs. There in fact may be little articular destruction, or the radiographs may be quite deceptive. This is an instance in which the appearance of an adequate joint space is often maintained, despite complete loss of articular cartilage, because of the weak cuff and swollen joint-lining tissues (see Figure 11–1). Motion and modalities are the primary physical treatments during the flare. Surgical synovectomy, via the arthroscope, is of some usefulness if medical treatments are unsuccessful. Postsurgical bleeding into the joint, as well as capsular pain and stiffness, require prolonged passive motion treatments; for most patients after rheumatoid synovectomy, 6 weeks of thrice-weekly treatments is required.

The destructive arthropathy of rheumatoid disease may ultimately produce intolerable pain and loss of motion. A situation similar to osteoarthritis then results. The primary difference in rheumatoid arthritis of the glenohumeral joint is that so many other structures around the joint are usually destroyed by the time articular surface destruction has occurred. The rheumatoid synovium attacks the rotator cuff, destroying it in the absence of any impingement phenomenon. The capsule is weakened, producing instability, and the bone adjacent to the articular surfaces is destroyed, making the implantation of prostheses, which rely on their anchoring to bone for stability, difficult or even impossible. Under attack by the rheumatoid disease as well as by most of the medications used to control it, the red muscles are weakened, further eroding the patient's rehabilitation potential.

Of course, not every patient develops all these changes, and they do take time to occur. It is therefore considered prudent practice with rheumatoids to be somewhat more aggressive in recommending early surgery, especially for shoulder arthritis. Although incomplete, there is an effect of lessening the severity of the rheumatoid attack on the joint when articular cartilage is removed; the articular cartilage is a prime target of the abnormal immune response of rheumatoid disease. The physical removal of synovium, which is usually accomplished at the time of joint replacement surgery, similarly decreases the attack on the remaining bone and ligamentous structures of the joint. It is therefore the recommendation of the author and most shoulder surgeons that joint replacement, before joint destruction, is the best way to ensure good shoulder function.

Surgical arthroscopy of the early rheumatoid shoulder undergoing a rheumatoid flare is sometimes used in place of, or as an adjunct to, medical treatments to control synovitis. A similar rationale for the same procedure is used in cases of early osteoarthritis of the shoulder with an acute inflammatory response. This is not the quick, easy procedure that arthroscopic glenoid labral resection often is. Rheumatoid synovium is hypervascular. It bleeds profusely when cut, and this bleeding obscures visualization within the joint. A reasonably thorough synovectomy can usually be accomplished arthroscopically, however, with persistence and high-pressure irrigation of the joint during the procedure. Some improvement in symptoms is usually accomplished with arthroscopic rheumatoid synovectomy, although rehabilitation after this procedure is slow, often taking as long as would be expected after total shoulder replacement. A number of reasons for this can be seen. The capsule is abraded by the shaving tool used to remove the synovium. Extracapsular tissues unaffected by the procedure are still undergoing the flare response. Most significant, the glenohumeral joint is filled with blood. Patients contemplating this procedure must expect 1 to 3 months of therapy, consisting simply of motion and modalities, before symptomatic relief is achieved.

Rheumatoid synovectomy is a reliable procedure when performed in the elbow, knee, or wrist. Although the synovium does eventually regrow, good symptomatic relief can be expected for 1 to 3 years postoperatively. Similar results have been obtained in the shoulder when adequate synovial resection has been followed by adequate rehabilitation.

Acute Inflammatory Arthritis

Osteoarthritis, Acute Synovitis, and Low-Grade Infectious Arthritis

Arthroscopic debridement of the osteoarthritic shoulder that is undergoing an acute inflammatory synovial response is less often performed, perhaps because the symptoms are less severe and more likely to be controlled medically. When joint surface destruction is severe and osteophytes ring the articular bearing surfaces, little or no pain relief is generally expected after arthroscopic joint debridement. Shoulder arthroscopy can be particularly effective for the osteoarthritic shoulder in one situation. A variant of the osteoarthritic inflammatory response that involves development of an acute, although generally low-grade, bacterial infection should be familiar to the shoulder practitioner. This condition is seen most often in older patients with advanced degenerative joint disease; a streptococcal organism has been most commonly cultured in these shoulders (and knees as well), which are already filled with debris from the ongoing degenerative process.

Capsular distention, which the examiner can best see by looking down at both shoulders of the seated patient, and capsular tenderness, both posteriorly and anteriorly, are the local physical signs of the infected arthritic shoulder. There are systemic signs of infection, including fever and elevated white blood cell count, although these have not been severe in the author's practice. Aspirated joint fluid is cloudy and filled with debris, although not quite containing the density of white blood cells that is typically considered necessary for there to be a classic septic arthritis (normally, infection is thought to produce a joint fluid white cell count of $50,000/mm^3$ to $100,000/mm^3$; these cases have had $20,000/mm^3$ to $40,000/mm^3$). Joint fluid cultures are consistently positive, however, unless antibiotics are being used. These low-grade infections of arthritic joints may be related to bacterial utilization of the abundant joint debris for growth and multiplication. They respond well to antibiotics and arthroscopic joint irrigation and debridement. This is in distinction to the classic clinical presentation of septic arthritis with high fever and frank, thick pus in the joint. Multiple irrigations and even open drainage of the joint, along with long-term antibiotic therapy, are necessary in these cases. The typical septic arthritis does not have a tendency to present in shoulders already affected by degenerative arthritis. It is therefore more likely to be confused only with the last type of arthritis to be described: crystalline deposition arthritis.

Pseudogout

Pseudogout is the term given to the intraarticular inflammatory response to deposits of calcium pyrophosphate crystals. This is the chalky, white calcium deposit that is often seen in osteoarthritic joints. Pyrophosphate is only seen to be crystalline under the microscope.

Pseudogout attacks are associated with pain, redness, swelling, and occasional low-grade fever. Physical signs are essentially the same as those seen with any process producing a joint effusion (build-up of fluid within the joint) and synovitis; posterior joint line tenderness, swelling, and motion limited by pain are similar to those seen in cases of infectious arthritis. No organism is found when the joint fluid is cultured, however, and microscopic examination of the fluid demonstrates pyrophosphate crystals. Most cases of pseudogout respond to antiinflammatory medication, but resistant symptoms may be treated quite well with arthroscopic irrigation and debridement of the glenohumeral joint.

Gout

Gout is a similar condition in which intraarticular deposition of crystals of uric acid produces an intensely painful synovial inflammatory reaction. Gout rarely presents for the first time with an attack of shoulder pain.[5] It is therefore unlikely for a patient without a known history of gout to have undiagnosed shoulder pain that is caused by gout. Conversely, a patient who has a gout attack of the shoulder will probably recognize or suspect the diagnosis of gout.

This is a painful condition. The shoulder is held absolutely rigid at the side, and little palpation of the joint is tolerated by most patients. Medication alone controls these symptoms in the majority of cases. Antiinflammatory agents are effective against gouty pain. Colchicine, a drug that inhibits white blood cell functions, is a traditional and effective treatment for the pain of gout. Subsequent attacks are avoided by the use of drugs that promote the secretion of urate, thus preventing its build-up within joints. Allopurinol is the most commonly used of these. Physical treatments and surgery only become necessary when long-term gouty disease has produced articular surface destruction and chronic, painful arthritis. Serious chronic gouty arthropathy of the glenohumeral joint is rare.

The diagnosis of gout is made definitively by the microscopic observation of needlelike crystals of urate in the aspirated joint fluid. This reinforces a basic principle in the work-up of any acute glenohumeral arthritic or synovitic process: Careful, sterile needle aspiration of the joint is an essential part of the diagnostic process. With the increasing incidence of sexually transmitted diseases (gonorrhea and acquired immunodeficiency syndrome are both potential causes of septic arthritis), the high prevalence of intravenous drug use, and the growing utilization of legitimate immunosuppressive agents, bacterial joint infection must be suspected in every "hot" shoulder. This is true even when a likely diagnosis (flare in a rheumatoid or hemarthrosis in a hemophiliac) is present. Practitioners for whom diagnostic aspiration is inappropriate should not hesitate to refer a patient to have this done.

AVN of the Humeral Head

AVN of the humeral head is not an uncommon problem. Pathophysiologically, it is most easily understood as a loss of normal blood supply to the cancellous (spongy) bone of the humeral head. This causes death (necrosis) of the bone, which is followed by softening and collapse. Loss of the roundness of the dome of the humeral head then produces articular surface incongruity, which in time produces the osteoarthritic pattern of joint destruction and reactive bone formation, first on the humeral surface and then the glenoid surface of the joint.

The exact cause of the original loss of blood circulation to the humeral head bone is unclear. There are frequent associations with the use of steroidal drugs, use of alcohol, sickle cell disease, and chronic wheelchair use.[6] These are certainly conditions that the history must elicit when AVN is suspected. The disease process is not well understood, however. Wheelchair use, the one mechanical association, does seem to involve increased pressure in the humeral head due to chronic joint compression. The most common historical finding with AVN in general (including AVN of other bones, such as the femoral head) is steroid use. The actual incidence of AVN among high-dose steroid users is so low, however, as to suggest a causative role in the production of AVN of the disease for which the steroid was prescribed.

Patients may present with AVN of the humeral head at any adult age and with a variety of complaints. The most usual is pain. There is a general tendency of the pain patterns to change with the stage of the disease. Early on in the disease, the humeral head is still round and firm with no changes in the articular cartilage. Pain felt during this stage tends to be the toothachelike bone pain that is associated with bone infarction (acute loss of blood supply or ischemia). This early pain of the actual AVN process is often worse at night and is largely nonpositional, although compressive stress across the joint does increase discomfort when the pain is severe. Many AVN patients pass through this stage with no pain at all, however.

Later, as the humeral head softens and collapses, the pain becomes more typical of the osteoarthritic pattern, with a few important differences. Pain is felt to be clearly in the shoulder or upper arm. It is related to motion and especially joint compression. Actively maintaining horizontal abduction is difficult because of this. Posterior joint line tenderness is usually present. The active range of motion is limited by pain. The important differences from pure osteoarthritis at this point are that passive motion is usually maintained and external rotation is not particularly painful. These differences then decrease with time as full-blown glenohumeral osteoarthritis develops. The earliest phases of AVN (bone infarction) do not produce bone changes that are visible on plain radiographs. MR imaging and nuclear bone scans are able to detect changes in the bone of the humeral head that are highly suggestive, although not absolutely diagnostic, of AVN. Later phases, in which bone reaction to infarction, softening, collapse, and arthritic changes occur, are easily diagnosed on plain radiographs.

Early AVN of the humeral head does not always lead to articular surface collapse. The exact natural historical statistics are not reliably known, but many cases of humeral head pain with biopsy- or MR-proved AVN have been known to resolve completely with time. This fact argues well against surgical treatment for early AVN unless symptoms are truly unbearable. Anti-inflammatory medications are quite effective against this type of bone pain. Other treatments should include pain reduction techniques and ranging to prevent loss of motion along with activity modifications to avoid unnecessary compressive forces on the humeral head. A variety of medical treatments have been used in attempts to halt the progress of early AVN. These have included drilling or decompression of the humeral head, medications, and electric fields. None has had prolonged, statistically proven effectiveness.

Late-stage AVN is best treated with replacement of the humeral head and possibly the glenoid surface if it, too, has been destroyed. These are often surprisingly easy shoulders to rehabilitate. If operated before advanced osteoarthritic changes take place, the soft tissue problems of contracture, cuff tear, and intracapsular inflammation and synovitis are not present. The only real problem with this shoulder is the articular surface; once it has been properly replaced, resumption of nearly normal shoulder function is usually only a matter of recovering from the surgical procedure itself. Rehabilitation after shoulder replacement is discussed below.

TREATMENT OF GLENOHUMERAL ARTHRITIS

As discussed earlier for the individual diseases, medical treatment appropriate to the specific arthritis-producing disease can be extremely effective in reducing symptoms. Returning to the osteoarthritis model, however, the only medications that can be used safely for some long-term symptom control are the antiinflammatory agents. With the usual warnings about side effects in mind, aspirin, acetaminophen, ibuprofen, naproxen, and the others on the market can make some patients with mild to moderate degenerative disease more comfortable. A problem with osteoarthritis of the shoulder is the large role of joint contracture in pain generation. Capsular pain is much less affected by the nonsteroidal agents than true articular degenerative pain. Oral narcotics are used by some patients without addiction and symptom amplification, but these are always concerns. Intraarticular steroid injections are helpful in controlling acute synovitis and similar arthritic flares, but their long-term effect on articular structures is negative, and they do not provide any true relief of pure articular surface pain; patients with late-stage osteoarthritis or AVN, for instance, enjoy little or no relief from intraarticular steroid injections.

The physical treatments that have been most effective in glenohumeral arthritis utilize heat and motion. The observation that heat feels good on arthritic joints is made quite frequently by patients with arthritic shoulders. These patients may take hot showers at midday for relief from pain. Moist heating pads and ultrasonation are therefore recommended at the start of every physical therapy session. Therapeutic motion is more effective at relatively high angular velocities, within the comfortable range, in forward elevation, abduction, and adduction. Progressive range maneuvers are best done passively or with active assistance to avoid the compressive load placed across the glenohumeral joint by the rotator cuff. Pendulum type exercises, which may be done with hand weights to increase axial traction forces, seem to permit motion with less of the grinding compressive stress that produces pain in osteoarthritics. Those osteoarthritics with audible glenohumeral crepitus (the noise produced by motion of the loaded glenohumeral joint is more accurately described as a squeaking) should be studied carefully. They provide the practitioner with an excellent opportunity to study the effects of different motion techniques on joint loading, which in their cases is clearly audible.

As the capsule warms up and stretches a bit, the ranges generally can be expanded. Forward elevation, extension, and abduction are most easily addressed in osteoarthritic shoulders. Internal and external rotation ranging is not well tolerated by most patients with significant glenohumeral degeneration; these motions seem to produce more grinding pain than the others, and impingement of the marginal osteophytes at the ends of rotational range is both unpleasant and not apt to result in any improvement in motion or long-term pain. Internal rotation contracture may be a chief patient complaint in many osteoarthritics, in which case progressive external range of motion work cannot be avoided. It is much easier to do this in mild forward elevation and abduction than with the arm held at the side.

In general, physical treatments for osteoarthritis of the shoulder are most effective for patients with mild disease or those with a transient synovitic flare. Once the glenohumeral joint is contracted in internal rotation and the articular surfaces are ringed by a thick fringe of osteophytes, it is difficult to restore motion or relieve pain with any treatment other than joint replacement. Although degenerative diseases do progress along a continuum, there is, as mentioned earlier, a distinct threshold in shoulder arthritis at which symptoms become intolerable and patients present for treatment. The patient group reaching this threshold earlier in the disease process (possibly those with lower pain tolerance) is the most likely to benefit from physical therapy, exercise, and activity modifications.

Strengthening of the shoulder girdle musculature, although generally helpful if there are apparent deficiencies in specific groups, should be a secondary, not primary, goal in treating patients with shoulder arthritis symptoms. Most strengthening exercises are painful and do nothing to relieve the symptoms of the patient with an arthritic shoulder. There is one exception, however: A modest but appreciable increase in range is often seen when motion is changed from passive to active assisted in osteoarthritics. This is true independent of the increased scapulothoracic components of active motions. One can, for example, employ strengthening exercises for the posterior cuff muscles when trying to increase the range of external rotation or anterior deltoid strengthening when working on forward elevation. This is in contradistinction to standard range-building techniques used with other underlying causes of stiffness.

The reasons for the effectiveness of this technique, although frequently an empiric observation, are purely theoretical. There may be true disuse atrophy of the agonists of the most severely affected ranges; arthritic pain with external rotation, for example, may cause the patient not to use the external rotators, leading to their weakness and subsequently decreased range of external rotation. Strengthening the external rotators in this case would serve to break the cycle of pain, disuse, weakness, contracture, and increased pain. Although this strategy is often effective in cases of moderate disease, the ability to tolerate strengthening exercises is eventually lost as articular degeneration and contracture become more severe. Patients who are able to benefit from physical treatments for glenohumeral arthritis generally do improve rapidly; pain decreases and motion improves in 1 to 3 weeks. Three months of treatment is not needed to find out that therapy is not going to be effective. If symptoms are serious and have not been relieved by medications and 4 to 6 weeks of physical therapy, surgical treatment is considered.

Surgical treatments for shoulder arthritis include arthroscopic and open debridements of the joint, resection arthroplasty (simple removal of the humeral head), and surgical fusion of the glenohumeral joint. The effective uses of arthroscopy in glenohumeral synovitis and the various bacterial, inflammatory, and crystalline arthritides have been described above. There is little usefulness of arthroscopic joint debridement outside of these. Arthroscopic debridement of the late osteoarthritic shoulder gives little or no lasting relief in most cases. Resection arthroplasty seems as if it might be an effective method of pain relief. Nearly asymptomatic shoulders are occasionally seen in patients who have had proximal humeral fractures followed by resorption of the humeral head. This happy outcome does not attend elective surgical resection of the arthritic humeral head. Resection arthroplasty of the AC joint is safe and effective. Humeral head resection neither improves function nor completely relieves pain.[7] It is no longer employed except in unusual circumstances where a shoulder fusion cannot be performed.

Glenohumeral fusion is an old operation that today is considered a salvage procedure. It is the procedure of choice in cases of deep infection around the shoulder and where there is total loss of cuff and deltoid function. There are many surgical techniques that can be used to achieve glenohumeral fusion. It is obvious that one factor, scapulothoracic motion, is important to functional rehabilitation. The functional loss and incomplete pain relief afforded by all these procedures stand apart from the generally good results achieved by the most commonly performed procedure for glenohumeral arthritis: joint replacement. It is the procedure of choice for the vast majority of patients.

Shoulder replacement surgery involves replacement of the humeral head and glenoid articular surface with metallic (steel or cobalt-chrome) and plastic (high-density polyethylene) prostheses, which are usually fixed to the bone with plastic (polymethylmethacrylate) bone cement. This type of surgery is similar, conceptually, to the joint replacement that is commonly performed for arthritic hips and knees, although shoulder replacement is a somewhat more delicate procedure that is much less frequently done.

Shoulder replacement was developed by Neer at Columbia University.[6] Despite a plethora of new companies manufacturing implants, no major changes in the procedure have come into widespread use since its final development in the 1970s. *Shoulder replacement* is a term used to describe procedures that replace only the humeral head and those in which both the humeral head and the glenoid are treated with artificial resurfacing (Figure 11–5). Many

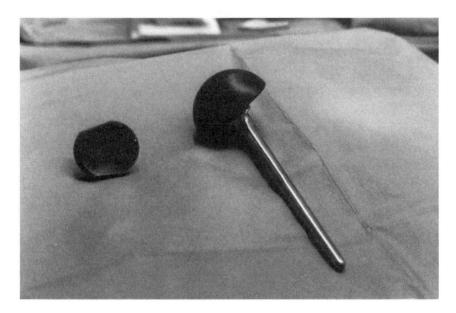

Figure 11–5 Prosthetic trial components: humeral head with stem and glenoid.

other procedures may be performed simultaneously during shoulder replacement surgery. Repair of a torn rotator cuff and AC arthroplasty are among the most common. These concomitant procedures may actually affect the postsurgical rehabilitation course more significantly than the joint surface replacement.

Shoulder replacement requires a cooperative patient who is free of infection and able to tolerate a major surgery and 1 to 6 months of postsurgical rehabilitation. Cooperation is absolutely necessary because of the surgical approach used. The deltoid is not usually taken down from the acromion, but the subscapularis tendon and anterior glenohumeral capsule are completely transected to give surgical access to the joint. Although they are sutured closed during the surgical closure, these structures must be protected for at least 4 weeks after surgery to prevent being ripped open, which will produce permanent anterior glenohumeral instability and weakness. Loss of the anterior repair is one of the most common problems after shoulder replacement surgery. It can occur up to 6 months postoperatively and results in chronic subluxation, which, although rarely painful, does preclude normal active elevation. Distinguishing this problem from rotator cuff dysfunction (or avulsion) and insufficient size of the humeral head prosthesis is essential to treatment of any unstable shoulder replacement.

Infection in the presence of a shoulder replacement is disastrous. Difficult (sometimes impossible) to eradicate, deep, bony infection around a surgical implant requires removal of the implant and much bone, making ultimate reconstruction, even with fusion, difficult or impossible. Patients with ongoing infections are obviously not candidates for joint replacement. Patients with high risk of bacterial contamination of the blood stream, such as intravenous drug abusers, are similarly not candidates. Diabetics, transplant patients, and other immunosuppressed patients and those on chronic steroid therapy may receive joint replacements safely, but liberal use of antibiotics and careful surveillance for infection must be a life-long practice after the surgery.

The ability of the patient to tolerate the surgical procedure is another important factor in shoulder replacement surgery. Although not involving as much blood loss as hip or knee arthroplasty, shoulder replacement involves reaming the intramedullary cavity of the humerus, a sizeable blood loss from bleeding cut bone surfaces, and extensive dissection of a highly vascular area of the body. Patients must be medically stable with satisfactory cardiac and respiratory function to be considered candidates for the procedure (Figures 11–6 through 11–10).

Rehabilitation after shoulder replacement involves at least 6 weeks of physical therapy in the author's practice. Patients must agree to this preoperatively. The surgery without the rehabilitation leaves a stiff, weak, and painful shoulder that may not respond to late rehabilitation efforts. Surgery must be planned around the rehabilitation course; patients must be in town for the 2 months after the procedure. It is reassuring for the surgeon contemplating a shoulder replacement to hear that his or her patient has been cooperative with physical therapy. Although the course after straightforward joint replacement for degenerative arthritis is usually smooth, shoulder reconstructions involving joint replacement and large, simultaneous rotator cuff repairs are among the most complex and extensive shoulder operations that are ever done. Their rehabilitation may be slow, sometimes painful, and, for months at a time, quite discouraging. Mental preparation of the patient for this is an important element of preoperative treatment.

The surgical procedure used to perform shoulder replacement is universally done through an anterior approach between the deltoid and the pectoralis major muscles. An extended version of the surgical approach used to correct anterior instability, this technique does not usually require any cutting or detaching of the deltoid from its bony origins. The deltoid does have to be pulled out of the way with some vigorous retraction during the procedure. This can cause some early weakness of the anterior deltoid (distinguishable from axillary nerve damage by the presence of intact epaulet area sensation and the ability palpably to set the anterior deltoid), but because it is only

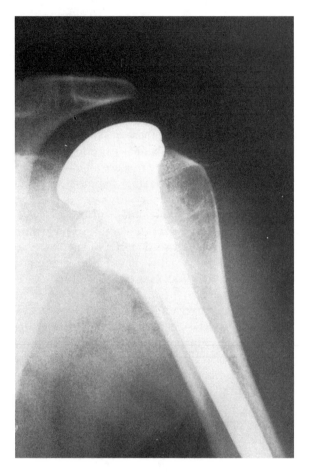

Figure 11–6 Radiograph showing modular humeral head replacement for AVN of the humeral head in a 34-year-old woman.

stretched and not detached it can be expected soon to regain full strength and does not need to be specially protected during the early postoperative phase of rehabilitation.

The large cephalic vein marks the interval between the deltoid and the pectoralis; it is otherwise sometimes difficult to distinguish. In procedures done to revise previous surgery or for posttraumatic arthritis, scarring and fibrosis of the deltoid can make it difficult to retract. In these cases, the deltoid insertion on the humerus may be released to gain surgical exposure of the shoulder. This is quite important to note during postsurgical rehabilitation

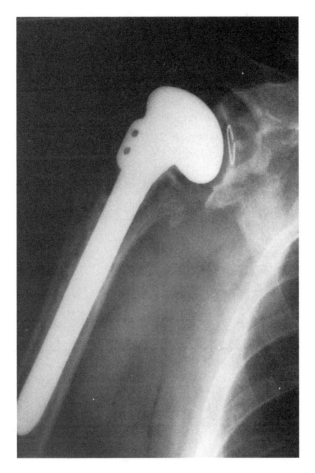

Figure 11-7 Radiograph showing humeral and glenoid replacement for osteoarthritis (compare with Figure 11-3).

because the reattached deltoid must be protected with pure passive motion (as after a rotator cuff procedure). In some tight shoulders, the humeral insertion of the pectoralis major is cut to enhance exposure. This is usually repaired in closure as well, but because the tissue is so strong and there are so many other adductors acting agonistically, there is no real need to protect the pectoralis repair during rehabilitation.

The nerves that are most at risk during the shoulder replacement procedures are the axillary and the musculocutaneous, although any and all of the brachial plexus branches can be affected. The musculocutaneous nerve, which powers the short head of the biceps, is retracted along with the muscles originating from the coracoid process. It is rarely cut, but the stretching with retraction can produce weakness of the biceps for some months after surgery. The axillary nerve, powering the deltoid and teres minor, is at particular risk during revision shoulder replacement procedures. As mentioned above, it should be considered if there is unusual deltoid weakness postoperatively.

The axillary nerve's sensory supply to the skin of the upper lateral arm (the epaulet area, if rather long epaulets are worn) is somewhat variable and is not to be entirely trusted as a sign of intact nerve function. The variable speed of return of muscular power after a long surgery is perhaps the most obvious reason, but there are many other reasons why discretion should be exercised in communications to the postoperative patient regarding what appears to be nerve dysfunction. The operating surgeon should simply be informed, pri-

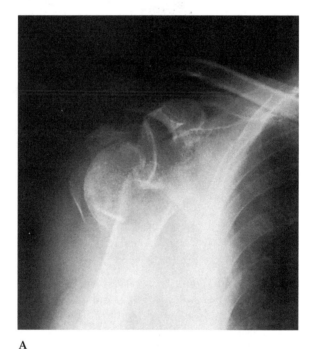

A

Figure 11–8 (A) Radiograph showing a fracture separating the humeral head and both tuberosities.

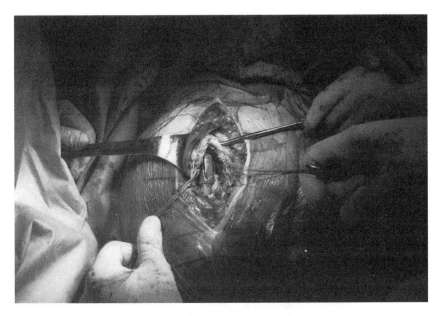

B

Figure 11–8 (B) Operative photograph showing reconstruction with a prosthetic humeral head and internal fixation of both tuberosities with heavy suture. Note the bundles of sutures attached to both tuberosities and the prosthesis between them. A fairly strong construct can often be achieved this way, permitting aggressive early motion.

vately, of any apparent nerve or muscle problem in the postoperative patient. The surgeon's lead, as long as it makes clinical and ethical sense, should then be followed in addressing the issue. If it does not make sense, the patient is still not the best person to whom to bring this; one should approach a medical superior, such as the department head or chief of staff. This is generally the safest and fairest approach for both the patient and the professionals involved.

The surgical decision of whether to resurface the glenoid is often made at the time the glenoid is exposed and palpated for surface roughness and cartilage cover. Satisfactory results can be expected from shoulder replacement without glenoid resurfacing when the glenoid surface is relatively intact. When the glenoid is irregular or devoid of articular cartilage, pain relief is more complete and more immediate when the glenoid is resurfaced. There are

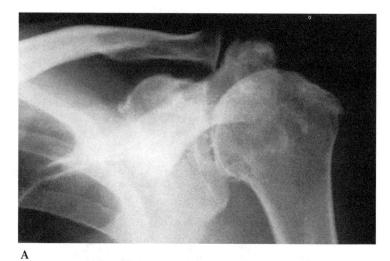

A

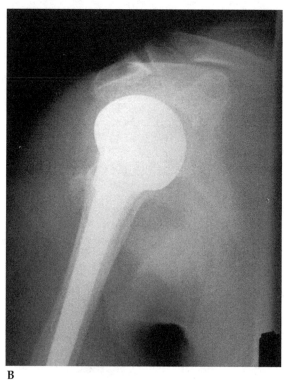

B

Figure 11–9 **(A)** Posttraumatic arthritis. **(B)** Reconstruction with a humeral head prosthesis.

times, however, when there is poor glenoid bone stock and, even though the glenoid is quite arthritic, there is not enough native bone left to hold the glenoid component securely. No resurfacing is done in this case. Because this is a problem that is usually faced in rheumatoids, whose weak shoulder girdle musculature and capsular ligaments do not create large compressive forces across the joint, there is little difference noted in postoperative rehabilitation. On the occasion that a true cuff-intact osteoarthritic shoulder is replaced without glenoid resurfacing, greater comfort will be had in postoperative motion therapy if distraction techniques, such as those used for motion in unoperated

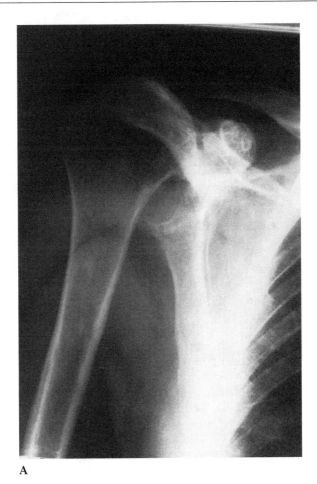

A

Figure 11–10 (A) Cuff tear arthropathy.

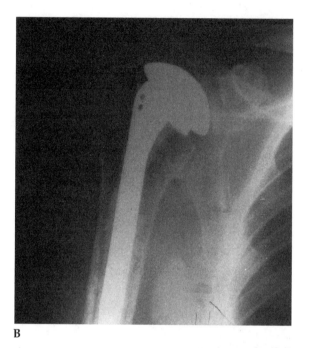

B

Figure 11–10 (B) Reconstruction with joint replacement.

---

osteoarthritics, are used. These shoulders eventually do improve significantly. The late result of humeral head replacement alone for true glenohumeral arthritis are only slightly inferior to those obtained when both glenoid and humerus are resurfaced.[6]

Rehabilitation after shoulder replacement surgery may be quite rapid and involve little pain, as is often seen after surgery for AVN, or may be slow and quite painful, as after revision surgery for cuff tear arthropathy. Rheumatoids generally have an easier time regaining motion and strength if they undergo shoulder replacement early in the disease course, while the rotator cuff and glenoid bone stock are still intact. Patients with cuff-intact osteoarthritis and preoperative contractures are usually treated with capsular releases and lengthening during the surgery. Nevertheless, they tend to be stiff postoperatively and demand the most aggressive range of motion therapy in the early postoperative period if the motion gains made at surgery are to be ultimately realized.

After total shoulder replacement, twice-daily in-hospital therapy is a great advantage. Hospital utilization policies denying hospitalization for intensive rehabilitation do these patients a significant disservice. Outpatient therapy is used after discharge until full motion has been achieved and strength is seen to be improving smoothly. The frequency of outpatient visits is adjusted clinically; stiff osteoarthritics may require five sessions per week for the first 2 weeks. Thrice-weekly sessions for 6 weeks followed by twice-weekly sessions for another 1 to 2 months are average. Achieving motion goals early carries a significant advantage; this generally cuts down on the total time in rehabilitation.

Limiting the motion and strength goals that are to be set for postoperative rehabilitation is common practice after shoulder replacement done in the absence of an intact or functioning rotator cuff.[8] Although little danger accompanies passive elevation above a current limit, there is often a problem with returning to active use of a rotator cuff that has been repaired at the time of shoulder replacement. Rotator cuff tendon tissue that has been stretched tightly over a large metal hemisphere is not likely to heal rapidly or well. Sudden, noticeable cuff rupture with secondary instability is seen up to 18 months after combined cuff repair–joint replacement procedures. Obviously, this may be unavoidable. The most important goal to limit, therefore, is not usually motion but rather the permitted contraction force of the deltoid and rotator cuff muscles. Eccentric contraction is most dangerous and thus is limited for as long as possible. There are certain situations, such as revision shoulder replacement surgery, in which limited motion goals are set to protect a scarred or stiff subscapularis and anterior capsule. These particular goals should be based on surgical findings (ie, how much external rotation was tolerated and safe with direct observation and palpation of the subscapularis repair).

The above caveats and stipulations notwithstanding, the postoperative rehabilitation of most total shoulder patients is straightforward and quite similar to the sequence used after rotator cuff surgery. The first or second postoperative day generally sees the beginning of passive forward elevation, internal rotation, and external rotation to early goals, with attention being paid to overall stiffness, cuff integrity, and subscapularis repair integrity, respectively. Pendulum exercises and elbow, hand, and wrist motion are permitted ad lib from the day of surgery. The arm is supported in a sling during ambulation and on a pillow in bed. The hand may be used for eating and grooming as tolerated. If no exceptional muscle work has been done, active assisted ranging can follow by the third week with pulley elevation, baton external rotation, and towel internal rotation exercises. Cold is helpful with early pain control. Heat is avoided in the early postoperative phase because there is already an inflammatory healing response in progress. Pure active motion is generally used as tolerated starting at postoperative week 6 and resistive strengthening by week 10. This is the rough time table for an otherwise uncomplicated course after shoulder replacement for cuff-intact osteoarthritics. It may be slightly accelerated for younger patients or those without contractures and of course slowed significantly if cuff problems, revision, instability, or neurologic problems are present.

REFERENCES

1. Neer CS, Craig EV, Fukuda H. Cuff tear arthropathy. *J Bone Joint Surg Am.* 1982;65:1232–1244.
2. Cofield RH. Degenerative and arthritic problems of the glenohumeral joint. In: Rockwood CA, Matsen FA, eds. *The Shoulder.* Philadelphia, Pa: Saunders; 1990:696.
3. Garancis JC, Cheung HS, Halverion PB, McCarty DJ. "Milwaukee shoulder": Association of microspheroids containing hydroxyapatite crystals, active collagenase and neutral protease with rotator cuff defects. *Arthritis Rheum.* 1981;24:484–491.
4. Rockwood CA, Burkhead WZ. Management of patients with massive rotator cuff defects by acromioplasty and rotator cuff debridement. *Orthop Trans.* 1988;12:190–191.
5. Kelley WN, Schumacher HR. Gout. In: Kelley WN, Harris ED, Ruddy S, Sledge GB, eds. *Textbook of Rheumatology*, 4th ed. Philadelphia, Pa: Saunders; 1993:1293.
6. Neer CS. *Shoulder Reconstruction.* Philadelphia, Pa: Saunders; 1990.
7. Cofield RH. Arthrodesis and resection arthroplasty of the shoulder. In: McCollister EC, ed. *Surgery of the Musculoskeletal System.* New York, NY: Churchill Livingstone; 1983:109–124.
8. Neer CS, Watson KC, Stanton FJ. Recent experience in total shoulder replacement. *J Bone Joint Surg Am.* 1982;64:319–337.

Chapter 12

The Shoulder in Sports Medicine

PAIN AND DYSFUNCTION OF THE ATHLETE'S SHOULDER

To the practitioner treating a general population of shoulder patients, it does often seem that the serious athletes experience a different set of problems than the rest of the population. Athletes often complain of pain that occurs only after intense exercise or with a specific part of a complex motion used in their sport. The psychologic demands of and on many athletes, especially school-age athletes, are complex and changing, alternately producing amplification and suppression of symptoms. Athletic shoulder problems can be, pathophysiologically, simple and seemingly minor, yet because of the high physical output involved they can produce extraordinarily severe symptoms. For example, a 17-year-old swimmer with bilateral overuse of the internal rotators (Figure 12–1), after a week of excessive training and competition, required narcotics for excruciating pain at rest and had to sleep upright in a chair for 5 nights. No structural or metabolic problem was found, and symptoms resolved completely after rest and a change in her training schedule. The converse of this example may also occur. Many swimmers have highly subluxatable, nearly dislocatable shoulders that are barely symptomatic through years of high-output training.

This is not to suggest that the shoulder problems of athletes involve completely different anatomic or physiologic phenomena. Overuse of various musculotendinous groups, impingement, instability, acromioclavicular (AC) joint pain, synovitis, labral tearing phenomena, and fractures make up the bulk of sports-related shoulder problems. The operative difference with sports-related pathology is that it is often more difficult to diagnose. The excellent strength and tone of the shoulder girdle muscles in shoulder-intensive athletes can render useless diagnostic signs that may otherwise help make the diagnosis. Instability or complex impingement pain may be entirely pre-

Figure 12–1 The posterior shoulder girdle musculature of a competitive swimmer. Swimming athletes place tremendous, repetitive strain on the active and passive elements of the shoulder girdle. Note the latissimus dorsi bulk in this 17-year-old regional butterfly champion.

vented by muscular action until fatigue occurs, forcing reliance on underlying inadequate passive stabilizers or uncoordinated use of the cuff. The challenge and interest of sports medicine in shoulder practice rest largely in diagnosis.

As mentioned in earlier chapters, a somewhat different set of treatment rules exist for traditional and sports medicine practice. Most simply, sports medicine seeks relief for pain and dysfunction that arise from sport and prevent optimal performance in sport. It follows logically that return to sport is one of its primary goals. Patient motivation must be assessed at every meeting because of this. Most sports practice does not involve professional or even varsity level athletics. The boom in sports medicine spending in the United States has been created by recreational athletics. Even within large sports medicine orthopaedic practices taking care of professional teams, the bulk of surgical patients are not team members. The recreational patients may not have the same die-hard resolution to perform at all costs and should understand their specific treatment goals and options, including decreased output and prolonged abstention from the offending sport (ie, rest).

A different set of rules (or expectations) also applies to the athletic shoulder in regard to diagnostics. Although all the data described in the previous chapters are still needed, historical detail should obviously include specific information about the particular sport involved. It is important to study the motions of each sport in relationship to the individual patient's symptoms because there are some typical sports-related presentations with which the shoulder practitioner can compare the individual patient's data. These are useful when diagnoses seem vague or overlapping.

A major category of athletic shoulder problems involves throwing motions. Pitching and throwing in baseball and football, serving in tennis, javelin throwing, and other ballistic motion sports produce a large percentage of shoulder patients in sports medicine. Although simple overuse is the most common cause of athletic shoulder pain in general, impingement, instability, and their stepchild complex impingement present commonly with activity-related pain in throwers and servers.

Throwers' shoulder pain should not be considered in a single category because the range of underlying pathomechanisms is quite broad. Loose anterior capsules and tight posterior capsules are common findings in throwers, but they are not universal. Neither is anterior instability the underlying cause of all throwers' shoulder pain.

Swimmers develop strong internal rotators and adductors with relatively weaker external rotators. They also tend to stretch the anterior and inferior capsule, creating instability. Soreness of the rotator cuff may be a deceiving feature of the swimmer's examination; cuff signs unrelated to impingement may arise that are simply due to the high-stress output of the shoulder girdle musculature during serious training. Weightlifters and body builders can develop hypertrophy of the muscular portion of the supraspinatus, which produces impingement under the AC joint. They also frequently have unstable glenohumeral joints with labral tearing phenomena. These two problems and musculotendinous strain are more likely to explain a weightlifter's shoulder pain than "weightlifter's clavicle" (distal clavicular osteolysis). Competitive cyclists, martial artists, skiers, and wrestlers get AC separations and clavicle fractures with late AC joint pain. Long gun shooters (shotgun particularly) tend to develop traumatic anterior capsulitis and bicipital tendinitis from the impact of recoil.

The historical details necessary for proper diagnosis of athletic shoulder pain range from general health, performance, and psychologic aspects to the complex technical aspects of the athlete's specific performance in sport. The practitioner should ask not only about general health and athletic performance but also about the patient's standing within his or her sport. Is there an important game or meet upcoming for which training has been increased? Is the patient's position on the team being threatened? Has a new position, technique, exercise, or stroke been introduced? Cross-training can bring out a new range of shoulder symptoms. Changed or increased demand on muscles is a common source of shoulder pain.

Secondary gain issues are as prevalent in sports practice as elsewhere, and their presence should be appreciated. It is good practice to make a subtle and discreet determination of the patient's true desire to continue to play. A use-related shoulder pain may become intolerable when the patient really (but not admittedly) wants a medical excuse for getting out of the sport. This is a common situation with high school and college athletes under external pressure to stay in sport; questions such as "How important is it to your family that you continue to play?" may help open the patient up to discussion of this topic. Countless social, political, economic, and legal problems can stem from this area of inquiry. A record of these issues is best kept in the mind of the practitioner. It is nevertheless quite pertinent to many problems of athletic pain and performance. Parents and coaches can be remarkably insensitive to the problems faced by "big jocks." A sympathetic therapist, trainer, or physician who understands the big picture as well as glenohumeral instability can do much for these patients.

Symptom minification or denial is another psychosocial issue in athletes of which the practitioner must stay aware. This is not exactly the opposite of the above situation, but careful, repeated examinations and a good patient relationship are nevertheless essential to identifying it. A particularly difficult diagnostic situation arises when severe instability on examination (ie, a nearly dislocatable shoulder) is discovered in a patient who is believed to be denying symptoms for secondary reasons, such as not wanting to be dropped from a team or position. There is little that can be done here until both patient and practitioner come to a realistic understanding of the symptoms and their underlying cause.

Asking specific questions about cervical and neurologic symptoms is essential, particularly with contact sport participants, who frequently experience spinal cord or brachial plexus compression phenomena (burners or stingers). Although there is no clear association of these with hyperligamentous laxity or shoulder instability, high cervical radiculopathy should be a consideration when trapezius or parascapular pain is seen in a contact athlete. An occasional patient will only complain of decreased performance, not pain. The fastball or serve may be slower or less controlled, or an older patient may simply complain that "I can't swim anymore." Although some neuromuscular disorders (eg, syringomyelia, muscular dystrophy, some tumors, and nerve diseases) may present this way, it is unusual for any of the most common mechanical shoulder problems to exist without causing any pain at all. It is far more likely that admitting to pain is the patient's difficulty. Because a pain history is so essential to diagnosis, every effort must be made to gain this information without putting words into the patient's mouth. Use of a more "athletic" vocabulary may help with this type of patient, who, although tough enough to be untroubled by pain, may admit to feeling a "pull," "catch," or "stitch" around the shoulder that keeps him or her from being able perform as well as before. Once its existence has been established, the location of this "stitch" has been quite demonstrable in the author's practice.

The special details of physical examination of the athlete's shoulder begin with sport-specific provocation of the patient's pain. A thrower may need to warm up and begin throwing to demonstrate his or her pain. Having the patient move slowly through the throwing motion while applying resistance may be sufficient to elicit the pain, but if it is not, the patient should be allowed to throw. Differential injections of small amounts (2 to 3 mL) of anesthetic solutions are sometimes invaluable in the evaluation of the athlete's shoulder. These are made into the subacromial space, the glenohumeral joint, or the AC joint. Repeated throwing after each injection can demonstrate which general areas are generators of the patient's specific pain. Throwers and swimmers often have positive impingement signs that are rendered negative by a subacromial injection even though provocative testing shows no change in the typical pain (ie, after subacromial anesthetic and negation of the impingement sign, there is still pain with throwing or the resisted stroke motion of the swimmer). It is important that the patient not be examined only once after a heavy workout. Muscle soreness in this situation can make accurate diagnosis impossible. This is especially true for cases in which eccentric loading of deceleration- or recovery-phase muscles makes them sore and tender the next day. Upgrading one's strength testing evaluations is another physical examination issue with athletes. The same torque in subscapularis isolation might be rated 5+/5 in a small rheumatoid but 4-/5 in a big power lifter.

Most of the tests used in examining the painful athletic shoulder are no different than those used with the general population. These have been described in chapters on the specific ailments. The athlete should be examined in just about the same way as any other shoulder patient, the examiner's mind kept open to mundane, non–sports-related pathology as well as typically athletic problems. Because they are so often seen (and confused) in shoulder-intensive athletes, however, impingement, instability, and complex impingement should be attended to particularly on physical examination.

COMPLEX IMPINGEMENT

Throwing athletes with shoulder pain have been a common treatment problem for many years. A certain percentage of them have clearly defined impingement pain; some have clearly symptomatic instability. There has always been a significant fraction of this group with signs of both instability and apparent impingement. These patients have been treated conservatively with occasional good results. When treated operatively for impingement the results have not been as good, however, and the nonoperative treatment has not always been sufficient. A variety of terms describing this situation have been used: *complex impingement, glenoid impingement, secondary impingement,* and *dynamic instability.* Careful examination of this subgroup of patients can generally yield an understanding of the pathomechanics involved (Figure 12-2).

As initially described in Chapter 8 and most thoroughly addressed by Walch,[1] complex impingement generally presents with the complaint of pain in the anterior or posterior (more common) shoulder that is maximal at the beginning of the acceleration phase of throwing. There is no history of dislocation or even symptomatic instability in most patients; no catching, dead arm phenomenon, or radiation of pain is generally present. The physical examination is remarkable for full range of motion, mild to moderate anterior instability on shear stress tests, positive anterior apprehension pain, and a positive anterior relocation test (the pain produced by abduction and external rotation is decreased by direct posterior pressure on the humeral head). There is also a positive impingement sign, some pain with supraspinatus isolation testing, and some pain with forced horizontal adduction. Labral signs are variable. Posterior cuff isolation is painful if the shoulder has been recently worked but is usually not painful after a few days of rest. The radiographic work-up may show labral pathology or slight magnetic resonance (MR) signal alteration in the cuff tendons.

The key to making the diagnosis of complex impingement is the use of differential injection tests. When this type of patient is seen, rest, antiinflammatories, cuff strengthening and stretching, subscapularis and biceps strengthening, internal rotation and adduction stretching of the anterior capsule, and modalities for the cuff muscles are used. If symptoms persist or return, a differential injection test is performed. The subacromial space is first injected. This usually takes away the positive impingement sign but does not take away the pain of throwing, which is the patient's chief complaint. If throwing pain is completely relieved, the diagnosis of subacromial bursitis or pure impingement is suggested. An injection is then made into the glenohumeral joint, and the anesthetic is allowed to circulate within the joint by passive ranging of the limb. The examination is repeated, and throwing is generally found to be more comfortable. This implicates an intraarticular source of pain. The pain of the anterior apprehension test, and concomitantly the relief of the relocation test, are also lessened. No improvement in throwing pain at all implicates a muscular source.

The pathophysiology of complex impingement rests on anterior instability that is too mild or too well compensated by muscular tone to produce typical

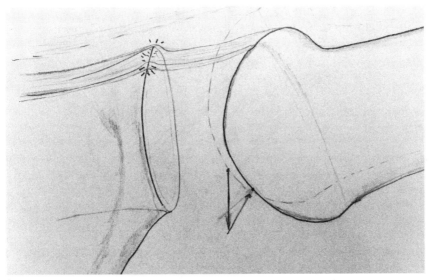

A

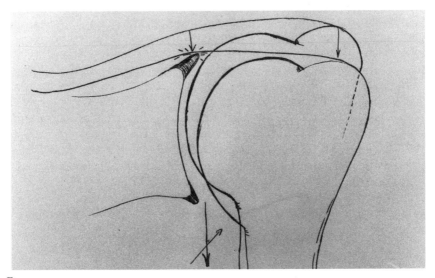

B

Figure 12–2 Complex impingement. Inferior (**A** and **B**) and anterior (**B**) translation of the humeral head during throwing motion causes impingement of the intraarticular surface of the cuff against the posterosuperior aspect of the glenoid labrum. Symptoms are similar to those of rotator cuff tendinitis. The underlying cause is mild dynamic anterior instability. Arrows indicate displacement of humeral head during throwing.

symptoms of instability (see Figure 12–2). In the absence of normal passive restraints to anterior translation of the humeral head, the rotator cuff is used reflexively to stabilize the joint. As mentioned earlier, the use of the cuff during the extremely rapid accelerations involved in throwing is not normal in high-performance throwers. As the cuff muscles fatigue, they fail to prevent anterior and inferior translocation of the humeral head. The cuff then gets dragged anteriorly and inferiorly, impinging against the posterosuperior glenoid. This impingement produces irritation of the cuff and the glenoid labrum somewhat posterior to the insertion of the long head of the biceps tendon. The actual pain of complex impingement is both that of the irritated cuff tendon (tendinitis pain) and that of the posterior capsule and labrum.

The best surgical procedure to correct the underlying instability that is responsible for complex impingement is a matter of considerable current debate in the orthopaedic community. The most basic reason for the debate is that truly high-performance throwing may not be possible after stabilization surgery. Although there have been published series in which the percentage of throwers returning to their previous level after stabilization surgery has been as high as 50%,[2] there is a good chance that return to throwing at the patient's previous level will not be possible after any open procedure. Because many complex impingers are still able to throw, albeit with significant pain, the surgery does carry the possibility of actually worsening athletic function.

Arthroscopy is often done on complex impingers; arthroscopic observations of the posterior labrum and cuff are often responsible for the discovery of the condition. Arthroscopic debridement is often done because it can be accomplished readily with little morbidity. Debridement of the ragged posterosuperior labrum and any hanging bits of the cuff (more cuff should not be taken) can give pain relief to some throwers. Nothing definite is accomplished toward stabilization of the glenohumeral joint by this, although there has been conjecture that some generalized tightening of the capsule results from the irritation of the arthroscopic procedure. Arthroscopic stabilization procedures done in the absence of a Bankart lesion include suture plication and laser cauterization of the anterior capsule. These have also been reported to be effective for instability symptoms (not complex impingement) in a few small series,[3,4] but doubt remains regarding their use in complex impingement.

In short, once the diagnosis of complex impingement is likely, every effort should be made to enhance cuff, subscapularis, and biceps strength and tone and to prevent anterior translocation during throwing using physical means because the optimal surgical treatment is not yet known. Only if, despite aggressive long-term treatment, the patient simply cannot play because of the pain should surgical treatment be considered.

GLENOHUMERAL PATHOLOGY AND ARTHROSCOPY

In addition to complex impingement, there are a number of other diagnoses of importance to athletic shoulder patients that are made primarily at arthroscopic examination of the glenohumeral joint. These include the superior labrum anterior posterior (SLAP) lesion, many cases of labral detachment and tearing that do not produce physical examination of MR signs, free bodies in the joint, and certain tears, stretches, or disruptions of the capsular ligaments (called thickenings of the anterior capsule). They do not include subacromial impingement, which is a diagnosis made on physical examination and injection test and confirmed, if necessary, by MR imaging. Arthroscopy is quite useful in the treatment of athletic shoulder problems because the procedure itself carries little long-term morbidity. An athletic shoulder (without significant pathology) can generally return to full, comfortable athletic performance within 2 weeks of a simple arthroscopic peek into the joint. Although it is certainly possible to overuse arthroscopy in general shoulder practice, with athletes whose diagnosis is not clear cut or who seem to have one of the problems for which arthroscopic surgery is an effective treatment, early use of arthroscopy can increase the efficiency and effectiveness of any physical treatment plan.

SLAP lesions have only been treated in the shoulder-intensive athletic population.[5] As mentioned in earlier chapters, the ability to detect these with any mechanism other than arthroscopy is questionable, despite the claims of MR arthrographers. A SLAP lesion includes any roughening, ripping, tearing, or avulsion of the superior glenoid labrum where it connects to the tendon of the long head of the biceps.[5] The symptoms of which patients who are found to have SLAP lesions complain are fairly typical labral tear symptoms. They include pain, catching, and snapping felt deep in the shoulder during abduction and overhead use in sports;[6] tennis and military press lifting exercises have been implicated in the author's practice. These patients have been brought to arthroscopy with the general diagnosis of intraarticular loose body and found to have SLAP lesions. There is no diagnostic physical examination sign for the SLAP lesion other than the click or thump felt on glenohumeral grinding that is indicative of labral pathology.

The underlying pathomechanics of the SLAP lesion are a matter of conjecture. The long biceps tendon and superior labrum are both stabilizers of the humeral head against superior shear, the one functioning as a check rein and the other as a doorstop.[7] Acute or chronic stress applied by the humeral head is believed to produce this damage to the tendon insertion and labrum.

The SLAP lesion is in a good location within the glenohumeral joint for arthroscopic debridement (done for low-grade fraying and degeneration) or repair with bone sutures (done for major detachments of the labrum and tendon). Postoperative rehabilitation must avoid glenohumeral shear and strong use of the biceps until healing is believed to be complete (2 months if there has been a repair). Full passive range is generally safe, however, and sling use is discontinued within 1 week of surgery. Treated thus, SLAP lesions generally have a good prognosis for return to full sports activity.

Capsular damage and intraarticular bony free bodies are often discovered in the same shoulders at arthroscopy. These are suspected when symptomatic instability, grinding, severe catching pain, and posterior joint line pain are found in an athletic shoulder that exhibits anterior or anteroinferior instability on shear stress testing. They are both the product of the anterior instability. Capsular damage or stretch in the absence of a true Bankart avulsion, as mentioned above, is not repairable by well-established arthroscopic means. Free bodies, which are often bits of the posterior humeral head or anterior glenoid (the fragments of the Hill-Sachs and Bankart fractures, respectively), can sometimes be extraordinarily difficult to find and remove arthroscopically. Occasionally, a bony free body can actually be sensed—not palpated but felt through the motion of the humeral head—on physical examination. Although many loose bodies eventually become synovialized and incorporated into the capsule, in the athlete they have the potential for causing significant damage to the articular surfaces. A serious attempt at arthroscopic removal is therefore the recommended treatment when free bodies are believed to be present.

MUSCLE AND TENDON INJURIES ABOUT THE ATHLETE'S SHOULDER

Overuse injury of muscle and tendon represents the most common cause of a painful condition about the shoulder in athletes. Although most athletes who experience an overuse injury do not seek professional treatment for it, there are sufficient numbers who do. This makes recognition and treatment of the common overuse injuries important tasks for the shoulder practitioner. A number of musculotendinous injury patterns are common; many are distinctly uncommon, although they are usually not difficult to diagnose if basic shoulder anatomy is kept in mind. The common injuries involve the rotator cuff, the biceps long head, the subscapularis (accompanying anterior dislocation), and the deltoid. The usual injury is intrasubstance tearing or stretching. Less common pathomechanisms include avulsion of the bony anchor points of the tendons, rupture or tearing of the tendons, and rupture of the red muscle substance itself. Much having been said about the unusual anatomy and pathophysiology of the rotator cuff tendons in earlier chapters, injuries to groups other than the rotator cuff are examined here.

The basic principles of muscular pathophysiology must be kept in mind when patients with overuse injuries about the shoulder are examined. A torn or stretched muscle generally exhibits three signs on physical examination: weakness, tenderness, and pain on contraction. Completely torn or avulsed musculotendinous units often exhibit a fourth sign: alteration in contour, a bulge or depression that is of new onset and is different from the surface anatomy of the contralateral side. Radiographic work-up for muscular overuse injury is often not necessary unless complete rupture or avulsion is a possibility. Little information about the muscles themselves is to be gained from plain film radiographs. MR imaging does demonstrate muscular anatomy and can give some information about the injury itself; bleeding, swelling, and tendinous disruption can be demonstrated by MR imaging of muscles. MR signal changes within muscle depend primarily on the relative water and fat content of the tissues. The signal changes are not specific; in fact, it is sometimes not possible to distinguish physical injury from tumor on MR imaging. The clinical situations in which MR studies are appropriately obtained include complete avulsions or ruptures of the biceps, the pectoralis major, and, of course, the rotator cuff. It should also be kept in mind that injuries to the musculotendinous structures about the shoulder should be diagnosed after fractures, metabolic disease, and neurologic disease are ruled out. The athlete's shoulder examination should not be any less complete than the nonathlete's.

Because musculotendinous injuries are common and not sports specific, the only historical detail that these problems have in common is a relationship to overuse. Complete ruptures generally happen acutely; stretch and strain injuries can often be linked to a particular episode of high output. Ruptures of the muscle belly do seem to be more likely when there has been direct, traumatic impact to this part of the muscle.[8]

A spectrum of overuse muscle injuries exists. Next-day soreness, traditionally considered related to the build-up in muscle of the chemical products of anaerobic metabolism (lactic acid), is the mildest form of overuse injury. Tenderness is diffuse, and symptoms regress within a week after simple overuse of red muscle. Muscle strain implies some physical stretch within the musculotendinous unit; *microtearing* is a term used to describe this. The actual damage is still microscopic, although serum values of creatinine phosphokinase, which reflect the destruction of muscle fibers, do rise as a result of the strain injury. Tenderness is still diffuse throughout the length of the strained muscle, and function (strength) is temporarily decreased. Strain injuries may take 3 weeks to regress, although regression is generally complete. The more severe the strain injury, the more likely it is that there will be shortening and fibrosis of the involved muscle. Rest and some stretching represent the general treatment.

Partial macroscopic tearing of the musculotendinous unit is the next clinical level of injury. Tenderness here is localized and rather severe. Macroscopic tearing typically produces ecchymosis (bruising) and pain in the location of the tear when the muscle is stretched. Although there is some current disagreement on this, immobilization traditionally has been added to the treatment formula when macroscopic muscle tearing has occurred. Complete disruption of the musculotendinous unit is at the most severe end of the spectrum. This disruption may be through bone, as in a tuberosity avulsion fracture; through tendon, as in a biceps tendon rupture; or through the red muscle belly. Treatment here must include reapproximation of the disrupted tissue if functional recovery of the musculotendinous unit is to be achieved.

Treatment plans for musculotendinous injuries of the athlete's shoulder should be based on a few simple principles, with clinical experience occasionally overriding these. First, patients must be reexamined at a time remote enough from the traumatic event for the generalized soreness of the shoulder girdle muscles to have subsided. It is then that the examination is capable of demonstrating specific areas of tenderness and weakness. The initial examination should be complete and rule out other acute problems as described. Second, rest is a must. Patients who have just injured their shoulder almost never benefit from exercise. A 30-second motion drill (forward elevation with external and internal rotation) done twice a day is sufficient to avoid preventable stiffness. Third, if surgical repair of a complete musculotendinous disruption is to be done, it should be done soon. Tendinous disruptions are not quite as emergent as ruptures of red muscle. The reactive changes after muscle ruptures are a part of healing, but delay of repair results in shortening of the musculotendinous unit. Contracture, scar, and fibrosis make both the surgical repair and the postoperative rehabilitation much more difficult and can compromise the final functional result.

Finally, acute muscle injury produces hyperemia and spasm. This is acutely (within the first 36 hours) best treated with cold application. Stretching and heat are generally best begun when local tenderness has just started to decrease. Stretching should be active assisted at first and then passive. Strengthening as a treatment and preventive measure against further overuse injury should not begin until tenderness is gone. Early strengthening exercises should be concentric and coordinated; eccentric isolation work is only done at the final stage of treatment.

Rupture of the long head of the biceps is the only acute musculotendinous disruption (besides rotator cuff tear) that is apt to be encountered with significant frequency. This problem may occur after a long history of impingement pain or bicipital tendinitis, or it may occur suddenly without any prior biceps symptoms. With or without symptoms, biceps rupture is usually the result of chronic bicipital tendinitis, which is usually related to subacromial impingement. Tendinitis of the long head of the biceps, related at least theoretically to overuse, is a common diagnosis in the athletic population as well and thus bears examination. Tenderness of the anterior shoulder (the area of the bicipital groove) that can be eliminated temporarily by injection of local anesthetic into this area is the most reliable sign of bicipital tendinitis (the long head of the biceps is understood in references to biceps tendinitis). Pain at this area or in the front of the arm with force supination of the forearm and a 90° bend in the elbow and pain with forced flexion of the shoulder while the elbow is straight and the forearm supinated are also seen in many, but not all, cases of biceps tendinitis. Because of variations in the depth and shape of the bicipital groove, subluxation and even dislocation of the biceps tendon may occur chronically and add to the mechanical irritation of the tendon. This can be detected by passively internally and externally rotating the abducted arm while palpating the bicipital groove.

A diagnosis of acute bicipital tendinitis should prompt a careful work-up of the shoulder. As seen earlier, impingement, rotator cuff tears, adhesive capsulitis, the SLAP lesion, and symptomatic instability can produce this type of anterior shoulder pain and tenderness. If the tendon ruptures before presentation, the same work-up and set of differential diagnoses apply. Rupture of the biceps tendon is usually noticed by the patient, who states "There was a pain in the front of my shoulder, and a lump appeared in the front of my arm."

The treatment for bicipital tendinitis is often the treatment of the underlying process that causes it, that is, impingement, frozen shoulder, subluxation of the biceps tendon (which can be corrected surgically), or glenohumeral arthritis. Modalities such as ultrasound and cold often provide symptomatic relief. These, coupled with antiinflammatories and rest, are able to control symptoms in about half the patients also being treated for an underlying problem that is thought to cause the tendinitis. Bicipital tendinitis as an isolated entity does exist, although it is less common.

When no underlying cause of the tendinitis is found, or if symptoms are severe, treatment by peritendinous injection can be quite gratifying. Injection of steroid and anesthetic agents into the sheath around the tendon is quite effective in relieving symptoms of the tendinitis. The symptoms of rupture of the tendon are said to be weakness of elbow flexion and supination as well as cosmetic deformity. Although the latter cannot be denied, the actual degree of elbow weakness is often quite mild. Surgical repair of the tendon rupture, once it has occurred, is recommended only for young athletic patients (in whom the rupture is more likely to be related to pure mechanical loading to failure during sport).The underlying reason for the surgery is to return strength to as close to normal as possible. There is often much pressure from patients to have this obvious injury repaired. Direct suture repair or insertion of the tendon into the bone of the upper humerus (tenodesis) can be accomplished surgically, although the repair must be protected for at least 2 months (no active elbow flexion or resisted extension and decreasing intermittent sling use for the entire period). The humeral head depressive function of the biceps tendon is lost after tenodesis. The weakness that results from loss of the long head of the biceps as an elbow flexor and supinator is negligible for most people, even serious recreational athletes. The cosmetic deformity of the permanent lump on the front of the arm is also well tolerated.

Patients with biceps ruptures who are treated nonsurgically do not generally require physical therapy unless they are having symptoms referable to rotator cuff disease and impingement. The loss of the humeral head depressing effect of the long head may intensify impingement symptoms, necessitating treatment for this.

Deltoid tendinitis is seen in kayakers and white water canoe enthusiasts, whose propulsive force is largely applied by pushing upward and forward on the upper end of the paddle. It is mentioned, among a vast range of shoulder girdle musculotendinous overuse injuries, because it produces pain in the deltoid insertion area, where so many other pathologic entities (see Chapter 8) seem to produce pain. The difference in the case of deltoid tendinitis is that the problem really is located where it hurts. This area is tender as well and hurts particularly when anterior deltoid isolation maneuvers are attempted (eg, forward flexion).

TRAINING, PROPHYLACTIC MEASURES, AND PREHABILITATIVE TREATMENT

Most patients treated in a sports medicine practice eventually graduate from rehabilitative treatment to sports training. This is an implicit goal of most surgical and rehabilitative treatment. It must be kept in mind that the goal of training is enhancement of athletic performance per se, whereas resumption of physiologically normal (and comfortable) function was the goal of rehabilitation. Return to coaches' and athletic trainers' supervision and leaving the direct care of physicians and physical therapists has often marked the end of rehabilitation and the beginning of training. This demarcation, in actual practice, is becoming increasingly blurred, with trainers being involved in rehabilitation and therapists participating in training exercise. Without casting judgment on the propriety of this, anyone involved with the athlete's return to sport—therapists, trainers, coaches, and even families of athletes—should be aware of the important clinical decision that is made with every shoulder patient at this point of beginning training. Serious athletic training involves a shifting of the athlete's focus of attention away from his or her shoulder and onto the sport. It implies the lifting of restrictions.

"Unrestricted activity," "full contact," "advancement as tolerated," and "activity ad lib" are perilous orders for the physician in sports medicine. Shoulders treated operatively and nonoperatively are injury-prone joints. Athletic shoulder practice includes many cases, as often seen in swimmers, in which nothing done in the rehabilitation setting even closely replicates the muscular output of the unrestricted workout. Athletic injuries related to glenohumeral instability are treated with strengthening of the stabilizing muscles. These can be expected to fatigue as training is advanced, permitting higher levels of subluxation than seen during rehabilitation and possibly being accompanied by recurrent symptoms. Contact sports introduce the elements of externally applied dislocating forces and eccentric contractions of the cuff, which must absorb the energy of running and falling bodies. Complete safety of any joint, especially the shoulder, cannot possibly be guaranteed in this environment.

Maximizing the safety with which the athlete returns his or her shoulder to training is the goal of the final phase of rehabilitation. This should always include sport-specific coordinating exercises and progressive rehabilitation level practice of the shoulder-intensive maneuvers used in the sport. These rehabilitation-training exercises are more sport specific than disease specific. Whether cuff disease, instability, or even a fracture has been treated, when it is no longer producing signs or symptoms with daily living activities it must then tolerate the sport-specific stresses with which it will be tested in unrestricted training. Throwers are given a graduated schedule of throwing starting with forearm tosses and working up to half-speed pitching. Tennis players start serve practice with throwing also, then progress to a slice serve without a ball, then to a flat serve, and finally return to the twist serve. Weightlifters with instability are often a problem because some of the exercises used in their training necessarily place concentrated stresses on nonmuscular elements of the glenohumeral joint (ie, the capsule and labrum). These structures cannot be expected to strengthen or hypertrophy significantly even if exposed to gradually increasing levels of stress. It is nonetheless the goal of most weightlifters to lift as much weight as possible in specific positions, which may injure an unstable glenohumeral joint or a torn glenoid labrum. The only logical resolution of this is either to restrict activity, prohibiting external rotation and abduction lifts and exercises such as flies and reverse flies (which are apt to injure a partially torn labrum), or to correct the instability or loose labral tear surgically before returning the patient to unrestricted lifting.

No professional in athletic medicine will argue against maintenance of a strong and toned shoulder girdle as a way to increase performance and generally minimize the risk of shoulder injury in sport. There has not been a study showing a decreased incidence of instability and cuff injury, the two most serious and common athletic shoulder problems, in patients with superior shoulder girdle musculature, however. It might be found that the incidence of these problems is actually increased. Weight trainers with glenohumeral instability are common. There are also many seen with chronic cuff pain caused by impingement of the thick, hypertrophied, musculotendinous junction of the supraspinatus on the hypertrophied AC joint. These patients do experience symptomatic relief when they stop training the cuff muscles or "debulk," but if they do not do this it is senseless to think that their impingement symptoms will respond to muscle strengthening.

A good deal is written and discussed about modifications of sports activities to accommodate shoulder disease. Strain or overuse injury may (theoretically) be avoided if muscular strength and elasticity (flexibility) are improved. Changes in swimming style (increasing body roll), pitching style (increasing weight transfer, lumbar motion, and lean), tennis style (also favoring body, spine, and leg motion over shoulder motions), and warm-up procedures (to include posterior capsular stretching and cuff coordinating exercises) have all been suggested as training modifications that might prevent further instability and cuff-related pain.[9] All these measures can be considered to have both training and prophylactic value. Proper training may be considered to have both increased performance and decreased injury as its goals. The role of the shoulder practitioner in sports medicine practice must therefore extend into the training phase of treatment. Even if not by means of actual patient visits, this can still be accomplished through imparting a clear understanding of the pathomechanical issues and an overall training-phase treatment plan. When the physical challenge of returning to serious sport is anticipated, training-phase treatment entails prehabilitation of anticipated injury as well as finalized rehabilitation of the injury originally treated.

REFERENCES

1. Walch G, Liotard JP, Boileau P, Noel E. Posterosuperior glenoid impingement—another impingement of the shoulder. *J Radiol.* 1993;74:47–50.

2. Bigliani LU, Kurzweil P, Schwartzbach CC, et al. Inferior capsular shift procedure for anterior shoulder instability in athletes. *Am J Sports Med.* 1994;22:578–584.

3. Caspari RB. Arthroscopic reconstruction for anterior shoulder instability. In: Paulos LE, Tibone JE, eds. *Operative Techniques in Shoulder Surgery.* Gaithersburg, Md: Aspen; 1991:57–64.

4. Tibone JE. The facts about arthroscopic stabilization. Presented at the American Association of Orthopedic Surgeons' Course on the Shoulder; March 1994; Marco Island, Fla.

5. Snyder JJ, Karzel RP, DelPizzo W, et al. SLAP Lesions of the shoulder. *Arthroscopy.* 1990;6:274–279.

6. Paulos LE, Graver D, Smutz WP. Traumatic lesions of the biceps tendon, rotator interval and superior labrum. *Orthop Trans.* 1990;15:85–86.

7. Rodosky MW, Harner CD, Fu FH. The role of the long head of the biceps and superior labrum in anterior stability of the shoulder. *Am J Sports Med.* 1994;22:11–130.

8. Heckman JD, Levine MI. Traumatic closed transection of the biceps brachii in the military parachutist. *J Bone Joint Surg Am.* 1978;60:369–372.

9. Jobe FW, Tibone JE, Jobe CM, Kuitne RS. The shoulder in sports. In: Rockwood CA, Matson FA, eds. *The Shoulder.* Philadelphia, Pa: Saunders, 1990:981–988.

Chapter 13

Fractures about the Shoulder

Fractures of the upper humerus, clavicle, and scapula are considered in this chapter. Fractures about the shoulder are common (the clavicle is the most commonly fractured bone in young people).[1] Their occurrence is usually traumatic and painful, and their diagnosis is generally straightforward, by means of plain film radiographs. Patients with acute fractures around the shoulder rarely leave a practitioner wondering why the shoulder hurts.

Fracture diagnosis and treatment may nevertheless be quite complex. For many shoulder fractures, the concomitant soft tissue injuries are often more serious than the bone injuries. Evaluation of these injuries may not be aided by much information from the physical examination. Instability of the fracture itself, as well as pain and muscular splinting, prevent much of the usual physical examination of the shoulder. Even in cases of nondisplaced fractures, the examination is limited by the desire not to cause displacement. Examination of patients with shoulder fractures should therefore stress neurologic function, skeletal deformity, and localization of tenderness, ecchymosis, and soft tissue swelling. Complete X-ray studies are obviously the most important radiographic examination. Magnetic resonance studies are not commonly obtained after acute fractures because they add little to bone imaging and because soft tissue imaging is likely to be confused by swelling and bleeding.

Reference to the corresponding chapters should be made when one is considering fractures with concomitant capsular injuries (dislocations or subluxations, Chapter 9), rotator cuff injuries (Chapter 8), acromioclavicular (AC) joint injuries (including distal clavicle fractures, Chapter 10), or the late effects of intraarticular fractures (posttraumatic arthritis, Chapter 11). Although a discussion of the definitive orthopaedic care of shoulder fractures is not the objective of this presentation (it is well described in a number of excellent reference texts).[2,3] the general principles of diagnosis, pathophysiologic evaluation, and treatment of the major shoulder fractures are important for each practitioner treating the shoulder patient. These are described, along with some surgical and rehabilitation specifics, on the more difficult and common bone injuries.

Reduction of a fracture or dislocation is the process of putting the fragments into anatomic, or roughly anatomic, position. The treatment sequence for most shoulder fractures is to reduce, immobilize until healing creates sufficient bony stability to permit safe mobilization, mobilize, and then strengthen. The actual need for anatomicity in reduction is quite variable, depending on the location of the fracture, functional demands of the patient, and concomitant soft tissue injuries. Fractures of the humeral shaft up to the surgical neck (that part of the shaft immediately below the tuberosities) can heal with tremendous angulation, shortening, and displacement without creating any noticeable functional deficit, deformity, or pain. Fractures of the humeral head's articular surface, on the other hand, can cause arthritic pain, loss of motion, and even joint instability if displaced by so much as 1 cm.

Reduction, when necessary, may be achievable by closed means (closed reduction) and then be stable (ie, stay reduced) or unstable. Geometric stability is the stability achieved by virtue of the shape of the fractured ends of the bone. Good geometric stability is achieved when the ends of the fractured bone (the fracture surfaces) somehow "lock" into each other. This can be seen with extremely irregular fracture fragments. Poor geometric stability is seen with a simple, straight, transverse, linear fracture. No interdigitation or locking can occur because of the geometry of the broken bone in this case.

Loss (or expected loss) of a necessary closed reduction and inability to achieve a closed reduction are valid reasons for performing open (surgical) reduction. Generally, some sort of surgical appliance, suture, wire, screw, rod, pin, or plate is used at the time of open reduction to stabilize the bone fragments, preventing loss of reduction. It is rare that the construction achieved at surgery is physically strong enough to permit significant use of the shoulder. Mobilization, in most cases, must wait until the natural healing of the fractured bone has created enough mechanical integrity (fracture stability) to permit stress and motion of the shoulder without loss of fracture reduction. It is a basic orthopaedic principle that, in the absence of bony healing, (most) surgical constructs used for internal fixation of fractures will eventually loosen, detach from bone, or break if subjected to the usual stresses applied to the bone in daily living activities.

Open reduction with internal fixation is not the only surgical procedure used for fractures about the shoulder. In addition to soft tissue reconstructions of the rotator cuff or other structures, replacement of the humeral head with a prosthesis is commonly performed in cases of proximal humeral fractures that destroy or render avascular (and therefore incapable of healing) the humeral head. These proximal humeral replacement procedures are similar to those done for degenerative disease (see Chapter 11) with the major difference of concomitantly involving reduction and internal fixation of the greater and lesser tuberosities. Rehabilitation of these patients must be done with greater attention to the replaced and internally fixated tuberosities than to the humeral head, which, once replaced, is strong enough for full usage. Avoidance of rotator cuff and subscapularis contraction for up to 6 weeks is therefore encouraged after this procedure or any procedure that involves reattachment of the tuberosities to the humerus.

MUSCULAR DISPLACEMENT FORCES

The muscular forces that produce the typical displacements of shoulder fractures cannot be controlled by voluntary or active means. All muscles around a fracture contract at some time, and if no geometric or surgical stability of the fracture has been achieved this will result in loss of reduction or fracture displacement. The major displacements are produced by the strongest, unopposed muscles. If positioning the arm to offset the effects of the displacing muscles is ineffective or intolerable, further surgical stabilization may be necessary.

The major displacing force on the upper humeral shaft is the pectoralis major. It pulls the shaft medially with respect to the humeral head and tuberosities when there is a fracture of the surgical neck. The tuberosities, when separated from the rest of the humerus, are obviously pulled by the subscapularis and rotator cuff; the lesser becomes displaced medially by the subscapularis, and the greater goes superiorly and medially under the influence of the cuff. If both tuberosities are attached to the humeral head (with a surgical neck fracture), this upper humeral fragment becomes rotated, as if the arm were abducted or forward elevated (Figure 13–1).

Glenoid and humeral head fractures are not displaced significantly by muscle pull because they are largely free of muscular attachments. Acromial fractures may be pulled downward a bit by the deltoid, but the trapezius provides some upward pull, and the tough, fibrous deltotrapezial periosteal aponeurosis also prevents wide displacements. The clavicle has a number of ligaments holding its distal end down to the scapula (or coracoid), the pectorals and deltoid pulling it downward and the trapezius and sternocleidomastoid pulling it upward. Displacement of clavicular fractures is well tolerated by most patients, and midshaft or distal fractures are not often widely displaced by muscle pull.

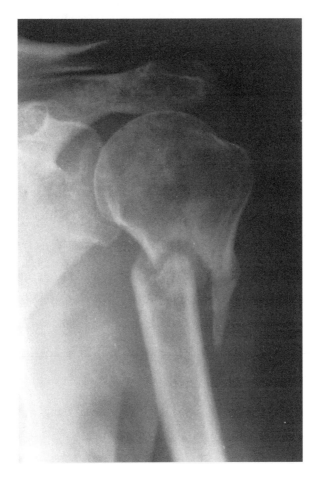

Figure 13–1 Radiograph showing a healed, displaced humeral shaft fracture.

A host of physiologic and metabolic factors influences the rate and strength with which fractures heal. The time that one must keep in mind as a baseline minimum for fracture healing (meaning initial bony stabilization with about half the ultimate strength) is 6 weeks. Fracture healing time is shorter in young children and longer in the elderly. Brain and spinal cord injury occasionally has a mysterious effect, accelerating the rate and vigorousness of the fracture healing response. Heterotopic ossification (the de novo growth of bone within soft tissues) is also commonly seen in these patients. Most other pathologic states do the opposite of this, slowing and weakening the healing of fractures.

The bone around the shoulder has a generally excellent blood supply, and fractures given adequate reduction and immobilization usually heal. The only bone that does not heal well is the actual dome of the humeral head if it is left as a free, unattached fragment. In this case it has no definitive blood supply and can be expected to die, necessitating prosthetic humeral head replacement. Nonunion, or the failure of a fracture to heal with satisfactory bony stability, is favored by distraction and motion at the fracture site. This is a serious complication that can often be avoided by sufficiently long immobilization and, of course, by never distracting or applying axial traction to an unhealed fracture.

Most shoulder fractures are immobilized in a sling or sling and swathe, the swathe being any strap that wraps around the body to hold the humerus to the trunk. Abduction or airplane splints are occasionally used with upper humerus fractures because the abducted or forward elevated position helps achieve or maintain reduction. These are removable orthotics that must not be removed until some fracture stability has been achieved. Because this usually takes at least 3 weeks and these are extremely ungainly splints, there is a tendency for orthopaedists to use nonremovable shoulder casts, called shoulder spicas, to immobilize this type of fracture. Spica casts are also rather uncomfortable and must be worn for about 6 weeks. Instead of the spica cast, the option of having the fracture surgically stabilized with a few pins or wires, permitting the use of a simple sling during the healing period, is often chosen by patients.

GENERAL PHYSICAL TREATMENT OF SHOULDER FRACTURES

Although there will obviously be variations based on fracture type and other clinical features of the patient, some general principles of fracture care apply to a broad range of shoulder fractures. These begin with elbow, wrist, and hand mobilization. Swelling and stiffness of the ipsilateral hand and forearm after shoulder fractures of every type are expected. The functional deficits created by loss of hand and elbow motion may be severe; especially in older patients, the stiffness and sensitivity of the hand and wrist created by the shoulder fracture may carry with them greater discomfort and functional disability than the fracture itself. It is therefore imperative to maintain as much motion as possible, both active and passive, of the hand, wrist, and elbow from the first contact with the fracture patient.

After an acute fracture, most patients are overwhelmed by the pain they are experiencing. The first lesson that their broken bone teaches is that it hurts to move it. This creates the instinctive tendency to hold the arm and forearm close to the body and to avoid any active use of the hand and wrist. Unless a truly extraordinary situation exists, such as concomitant fracture of the wrist or elbow, the elbow can be slowly extended to $0°$ and flexed to $120°$ without moving the fracture site or causing an unbearable increase in fracture pain. Similarly, the wrist can be slowly dorsiflexed and volar flexed, and the hand can be made into a fist and fully opened. These are important exercises to begin as soon as possible; it is especially true of shoulder fractures that stiffness is much easier to prevent than to reverse.

Changes of local circulation to the entire involved upper extremity, including skin temperature, sensitivity, and sympathetic tone, are common, being the rule rather than the exception after there has been a fracture around the shoulder. A gradation of this phenomenon may be observed from normal (mild) postfracture hypersensitivity to a full-blown reflex sympathetic dystrophy of the upper extremity, or shoulder-hand syndrome. Stiffness and weakness of the hand, wrist, and elbow are among the most detrimental elements of this problem. If they are anticipated early on in every shoulder fracture patient, the frequency with which the practitioner treats postfracture sympathetically mediated pain syndromes will be decreased. There are many psychologic elements involved in reflex sympathetic dystrophic pain and dysfunction. Knowing that the hand and elbow of the fractured upper extremity still work, the patient may avoid some of these. In the author's practice, hand, wrist, and elbow range of motion exercises are taught on the day of fracture.

Deciding scientifically when to begin passive range of motion after fractures around the shoulder is difficult for the orthopaedist. Insufficient immobilization increases the risk of nonunion or fracture displacement and malunion. It also is uncomfortable for patients to move unstable fractures, which may lead to higher levels of sympathetic tone in the extremity. Overlong immobilization may result in unnecessary stiffness or muscular weakness. It is generally safer to err on the side of too much immobilization because the problems it causes are more readily reversed.

One of the traditional methods of deciding when to permit gentle passive motion of the shoulder after upper humerus fractures has been to palpate the humeral head above the fracture line while passively moving the arm from the elbow. If the upper and lower humerus are felt to move as a unit, then passive motion is begun. It is commonly seen that fresh fractures of the upper humerus can move as a unit if some gentle upward pressure is applied to the arm during rotation but not if the weight of the arm is left unsupported. Similarly, contraction of the deltoid by pulling the shaft of the humerus upward may produce some compression of the fracture site, promoting motion as a unit. Clavicle fractures are treated similarly by some practitioners. Clavicle fractures are subcutaneous and easily palpated, and motion is permitted within the range that is believed not to produce any motion at the fracture site.

The surgical experience of exposing proximal humeral, scapular, and clavicular fractures at various time intervals after fracture has shed some light on the decision as to when passive motion is safe to begin. Before 7 days in middle-age patients, nonimpacted fractures do not really have any stability due to fracture healing. The muscles, tendons, and ligaments around the shoulder can provide some stability for small bony fragments, and of course impaction of fracture fragments (jamming or crushing of bone fragments into one another) does tend to stabilize them. Impaction is not uncommon around the shoulder because most of the bone is cancellous (spongy), capable of being reduced in volume by crushing forces. During the second and third weeks after fracture, initial fibrous changes in the blood clot that fills the spaces between fractured bone ends do impart some degree of mechanical stability. At surgery, fractured bone fragments after approximately 10 days must be pried apart to be manipulated. There is also a noticeable contraction of the soft tissues around the fracture site, which also imparts some stability to the fracture. Cortical bone is much less stable than cancellous bone at 3 weeks; shaft fractures of the humerus are still quite unstable at 3 weeks.

Given the wide range of personal preferences among orthopaedists, and of course taking patient age and clinical factors into account, it is possible to make a rough time table for when passive motion should be started after various shoulder fractures. These are described with the specific fractures. Patient and practitioner alike must be aware of the arbitrariness of these figures, however, and not be reticent to abandon or decrease motion maneuvers temporarily if they appear to be producing fracture motion, increased swelling, or excessive pain.

The general care of patients with shoulder fractures also involves much of the consideration of activities of daily living and nightly sleeping. In the middle of so much muscle and fat, relatively unconstrained by any external apparatus, and sliding around on a thorax that moves with every breath, shoulder fractures are difficult to immobilize. As a result, patients with shoulder fractures, especially in the first week, are an uncomfortable lot.

A few tricks can be used to increase their comfort. Most basic is the swathe. Although the strap that goes around the patient's waist that is supplied with many commercial shoulder immobilizers is properly termed a swathe strap, it is not as secure as one that is made specifically for the purpose of pinning the humeral shaft to the thorax. A simple, wide (15-cm) elastic bandage, wrapped around the affected humerus and trunk, makes many patients more comfortable than the sling alone. Sleeping is easier for most acute shoulder fracture patients in the semiseated or upright position. Many pillows, taken off the sofa if needed, may be stacked at the head of the bed to keep the trunk upright. A large, soft lounge chair may be a preferred place to sleep. Patients with clavicular or acromial fractures often experience some pain relief with scapular retraction. A small rolled towel placed between the scapulae while sleeping supine can benefit these patients. With most other shoulder fractures, a pillow under the affected side's elbow in bed provides comfortable support. Obese, short, and large-breasted patients may do better with the elbow extended and the shoulder a bit more abducted on the pillow.

Finally, cold therapy is effective around the shoulder, but the traditional bag of ice is a rather ineffective means of delivery. The commercially available, anatomically formed ice water bladders (eg, the Cryo-Cuff) have been of greater benefit to patients with acute shoulder fracture pain.

Modalities other than cold have limited usefulness for patients with acute shoulder fracture pain. Although an occasional report is made of great pain relief with early use of transcutaneous electrical nerve stimulation, this is not reliable and is infrequently prescribed. Muscle spasm associated with acute fracture may be severe, and limited application of heat, electrical stimulation, and ultrasound to the palpably spasmodic area only (these should not be applied to the fracture site itself) can be helpful. Acute fracture pain is more appropriately treated with medication than most other chronic painful conditions about the shoulder. The pain of fracture is expected to be limited in duration, and it is quite severe; this is a good indication for limited use of mild narcotic analgesia. Similarly, oral or intravenous muscle relaxant medications may be easier to use and more effective than physical treatments. Physical therapy for the fractured shoulder is more useful in the later stages of healing and rehabilitation.

Admission of patients with acute shoulder fractures to hospital beds is becoming less and less frequent as hospital utilization review departments make admission criteria more stringent. Older patients with upper humeral fractures (and no other significant injuries) are still often admitted because they are simply unable to take care of themselves. The pain of these injuries is often quite intense, and admission is justified for a short time by the need to administer injectable narcotics. Physical medicine consultation may be made during these hospitalizations for treatment of the shoulder injury and may serve as another justification for inpatient treatment. There is little besides hand, wrist, and elbow range that can be done for the fracture itself. Early range of motion for the shoulder will not be appropriate for at least 1 week (and generally longer) after the fracture. Physical treatment may be quite valuable to the patient if assistance with and practice of activities of daily living are stressed. Merely getting dressed and putting on the shoulder immobilizer are major tasks for many older patients with shoulder fractures. An already unsteady gait may become much more so with the arm in a sling, and the use of a cane or walker may become impossible. It is therefore quite common for shoulder fractures to render patients incapable of unassisted ambulation and therefore incapable of independent living. Although most shoulder fractures in this older age group are treated nonoperatively, a surgical procedure, if necessary, may certainly decrease further the frail elderly patient's ability to return to independent living.

Platform walkers or hemiwalkers are sometimes more easily managed by this type of patient. As long as the walker is being used for stability only (ie, the patient is bearing full weight on both lower extremities), early "cheating" out of the sling and onto the walker is often well tolerated with the impacted upper humeral fractures that are common in this osteoporotic group. A highly comminuted (broken into many pieces) or widely displaced fracture may not permit this. A cloth loop around the neck may be used as an accessory sling during bathing or changing clothes. Reach-extending devices as well as active hand and elbow exercise equipment may be helpful. (No significant resistive strengthening is done here, but confidence in and function of the hand and elbow are improved with exercise within the patient's ability.) The increased disability that shoulder fractures bring to this fragile group of patients may be addressed quite effectively by physical treatments in the inpatient as well as outpatient settings.

SPECIFIC FRACTURES

Humeral Shaft

Fractures involving the cortical tube of the humeral shaft are not properly shoulder joint fractures but require much of the same type of care. This type of fracture is usually the result of direct trauma to the arm (Figure 13–2). Throwing athletes occasionally experience a sudden displaced fracture of the midshaft of the humerus while throwing hard (Figure 13–3). Nondisplaced stress fractures may also occur in the athletic population. The humeral shaft is also a common site of pathologic fractures caused by tumor destruction of the bone (Figure 13–4). These fractures may damage the radial nerve as it wraps around the humerus in close apposition to the bone. The ability to dorsiflex the wrist as well as light touch sensation on the radial dorsum of the forearm and hand should always be checked. Humeral shaft fractures are usually treated nonoperatively; quite a few good studies have demonstrated that complications are significantly less common when these fractures are treated closed.[4] Techniques for immobilizing the humeral shaft vary quite a bit among orthopaedists. The hanging cast, a plaster or Fiberglass circular cast from the upper arm to the hand with the elbow flexed 90°, was a standard treatment method until good studies showed it to produce a much higher rate of nonunion than

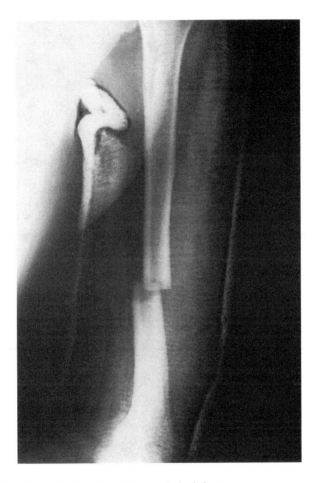

Figure 13–2 Radiograph showing a humeral shaft fracture.

other methods.[5] Early immobilization of the humeral shaft in coaptation splints (plaster or Fiberglass splint slabs on the medial and lateral surfaces of the arm and forearm) is now popular. These are believed by most clinicians to be the early treatment of choice. They do not allow elbow motion.

As soon as there is some radiographic evidence of healing (2 to 4 weeks), the coaptation splints may be changed for a Sarmiento type humeral orthotic. This is a plastic cuff that can be tightened around the entire arm (Figure 13–5). It does not rely on bone contact for control of motion as a tibial or forearm cast does but rather attempts to utilize a fluid containment principle to prevent

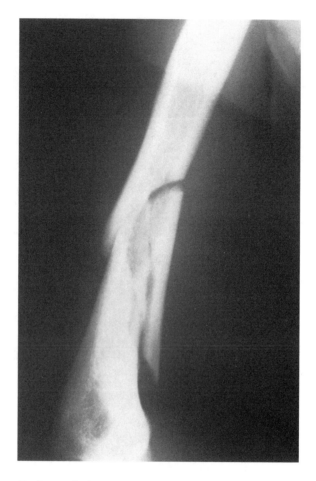

Figure 13–3 Radiograph showing a spontaneous distal humerus fracture that occurred in a 27-year-old athlete while throwing.

gross motion of the fracture. The fleshy arm is encircled by the cylinder of the orthotic like a balloon in a pipe. The bone in the center of the arm is thus protected from bending and twisting stress, although it is still subject to muscular forces and quite a bit of micromotion, which is believed to be physiologic and a stimulant to fracture healing. Patients usually require 2 to 4 months in the Sarmiento type orthosis before it can be safely removed, the fracture being healed sufficiently to resist normal living stresses.

Nonunion of humeral shaft fractures is a significant threat and is considered every time this fracture is treated. Early motion is not a major consideration

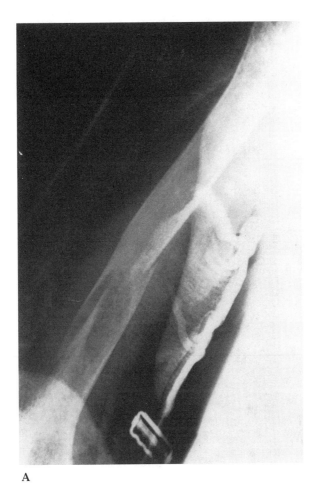

A

Figure 13–4 (A) Radiograph showing a pathologic fracture. Note moth-eaten quality of bone. This is due to invasion by tumor.

because the fracture does not actually involve the shoulder joint; shoulder motion will eventually be restored with physical therapy, whereas nonunion, resistant sometimes to multiple surgical procedures, has been seen by every orthopaedist. Traction on the arm, carrying, and twisting are obviously not allowed while the orthotic is worn. Gentle elbow motion is permissible when further healing is seen. This is detected on serial radiographs and clinical examinations as increased stability and decreased tenderness at the fracture site.

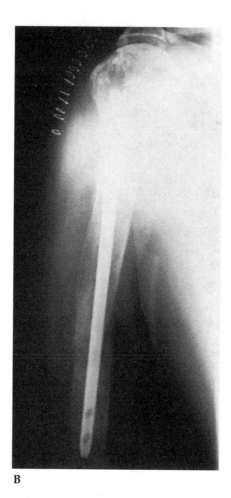

B

Figure 13–4 (B) Radiograph showing a pathologic fracture treated with intramedullary rod fixation. After fixation with a titanium intramedullary rod, stability and alignment are restored.

Humeral shaft fractures treated operatively have traditionally been fixed with metallic plates held fast with screws to the humerus. These constructs are notoriously weak in torsion. They are best protected with the same orthotics that would have been used had the surgery not been done. Special indications for open reduction and internal fixation of humeral shaft fractures usually include the presence of other injuries besides the humeral shaft fracture. These include nerve injuries that appear to involve actual laceration of the nerve and concomitant fractures below the elbow (the "floating elbow"). The plates can

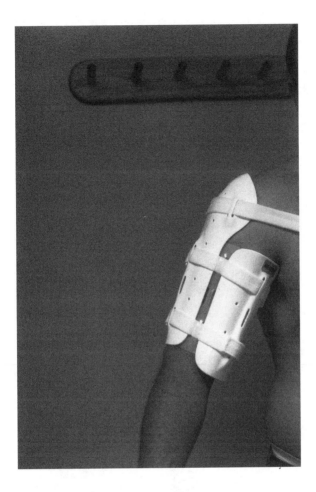

Figure 13–5 Sarmiento type orthosis used for humeral shaft fractures.

break, the screws can lose their purchase on the bone, and the fracture can fall apart months after the surgery. Humeral shaft fractures treated with plate fixation therefore must be protected from stress until healing is ensured. This may take 4 months. Other methods of internal fixation of the humerus are used less frequently because not all fracture patterns are amenable to these methods of fixation. The intramedullary fixation techniques may be more stable in terms of permitting earlier motion of the shoulder because they are less prone to mechanical failure. Humeral shaft fractures may be fixed with intramedullary rod fixation, external fixation, and simple pinning. The caution with all these is against distraction of the fracture because nonunion rates are still higher than those seen with nonoperative treatment.

Proximal Humerus

Upper humerus fractures, including those discussed earlier, represent the most important group of shoulder fractures in combined terms of severity and frequency. When the humeral head itself is significantly damaged or broken off from its blood supply (which comes only through adjacent bone), it must be replaced with a prosthesis (Figure 13–6). Failure to do this leads to a chronically weak and painful shoulder. The humeral head replacement operation usually entails surgical reattachment of the tuberosities to the humeral shaft (Figure 13–7). The results of this procedure are variable. Although the majority of patients are made comfortable, functional return is often poor. Because it is most frequently done in older patients, there may be problems due to age-related factors such as weakness, preexisting cuff disease, and the like. A good proportion of patients treated with proximal humeral replacement for fracture

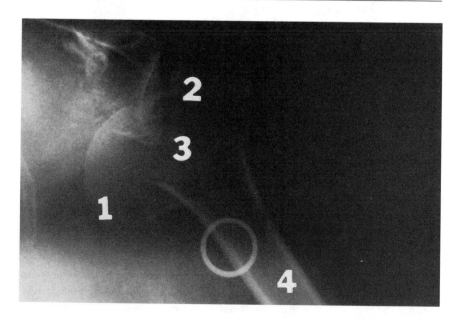

Figure 13–6 Four-part fracture-dislocation of the shoulder. 1, Humeral head; 2, greater tuberosity; 3, lesser tuberosity; 4, humeral shaft.

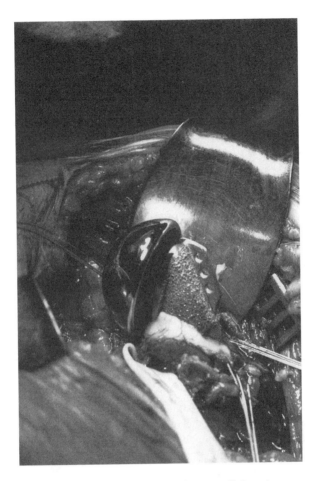

Figure 13–7 Reconstruction of the four-part fracture-dislocation.

never regain more than 100° of active forward elevation despite massive physical therapy and rehabilitation efforts. Cuff and subscapularis weakness seems to be one reason for this. Another seems to be difficulty in coordinating the deltoid with these other two groups. Improved results in rehabilitation have been obtained with early use of overhead pulley elevation exercises. In the past these were not allowed because they do involve some active assisted use of the cuff muscles. With greater confidence in the surgical stabilization of the tuberosity fragments, earlier, gentle use of these muscles has been permitted with appreciably better ultimate cuff and deltoid function.

A number of technical and surgical factors may account for some patients' inability to elevate actively after humeral head replacement. Shortening the humeral head's thickness by putting in too low or too short a prosthesis loosens the myofascial sleeve within which the fulcrum of the glenohumeral joint functions. This may create relative deltoid and cuff weakness. The other problem, making the head too long, also prevents motion by making the joint too tight. These length differences are small and cannot be appreciated on physical examination, although they may be on radiographs. Humeral head damage is often seen in fracture-dislocations of the shoulder. Axillary nerve injury occurring with fracture-dislocations may be obvious and may explain late deltoid weakness, or it may be more subtle, requiring electromyographic evaluation. Neurologic function of the cuff and deltoid should be considered whenever functional return is slow after proximal humeral replacement.

Early passive motion, with the possible use of pulleys as mentioned above, should be started while patients are still in the hospital after proximal humeral replacement for fracture. Pendulum exercises are begun on the first postoperative day, as are hand, wrist, and elbow motion exercises. By 6 weeks, patients should have nearly full passive range in forward elevation and external rotation and internal rotation to the base of the spine. It is at this time that active deltoid and cuff strength is critically assessed and active assisted use of these groups is begun. Patients should expect to be in formal outpatient physical therapy for at least 3 months and possibly for 6 months after humeral head replacement for fracture. Some patients, especially younger ones, may go through rehabilitation much faster, but as a rule the reattached tuberosities leave the cuff and subscapularis weak for at least 2 months.

Fractures of the proximal humerus that do not devascularize or otherwise irreparably damage the humeral head may still require surgery for open reduction and internal fixation of the tuberosity fragments or, occasionally, for reduction of the glenohumeral joint and repair of the capsule and/or rotator cuff. The indications for this type of surgery are based on the expected outcome when the fracture is treated closed. Significantly large displacement of the fragments and rotation or angulation of the upper humeral segment with respect to the humeral shaft can be expected to result in permanent loss of motion or subacromial impingement. The displacing muscle forces described above are most often responsible for the inability of closed reduction to address these displacements adequately; redisplacement is likely to occur unless secure surgical fixation is achieved.

A great variety of fixation methods have been employed in dealing with proximal humeral fractures. Plates and screws are useful in younger patients with hard bone; in older patients the bone of the upper humerus is often extremely soft, deformable by a hard pinch with the fingers. Screws do not achieve much purchase in this soft bone and may cut out, leaving the fracture to fall apart and sharp metal loose in the shoulder: an unhappy outcome. Wires and heavy sutures are used when soft bone is encountered to tie down the tuberosities and the humeral head–bearing fragment to the humeral shaft. Pins or solid rods, from coat hanger wire to soda straw thickness, may be laced longitudinally down through the upper humeral fragment and into the shaft. These do not provide rigid fixation on their own, but when used to anchor one end of a loop of wire or heavy suture (Figure 13–8) they can create a construct that is strong enough to permit early shoulder motion. Upper humeral frac-

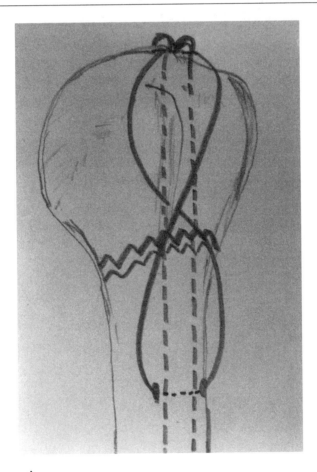

A

Figure 13–8 (A) Tension band construction diagram.

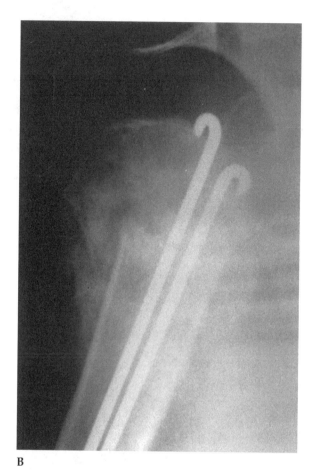

B

Figure 13–8 (B) Tension band construction radiograph. Only longitudinal pins are visible on the radiograph because the suture is radiolucent.

tures are properly considered shoulder joint fractures. Early passive range of motion is a significant benefit in their rehabilitation if it does not result in displacement or angulation. A strong construct is thus quite an advantage. Only the surgeon can determine whether and how much early motion is safe to use after a particular operation (Figure 13–9); ranging the shoulder during the procedure and testing the rigidity of the fracture construct under direct vision constitute how this determination is made.

Rehabilitation after open reduction and internal fixation of a proximal humeral fracture goes through the same phase as most postoperative shoulder work: rest, passive motion, active motion, and resistive exercise. If sufficient

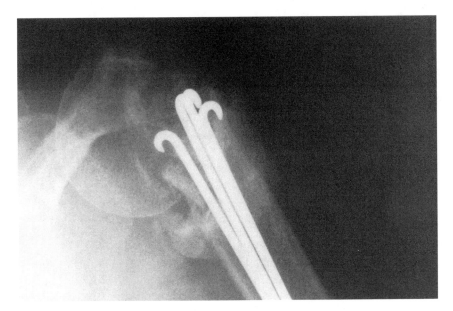

Figure 13–9 Radiograph showing a failed surgical reconstruction of a proximal humeral fracture given early motion with loss of surgical fixation.

stability has been achieved at surgery, passive elevation may begin the day after surgery. The orthopaedist should be asked about this to prevent myriad problems for patient, physician, and therapist alike. The shoulder motion that is least likely to produce displacement is generally believed to be pendulum exercise, but even this must be ordered by the operating surgeon. In practice, many surgeons put the operated arm into a sling and leave it there for 6 weeks. This may actually be necessary with certain fracture constructs to prevent displacement or angulation. A stiff shoulder will be found at the end of this period. Progressive range of motion exercises are obviously needed; they must be done with fracture stability still in mind, however. The quality of healing at 6 weeks after surgical fixation is not always good. Starting here with pendulum exercises and advancing to oval (anterior cuff) pendulums and passive forward elevation is generally safe.

There may have been significant elevation of the greater tuberosity or the soft tissues covering it as a result of fracture, surgery, and healing. Impingement of this tuberosity on the anterior acromion or undersurface of the AC joint is common and may limit forward elevation in some patients. Emphasis on scapular retraction during elevation is helpful when this occurs. The impingement is of a different nature than that seen with most rotator cuff patients. A soft tissue component seems to be present, perhaps of postfracture reactive tissues around the tuberosities. It may also be difficult to distinguish true impingement pain from the general pain of the fracture and attached and contracted cuff and capsular tissues. The impingement pain and impediment to forward elevation often diminish spontaneously as cuff strength improves. The problem remains in the early postoperative period, however, so that resistive work on the cuff cannot be done until fracture healing is secure. When patients are begun in therapy 6 weeks after surgery, active assisted motion may be used with the added benefit of decreasing this impingement phenomenon.

Acromioplasty with resection of protuberant tuberosity bone after fracture healing and strengthening is occasionally necessary. Acromioplasty at the time of open reduction and internal fixation is not often done because clearance of the acromion by the tuberosities seems to be adequate during the initial procedure. Statistics have not been compiled to justify the routine use of acromioplasty, although its use in selected cases has been associated with rapid return of motion. Waiting at least 6 months after open reduction of upper humerus fractures before considering any secondary procedure is advised. A period of complete cessation of physical therapy and exercise is recommended for patients who continue to have impingement-related pain and stiffness for more than 4 months after open reduction and internal fixation. This "therapy vacation" can help symptoms dramatically in a subset of patients.

Upper humeral fractures treated nonoperatively are the most commonly encountered and display the widest range of clinical courses. Some patients with slightly displaced surgical neck fractures (the most common pattern, with the fracture line occurring just below the tuberosities) have tremendous pain and stiffness, requiring long, difficult rehabilitation to regain motion and strength. Others may wear a sling for 10 days and have a sore shoulder for a few weeks more but otherwise require no therapy of any sort to return to full functional use of the shoulder. Fracture stability must be judged from radiographs and clinical examination with motion permitted accordingly. Subacromial impingement of the greater tuberosity may be a problem with nonoperatively treated upper humeral fractures even when the degree of displacement of the tuberosity is minimal on radiographs. With the same considerations given to this phenomenon as in the operatively treated fractures described above, after 6 weeks of fracture healing time progressive ranging should be quite aggressive. A postfracture syndrome of pain, sensitivity, and stiffness has often been observed by practitioners treating patients who have had minimally displaced tuberosity and surgical neck fractures of the humerus. Contributing elements theoretically include impingement as described above, sympathetically mediated pain, and idiopathic adhesive capsulitis.

Prolonged, aggressive stretching and strengthening have always been used with these patients with eventual return to normal shoulder function.

A full range of motion that is otherwise attainable should not be foregone because the patient (or therapist) is squeamish about some (possibly) impingement-related pain. The rotator cuff will not be torn by stretching in elevation. The actual mechanism by which this pain abates may be that the proud tuberosity is somehow "massaged down" by the impinging acromion during elevation stretching. Strong antiinflammatories and other pain medications are useful during this phase of therapy. Early, gentle motion is obviously desirable after upper humerus fractures, as long as bony stability is adequate. A completely different level of aggressiveness is necessary once contracture has developed. Fractures must be healed (6 weeks) before this type of aggressive ranging is done.

Scapula

The acromion, glenoid, coracoid, and scapular body (the shoulder blade itself) are all considered here parts of the scapula. Besides the Bankart type fractures mentioned in earlier chapters, scapular fractures are not an enormous clinical problem. They are not common. They heal reliably within 6 weeks and, with some glaring exceptions, usually do well clinically regardless of how they have been treated. The scapular fractures that pose the greatest problem are those associated with serious multiple trauma, those associated with chest and neurovascular injuries, and those that destabilize the glenohumeral joint. The articular surface of the glenoid must be surgically reconstructed if more than half of it is significantly displaced by a glenoid fracture. This is primarily to prevent instability of the joint. Posttraumatic arthritis due to glenoid fracture is not a major concern because it has only rarely (and questionably) been observed. As long as the humeral head is centered within the glenoid fossa, open reduction with internal fixation of glenoid fractures is an elective procedure, done to restore anatomicity and to prevent possible long-term joint problems. To a practitioner used to seeing symptomatic relief from resection of a glenoid labral tear, the urge to fix a fracture of the glenoid itself is quite strong. Clinical evidence of poor shoulder function resulting from failure to fix even displaced glenoid fractures simply has not accumulated, however.

Similar considerations exist regarding fractures of other parts of the scapula. Acromial fractures generally result from direct impact, although there are some avulsions that occur at the AC joint capsular insertion sites. Loss of the deltoid origin and impingement on the rotator cuff are problems that can be avoided by anatomic surgical repair here. The fractured scapular body can heal with a frighteningly large displacement and not be a source of any symptoms. Sling immobilization until comfort permits active and passive motion of the shoulder is the treatment of choice in this country. A number of European surgeons do perform extensive plate and screw reductive procedures for scapular body fractures, for reasons that are unclear. The scapulothoracic pain and crepitus that radiographs of jagged, malunited scapular fractures lead one to expect have not been a clinical observation.

Coracoid fractures may occur as part of an AC separation (intact coracoclavicular ligaments avulsing from their coracoid insertion) or from direct trauma, especially in individuals who shoot high-power rifles or shotguns.[6] If displaced, these heal with a fibrous union that, in at least one instance in the author's practice, has been a source of chronic pain and tenderness (Figure 13–10). Coracoid fractures differ from other scapular fractures in their treatment; longer immobilization (6 weeks in a sling or abduction splint) is recommended for this truly extraarticular apophyseal fracture. Use of the coracoid-based muscles (biceps and coracobrachialis) is obviously discouraged during this time.

Clavicle

The clavicle is a unique bone. Those born without clavicles seem not to experience any particular shoulder problems other than the ability to bring their shoulders together under the chin. Large, displaced fractures, nearly poking through the skin, generally heal with only a bump to remind the patient of the experience, whereas small avulsions and even microscopic cracks near the end of the bone (eg, weightlifter's clavicle) can cause pain that requires surgery. Fractures of the clavicle that are treated closed and are not AC separations through bones (see Chapter 10) can be expected to heal completely without long-term sequelae (except for the bump) about 99.9% of the time.[7] Neurologic, vascular, and pulmonary evaluations are, of course, necessary in the work-up of acute clavicle fractures because of the proximity of these structures to the traumatized bone. Many types of immobilization, including slings, harnesses, casts, and bandages, can be used to treat acute, closed fractures of the clavicle. A butterfly or figure-of-8 harness and arm sling used together are the author's usual choice. Although some orthopaedists believe it is important to achieve reduction and to hold it while the fracture heals, most agree that the clavicle is difficult, if not impossible, to hold reduced in the ambulatory patient without internal fixation. The main purpose of the devices applied to patients with acute clavicle fractures is to make them comfortable while the fracture heals.

There are specific indications for performing open reduction and internal fixation on clavicle fractures. They include open fractures and those in which

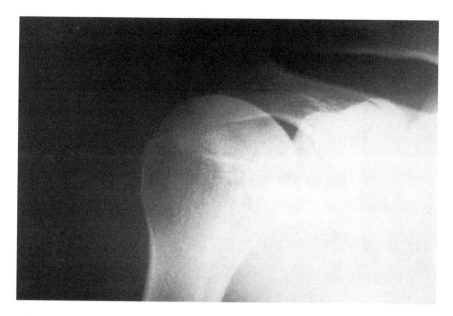

Figure 13–10 Radiograph showing a fracture of the coracoid (dark line), which is just visible at the superior surface of the coracoid process.

the skin is nearly broken by clavicular fragments as well as neurovascular compromise created by pressure of the fracture fragments on the subclavian artery, subclavian vein, or brachial plexus, all of which are nearby. The distal clavicular fracture that is just medial to the clavicular insertions of the coracoclavicular ligaments (the AC separation through bone) is another relative indication for open reduction and internal fixation because of its high rate of nonunion and permanent shoulder girdle deformity. Its pathomechanics are well understood.

The type II fracture of the distal clavicle is caused by a mechanism similar to that of AC separation. Downward force on the shoulder girdle causes failure of the passive suspensory apparatus of the shoulder girdle. In the case of AC separation, the coracoclavicular ligaments and AC joint capsular tissues fail, permitting the shoulder girdle to fall relative to the clavicle. In the case of this special type of distal clavicle fracture, the ligaments and AC capsule remain intact, but the clavicle itself, just medial to or within the insertion area of the ligaments (there are two coracoclavicular ligaments: the conoid medially and the trapezoid laterally), fractures (Figure 13–11). This permits the outer end of the clavicle to fall down with the shoulder girdle while the inner end is held up by muscles (such as the sternocleidomastoid and the trapezius). This fracture

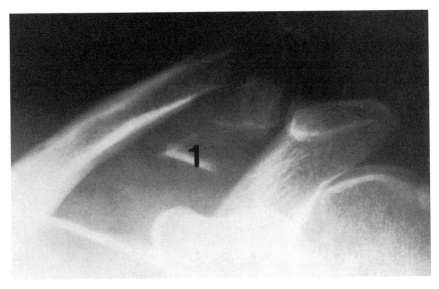

A

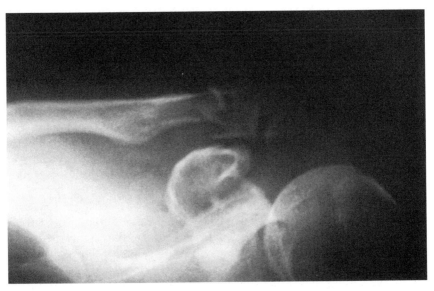

B

Figure 13–11 Radiographs showing distal clavicle fractures (AC separations through bone). **(A)** Grossly displaced with fragment coracoclavicular ligament (1) clearly visible. **(B)** A more common pattern with less displacement.

might heal if immobilized and reduced using an externally applied brace, such as the Kenny-Howard brace (see Chapter 10), but it does have a strong enough chance of going on to symptomatic nonunion. Barring medical contraindications, surgery is recommended as soon as the diagnosis, which is by simple plain film radiographs, is made. This surgery involves reduction and pin, screw, or suture fixation of the fracture as well as fixation of the medial clavicle down to the coracoid in many instances (Figure 13–12). This type of surgery accounts for the majority of clavicular fixations that are done, perhaps because, although these fractures represent less than 10% of clavicle fractures, they produce the great majority of clavicular nonunions.

Rehabilitation after open reduction and internal fixation of clavicle fractures, including the type II distal clavicle fracture described above, is most dependent on adequate healing of the fracture itself. These are all extra-articular fractures that do create some muscular stiffness and weakness but, when healed, do not leave specific capsular or tendinous contractures, as upper humeral fractures do. Bone healing is most threatened by motion that is too aggressive or too early. As with humeral shaft fractures, these patients will get their shoulder motion and strength back eventually as long as the fracture heals and the surgical construct is kept intact. Any surgically treated clavicle should have at least 6 weeks of sling immobilization with regular elbow, hand, and wrist motion as the only exercise. Isometrics are not particularly desirable during this first 6 weeks. If they are done forcefully, they can place excessive strains on the internal fixation devices. The clavicle is mostly cancellous bone that does not offer a particularly secure purchase for screws or pins placed in it. Motion is usually begun at 6 weeks or later if radiographic healing has not yet taken place (more distal fractures often take longer to heal). The usual sequence of passive, active, and resistive exercise can be followed with rapid advancement in most cases once bone healing is secure.

A specific activity restriction that should be maintained for at least 4 months after surgical fixation of a clavicle fracture is avoidance of contact sports. The clavicle is a frequent site of reinjury after fractures have ostensibly healed. This may be due to the disuse-weakened arm's decreased ability to fend off danger or to the relative fragility of the healed clavicle. Cyclists frequently have clavicle fractures. Going over the handlebars again in the 12 months after a clavicle fracture carries a greater than usual chance of breaking the same clavicle again.

Rehabilitation after closed treatment of clavicle fractures may simply be a matter of gradually permitting full activities of the shoulder. Many patients continue to have night pain and difficulty sleeping on the affected side as their only symptoms once the initial fracture pain has subsided. This night pain is relieved by sleeping supine or with a rolled towel between the scapulae. Tran-

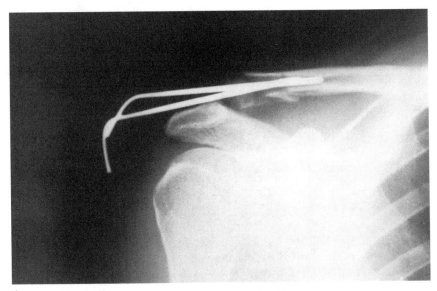

A

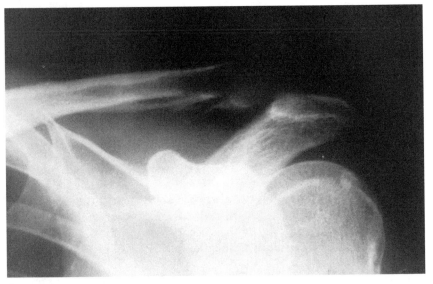

B

Figure 13–12 (A) Surgical reconstruction of a distal clavicle fracture with pinning of the fracture and repair of the fragment bearing the coracoclavicular ligament to the clavicle. (B) Same clavicle after removal of pins and bone healing.

scutaneous electrical nerve stimulation has been quite effective for night pain in the few patients who have required help beyond mild narcotic analgesia. A circulating cold water bladder has been similarly effective in a few instances. Quite a few patients with clavicle fractures are never referred for physical medicine treatment. Return of normal shoulder function is usual after the clavicle heals as long as the patient is motivated to resume normal function and does not have other shoulder disease. Early pendulum or passive motion exercises are often prescribed to decrease the duration of shoulder stiffness. Their efficacy has not been established scientifically. Care should be taken to avoid traction on the arm and horizontal abduction/adduction, which tend to create fracture site motion. Scapulothoracic stiffness is a common finding after clavicular fractures have healed. Rehabilitation should emphasize scapulothoracic as well as glenohumeral motion in coordinated exercises for the entire shoulder girdle. Neck pain and stiffness are similarly complaints of many patients whose clavicular fractures have healed. Neck motion, especially in patients with cervical arthrosis, may be started early (7 to 14 days after the fracture) to avoid this.

REFERENCES

1. Neer CS. Fractures of the clavicle. In: Rockwood CA, Green DP, eds. *Fractures in Adults.* Philadelphia, Pa: Lippincott; 1984:703–713.
2. Rockwood CA, Green DP, eds. *Fractures in Adults.* Philadelphia, Pa: Lippincott; 1984.
3. Crenshaw AH. *Campbells' Operative Orthopedics*, 7th Edition. St. Louis, Mo: C.V. Mosby; 1987.
4. Scientific Research Committee, Pennsylvania Orthopedic Society. Fresh midshaft fractures of the humerus. *Penn Med J.* 1959;62:848–850.
5. American Academy of Orthopedic Surgeons. *Orthopedic Knowledge.* Update 3. Chicago, Ill: AAOS; 1990.
6. Boyer DW. Trap shooter's shoulder: Stress fracture of the coracoid process. *J Bone Joint Surg Am.* 1975;57:862.
7. Neer CS. Non-union of the clavicle. *JAMA.* 1960;172:1006–1011.

Chapter 14

Less Frequent Disorders of the Shoulder

STROKE SHOULDER

The combination of motor and proprioceptive loss, pain, and stiffness in patients who have experienced a cerebrovascular accident (CVA) often represents a truly mysterious disease entity recognizable by any practitioner who treats stroke patients regularly. Stroke shoulder follows brain damage and is typically produced by loss of blood circulation to specific areas of the brain that control motor function. Brain damage occurring through other mechanisms, such as head injuries, viral or bacterial infections, anoxia, degenerative neurologic disease, or multiple sclerosis and tumors, may present with aspects of stroke shoulder with similar contractures and pain. These, too, are upper motor neuron disease states affecting voluntary control of the shoulder girdle musculature. Stroke shoulder tends toward a specific presentation, however, whereas these other entities have more variable signs and symptoms.

After a stroke affects voluntary motor control of the shoulder girdle musculature, many patients experience no shoulder pain (other than weakness or paralysis) at all. Those who develop stroke shoulder may do so at any time after the stroke, although it is most common within the first 18 months. Spasticity of the involved muscles is usually seen in these patients, but this is not universal; flaccid paralysis can be accompanied by the exact pain and stiffness seen in patients with pronounced spasticity. Contracture in internal rotation, adduction, and neutral elevation is by far the most common pattern after a stroke. The pectorals and subscapularis seem to over-pull the cuff muscles and deltoid in the vast majority. Occasionally the cuff muscles contract more powerfully than the adductors, leaving an abducted and externally rotated arm, but this pattern is more common in head injury and multiple sclerosis. Pain is usually the symptom that brings the patient to the shoulder practitioner, how-

338

ever, and it is this pain that is the least clearly understood element of stroke shoulder.

The pain of developing stroke shoulder is not clearly related to traction on the glenohumeral joint capsule or brachial plexus, although the humeral head does sag down inferiorly out of the glenoid, and the scapula often rotates to point the glenoid more inferiorly.[1] The pain may seem to be related to traction on the plexus because of its character. Downward traction increases pain in some stroke patients. Elevation of the humerus to its usual station within the glenoid should be tried, but slings and splints should not be used excessively, especially if they do not improve the pain. This is to avoid increasing stiffness. Stroke shoulder pain is not clearly related to the developing contracture of the shoulder, although there are many patients in whom this would seem to be true because their typical pain is most intense at the ends of range. In addition, there is often a phase in its development in which the entire glenohumeral capsule is tender, resembling the early inflammatory phase of adhesive capsulitis. The pain of stroke shoulder is not clearly related to acromioclavicular (AC) joint arthritic changes or rotator cuff tears, both of which are often present in these patients. It does not respond reliably to periarticular or intraarticular steroid injections. It may increase, along with the contractures, even while prophylactic physical therapy is being done to avoid contracture. Stroke shoulder may also be a self-limited disease, at least in terms of pain, because few patients are seen who have had significant pain for more than 3 years in the absence of another diagnosis.

The first step in treating stroke shoulder is to avoid wrongly jumping to the diagnosis. There are other entities that produce pain and stiffness in the affected shoulder of patients after CVA. Cervical radiculopathy and infection have been discovered in patients thought to have stroke shoulder. The neurologic examination of the stroke patient will present many positive findings that generally require a neurologist to sort out; attention to the sensory findings of the upper extremity may suggest a peripheral nerve lesion, such as cervical radiculopathy. Hyperactive deep tendon reflexes are common after strokes because the spinal reflex arc is intact but the nerve pathways that are involved with modulation of the reflex are defective. The examination of the neck is obviously important as well. A flabby, fluid-filled swelling around the shoulder is usually due to a longstanding rotator cuff tear; if this is hot and tender, however, it must be aspirated to look for infection.

The AC joint is often somewhat tender in stroke patients. When tender, it may be the underlying cause of the frozen shoulder and most, or even all, of the patient's pain. Injection testing with local anesthetic is then indicated. Subacromial injection testing is similarly appropriate if signs of cuff disease are present. It is difficult to theorize how impingement-related phenomena can occur with the humerus drooping down and active elevation lost, but the cuff is often tender and sore in these patients. Spasm of the cuff musculature may be involved. The biceps groove may similarly be a source of inflammatory tendinitis if it is tender in the stroke patient; a mechanical irritation caused by abnormal muscle mechanics may be similarly invoked as a cause without any real underlying evidence.

The diagnosis of various neuropathic pain syndromes in stroke patients with shoulder pain is made problematic by the fact that stroke shoulder itself is probably a neuropathic pain syndrome. Sympathetic mediated pain (reflex sympathetic dystrophy) and thalamic infarction pain syndromes may certainly be present as distinct pathophysiologic causes of the patient's shoulder symptoms. Local vasomotor changes, cutaneous hypersensitivity, and hyperalgesia with mottled osteopenia on radiographs and local increased isotope uptake on bone scan suggest sympathetically mediated pain. The evolution of the neurologic deficits (especially the significant sensory loss after the stroke) and the detailed neurologic examination itself suggest the thalamic pain syndromes.[2,3] Despite the complexity of these and other pathophysiologic mechanisms, all of which may produce shoulder pain in the stroke patient, physical treatment is generally straightforward. The stroke shoulder needs motion.

Thermal modalities, hot and cold, help decrease pain during mobilization exercises. With stroke shoulders, both should be tried and the results compared. Many stroke patients do better with cold before passive ranging, a finding that is not seen with other causes of contracture. Ultrasonation is useful in those patients who do better with heat. Electrical stimulation has not been helpful; neither has transcutaneous electrical nerve stimulation (with the rare exception). Motion is necessarily passive with these patients because they generally have no active control of the shoulder girdle muscles. Unlike mobilization of other types of frozen shoulders, mobilization of the stroke shoulder should not include axial traction on the humerus. Simple but persistent supine forward elevation, external rotation, and internal rotation are done passively with modalities, pain medication, and muscle relaxants as needed and as tolerated. The sling may be used for pain relief before and after therapy, but its use for more than 1 month is avoided.

It must be kept in mind that the end points of treatment are quite specific with stroke patients. Motion sufficient to bring pain down to tolerable levels is the primary goal of treatment. It is generally true that restored motion is associated with decreased pain. Active motion or strength goals are unrealistic and most often unattainable for stroke patients with paralysis of the shoulder girdle musculature. The functional demands on the shoulder may include little other than ambulatory aid use. In this case, the adduction and internal rotation must be decreased sufficiently to get the hand to a walker or cane. Elbow flexion contracture may prevent this as well. It is a typical concomitant. A good-quality arm sling is regularly tried if traction on the arm increases pain or if axial force directed superiorly seems to relieve pain. Sufficient padding of the shoulder strap is needed to prevent pressure problems with the skin over the trapezius; if effective, this sling is worn quite tightly. Straightening of the elbow should be practiced at least three times daily while the sling is in use.

Orthopaedists with interest in performing surgical releases for the tissue contractures that attend stroke shoulder believe that they are often necessary.[4] The majority of orthopaedic surgeons do not, however, and believe that satisfactory functional return and pain control can be achieved through physical therapy. Avoiding contracture of the shoulder through prophylactic range of motion exercises is a basic concept in the treatment of any joint that has lost active control. It certainly applies to the shoulder, and daily ranging of every shoulder affected by a stroke is recommended. Stroke shoulder often develops despite dutifully performed daily motion, however, and must therefore be treated with a significantly higher level of aggressiveness. Respected sources have in the past recommended the exact opposite of this, however,[5] with rest being the recommended early treatment. The idea of relieving the pain of stroke shoulder by letting immobilization-induced contracture occur seems to be based on the contracture's ability to prevent the downward subluxation of the humeral head. This is questionable.

The appropriateness of surgical releases for rapidly developing contractures and intolerable pain must be determined individually. Intellectual humility in the face of this disease process is necessary. The excellent (long-term) results that have been achieved by some practitioners[6] using only non-surgical treatments for stroke shoulder do stand against the findings of others who, in the treatment of longstanding, painful contractures, have made extensive use of surgical releases with good relief of symptoms as well.[4] These latter findings prevent the blanket statement from being made that all patients eventually regain passive range and stop experiencing pain without having to undergo a surgical release.

The therapeutic implications of our paucity of true understanding of stroke shoulder are easily summarized. First, the pain of stroke shoulder does seem to be related to loss of motion; therefore, efforts should be aimed at maintaining or increasing range. The pain itself has some neuropathic character and some mechanical character related to periarticular inflammation, inferior humeral subluxation, and soft tissue contracture. Therapeutic motion should therefore be accompanied by appropriate modalities and should not be so rough as to overstimulate neural or inflammatory pathomechanisms. Second, other shoulder pathology must be considered, both mechanical and neurologic. Third, immobilization or rest and surgical releases are available as alternative treatments for patients whose symptoms are unrelieved by persistent physical treatments.

CALCIFIC TENDINITIS OF THE ROTATOR CUFF

This is a common cause of the "hot" shoulder. Patients with calcific deposits may have truly severe pain and may be actively splinting to the extent that walking, coughing, or even breathing deeply is avoided. Less dramatic presentations of calcific tendinitis are also seen with cuff pain and tenderness that are intensified by use (but, significantly, not completely relieved by rest). The shoulder with calcific tendinitis is tender; the actual tenderness is maximal in the area of the deposits themselves, but the level of tenderness may be so high as to produce a shoulder that hurts, and is tender, "everywhere." There is no typical history; chronic subacromial impingement would seem to be a causative element, but usually it is not present. Patients do experience some relief with oral antiinflammatory medications in most cases. Pain develops over days or months and may resolve spontaneously and completely, especially if there has been a rapid development.

The biggest sources of diagnostic confusion in calcific tendinitis are the rotator cuff weakness and soreness and the positive impingement sign that are often present when the pain is acute. There may even be partial improvement in all these upon subacromial injection testing with local anesthetic. The distinction between rotator cuff tear and calcific tendinitis of the rotator cuff is based on both the presence of acute pain with rest and radiographic findings (Figure 14–1); calcium deposits are readily visible on shoulder films, although special views may be needed with the arm in different rotations to visualize the calcium.

The pathogenesis of calcific tendinitis is poorly understood. The insoluble calcium salts seen on radiographs precipitate out in areas of the rotator cuff tendons (all three may be involved) in which the normal tendon tissue has been damaged in some unknown way. Mechanical, vascular, and metabolic theories have been advanced with no clear favorite. There can be some resorption of the salts through cellular phagocytosis. The radiographic appearance of resorption, breaking up, and partial disappearance of the deposit is associated with increased pain and locally increased vasculature around the deposit. Pain during the growth of the calcific deposit (the formation phase) is generally less or absent.[7] Rotator cuff tears are often seen at surgery for calcific tendinitis, but the deposits are not necessarily near the tears. Longstanding tears of the cuff may produce calcified deposits within the tendons that are

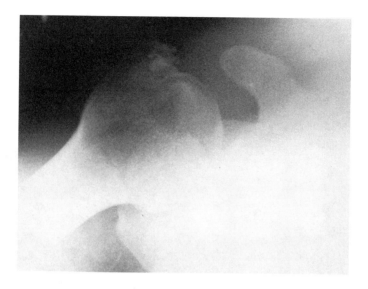

Figure 14–1 Radiograph showing calcific deposits in the rotator cuff (calcific tendinitis).

visible on plain film radiographs. These are streaky and stippled (Figure 14–2), however, as opposed to the lumpy and rounded deposits seen with calcific tendinitis.

The treatment of calcific tendinitis is far better understood than its cause. The most direct method of relieving the patient with acute pain is termed needling or barbotage; a rather large-bore (18-gauge) hypodermic needle is used to poke and pierce the deposit repeatedly, disrupting and sucking up the calcium as much as possible (its consistency varies from that of loose toothpaste to that of farmer's cheese) and bathing the area with local anesthetic and steroid. Radiographs and physical examination are used to localize the deposit for this needling; as usual, the injection is made at the exact point and in the exact direction in which tenderness is maximal. This is usually lateral to the middle third of the acromion. The needling is followed by sling rest for 7 days and the strongest antiinflammatory medications that are tolerated. Indomethacin is often preferred in this situation and is used for about 2 weeks. Needling works most reliably with the acutely painful case. It is recommended over the physical methods when the shoulder is "hot."

Ultrasonation of deposits has been used with good relief of symptoms in some patients. It is recommended, along with cuff stretching and strengthen-

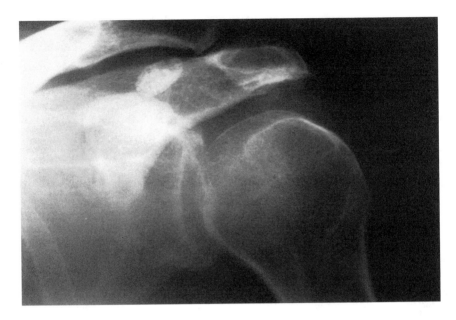

Figure 14–2 Radiograph showing cuff tear calcification (lacy or streaky appearance). This is distinct from the appearance of calcific tendinitis. A well-defined, oval free body under the clavicle is an ossified free body (true bone, not a calcium deposit).

ing, for milder, chronic symptoms, which are less likely to be permanently relieved with needling. The usual physical therapy prescribed for patients with chronic calcific tendinitis consists of active assisted range exercises in forward elevation, adduction, extension, and internal and external rotation; cuff strengthening exercises; ultrasonation of the cuff; and hot, moist packs.

Surgical excision of calcific deposits is done if physical therapy and needling fail to relieve symptoms. More than half the cases respond well to nonsurgical therapy. Surgical treatment is most useful, and most necessary, with chronic cases. Here, resorption of the calcific deposit fails to occur spontaneously, perhaps preventing the acute, severe pain that is associated with resorption but necessitating surgical removal to put an end to the chronic pain and tenderness.

Surgery is done through a small deltoid splitting incision made as directly as possible over the deposit. The actual deposit is often unimpressive when encountered at surgery; less than 5 mL of crumbly, white paste is removed in most cases. This is actually within the substance of the cuff tendon, and removing it may leave a small cuff tear. This is easily repaired if encountered; because it is a longitudinal tear and is repaired side to side, it does not necessitate total cuff protection during healing. The cuff in the region of chronic calcium deposits is not impressively inflamed; subacromial bursal tissues are similarly unimpressive in most instances. The surgery can usually be performed without detaching a significant portion of the deltoid origin from the acromion. The deltoid, too, can be used gently during the postoperative period if this was the case at surgery. Subacromial decompression is commonly done as part of this procedure when impingement is believed to contribute to the symptoms or pathogenesis. It is performed by the author if the calcific deposit is found in the impingement area of the supraspinatus. Postoperative rehabilitation should then proceed as usual for open subacromial decompression surgery (see Chapter 8).

Excellent success rates have been achieved with surgical excision of calcific deposits in the rotator cuff. Surgical morbidity is low. Although pain relief is gratifying, functional recovery of full rotator cuff function may take up to 6 months. It is therefore recommended that postoperative rehabilitation be somewhat prolonged until cuff strength returns to normal. Patients undergoing this surgery are similar to those with cuff tears insofar as strong contraction of the cuff has been avoided for a long time. Wasting of the spinatus fossae is a common finding in patients with chronic calcific tendinitis. Aggressive strengthening should therefore continue until normal cuff strength is achieved because, having adapted to minimizing their cuff use, patients may not strengthen adequately in daily activities. Functional and even training exercises (eg, throwing), continued for an extra month after the usual 6-week passive, active, and resistive sequence, may avoid perpetuation of cuff weakness for years.

CHARCOT'S SHOULDER AND SYRINGOMYELIA

Seeing large numbers of shoulder patients, the examiner may have the opportunity to make the neurologic diagnosis of syringomyelia because it is the most common underlying cause of neuropathic arthropathy of the glenohumeral joint (Charcot's shoulder). Although an unusual condition, it must be kept in mind because it is likely to escape detection by many other specialists who happen to treat the patient. Important, unusual, and striking, this is always a memorable diagnosis.

A syrinx, or long, hollow cavity, may expand within the cervical spinal cord. Filled with the same cerebrospinal fluid that bathes the entire central nervous system, the syrinx, whose presence in the cord is termed syringomyelia (Figure 14–3), may produce surprisingly subtle neurologic findings.

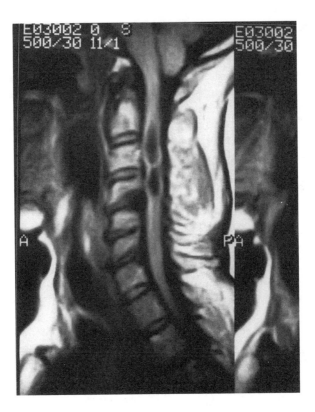

Figure 14–3 Magnetic resonance image showing syringomyelia, which appears as a dark area within the spinal cord. The neurologic deficit produced may create characteristic changes of the glenohumeral joint (neurotrophic or Charcot's joint).

Affecting proprioception, temperature, and deep pain sense, the syrinx may be discovered by the shoulder practitioner because it is the most likely cause of the Charcot shoulder (Figure 14–4).

Charcot's joint is a term given to any joint that undergoes destructive proliferative changes due to neurologic loss of normal pain sensation and proprioception. This characteristically includes free fragments of periarticular bone, malalignment, and severely decreased articular cartilage space on radiographic examination. Increased joint laxity, effusion, impressive crepitus, and surprisingly little pain with motion are encountered on physical examination. The Charcot shoulder looks like the worst possible case of osteoarthritis on

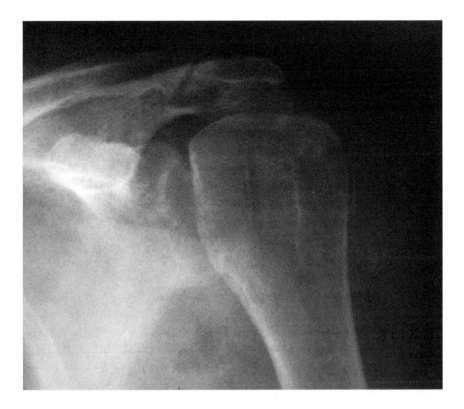

Figure 14–4 Radiograph showing Charcot's shoulder in a patient with syringomyelia. This shoulder is often less painful than the destructive, degenerative radiographic appearance would suggest.

radiographs, but it is unstable (glenohumeral instability may be the presenting complaint) and has little contracture. It does produce some pain; this is generally what brings the patient to seek help, but the pain is distinctly less than would be expected from the physical and radiographic findings. The changes in the glenohumeral joint are often present bilaterally.

Charcot's shoulder may be caused by neurologic diseases other than syringomyelia, although syrinx is by far the most common cause and the only cause that is likely to be discovered by the shoulder practitioner. Late syphilis (tabes dorsalis) and diabetes are two of the other possible causes of a Charcot joint. Syphilis is almost never seen this advanced in the Western world. The diabetic who is developing neuropathic shoulder changes is almost certain to have severe diabetic peripheral neuropathy and several other Charcot joints, probably in the lower extremities. These should be detectable in the history.

Neurologic examination of the upper extremities is essential to making the diagnosis of syringomyelia. Inability to detect temperature normally and relative insensitivity to painful stimuli such as a pin prick are the earliest signs of syringomyelia. The arms, forearms, and hands are tested specifically for these sensibilities; light touch is not affected and will not detect the syrinx reliably. Any loss of pain or temperature sense should make the examiner suspicious of syringomyelia. Sensory loss over the trapezius and upper back is another sign of syringomyelia.

The syrinx and neurologic deficit necessarily precede the development of Charcot's shoulder; it is therefore the characteristic neurologic examination with pain and temperature insensitivity that is most helpful in early cases where instability and destructive, fragmenting arthritis have not yet developed. Plain film radiographs can eventually make the diagnosis of a Charcot shoulder, however, and magnetic resonance imaging of the cervical spine confirms the diagnosis of syringomyelia.[6]

The pathophysiology of the Charcot joint is believed to involve the joint's loss of protective sensation, both pain sensation and proprioception. This leads to multiple episodes of trauma and subluxation, which if undetected create the joint laxity and arthritis. Major fractures may occur in neuropathic shoulders without detection. A fresh fracture on a radiograph in a smiling patient who is moving the arm without pain is another sign of Charcot's shoulder and possibly a syrinx.

Therapeutically, there is little that can be done to reverse the changes of Charcot's shoulder. Fusion and shoulder replacement have been attempted with poor results. They are generally not recommended. Physical treatment consists of activity modification and supportive use of a sling or other immobilizer. Great care must be taken with any use of modalities because of the possibility of causing thermal or electrical damage; protective reflexes are necessarily blunted in the Charcot shoulder. Motion is similarly precarious because of the threat of creating further damage (ie, causing fractures or a dislocation or simply grinding up a joint filled with fragments of bone and cartilage). Neurologic consultation should, of course, be obtained as soon as the diagnosis is considered. It is occasionally possible to treat the cause of the syrinx, which may be a spinal cord tumor or downward overgrowth of brain tissue (specifically the cerebellum in Arnold-Chiari syndrome) into the spinal canal.[8] Most cases are not specifically treatable, however, and receive supportive and assistive care only.

SCAPULOTHORACIC DISORDERS AND MYOFASCIAL PAIN ABOUT THE SHOULDER

As mentioned earlier, fractures and bony growths of the scapula, such as osteochondroma, may rarely be the cause of a painful grating or snapping as the scapula moves on the chest. Radiographic work-up, often using special scapular views, establishes this specific diagnosis. Physical treatments that have been useful in these circumstances have included immobilization, stretching of the ends of scapulothoracic range, local ultrasonation, and glenohumeral emphasis in shoulder motion. Only rarely is surgical excision of the offending bony projection of the scapula necessary. This may not relieve the snapping.[9,10] Scapulothoracic crepitus and pain due to true scapulothoracic bursitis have been treated with exactly the same physical regimen with the addition of steroid injections, which are done with a long 25-gauge needle (with some risk of creating a pneumothorax). Patients have required long courses of therapy and up to six injections, but in the author's experience all have eventually achieved symptomatic relief with conservative treatment. There are shoulder surgeons who regularly perform open surgical scapulothoracic bursectomies, although their opinions on the need for this procedure are not widely held.

The most common cause of periscapular, subscapular, or scapulothoracic pain is probably the muscular pain of unclear etiology that has been termed myofascial, fibromyalgic, or myotomal pain. These pains are common around the scapula, often in the regions of the insertions of the rhomboids or levator scapulae on the scapula. They are by no means restricted to this area, however. Other common areas include the trapezius or superior spinatus fossa, the base of the neck about 2 cm lateral to the midline, and higher up the neck in the erector spinae group. These muscular pains often radiate into the arm, up or down the spine, and into the shoulder blade. The pains are positional, changing with various movements of the neck and shoulder. They present with the fairly constant finding of a tender spot that has a thickened, cordlike, lumpy, or bandlike character on light palpation. Stimulation of the spot often recreates the radiating pain. These are referred to as trigger points or nodes in the physiatric literature.[11]

Various physical methods may be employed to treat pain and tenderness. Spray and stretch techniques have been popularized by Travell et al.[12] These consist of slowly spraying a skin refrigerant on the area, then stretching the specific muscle in which the spot is believed to be located, and then applying heat or other modalities. This has been variably successful in the author's practice. High-dose nonsteroidal antiinflammatory treatment has been effective, as has enforced rest and restriction of caffeine intake. Simple massage, with or without thermal contrast applications, usually helps transiently, as does a hot shower. The most direct and, in the author's practice, successful method of eliminating the symptoms of these local muscular pains is direct injection of the tender area with local anesthetic. Dry needling seems to help as well, but not as reliably. Conjecture as to the pathophysiology here is left to the voluminous, although often contradictory, literature on the topic.[12-14] Muscular pain of this type is common. It should nevertheless be a diagnosis made not only by discovering a tender lump that produces radiating pain but also by ruling out other neck and shoulder pathology.

REFERENCES

1. Smith RG, Cruikshank JG, Dunbar S, et al. Malalignment of the shoulder after stroke. *Br Med J.* 1982;284:1224–1226.

2. Vick NA. *Grinker's Neurology.* 7th ed. Springfield, Ill: Thomas; 1976.

3. Head H, Holmes G. Sensory disturbances from cerebral lesions. *Brain.* 1911;31:102–254.

4. Mooney V, Perry J, Nickel V. Surgical and nonsurgical orthopedic care of the stroke patient. *J Bone Joint Surg Am.* 1967;49:989–1000.

5. Turek SL. *Orthopedics.* Philadelphia, Pa: Lippincott; 1959.

6. Neer CS. *Shoulder Reconstruction.* Philadelphia, Pa: Saunders; 1990.

7. Uhtoff HK, Sarkar K, Maynard JA. Calcifying tendinitis. *Clin Orthop.* 1976;118:164–168.

8. Berkow R, Talbott JH, eds. *The Merck Manual of Diagnosis and Therapy.* Rahway, NJ: Merck, Sharp and Dohme; 1977.

9. Cooley LH, Torg S. Pseudowinging of the scapula secondary to subscapular osteochondroma. *Clin Orthop.* 1982;162:119–124.

10. Milch H. Snapping scapula. *Clin Orthop.* 1961;20:139–150.

11. Simons D. Myofascial pain syndromes due to trigger points. In: Goodgold J, ed. *Rehabilitation Medicine.* St. Louis, Mo: Mosby; 1988:686–723.

12. Travell J, Rinzler SH, Herman M. Pain and disability of the shoulder and arm; treatment by muscular infiltration with procaine hydrochloride. *JAMA.* 1942;118:120.

13. Travell J, Rinzler SH. The myofascial genesis of pain. *Postgrad Med.* 1952;11:425–434.

14. Simons DG. Myofascial trigger points: A need for understanding. *Arch Phys Med Rehabil.* 1981;62:97–99.

Index

V

Vascular causes of pain, 64–65

W

Weaver-Dunn procedure, 258
Weightlifter's clavicle, 251, 295, 332
Workplace modifications, 189, 191

X

X-rays, 46–53, 54–55
   anteroposterior view, 47
   axillary view, 47, 50
   glenohumeral joint instability on,
      183–184
   lateral view, 47, 50
   rotator cuff disease on, 134–135